Sweet Remedy

A Novel

Linda
Phillips
Ashour

Simon & Schuster

SIMON & SCHUSTER
Rockefeller Center
1230 Avenue of the Americas
New York, NY 10020

Simon & Schuster and colophon are registered trademarks
of Simon & Schuster Inc.

Designed by Deirdre C. Amthor

Manufactured in the United States of America

10   9   8   7   6   5   4   3   2   1

Library of Congress Cataloging-in-Publication Data

Ashour, Linda
    Sweet remedy: a novel/Linda Phillips Ashour
        p. cm.
    1. Man–woman relationships—Fiction. 2. Middle-aged women—
Fiction. I. Title.
PS3551.S416S9   1996
813'.54—dc20   95-52406
                                                    CIP

ISBN 0-684-81833-7

Acknowledgments

*M*any people helped me through the writing of *Sweet Remedy*. Thanks to my mother, for the quiet confidence that I could do it again. I owe much to Linda Upton, patient friend, skilled reader and writer. Without those phone calls and fax messages, this book would have gone down in round one. Aimee Liu offered tireless readings and, best of all, kind, tough advice. Eve Babitz, writer and dancer extraordinaire, pitched in at the last minute with great insights. Jimmy Dunne, my songwriting mentor, has been so generous with his time and talent. I'd also like to thank B. J. Robbins, my hard-working agent, and Melissa Roberts at Simon & Schuster for expediting things so beautifully. Greatest thanks of all goes to my editor, Bob Asahina, for taking one more leap of faith.

For
Savannah
and Christopher

I want to share an orange, a pot of black cowboy coffee, the calm and common sense of breakfast talk, the smiles, the touch of fingertips, the yearning of the flesh, the comradeship of man and woman, of one uncertain human for another.

Edward Abbey

One

I was just beginning to consider love again when pounding on the front door punctured my reverie. My thoughts were wildly unfocused, but something was undeniably stirring in me and I sensed that a forty-year-old woman was as alive as a young girl in important, mysterious ways. I threw open the front door to see about all the commotion and found my friend Beth, struggling with bags and bowls. She was glaring at my doorbell.

"You could always break down and just have it fixed, Polly."

"One of these days, I'm going to have *everything* in this house fixed."

"Did your grandmother arrive in one piece?"

"Oh, sure. She knows the route to California by heart. Let me have that."

She handed me an oval platter filled with roasted vegetables and a perfect mound of wild rice, then stepped inside the living room and shook her head.

"Good God."

Granny Settle slept on the couch, snores rolling painfully down her chest. She sat propped up on pillows, looking just like an eerie homespun doll. Her hair could have been fashioned from the insides of an aging down pillow, feathery white strands pressed to her skull and put to a decent use. She wore overalls and a red shirt. Fire engine red, the kind that pulls mad bulls to the center of the ring. Because my living room flirted with so many styles of furniture and accessories, she wasn't even a startling sight. At least not to me.

Beth waited until we got into the kitchen, then closed the door firmly behind her.

"This is not what you need to be doing now. You're supposed to be living the single life."

One thing Beth has not properly researched is what it's like to be single when you're forty years old. I tell her and tell her, but she lectures me on my poor attitude. Her campaign began the day Tom moved out six months ago. She has been married forever and even tends to romanticize adultery. She relies heavily on *Cosmopolitan* for this faked-out view of things, the crazed concept that adultery brings couples closer together. She doesn't understand that adultery pulls out every stop and can blind raging partners temporarily or even forever. And that marital Armageddon isn't sexy at all. Beth doesn't understand that going out on a date at this age is an act that defies God and nature. At a point when I should be dispensing timeless wisdom to my teenage daughter, having long ago made the kinds of moral decisions that she is up against, I find myself completely tongue-tied or, worse, asking if I can borrow her white T-shirt.

"I don't see how a little visit from my grandmother is going to hold me back." My stomach fluttered uncomfortably as I spoke. Food would probably help.

"Polly." She stopped unloading the sack and put her hands on her hips. "You need romance. You need love. You don't need a grandmother camped out here. Where's your can opener?"

We worked in silence for a while, listening to the sounds of U2 seeping softly from Kate's room. My daughter had voluntarily toned it down for our visitor. Beth gave me a hard look before asking her question.

"So how was that gallery opening the other night?"

"Something came up. I couldn't make it."

She spun the lettuce faster and faster, one corner of her mouth turned down.

"You've got to get out of your house, Polly. You're withering away in here. Put the word out that you're separated, single and *looking*. Hey, handsome."

She bent down to greet my son, his face hidden under a baseball cap. He brushed his cheek against hers. At twelve, Toby no longer permitted any other kind of kiss.

"Mom, where'd you put my history book?"

"*I* didn't put it anywhere."

"Can you at least help me look?"

"Not if you want dinner."

"Are you gonna be in a bad mood the whole time she's here?"

I turned to face him. He'd started wearing Tom's old St. Christopher medal again. St. Christopher, patron saint of travelers. I couldn't stand the way he fidgeted with the chain.

"Don't be so fresh."

"Because if you are, I can just go to Stewart's to live. They wouldn't mind. They like me."

"Go wake your great-grandmother. Time to eat."

The door slammed behind him. The other corner of Beth's mouth turned down and I cut her off at the pass. "This is going to work out beautifully, just wait and see."

"Your grampa sure left me holding the bag. Dying like that with forty acres of grub land nobody wants to buy. Once I give away all my things, I can join him."

Beth's back straightened suddenly and she pushed a piece of bread into her mouth.

"Granny! Don't talk like that."

"The truth always stings some."

"Could you pass the stuff with the corn, Mom?"

I was so pleased that Toby was eating vegetables, I didn't comment on his manners. He should have expressed some sorrow over his great-grandmother's imminent death, but that would come, once he got to know her.

Granny Settle didn't believe in lawyers and fancy papers, as she called them. So she had taken to the road when my grandfather died to divvy up prized possessions between my cousin Rory and me. The interior of my garage now looked like a displaced graveyard. Tall, indeterminate shapes were hung with white sheets and cinched on the bottom by an elaborate rope. Maybe the same rope she used to tie my grandfather to a tree that legendary day back in Granite. He couldn't make up his mind who to marry, her or Eveline Parker, so Granny Settle tied him to a tree until he could decide.

She was working a toothpick into a tough spot and I had to wait for her to extract whatever was giving her trouble. I spent every Christmas serving dinner to seniors and I knew how terrible it was to grow old. Everything wound up in your teeth or on the front of your shirt. There was no helping it. Kate started to cough and Toby put his face in his sleeve.

"Aaah. There." She swiped at her mouth with a napkin, then frowned accusingly at Beth. "What'd you say that was?" She pointed at what remained of her vegetables. She'd picked out bits of what she didn't like.

"Sun-dried tomatoes."

"Sure doesn't taste like any tomato I've ever eaten, canned or otherwise." She scratched the side of her face and considered each of my children. It was the first time she'd really looked at either of them since she'd arrived. She was the most unsentimental woman I had ever known, apart from my own mother.

"You kids like old people?"

I started to pray, but I didn't get past Dear Lord. I open all my prayers that way, like they're letters written on fine stationery.

"Depends on the old person." One thing about Kate, she didn't mince words.

"What about you, son?" It was Toby who finessed things, Toby who smoothed the feathers Kate ruffled.

He was terrified. I could tell by the way he ate. His plate was practically wiped clean and I usually had to fight to get him to eat anything that couldn't be ordered at a drive-through window.

"He loves senior citizens, Granny. Toby takes care of several lawns on the street. Why, he—"

"Let the boy talk for himself." My granny's eyes were blazing and she had put her hands inside the front of her overalls. "Do you like *old* people?"

"Kinda. I guess."

"Toby's a suck-up. That's how come he does their lawns. Plus they *pay him,* Mom!"

"That will be quite enough, Katherine."

"All right then. Listen, both of you. I'm a bother to no one even though I'm eighty-two and about to die. I have to get up in the night, but I still have control of my bowels and my mouth. I don't talk unless I've got something to say. I'll be cooking my own meals while I'm here and eating off my own plates. If you want to know anything about the rodeo or Granite, Oklahoma, you both better ask while there's time." She took her hands out of her overalls and put them on the edge of the table.

"Now, Polly. I'm not a senior citizen. I'm plain old. It's been years since we last visited and I see from your face you've had some hard times. I expect that's because Tom's gone."

I ran a quick mental survey. Brown eyes, shoulder-length dark blond hair, graying a bit near the face. And the Settle forehead, lightly lined, peculiar and clannish as a mason's handshake. What else did my grandmother see?

"Granny, I really—"

"Let me speak. You want to find out how long I'm staying, but you're too polite to ask. I'll leave when I'm ready and that could be day after tomorrow or next year."

I started to answer, but she'd already lost interest.

"I expect you people watch television after supper."

She stood up, so we did, too. Beth gave me a quick hug and made me promise to call. I began to clear the table and noticed a little mound of dirt on the floor under my granny's place.

I turned on the wrong switch in the dining room, the one that only worked occasionally, then remembered how Tom had rewired things years ago. It had been a disaster, complete with blown fuses and hours of candlelight and cursing. Tom loved tools and tinkering, but he had no natural aptitude for fixing things. Everything in our house was held together by a pin. Manuals and instruction books were tucked everywhere, their pages now yellowed and curling with age. I crossed the room to hit the lights, ramming my leg into the bed that jutted from one wall.

I ran my finger over the edge of the spare mattress; it was as full of old memories as I was. Tom and I found it tucked away in a hidden corner of a Simmons outlet when we were just a couple of kids. Married, but kids all the same. Once we got it home, we discovered it had been relegated to a far corner for a reason. The mattress was an odd size, somewhere between a queen and a double, and we learned to fall asleep in a hot jumble of arms and legs. This was a habit we hung on to for a long time, even after we had graduated to larger beds and sheets that were finally a proper fit.

"Mom. Are you just going to stand there staring at the mattress or what?" Toby's voice broke in the middle of his question.

"I'm getting ready to make the bed."

"We should put the table by the window."

"She doesn't like views. At least she didn't like them in Granite."

"It's mean to put the table in a corner, Mom. It's like you're punishing her for being here."

I did what my son said, putting the table and Granny Settle front and center of our lives, and wondered where his sense of outrage came from. He was a miniature police state, a conscience monitor that only slipped when it came to his own behavior. I knew the principal of his school very well and, during the past two years, had never had anything different to say when he phoned me. He would go through the list of classroom crimes I could tell he was reading by the lack of inflection in his voice. Toby had a kind heart, I reminded him, and that gentle spirit would eventually triumph. I always ended our conversations on a comic note, hoping to cheer him or add a little something to his dull day of disciplining unruly children and placating outraged teachers.

"The house is sure gonna look different for a while." Toby sat down on the edge of the new bedroom suite. "She can sit here if she gets bored with being at the table. Do you think people can see in this far?"

"Nah. Too far back, plus it's a pretty dim room."

He stared at her old sewing machine, covered with a soft cloth. "What's she gonna sew?"

"Toby, honey, I don't have a clue."

He lay back on the bed, his huge basketball shoes seemingly set in cement.

"Dad said to call when she got in. He was worried she wouldn't remember the way out here."

"So did you phone him?"

"Yep. He's still worried."

"Your father has trouble with change."

I didn't have wisdom, but I did have a three-thousand-year-old voice I used when I talked about Tom with the kids. It rose Tut-like from a buried tomb, where I stored most of my thoughts about the marriage. I tried to keep things even and fair. In doing so, in trying not to speak badly of their father, I produced stiff artifacts like that one about Tom.

I sat down next to Toby and tapped the top of his hand. "Go do your homework."

"Not yet."

"Now. No argument. I'm not in the mood."

"I'm not in the mood." I hated his version of the way I spoke, because he did it so perfectly. The virtuous tone made me sound like a prig.

I made up the bed, using hospital corners, thinking about Beth's admonishments and slapped at the bed suddenly, aiming at a wrinkle. I slapped again in a different spot, then again. Again. It felt good. Hitting the bed felt good.

"Gal, when did you start beating on beds?"

"You scared me, Granny! You sure don't make much noise when you move."

"You and your grampa. He used to say I moved like a slithering snake."

"You look exhausted."

"I am."

With that, Granny Settle unhooked her overalls and let them drop where she stood. I shuddered, seeing her body bared, and hoped the kids didn't walk in. Droopy underpants gave way to legs that were melting, melting with blue-veined flaps and pockets. She moved painfully to the edge of the bed, still in her red shirt, and dropped down exhausted. She stared at her own image in the darkening window.

"Looks like I'll be the first thing the mailman sees at this address."

It passed over me so quickly, I thought I imagined it. Rage, but just a sprinkling. Like pepper passed over boiling soup, then completely absorbed. She'd stepped out of her pants, just like a thoughtless kid. She was gone, curled into a tiny knot of sleep, by the time I had them up off the floor.

Two

I had to empty her overalls before I could even think of washing them. At first I thought they were just dusty, but then I realized every pocket was filled with dirt and small, smooth pebbles. Even small pockets that buttoned were filled to the brim with bright red dirt, suggesting she had fled a latter-day dust bowl. I stepped out the back door, slapped the overalls against the side of my garage and swept up what dirt had fallen, tossing it into a patch of night-blooming flowers, just then opening their blossoms for me. I was a fickle gardener, seeding one narrow patch of dirt with whatever the season suggested. I would clear the patch the instant it looked tired, haunting the aisles of the hardware store for another packet of seeds. Otherwise my garden was unchanging, given over to the reasonable, the drought-resistant, the gray-green fitting to California soil. Save this slim finger of riotous color, my garden was severe and predictable. I stuck my hand in the soil, checking the moisture. It was fine, still wet from last night's dousing. I bumped into an oily worm with my fingernail. A pigeon, plumped and sleepy, eyed me from the top of the fence.

The lights from the back bedrooms fell on the garden, turning it white and wintry, full of shapes and shadows it didn't have by day. I sat down in a metal chair to exult. I had bought the chair for that purpose. It was a chair from another time, suggesting croquet and chess, old roses and the time to prune them. I only had one chair like that, but it worked like a charm. Looking out over my tiny plot, I felt truly rich, lucky and lordly as a seigneur. Once inside there was always an inflated phone bill or a property tax installment to remind me that I was anything but that. However, from my chair, I could watch it all . . . the hammock, coming slowly unwoven from weather and boys, but still idling between a jacaranda and a sycamore, a broken-down pavilion flying in the face of good design. Sporting a pointy roof with rotting green wooden shingles, the pavilion was an eyesore, but I never saw it like that. The floor of shattered concrete slabs had long been destroyed by tree roots. Tiny white Christmas lights were strung along the outside of the structure and only a few of them needed replacing. The floor rose and fell, creating a kind of rolling ship deck, and sometimes I drank blue drinks out back, paper umbrellas plunged into crushed ice, and imagined myself heading into yet another strange, foreign port.

"Polly, is that you out there?"

I looked up to find my neighbor on his second-story porch, peering over the top of the hedge as usual. Even though a FOR SALE sign had stood in his front yard for months, Russell felt like a permanent installation.

"It's me."

I tried to make my voice sound friendly. Inflated phone bills weren't the only thing that reminded me I wasn't lord of the manor. We shared dear space on the planet and the fact of a neighbor whose hulking freighter looked on to my pipsqueak pleasure boat never let me forget it. I liked him well enough, but I did wish the hedge were a little higher, his house a little lower.

"Congratulations, Russell. I read about you in the Metro section last week."

"You did? You saw that?"

"Girls, girls, girls."

I could see him grin from where I sat. Russell was a contractor and the article commended his development in Long Beach. The residents featured, all female, praised Russell. His willingness to rectify their problems right away, his no-fault approach to any difficulty, large or small, during the first two years of occupancy. Customer relations in Long Beach appeared impeccable.

"Oh, that. They've been real happy with my work. One of them called a friend of hers at the *Times* and two weeks later we had a journalist out there. Cheapest ad I ever ran. Most effective, too. I've been getting calls since it came out." He paused and leaned way back in his chair. "About time I had some good women in my life."

Because I was older by a few years, he told me all about his love troubles. He had a ringing voice and he projected not only over the hedge that divided our property, but over my house to the neighbor on the other side. He would often finish a piece on his latest misadventure and I would hear the spigot squeak on the other side, which meant my other neighbor had stopped hosing down her deck to listen. Once in a while I had him over to dinner. He was an enthusiastic audience, smacking his lips over the simplest dish. Afterward, he would wander around my house to check windows and doors, fussing about my safety, my lack of a security system. I wasn't concerned, since Russell functioned as a one-man neighborhood watch. If I didn't actually see him each time I ventured into my backyard, I heard him rustling around on the other side of the eugenia hedge, the green barrier that gave me what little privacy I had.

"I got my friend to lower his prices for you, Polly. Told him how many square feet you got over there, how many doors and windows. I've got all the material for you. Very reasonable for the kind of motion detectors he's got. No armed response, but hey, you've got me." He was armed to the teeth and slept with a bat under his bed for good measure. Every time a woman rejected him, he added something. A new intercom. Bigger, brighter floodlights. "Whose truck is that in your driveway?"

"It's my grandmother's truck. She drove it out from Granite, Oklahoma. She's kind of touring the country to see her great-grandchildren. Can you believe it? I bet by tomorrow she'll have the kids pitching horseshoes and shelling peas on the back step."

That would work, that tone, the pleasures of a joyful extended family. Granny Settle on a zany, charming tour of the U.S.A. to see the family. I thought of her dirty pickup truck, the crunch that included most of the left side and the license plate dangling vertically from the window of the cab claiming "Oklahoma Is O.K."

"Gee." His chin was cupped in his hands. He seemed to be growing a beard, though it could have been the play of shadows on the porch. "You seem a lot happier down there than I am up here."

He didn't mean to be patronizing. He genuinely wondered why having pots of money didn't make him a happy man and it had become my policy to take his happy native comments lightly. A bachelor had no business living alone in an enormous house fit for a family teeming with kids and dogs and in-laws. The house had a Roman bath with ten Jacuzzi jets and arched golden fixtures. I knew. I'd sat in it before he moved in. You could see the airport from his bathtub, but that was all right. I could see a sky full of planes from my metal chair.

I was usually short of money and sometimes short of patience. My children were frequently rude and my household was either too sexy or not sexy enough. I wasn't actually dating yet, but I was making steady progress, whether Beth thought so or not. Signs of change were everywhere.

The lyrics I'd written all my life seemed like touching, quaint stories to me now. I was working on new material at top speed, and my songs finally bore some relation to modern life. I had lyrics stuffed everywhere, just like Granny Settle had dirt, and if I even so much as bent over to pick up a fallen sock, a country song would fall out of my pocket. So I had a lot on my mind, a lot more than somebody in a mansion on the hill. Still, sitting on the crazy deck of my crazy ship heading God only knew where, I sometimes found that I was unreasonably happy.

"Polly Ann, you chickenshit sonofabitch. Where are my pants?"

"Coming, Granny."

"Now, *that's* some grandmother."

For there she was, fist raised and spindly, knotted legs trembling with fury, on the back step. Lit from behind, her thin hair aglow, my granny seemed to fill every shadowy corner of my tiny pleasure port. I folded her overalls carefully over my arm and started to head inside.

How she hated chickens. She told me so again and again as she held the flashlight over me. Gathering up the dirt wasn't as hard as I imagined. Even under the thin beam of light, the difference between Granite dirt and Los Angeles dirt would have been obvious to a neophyte.

"You missed some. Yep, like I say, I'd rather keep company with a dead man than a chicken. Those dirty, filthy things do nothing but shit up a place and litter it with stinkin' feathers."

I knew the story by heart. I'd heard it all when I was a kid and knew every detail of the stories that fired her prejudice. Everyone had been called "chickenshit sonofabitch" at one time or another, my mother, me. Just about everybody except Tom. The term popped out of her mouth when she was angry or excited. It could signal rage or glee or anything that was simply too hot for my granny to handle at the moment.

"As far as I'm concerned . . ." The light wobbled unsteadily for a minute, then landed on a far spot behind a burst of exuberant pink flowers. ". . . that friendship your mother had with Minah Overstreet was a real stain on her character. I suppose she is still driving to Nevada to see her."

I kept my eye on the task at hand, separating out dirt and putting the righteous kind in a Baggie. L.A. dirt fell straight through the holes of my colander, while Granite soil globbed up and clung to the sides.

"Only in December. They go to the National Finals together every year. It's kind of a ritual."

"That ritual's got nothing to do with rodeo. That ritual is born of the blood of chickens. Born out of their entrails and their nasty pecking ways."

Russell had left the porch, overcome by the sight of my nearly naked grandmother. From where I knelt I could see him, pacing inside the master bedroom outfitted, I happened to know, in the very latest bachelor high-tech. Everything at his fingertips, everything stylish and easy and mechanized, the very things Russell didn't need, if you asked me. He needed his own brand of blood and bones, something to reach for at night besides the remote control. Granny Settle kept right on talking.

"Nothing good can come out of that Overstreet clan. I don't care how much money they have."

The arrival of the Overstreets and their chicken farm drove my granny into town against her will. Her spirit belonged to the dry, thirsty pastures she had so long inhabited with my grandfather and their scrawny ponies. The land she needed to sell had long been defiled by chickens. Granny's place was downwind of the chicken farm, and the stink, the squabbling of the Overstreets and their hugely profitable poultry operation made habitation of the "sweetest forty acres south of Granite" virtually impossible. My grandparents continued to operate the riding ring, wearing bandanas over their noses and looking like bandits on windy days. But heady, pint-sized equestrians didn't mind the smell and, even if they did, the Settle Ring was the only show in town. In those days, nobody knew how hugely profitable a chicken farm could be. When the Overstreets slaughtered off every last chicken and closed up their long, metal barns, then sold the parcel of land to a developer and moved to Las Vegas, my granny had already left for Granite city limits. And for nothing. Chickens still haunted her dreams. She woke up at four A.M., hearing their cries even in her sleep. She sighted them from every window of her one-story "town house" and smelled their blood on the linoleum floor of her kitchen. My grandfather tore it up twice to no avail. Two brand-new floors later, she still smelled blood, chicken shit and feathers in her own home. It didn't matter that the Overstreets had abandoned chickens for Vegas and bigger money still. That her own teenage daughter sat at the dining table writing lovesick letters to Minah Overstreet only added insult to injury.

"I never understood what your mama saw in that child. Washed-out little thing. A cheater, too. Copied off your mama's arithmetic lessons until it got her tossed out of school on her ear. Don't mix the dirt up so."

"I can't help it."

Minah had always been an unabashed good-time girl. She was currently on her fifth husband and he was just as pretty as the last one. She liked them younger by a few years and pretty, just this side of effeminate. Minah Overstreet had been "easy" as a young girl and she still traveled fast. My infatuated mother was only too happy to go along for the ride. She learned every trick she knew from Minah.

"Now then, Polly Ann."

I rested my weight on my heels. I hadn't been called Polly Ann in the longest time and being called that now made me think of straight lines and right angles, polished apples and hair rinsed with lemon juice and rainwater.

"Maybe now I can get some decent rest. If I need help washing my pants, I reckon I'll ask."

She went back inside. I sat back in the chair to watch the sky for a little bit before I followed her. I finally had my kingdom to myself, just as Granny Settle had hers, meted out in five plastic bags. I guess having that coarse, red dirt right beside her in the cab of the truck or the seat of her pants kept her comfortably tied to Granite, no matter how far she happened to travel.

The smell of fried meat woke me up the next morning. Granny Settle's tough little breakfast steaks and scrambled eggs were as predictable as the first freeze. She didn't believe in lunch. She thought it was a mean invention, a way to keep women tied to the stove all day. My mother cried on her first day of school. That was when she found out other people got to eat three times a day instead of two. I stayed in bed as long as I could, smelling the meat through the layer of sheets and blankets. I pulled on my pink Isotoners and did a few stretches.

"Morning, Granny."

She nodded hello, her eyes slightly glassy. Her hands were curved around a red enamel coffee cup. She took a noisy slurp and parted the kitchen curtains with one hand. A dog was doing its business in my front yard and she rapped on the window, shooing it away. She was wrapped in a wool plaid bathrobe

23

and her hair was combed away from her face. She was a welcoming presence. I'd forgotten how good it felt to have another adult in the house. For a second my kitchen felt just like a television commercial.

She hummed snatches of the old songs, the ones I'd listened to for as long as I could remember. She knew melodies to cure fevers and melodies to pass time. She used the same uneven bars to calm horses and humans; hearing them in this setting comforted us both.

The smell of food still hung in the air, but everything was spotless. Several new pieces of equipment sat on my countertop. A battered tin coffee pot and a cast iron skillet, some aluminum plates and dented cups, the kind I'd seen in sporting goods stores, were piled beside my canister set. Kate and Toby came into the kitchen. They rubbed their eyes and stood in the same sunny square. The rhythm in our house had changed and they didn't quite know what to do.

"What smells, Mom?" Kate turned up her nose, though she didn't need to. There was enough disgust in her voice to make the point. "What's all that camping stuff doing on the counter?"

"Say good morning to your great-grandmother."

Toby mumbled something and Kate kind of waved. Granny Settle didn't acknowledge either of them, but kept peering through the curtains. She looked hunted, like there was a long line of Feds on her trail. I looked at the kitchen clock and started sandwich making, toast making.

"Kate, pack chips for the lunch bags. Toby, go shower."

"Mom! I'll miss the bus."

"You will if you argue." He stomped off and I looked at Kate, sternly dividing up a few potato chips. I really needed to go to the store.

"He's a dick, Mom. Your son is such a lowly dick."

"Are you actually counting those chips?"

"If it looks like I get more, he totally spazzes. I think the toast is burning."

It was. Our highly calibrated mornings didn't permit toast burning. They were too black to scrape and there was no time to make new toast. I started pouring cereal. Granny Settle rapped again on the window, but harder this time. My television morning was disintegrating before my eyes.

"Cap'n Crunch? Do you really expect me to eat Cap'n Crunch for breakfast?" Kate was tapping a spoon against the sink. I didn't remember buying Cap'n Crunch, for some reason. Usually I picked out Cheerios or Wheaties.

"If Dad hadn't dropped off juice this morning, we wouldn't even have had that." Kate wiped her lips with the edge of a dishtowel.

"Your dad was over?"

"He dropped off my history book and some fresh juice. Oh, I forgot." She left the kitchen and came back with a copy of the *New York Times*. A note from Tom was attached about an article on country music. Page twelve.

Granny Settle stopped rapping on the window. My stomach was growling. It must have been the smell of meat. She set her red cup down, rose with great care and made her way over to Kate. Kate was knocking the hell out of the kitchen sink with her spoon. She was tall for her age. With or without her baseball cap, she was a lanky child and still uncomfortable with her new height. She slouched and this gave her tiny great-grandmother an advantage. Toby had appeared in the doorway. He was wrapped in a gym towel that seemed a smaller and smaller white rectangle every day. His wet hair stood up in stiff, jellied spikes.

"What smells is a piece of breakfast meat." She got up from the table and moved closer to Kate. They had exactly the same profile. The years between them didn't matter and neither did the baseball cap pulled low over my daughter's face, hiding the deep brown eyes and curiously flat forehead the Settle women all share. We can try to hide it with bangs or ball caps, but it's always there, glinting as wide and white as the marking on a blaze-faced mare. Granny Settle seemed like my daughter's strange, older sister. I took a couple of steps to one side.

"I ate my meat this morning like I've done nearly every waking morning of my life. You smell meat and gristle, child."

Kate didn't bat an eye. She glared into her own ancient face and didn't back down. Granny Settle grabbed her cast iron skillet with both hands and held it out in front of her.

"This old skillet's what I cook it on. It never needs greasing. I always saw to it my husband and I had our breakfast meat, even if one piece of meat had to last us all day and all night. I'll cook on it so long as I'm strong enough to pick it up."

Her arms trembled with the effort and so did her voice. I knew she was yearning for a birch tree and a birch switch, the one she brought down between an ornery horse's ears to bring the animal into line. Granny Settle was not a morning person. Neither was Kate. She stared into her great-grandmother's narrowed eyes.

"I never eat meat for breakfast. It's part of my religion."

"What religion would that be?"

"I haven't eaten meat for two years. Just smelling it makes me want to puke."

"Seems like there's a whole bunch of things you don't eat. There's meat, there's your mama's cereal. I'm going out this morning for supplies. Tell me what it is you do eat and I'll be happy to buy it for you. Polly, I believe your son is too old to waltz through the kitchen naked."

Toby was dancing around in his towel, dying to get into the act somehow. I sat down at the kitchen table, pointing my toes inside the Isotoners. I would be driving them to school.

"Toby, go put some clothes on. Congratulations, guys. You managed to miss the bus."

"No sugar. No meat—"

"Katherine!" The third thing on her list was No Shit, the skateboarder's guide to good nutrition. How many times had I heard it yelled from the back of the house when I called her for dinner? I grabbed the canister and started doling out what chips remained. It was almost empty.

"I'll finish here. You're going to be late for school."

She was still tapping the sink with the spoon. Granny Settle grabbed her wrist.

"Seems like everybody in this house has just got to *hit* something. Your mother hits beds and you seem to favor sinks. Now I'm wondering why this is."

Kate whirled away and stomped off to her room. Every footfall resounded as Granny Settle took up her seat again at the kitchen table.

"Polly Ann?"

"Yes?" How had I become Polly Ann with golden rain-washed hair in less than twenty-four hours?

"What does the child mean by 'lowly dick'?"

I sighed loudly. Kate had won the language war in our house. It had been a long, hard campaign. For months I punished each bad word, then the war moved to a different battlefield. Kate began painting bad words on banners, connecting them until they made no sense at all, and hung the banners in her room. Toby shredded them routinely, with Stewart's help, but the black banners kept reappearing. Now I only noticed her language when someone pointed it out to me.

"I'm not really sure, Gran. 'Dick' means penis and I think the 'lowly' is a touch of Shakespeare. Kate's studying *Taming of the Shrew* this year."

"That so."

"I think."

"And what church does the girl go to that makes her hate meat so?"

"No church exactly, Gran. She's got her own set of beliefs. Like most kids this age. Oh, you know."

"If I did, I wouldn't be asking. Now would I?"

Toby tucked into a bowl of Cap'n Crunch. A great fan of meat, sugar and shit, he couldn't have been happier. Granny Settle lifted my watch from the table and frowned, then asked what time they had to be at school.

"Either of you two ever taken a ride in the back of a truck?"

"I haven't. I don't know about Kate."

Granny Settle blew hard on the top of her coffee and announced it was high time they did.

I dressed fast, anxious to finish a song I'd been struggling with for days. On mornings when I didn't have to be a temp, I headed straight for the coffee shop where I got most of my real work done. The phone rang and I must have sounded a little sharp.

"It's me, darling. My, your voice sounds funny or is it this connection?"

"Morning, Mother. I'm in a bit of a hurry."

"Perfect. Me, too. Bobby and I are catching a cruise this afternoon. Mazatlán, can you picture it?"

Of course I could. I would look up Mazatlán later, refine my image of the coastal city slightly, and insert my mother, half a dozen Louis Vuitton suitcases and burly Bobby Denario. It was an easy exercise.

"Big news." She was panting a little. Probably fanning her face a bit or holding her hair in a twist she would release for great dramatic effect once she hung up the phone. My mother was a plush velvet curtain idling down to the theater floor, a handsome schedule of events. She was pure entertainment, if you were in the mood. I wasn't. I put a piece of chewing gum in my mouth and chomped.

"Are you chewing gum again? Didn't we talk about that the last time we spoke? Well, it's your life and your jaw. I'll make this quick."

I heard the Forester Sisters' voices floating through the new sound system Bobby had installed in the Palm Springs house. The old school twang seemed an insult to the elaborate setup.

"We've come up with the solution."

"To what?"

"To what to do about your grandmother. Bobby's putting in a bid today on that silly acreage in Granite."

"The riding ring?" I thought of that ring, stuck outside Granite city limits, where the horses only trotted when threatened with a birch switch. They knew the sound of the whoosh above their ears and without it they would just stand biting flies, their eyes half closed.

"There is no riding ring. But there is land and we're just tired of her carrying on about it all the time. Once the deal's done, you and I will have to talk. Your grandmother will be getting a nice little check and we can't have her just floating around, for heaven's sakes. We're going to have to *act*. Did she get in all right, by the way?"

"Yeah, no problem."

"That's a relief. Kiss, kiss."

I hung up the phone, in a bigger hurry than ever to leave my house.

Three

I nearly tripped over Tom as I ran out the front door. He sat on the front porch steps, working with a calculator. He'd cut himself shaving; I could see a little patch of Kleenex just above his collar. He grinned at me and turned back to the calculator.

"Like your shirt."

It was his shirt, a good sturdy blue, one that I'd appropriated from the back of the closet before he moved out. He hadn't slept. I could tell exactly how he'd spent the night. The preliminary prowl at midnight. Junk food at one-thirty and a paperback by two o'clock that would finally let him drift off. There was a deep crease in his cheek and I knew it would be a bad day. He went through periods of insomnia that lasted weeks. He pushed clear and stuck the calculator in an inside pocket.

"Do I look like somebody who dyes his hair?"

"Not particularly."

"I was thinking the other day how a guy with my face oughta have some gray hair except I don't. So that maybe people look at me and assume right away I dye it or something. I'm not starting to look like Reagan, am I?"

"Not even close."

His dark, undyed hair needed a cut by his standards. But I preferred it messy, flipping slightly over the edge of his collar the way it did now.

"Tom, why are you here again?"

"I came to see if Babe's awake."

"She's gone." I bit the tip of my tongue. Hearing him use the nickname reminded me of my grandmother's fondness for Tom. She had always been crazy about him, even when he was just a kid in her yard back in Granite, back again to load up his pockets with her cookies. She claimed to have fallen for him way before I ever did.

"Where's she sleeping?"

I pointed at a dining room window.

"So everyone's going to go through Kate's room to get to the kitchen? How'll that work?"

"It just will. The kids won't die because their traffic pattern is disturbed for a little while."

"If you ask me—"

"I didn't."

"Polly, they're *our* kids. When there's a disruption in their lives I'm affected, too."

"Disruption? You call this a disruption after what you've put us through? This is a cakewalk, Tom."

He winced slightly and ran his hand over his hair. My own scalp tingled, almost as if he were touching me. He'd begun using a new kind of soap with a heavy pine scent. I could just see it—dark green, curved deep as a back and dangling from a thick rope cord in his shower. He probably passed it right over his arms and chest under a hot blast of water. He almost never used washcloths.

"Polly."

"Yes?"

"What do I have to do to make this work?"

I'd been a good student all my life. Answers to everything. Tom's career agonies, Little League sponsorship woes, the midlife details that threatened to derail my friends. But now there seemed to be a cold wind blowing through my head that swept it clean of any solutions. I jammed my hand in a pocket and found a washed dollar bill curled inside. There wasn't much to say right then.

He took a deep breath and put his sunglasses on. They were pretty cockeyed by now. They'd been sat on, tried on, lost and found. Now they tipped unevenly to one side making him look like he was smiling even when he wasn't. He pushed hard on the buzzer; it didn't make a sound.

"Somebody could stand out here forever and you wouldn't even know. How would you know, Polly?"

"They'd knock eventually. That or go away. Are you traveling this week?"

"Till Wednesday. Tell the kids I'll call from the hotel."

"Oh, thanks for the juice. And the article."

"No problem. So long, Polly." He tugged on his collar and stepped off the porch, working a loose brick back into place before continuing down the path.

I sat down at a booth and sighed. Was my domain always going to consist of kitchens and dining rooms, tables and chairs? A waitress sailed over to pour me a cup of oily coffee. An iridescent ring sat on the top and, if I didn't add cream, I wound up being sidetracked by thoughts of why that ring was always there, instead of unlocking the songs in my head. None of this stopped me from drinking cup after cup. Tully hurried over to my table, sweating as usual.

"Polly. Whatchee asked for your phone number the other day."

"Who's Whatchee?"

"The idiot with the goatee. Don't tell me you don't remember him. Hair on his head's a different color than the goatee. You believe that? Like I would give out even the *names* of my customers. He ever bothers you, lemme know. On the street, anyplace. You just tell me, I'll break him in two."

"Thanks, Tully. Are there any sweetrolls left?"

"For you? Always."

The best table was near the back, where waitresses made dates for the movies and exchanged news about important shoe sales. If anybody decided to walk off the job in a huff, they did it there. There was plenty of light, but the table wasn't near the sidewalk where people could watch me. I'd had people stand in front of my table from time to time and the experience was unnerving. This wasn't performance art, after all. Sitting in the back was like being home with the phone off the hook. I had the human buzz without the sting—usually nobody bothered me. If anybody did disturb me, Tully took care of it right away. He was back with my order. Caramel oozed over the thick-lipped edges of the roll.

"Say, the one I liked, the one where the trucker is on his way home with a dozen roses? I heard it the other day on the radio. Beautiful song, what a beautiful goddamned song."

"I told you, Tully, I haven't had a song published yet. But I will."

"Damn right you will. You don't have any water. What the hell is the matter with him?" He jerked his head at the busboy, laboring under a tray of empty glasses. "How old is Toby again?"

"Twelve."

"Next year I get him. I could use a decent busboy in this place."

"He's all yours."

There was something about Tully's cinnamon rolls. While the rest of the city was dipping into yogurt and granola, I was wolfing down all the refined sugar my poor body could sustain. The first and last time I ever set foot in a health food store, I bought a bag of trail mix and broke a crown on one of the unsalted nuts. I could go all day on one of Tully's sweetrolls and often did. Granny Settle's own, I wasn't much of a lunch eater.

I took out a notebook and looked at what I had so far. Last week looked this way:

> Packin up my leavin things,
> Putting everything inside.
> Never know what I'll be needin,
> When I reach the other side.

I licked the top of my lip and imagined a woman my age taking a hurried turn around her bedroom. What if *I* had been the one to leave instead of Tom? What would I have needed on that chilly journey?

> Got a clock to tell the time with,
> There's a brush to fix my hair,
> Plus a coat to keep the cold out,
> And some stylish things to wear.

> Damned if I'll go barefoot,
> With no hat upon my head,
> Darlin when I close this door
> Just picture me in red.

> I'm finally gettin off this train,
> This sorry, low-class ride,
> Cause, honey, after all this time,
> I'm still big on pride.

I took another bite of my sweetroll and wondered if she really had to be that remorseless. I decided she did.

> Puttin on my leavin shoes,
> The ones with heels too high,
> They'll be clickin down the sidewalk,
> Lookin for a better time.

I could see the woman. I could also see her shoes glimmering in front of me. I'd never guessed that shoes baring the top of the toes were sexy and evocative until my mother brought it up. She had described the shoes she wore the night she met Bobby so many times, I felt they belonged to both of us.

I couldn't write for months after Tom left. After I got the kids off to school, I just lay around, literally. It was spooky. We couldn't maintain two lavish households and the money Tom could give me was just enough to live on if I did nothing extra and really watched expenses. If I wanted to, I could have stayed naked and drunk all day, as long as I was sober by three o'clock when the kids came home. Nobody would have known. The possibilities for self-destruction were endless and I thought about all of them from my favorite perch, an armchair as soft as a worn flannel shirt. Tom had taken the other chair upon my insistence. His apartment was furnished with a lot of tragic stuff he bought to induce pity, but I saw to it he had at least one great armchair. Even though I tried to stay clear of beds, for months I couldn't look at a sofa or chair without plopping down for a minute. Then the minute would turn into an hour or two. I couldn't believe my own lethargy. The telephone would ring and I would figure it was Beth or my mother calling to find out how I was, so I just let the phone ring on and on. Later I bought an answering machine to further refine my lethargy. I accumulated messages that I would never return and sometimes I erased them all without even listening.

But then one day I leaned over and snapped the radio on again, ripping through all the afternoon talk shows that featured phobias and fetishes or interviews too cerebral to hold my attention for long. I stopped fussing with the dial the minute I hit KZLA. Garth Brooks was singing about his friends in low places and all of a sudden I jumped from my comfortable chair, the music literally raising me up. I started swaying a little bit and this somehow turned into a dance. Before long I wasn't alone anymore. I'd just entered a room filled with people I'd known my whole life. They were simple people with simple troubles. They'd had enough of big-city life, people who drank expensive wine and paid their bills with home computers, and they were going home to a better class of losers. Or their daughters were going off to college and even though they'd been preparing for the moment for eighteen years, that departure was still a huge, yanking grief. They had terrible, broken-down cars, just like the ones that crowded my father's shop, and found a functioning radio cause for comic celebration and song. The music I loved best contained no surprises and I guess that was the attraction. I'd had my fill of the inadvertent; the steadiness of country brought me back to life. I began writing again and picking up the phone the minute it rang.

"Where do you put it?"

I looked at my watch. It was much too early for the lunch crowd, though the man asking the question looked like he was a card-carrying member. I liked his suit. It was handsome, but lived-in. Maybe he bought things like I did, to last decades. He put his arm on the back of the booth that divided us and I liked him even better. The jacket had brown suede arm patches, but not the contrived kind. These probably hid fabric that was thinning as fast as the hair on his head. It all made up for his dopey question.

"If you mean the roll, I put it in my stomach."

"You must have great metabolism. Mind if I ask what you're writing?"

"Song lyrics." He turned further in his seat and I could see he was reading *Billboard.* And that he wore clear nail polish. I felt a little stab of hope in my stomach.

"Got an agent?"

"Funny you should mention that because—"

"Because the thing is, I might be in a position to help you. Shel Elliot."

"Good to meet you, Shel. I'm Polly Harrison." I shook his hand over what remained of my roll. His hand was cushiony and damp and I let go right away. "So, who do you represent, Shel?" I drank some water and stared at him over the rim of the glass.

"Ever heard of Cactus and Ivy?"

"You bet! I love their sound." I'd head for Tower Records on Sunset this afternoon. The sales clerks there loved me and called each time an interesting, obscure country cassette came in over the transom. Tower Records was my night school and my music guild. They would absolutely have heard of Cactus and Ivy and anything else Shel Elliot might throw at me. They'd even give me reasons to like the group, assuming there were any.

"You do?" Little beads of sweat had begun to form on Shel's upper lip and one eyelid twitched suddenly as he reached over the booth with a business card.

"I'm crazy about their stuff."

"You know, there really might be something I can do for you. How do you feel about dropping by my office sometime? Showing me some of those lyrics of yours?"

"I'm out of town tomorrow and the next day, but next week is wide open." The image of a frantic schedule with a serendipitous break next week was a fantastic lie. Shel Elliot narrowed his eyes and I locked my ankles together under the table. Tully was making his way over and his teeth were bared. He was slapping at the side of his leg with a dishcloth, probably rehearsing some line he felt would liberate me.

"Then I'll expect you. Just tell my assistant it's Polly from the coffee shop to help me remember. I'm so fuckin' old that's what it takes these days. Hey!"

He grabbed a waitress for a side of home fries and more Postum. I went on with my work, saying yes to more of Tully's oily brew, yes to the Shels of the world and yes to the man who had just appeared in my mind. A big, beaming man with a limp and a hat in his hand. That's how I got most of my songs. By greeting someone in that room full of people I already knew and pulling up a chair to have a visit. Writing lyrics meant I didn't have to be by myself anymore. In a little bit, I would call my dad and see how he was doing. Where would I go to make that phone call? I pictured Granny Settle's expression as she listened to me chatting away in the kitchen. Or how that expression might change if I closed my bedroom door for some privacy. My father would probably just be pulling up to a house he shared with no one but dogs, either opening some food for them or some food for himself. It was pretty much interchangeable since my mother had left him for Bobby Denario, even though ten years had passed.

• • •

My father was drinking coffee when I called from a pay phone in Tully's lobby. He'd come in from the cold front porch to get the phone.

"What are you doing outside if it's so cold?"

"Wishing it was warm. Tell me again what she's driving."

"A Bentley."

"Hot damn. That mother of yours."

It was weird. He hated her for leaving, but news about my mother kept him going. If I could have sent him some of her over the pay phone, I would have done it. He hungered for details . . . whether she'd lightened up her hair, what the utilities bill must have been in a house that big, whether she still sang in a church choir now that she had Bobby and such a shimmery, cosmopolitan life. For as long as I'd been alive, my mother showered off whatever remained of her feverish Saturday nights with scalding hot water, and staggered off bright and early to sing in the choir. Bobby had changed lots of things, but he hadn't changed that.

"She's livin' the life, all right. And I'm fixing fenders. If that don't beat all, Polly." He was an auto mechanic, the best and most honest for miles around. People came to see him from all over. They came driving every kind of car, but apparently not Bentleys. At least not yet. "You tell her if she ever cracks that car up, she can ship it back here to me and nobody'll ever be the wiser."

Collusion continued and that was the other weird thing. When my mother was ready to call it quits with Bobby, she phoned my dad, whining and carrying on. Then he counseled her until she and Bobby patched it up. I never thought my parents were an award-winning couple. In fact, wishing they would break up got me started praying when I was small. I thought their anger would make the house blow up and the walls collapse and I'd be smashed inside. Then I saw a movie about Pompeii and I supposed their final rupture would be exactly like a volcanic eruption, with everybody scrambling down off the mountain to escape being burned alive. My childhood reveries featured blowups of all kinds and even when they didn't, even when they embraced the queasy peace that followed rage, I didn't kid myself about any rosy ending for my parents or for me. Even a child knows a man who has chased his wife with a tire iron can't expect love in return. On the other hand, this same child knows a woman can't make eyes at everyone in a small town and expect her husband won't chase her with a tire iron. It made me tired to think that Bobby Denario's money and my mother's teasing style now titillated Dad. Things were even worse than I thought in the mental health department. Each of my parents had a different strain of the same moral sickness and like everything going around, I was always afraid to catch it. I tried changing the subject.

"Business good, Dad?"

"Business is the same. I'm thinking of taking a partner. That way I'll have somebody to buy me out when I'm good and ready. Unless you're interested, that is."

"I'll pass."

"You were always a fast learner, Polly."

"Thanks, Dad. I'm pretty happy here."

"You don't always sound it. But your grandmama's come, hasn't she?"

"What does Granny Settle have to do with it?"

"She was meaning to come out there, ever since the troubles. So was I."

"The troubles" still lived in my father's mind. Oklahoma newspapers took AP releases about the riots and turned them into a range war or some version of a modern Dodge City, where basic justice was carried out with a rifle or a Bowie knife. My father tried to fly in and was embittered forever when he learned he could only get as far as the Ontario airport east of L.A. He couldn't arrive with the family arsenal and protect me because Mayor Bradley wouldn't let him. So it wasn't the riots that astounded him, it wasn't the fact of human misery and anger so diffused and long in the making that it could make a whole city implode, collapse into itself for long, bitter days. That he couldn't ride to his forty-year-old daughter's rescue was the most punishing lesson he learned from the Los Angeles riots.

"How is her disposition after the drive? It's Mama wanting to know."

"Tell Grandmother Jewel she is none the worse for the long trip."

"That'll disappoint her some."

Oh, didn't I know. The pair of old women would keep each other alive for hundreds, perhaps thousands of years. Neither woman was free to die, no matter what Granny Settle insinuated. She wasn't about to pass on before Jewel and vice versa. Maybe spite was the key to longevity.

Grandmother Jewel and Granny Settle lived on the same street in Granite and hadn't spoken for the past thirty years. I remembered Granny Settle's house, so different from Jewel's. Grandmother Jewel taught me how to do needlepoint, but it was Granny Settle who taught me to play poker. We drank sweet coffee and had shortcake we would eat plain when strawberries were out of season. She loved chocolate candy, the kind filled with rich, squirting surprises, and baked twelve kinds of cookies. I would come to her with my troubles, moaning about math or the pain of a bee sting or one more small treason committed by somebody at school. There was little that a cookie wouldn't cure and her sweet remedy was constant solace as I grew older. Long after my friends openly referred to their "cycles," I had only Granny Settle's cycles to refer to. I didn't menstruate until I was fifteen, but I kept good track of time by her cookies . . . Chocolate Crinkle one month followed by Meringue Drop the next and so on. They were just as dependable and less scary than blood.

"What did she bring you, Polly?"

"Is that still Jewel wanting to know?" I could hear a dogfight in the yard and wondered if he'd brought it on. Sometimes on the weekend when the shop was closed, he'd throw them a piece of meat to fight over for the fun of it. My father didn't have any hobbies to speak of.

"I was just wondering myself. You don't have to say if you don't want to."

"I'm not sure. She and Toby hustled a bunch of stuff into the garage. It's covered with sheets. Very hush-hush. Fact is, I don't even know how long she's planning to stay."

"If it was my house and she was my grandmother, I'd make it my business to know. She's somethin'. It *is* your house, isn't it?"

"Half of it is mine."

My dad thought Tom hung the moon. He'd always trusted Tom. What father wouldn't trust a son-in-law who'd gone to grade school with his only daughter? My dad loved to point out I learned to spell Tom's name the same week I learned to spell my own. Even after everything we'd been through, Tom's character was untarnished, packed away in that blue felt material that prevented the slightest stain on heirloom silver.

"You all right on money?"

"Fine, thanks."

"Kids okay?"

"I think so. Granny Settle thinks so." I heard him thump his foot on the ground and knew the thumping came from many things. Boredom with the conversation, resentment that I wouldn't fill in the gaping spaces in my mother's life with garish colors. Impatience with a daughter who still didn't know what she was getting, even when it was in her own garage all covered with dirty sheets.

"Our marriage wasn't much, but at least we *knew.*" The thumping was louder now, designed to bring the phone call to an end.

"Knew what?"

"That our kid was okay."

I didn't bother to correct him. I said goodbye and promised to call again in a week. My watch said it was one-fifteen in Granite and that meant there were already a few people standing outside Dad's shop with bashed cars and stories suggesting none of it was their fault.

Four

When I got back to the house the truck was gone. I wondered what supplies she was off buying. Maybe I could figure out how long she would be staying by what she loaded onto my pantry shelves. The morning had been productive and I wanted to keep up the momentum somehow, even if that meant humming in the kitchen or not talking to anybody and just letting the lyrics knock around some more while I got used to them. The kids were early, though, and this didn't get to happen.

"You guys cut class or what?"

"Minimum day, Mom. We *told* you." Kate's face was too pink, too bright and I knew she was feeling orphaned again. She once told me, in the middle of a Dickens period, that she felt orphaned at least once or twice a month. My forgetting important details like when half-days were scheduled was one quick way to make her feel that way.

"Well, here we all are."

Toby piped up. He had to, if only to lend balance to the scene. Two against one was usually the order of the day.

"We have a pupil-free day next week, Mom. Do you think you can be here?"

"Of course I'll be here."

Kate pulled on Toby's baseball cap and tipped the bill up slightly.

"Hey, cut it out!"

"Stop mimicking gangs, you idiot."

Kate handed me a note, carefully penned on yellow paper. Lorraine Middleton of Professional World had called. I must have made a sour face.

"You have to call her, Mom. I told her when I thought you'd be back."

"I don't have to call her. Especially if you guys are out of school next week."

"You're using us as an excuse. You can't say no to Lorraine anymore, Mom. You can't afford to. She's the only one from all those agencies who keeps calling you back. You need the money."

"Why don't you practice being fifteen and I'll practice being forty?"

Kate had drawn all over her hands and Toby's were so filthy I couldn't see what was under the layer of dirt. Inked-in faces appeared when she closed her fist and red Bic mouths opened and shut when she worked her thumb and forefinger. There was a full wreath of flowers sketched on the palm of her hand and skateboarding slogans too small to read. She looked dirty, but I guess I should have been grateful they weren't tattoos.

"Do me a favor, Mom." Her face was poppingly bright. Anger ran to Kate's northernmost point. Her whole head turned hot and red at the first sign of trouble. "Tell Granny Settle to mind her own business. Tell her not to take us to school anymore in her goddamned truck and especially tell her not to point at my friends."

"Honey, she doesn't mean to upset you."

"You're wrong. She means to upset everything in this house. Once and for all."

"Yeah," Toby chimed in. He pushed his hair out of his face, using both hands. It was a mighty effort. "She told us that this morning. 'Everything is going to change,' she said. Who told her she could come here anyway?"

"She's family."

"Oh, that's great! That's just great." His big eyes thickened so fast when he was about to cry. I knew he couldn't see anything from behind that glistening sheath of tears. "You call this a family? A mother, a sister, a great-grandmother and me? Two hundred thirty-five thousand boys annually become juvenile delinquents and guess what they all have in common? They all come from N.F.P. households."

Fact Man was back. Swatting, butting, kicking Fact Man, full of fictitious statistics.

"What's an N.F.P. household?"

"No Father Present! Cut it out, Kate."

It had been a while since we'd had an episode and I thought that was over for the time being. Kate tried to put her arm around him in a rush of sibling something . . . affection or, at least, recognition. It didn't work and she wound up dodging his flying fist.

"If you won't protect us from Granny Settle, Dad will."

"Yeah. Dad will." Toby was wiping off tears, leaving smeary tracks from the dirt on his hands. The storm cell was still there, but it was growing weaker. "I should be around men, Mom. I'm going to probably be a social psychopath when I grow up."

I had heard Toby's argument many times. It always meant he had said his peace, basically, but there were still a few zingers left over for me. He had never actually come out and said he wanted to live with his father. That had never been an issue since Tom was on the road so much. Instead he talked about men with a capital M.

"Instead of writing those songs, you should be going to a psychiatrist. Because maybe if you did, maybe if you did something other than write and sit around just being a nutcase, I would have a chance of growing up normal."

"Stick to one accusation at a time. We've gone from Granny Settle's strong personality to—"

"—your insanity, which is why I'm having a terrible childhood."

"Go to your room."

"Granny Settle said the truth always stings some."

He held his head high as he left the kitchen. Kate was torn between comforting me and siding with her brother. It was always confusing when the argument turned directions or grew nastier than it should have. She took a wooden kitchen spoon and started flipping it into the air. Kate was a master flipper. She had started with her baseball cap and advanced to anything that could be tossed into the air repeatedly. My productive morning had vanished and songwriting suddenly did seem crazy, but I couldn't see how doing it might turn my son into a psychopath.

"Want some tea, Mom?"

"That would be nice, yes."

"I'll bring it to your bedroom." This was an apology, as eloquent as they got. "Then you can call Lorraine back."

• • •

I didn't have to call Lorraine back. When the phone rang an hour later and I picked it up, she was already having a conversation with someone else. Lorraine, an ex-temp herself, "liked irregulars." She had children of her own, so she understood that, and she also had a deskful of unsold scripts at home. She liked being a kind of patron saint and thought of me as one of her struggling artists. Besides, she knew I could use the money and the work experience. I nearly always said yes to her lousy, last-minute jobs.

"—so tell him to drop dead. That bastard, just who does he think he is?"

"Hello?"

"That guy really pushes my buttons. Sally, pour me hot coffee, that's a good girl."

I tried again, this time cupping my hand around the mouth of the phone so she could hear. "Hello, this is Polly."

"Polly, there you are! Feel like a success package this week?"

"Not really, not too much."

"Because I've got a great job for you. A monkey could do it. Plus they pay your parking and you get to work in a nice building. Mid-Wilshire, you're gonna love it."

"What kind of work?"

"Believe me, a monkey could do it."

I pictured myself as a chimp, one who could talk on the phone and carry coffee; it wasn't a pretty image at all.

"Could you be more specific, Lorraine?"

She gave me the address on Wilshire Boulevard and said to be there the following day at eight-thirty sharp.

"If Martinez asks you back, the job ends Friday."

"It's by invitation only?"

"You know, if I could talk to people like you all day, I'd be a happy woman. You're smart, you're full of piss and vinegar. You wouldn't believe the level of humanity I put up with in this business. Don't forget to make them pay your parking. Remember, success package, success package."

I tried one last time. "Why can't you tell me what the job is? Am I going to work for the FBI?"

"I wish. It's a bank. Your daughter would make a crack receptionist. Tell her I said that."

"Goodbye, Lorraine."

The phone crashed down. She was always in such a rush. I should have gotten a phone number for Granny Settle in case she needed me. A complicated life had just become more intricate. As I thought of this, I imagined Beth saying See, See, See?

Kate brought tea and I took it into my closet for a look around. I had two choices for tomorrow and both were a shade of green that was very snazzy a few years back.

The bank was east of the Miracle Mile. I drove as quickly as I could, slowing down only once for a little Art Deco. The glassy green of the Wiltern Theater suggested water in a parched landscape. Occasional churches appeared along the way, but they reminded me of Kate's melted candles. My Pacer didn't turn any heads here and traffic grew a little meaner the longer I drove. I was relieved to spot the address Lorraine gave me. Tall, done up in requisite dark tones, the bank building cast a cold shadow of the same color over the parking lot.

The seatbelt had given my sheer dress a whopping crease that looked just like a banner. I tried to smooth it out as I rode the crowded elevator to the twentieth floor, but it still looked like I was a contestant for something. The suite I was looking for faced the elevator. There were no chairs in the waiting room. Just a woman and a desk.

"You Polly Harrison?"

I flashed a grin at the woman with the headset on. She seemed to be doing about five things at the same time, writing something down and then turning to her computer or the telephone. She stopped all operations and stood up, still wearing the headset.

"Yes."

"I'm Martinez. The others are already here." She turned and led me down a busy corridor. Everybody was hunched over computers or else carrying heavy boxes. They must have been heavy because people were complaining about their backs, but they didn't really complain *to* anyone. The people with boxes seemed to be talking to themselves.

"We're all going crazy," Miss Martinez explained as she walked. "This time of the month we all go crazy."

She walked very fast and I had to trot to keep up with her. "I never knew my bank statements were done by hand. It's funny, isn't it? We just take some things for granted."

Miss Martinez stopped dead in her tracks and I almost ran her down. "You're telling me you've never done this?"

"Oh, I've done things *like* this." I didn't know where the lie fell, which zone. Little and white, probably, if it was even a lie. I'd been around lots of paper, thanks to Professional World, and that was the solid truth. Miss Martinez looked unconvinced. It surprised me that she could hear me through her headset. It was a monster, a set of rubber earmuffs solid enough for the Arctic. She shook her head and pushed through the final door.

Five women sat slumped at individual folding tables. I could barely see faces behind the piles of paper on each station. Plastic bins, the ones mail carriers used in their trucks, stood to one side of every table. There was a long table in back with a pitcher of water and a thermos. Miss Martinez motioned to one of two tables.

"You get thirty minutes for lunch, plus a ten-minute break in the morning and one again in the afternoon. You need to fill one of these boxes up every hour. Instructions are on the board and don't seal your envelopes. Just crease the top. Any questions?"

"Not yet. Where can I find you if I do?"

"I'll be around." She adjusted her headset. "I'll be around." Miss Martinez smirked when she said it the second time.

In front of me were stacks of checks, divided by statements. Easy enough. My stomach began to relax. I looked at five things written down on the blackboard, each marked with an exclamation point.

"Hi." I peered over the top of my neighbor's stack of work. She grinned with one side of her mouth and kept counting checks. I watched her for a second, not wanting to throw off her count. One of the things we had to do was verify the number of checks against what was printed in the statement. Her right hand was in a splint, but it didn't seem to handicap her.

"Oof. One seventy-seven, this thing is a bitch. My name is Ann. I didn't catch yours."

"Polly Harrison. What's wrong with your wrist?"

"Carpal tunnel syndrome, but I get to take this thing off next week. Polly, this is Sealy, Jessica, Tanya and LaVonne." Everybody looked my way and I thought we'd have a friendly morning ahead. "I'm a singer. Once I get finished here, I've got a gig in Ventura, then back here tomorrow."

"Wow. What do you sing?"

"Blues, mostly. Especially since I got so much to be blue about, this damn job for one."

"I write song lyrics myself."

"No kidding."

"Country, mostly."

Ann made a sour face and I explained I wrote modern songs with modern themes.

"Well, I hope your music makes more money than mine does. Once I get my car paid for, I'm gonna have my number changed so Lorraine can't call me anymore."

"You're from Professional World, too?"

"We all are."

Well, that was great. That meant we were a team. I started in, looking over the bank statement for errors and making sure the name on each individual page matched. That took care of two things out of five. I started counting checks. This wouldn't be bad at all. We were all from Professional World, so it wasn't like we were warring temps. I heard plopping as I turned checks over, rhythmic plopping. The kind conducive to thought. I turned around and saw it was the completed statement dropping into each box. I watched LaVonne for a few seconds. She was a machine, making the barest movement as she ran through her checks. She was looking very refined with a bright orange suit and a scarf knotted at her neck. Her hairstyle, too. The tight chignon was perfectly understated office chic. Maybe that calm exterior hid tragedy and loss. Maybe LaVonne, like my lady determinedly pulling on her high-heeled leaving shoes, was sick and tired of fooling with her man. *Tired of foolin' with it, baby. It's time to let it alone.* I jotted that down on a little piece of scrap paper, stuck it in a pocket and licked my finger. This was going to be a terrific day, I could tell.

Miss Martinez was back. This time she was lugging a box herself. It was filled with more statements and I watched her in wonder.

"Aren't you using Stick Em?" She set down the box, moaned and glared at me. Then she grabbed a little jar that was on top of my table. "Use this. Otherwise you'll just tear your hands up. It'll increase your speed."

She leaned over my desk and looked at my carton. It was empty. I wiggled my fingers, then rubbed my hands together.

"You got any questions?"

I shook my head no and she left the room, this time with the headset around her neck.

Plop, plop, plop. The girls all worked fast, but there was so little visible effort. Not all the envelopes were white, either. Some of them were manila, like the ones I had in a separate tray. They were built like accordions inside, divided with frosted paper. I started my counting again. The statement said I ought to have fifty-eight.

"I once did Michael Douglas."

"Girl, I've done Shirley MacLaine. The councilman for my district, too. I've got stories to tell. With what I know, I could bury the man in his own dirt."

My first plop was rather thin. I needed to hurry, to go at least as fast as Ann, who clearly favored singing to stuffing anytime, but was getting the job done despite her disdain. I put some Stick Em on my middle finger and watched it glide over the checks. I was beginning to feel like a real pro.

"Used to be they'd order us a pizza for lunch."

"Yeah. Domino's. Jacopo's sometimes if there were enough people who didn't mind waiting a long time. I love their thin crust."

"I'm getting hungry just thinking."

I couldn't turn my head to see who was talking. I couldn't even put in my two cents without losing the motion. I was in the middle of a horror. It said there were two hundred and thirty-two checks in Dr. Santoni's statement and I was in my second recount. I began to imagine Santoni, who undoubtedly drove a black Mercedes and terrorized his nurses just as he was terrorizing me. I looked at the clock on the wall. I had been at it for nearly an hour. My carton was only half full.

"You think she meant it about the break?"

"No way."

I turned my head because stupid Santoni had come up shy for the third time. I hoped I'd bump into him one day. Maybe I'd be at a party sometime and meet a mustachioed Dr. Santoni and I would sit there knowing where every declared penny went. I started reading the checks. One of the amounts, made out to a department store, was what I lived on every month. I felt dizzy. The intervals between plops had decreased. I didn't need to turn around to know who spoke next. It was Ann.

"Ask me, you either give 'em speed or accuracy. Ain't nobody givin' both."

"Go on."

"Amen, girl."

I made a dizzying decision and closed the file on Santoni. I couldn't get anything to agree and I didn't care. I couldn't fit all the checks into the white envelope, so I grabbed a manila one, smashing the checks between the rows of frosted paper. His address showed in the window and anyway, it was unlikely that Santoni would balance his own checkbook. Minions would do that for him and they probably hated him worse than I did. Santoni made a big thunk as I dropped him into my carton.

"Time." It was Martinez, sans headset. She looked at my carton.

"That's all you've done?"

"Yes, but I've finally got the system figured out."

"I'll just take what you have. Even though it's incomplete. You need to work faster."

"I will, Miss Martinez."

She took my batch out of the room.

"I'm taking a break and I don't care if she asks me back or not. My contract says I get two breaks—"

I couldn't get up to join LaVonne. I was in the midst of a fat statement and had to continue.

"—and I'm gonna take them. Anyone like a Tic-Tac?"

She set one on my table and left the room. Her carton was the fullest and she knew she was coming back. I thought she ought to take twelve breaks and was about to say that to Ann when the wall phone rang. I hadn't even been aware that there was a wall phone until it started ringing. Miss Martinez didn't come in and nobody moved to answer it. I was the closest to it.

"What should I do, Ann?"

"Get it, I guess."

"Colossal Bank, Polly Harrison speaking."

"Polly! Just who I wanted to speak with. It's Lorraine."

"Hey, how are you?"

"Never better. Listen, honey, there'll be other jobs. You're still my A list success package. But this particular job is ending today."

"What do you mean?"

"I mean you're fired. Her commandos say you forgot page two on one of the statements, plus Santoni's a disaster. This is not the place for you. Get a time card from the bitch and go home. Look at it this way . . ."

I could hear her smoke, taking a long draw on the Virginia Slims she loved.

"I'm sure you can make a song out of this day. Now can't you, Polly?"

I was too depressed to answer. I thought of the monkey again. This time he was standing on the unemployment line. I forgot to get my parking ticket stamped and was out ten bucks, somewhat less than I earned for the day after deductions.

Five

*R*ight after getting fired from bank statements, I decided to drive over to the Sovereign. Parking outside the oddball beach hotel and glaring at it from the curb was always cathartic. Feeling mildly depressed never quite did it for me. I had to touch bottom, feel truly miserable, before I could think of swimming to the surface toward life and light.

Six months ago, I was a high-profile mom. I took on any task, great or small, for the school and that meant making a good many speeches. I talked to teachers, school board members and fellow parents. Public speaking got to me. The authority went not only to my head, but to my shoulders, knees and toes. I tapped at microphones with my finger, checking the sound, and my whole body would ring. Snapshots from the period showed alarming lights glancing off my head, as if I had swallowed radium. Besides speech making, I loved rooting around in the school library, sorting books and helping giggly girls find the latest Judy Blume or being the liaison with our neighbors, 20th Century-Fox, when we convinced them that a spring festival should be held on their lot. I could always be found at school or at home. At Parent Appreciation Night, I received a standing ovation and a gift from the president of the PTA. The gift was a beeper. Some of the emergency calls that came in were brownie shortages at school bake sales or a parent who didn't show up to man a booth, but it didn't matter that the beeps signaled small concerns. That I was the only volunteer with a beeper was a symbol of power and completely wowed everybody. But one day, when two women started going at it tooth and nail about what kind of name tags should be used at Back to School Night, I practically ran from the room. I felt like a single parent since Tom was traveling so much. He had just been given Nevada and though it was a great market for Zeemie Protein Powder and Zeemie Power Bars, the whole Zeemie product line, it meant a lot of new responsibility for me. So I decided to play hooky and just go to the beach for a day. I didn't even bring a transistor, that's how quickly I made the decision. I threw a towel and hat in the car and decided to conk out in the sun for a few hours before picking up the kids.

I took the same surface streets Tom and I had always used to take the kids to the beach when they were small. I saw a lot of skaters that day. They seemed welded to their boards, their sloped shoulders and dangling arms registering every shiver in the sidewalk. About five blocks from the Sovereign, I had to swerve hard to miss a boy who blew right into the intersection from nowhere. The kid looked at me accusingly, as if I were the one who hadn't heeded the stop sign, as if I were cutting school. I made a big show of looking at my watch and he disappeared down an alley. I didn't let it get to me. I was busy picturing myself at the beach. I was sorry tans weren't in fashion anymore. I would be white Polly forever and ever, never changing colors again in the course of the day. But public disdain for a deep tan didn't mean you had to boycott the beach. I couldn't wait for the great assault of odors. When I was a kid in Granite watching Annette Funicello in those bathing suit movies, I would pull on my turquoise swim cap, mix salt and water together in an old milk bottle and sniff until I got dizzy. My experiments didn't work. I could never make Granite smell quite like the California coast.

I stopped before I got to the water, though. Something embarrassed and delighted me about the Sovereign and I pulled my car over to try and figure it out for myself. It reflected someone's true taste. It was darling in the way France could be darling. Parasols sprouted on the lawn at random, there was a modest rose garden and porches were crammed with bicycles and the occasional hibachi. Clothing dried on a line in certain of the windows. I was enchanted. I wanted to be a guest there and dawdle over coffee, if they even served it. They did. I rolled down the window and saw several people lingering outside in the garden with cups and saucers in their laps. I studied a few of the guests. Then I put on my enormous beach hat and scooched down low in the seat. I prayed loudly. It opened in the usual way with *Dear God,* but a very testy tone was evident:

You have apparently decided to put me in hell or a good facsimile of same. Why did this have to happen to me? I may be a wobbly believer, but I certainly didn't deserve this. However I am—

Still Yours,
Polly

Instead of dying in the seat of the car as I watched Tom with a woman who was older and less pretty than I was, it occurred to me to make a little list of impressions. It put a crisp edge on the whole experience and writing stuff down helped lead me away from chaos. My natural curiosity was enhanced in a creepy way. I must have sat there, hiding under my giant hat, for a very long time as I watched eighteen years of marriage topple over like a giant redwood. Six months ago Polly Harrison reported this from the field:

1. She stirs his coffee for him and licks the spoon.
2. She sits all the way to the front of the bench.
3. She covers her mouth when she laughs.
4. She doesn't have large breasts.
5. She has had her hand on his knee for seven and a half minutes.
6. They look married.
7. They look banal.
8. They look alike.

I could have put lots of things on that list. It could have continued ad nauseam with my feelings of rage and my new sense of what dying was all about. But I liked the way the list looked. It was sleek, to the point and clearly written by somebody very much in command. I wasn't falling apart, though I could have, easily. I had to use the bathroom and I knew, because of the crazed thoughts running loose in my mind, that I'd better be really careful. For the first time in my life I suffered from penis envy. To march wordlessly forward, unzip my fly and piss on the two of them would have been a truly beau geste. But to stand there furiously dribbling all over the ground and my shorts suggested a madwoman. To do that would simply justify the whole affair. I locked the list in the glove compartment, put on some Chapstick and squeezed gently on the door handle. I didn't want to make any noise.

They were talking about Zeemie Powder. I rolled my eyes because so far everything but me was predictable. I was the only element that could have gone off in any direction. She was sitting on the edge of her stone bench, eager for news of Zeemie Powder, and Tom was blathering about the force of Zeemie. There was a time when he was ready to launch Zeemie missiles at Iraq. The actual composition of Zeemie was a secret as heavily guarded as the deadly recipes of the Manhattan Project. There were competing protein powders, certainly, but no company could make quite the same claims as his. He's calmed down some since then. I think being around bodybuilders all the time has had kind of an adverse effect on him. But back then, Zeemie was the grand march and Tom was the commanding general.

"It looks like we've got the endorsement."

"From Olympia McMichael?"

"Her agent's making a big thing over her fee and travel limitations in her contract."

"She doesn't like traveling?"

"Scared of planes."

"No!"

"It's weird, isn't it? The woman breaks bodies for a living and she's never flown before. Would you like to know what I think?"

"Always."

"There is no reason this can't be every bit as successful as The Wafer."

They exchanged a sober glance, then smiled at the same time. I was standing off in the shadows. I couldn't see too well or hear much better. It seemed like all my senses were short-circuited. There were a couple of Toms and about ten of her swimming around in front of me. He was wearing my favorite shirt. It was the gray-blue that brought out his eyes, the gray-blue *I* had taught him to wear. If my mind had been working, I would even have been able to say what day I had picked it up from the laundry. Another hotel guest was eyeballing me. He was Persian and rather diffident about eyeballing me, but doing it all the same. I curled my lip and put an end to that. I *knew* Olympia McMichael. I had sat next to her at an awards banquet and listened to her moronic opinions until I was practically catatonic. I decided to act, because if I didn't, I would wind up dribbling urine or breaking bodies, à la Olympia

McMichael. I not only had the penis envy thing, I had something new: a business suit complex. This woman made a real living and it gave her clout. I could tell that she had investments, a serious salary and a car phone. She would finish with my husband or somebody else's and then grab her suitcase and go back to some elaborate business palace where she had a whole staff. She had a crippling weakness for the offbeat. Thus, Tom. Thus, Zeemie and endorsements from muscle-bound lesbians. I could tell she made more money than my husband.

"I wouldn't mind meeting her. Could you arrange that? Swear you won't tell if I share something with you."

I was on the verge of gagging, but moving forward now.

"I swear."

"Not a single living soul."

I looked as attractive as a mutton chop in my big hat and shorts, but it wasn't going to stop me. I was right behind the two of them.

"I was seriously into mud wrestling in college."

That did it. I had just the right grip on the situation. I lay a chilly hand on my husband's shoulder and he dropped his coffee cup as I squeezed it. One good thing about the Sovereign was the total absence of Limoges. The cheap cup shattered all to hell.

"Hi, hon." He leaped to his feet and the sunglasses, always perched on his forehead, clattered to the ground along with the cup. "Polly! What are you—"

"—I was just in the neighborhood. Do me a favor, love? Pick the kids up from school for me? They've both got appointments at the dentist. I'm going away for a few days."

"Polly, we need to talk."

"I'll leave you a copy of their schedules. I don't believe we've met."

I took her hand in mine and thought of those metal buzzers Toby had at home that gave you a real jolt. I did very well and so did she, which is where her professional background came in handy. I was deeply grateful for my years of school service. At least I wasn't just a lumpy old housewife. I had skills, I had civic concerns and responsibilities. I could stand as tall as she did. I pulled at the hem of my shorts.

"I'm pleased to meet you, Mrs. Harrison."

"Ah, then you do know Tom has a family."

"Oh, yes. In fact, I've seen a picture of you."

I had a bad moment then. I felt completely exposed, as if a Peeping Tom had been leering at me. I had been mindlessly going about my daily business, whistling, bathing, shaving when I couldn't go another day longer and all the while someone had been peering in my windows. She knew me.

"I dislike scenes, don't you?" My voice sounded miles away from my body.

"Oh, hate them."

"I didn't get your name."

"Frankie Doray."

"It was a pleasure, Frankie. I bet you were something else in college. I can definitely see you all smeared with mud. Bye, now."

My breathing was all screwed up. I was due for an allergy shot and imagined that was it, although this was a new sensation. I couldn't take in enough air and it kind of ruined my parting shot. I was backing away from the two of them, backing away slowly as if my feet were part of the earth and it was the earth itself that was tearing, not me, as I took each hard step. Nobody moved. I saw because I only turned around when I had to, when it was clear that the only one doing anything was me. Then I turned my back on both of them and headed toward the lobby of the Sovereign. I still had to use the bathroom and, more importantly, I had to get a look at the hotel itself. She had looked in my windows and it was my turn to look through hers.

I was in trouble. There was nobody at the front desk and what people there were were scattered around bent over newspapers or guides to Los Angeles. I was wheezing, there was no air anyplace and I was sorry for my children. They would become one of those tragic newspaper stories with a dead mother and a father burdened with his staggering guilt. I didn't have time for a prayer, but I did see a bathroom on my left. I had to find some place to quietly die and I hoped nobody was in there to get in my way.

I kneeled down on the floor. Pressure forced my shoulders and head to the cold tile. Someone else was in a stall, I could see by the shoes. But she was too frightened by the sounds I made to do anything. Liability or she was repulsed by the idea of CPR with a stranger, I don't know. I didn't think I was dying, I knew it. I was somebody who needed oxygen and wasn't getting any and that meant I was going to die, but before I went, I needed to vomit. So I crawled to the other stall and did that. Suddenly I could breathe. My doctor later told me I'd had an asthma attack, my very first despite a lifetime of seasonal sniffing and sneezing. Vomiting cleared the air passages and was the body's automatic response if the asthma victim was lucky. I didn't know all that then, though. I cleaned myself up, feeling very self-conscious, and spoke to the pair of shoes next door.

"I must be coming down with something. I'm okay now, though. I'll be just fine." Nobody answered me, so I cleaned up as best I could and stuck a few Sovereign courtesy soaps in my bag. The gardens were empty when I peered through the entrance to the hotel. I went to the front desk to check in.

I paid cash for my stay at the Sovereign. It was a bargain at seventy-five dollars a day. After a continental breakfast, no food was served in the hotel and Beth ferried meals to me from a deli on Ocean Boulevard. She looked unsure on the first day. She worried over the pastrami sandwich and the scratchy towels. She wondered out loud what insects might be nestled inside the gold shag rug in my room. The Sovereign was a leaky old vessel. Cold air seeped in all day long, no matter that the windows were shut.

"You're going to catch pneumonia on top of everything else." She fussed with the latch on the window but didn't get anywhere. The Sovereign was drafty and there wasn't a thing to do about it. "Are you sure you're not shooting yourself in the foot? Look, I'm totally into the idea of revenge. It just seems like you should be having more fun while you're at it. This place is a dump."

"It's not that bad. I want Tom in agony and this ought to do it. I want him to think of me having my way with legions of men. Do you think he will?"

"Maybe. He might." Beth sighed and pulled on her ponytail.

"You didn't tell him where I was staying, did you?"

"Oh, no."

Her answer was too quick. She wasn't looking at me. Fury or fear was rushing into my head and my chest. Whatever it was felt too fierce to uncap, so I pushed and pushed until it was compressed and hard, dense as a rock in my heart.

"Beth, doesn't he even want to know?"

I knew her so well. She was deciding one of two things: whether I could handle the truth or whether she could handle telling it. I didn't give her a chance to find out.

"What's in there?"

She reached down and opened a totebag. She was like some wonderful fairy godmother. Every day she brought food and treats, plus travel magazines designed to make me think I was in Hawaii. She lifted silk pajamas out of the bag. They had white piping and some fancy emblem on the front pocket. She tore the price tag off with her teeth and shoved them at me.

"At least wear something nice. I can't stand to see you like this, Polly."

I couldn't either, so I didn't argue as she brought me extravagant oils and ointments, bedclothes fit for a princess. I wasn't leaving the bed at the Sovereign. I had told the desk clerk that, to make sure I stuck to my guns. The housekeeper was a nervous little woman who didn't like cleaning around me, where I lay sprawled for five days, but she was too frightened to argue. From my outpost, thanks to several guidebooks, I could see whitecaps on the Pacific and the white sand that lay stretched about a Hawaiian hotel, sparkling like a skirt of ground glass. I lay the silk pajamas on top of my blanket and opened the *Condé Nast Traveler* she held out to me.

"Did Kate seem all right to you?"

"Quiet. Poor Toby. He's like this miniature statistician. What was he telling me yesterday? All these horrible figures on prostate cancer."

"Did they buy the letter I wrote?"

"Pretty much. But they know something's up. You're going to have to talk to them eventually."

"Oh, Beth." I put the *Traveler* to one side and covered my face with both hands. "What am I going to do?"

She let me stay like that for a few moments, then gave me a brisk hug. I knew the pragmatism was phony, I knew she felt horrible, but I appreciated her approach anyhow. Nothing would have been worse than two women lying around being sorrowful. Having one of us that way was hard enough to take.

"You're going to imagine biting into this nice opakapaka with soy ginger herb sauce. Jeez, this stuff looks fantastic. And I'm not even a big fish eater."

It was true. Since I couldn't foresee the future, I sunk a grappling hook into an imaginary present. Maui and opakapaka would do just fine. I ate and drank up a storm, all from my bed at the Sovereign.

But as soon as Beth left me each day, I got down to my real task . . . imagining Tom and Frankie Doray in flagrante delicto. I did it to save my own life. I loved my home and my kids. I loved how I spent every living minute of my days. I had loved Tom, though I didn't know what I felt about him now. How did you examine love anyway, check that it was the right kind and the right strength? How could anybody make sure there was enough of it to last the minutes, hours, days rolling over days that made up a lifetime? I had once longed to crawl inside Tom's wonderful skin, share one body, one blood, and if that wasn't love, then I didn't know what was. But when did I feel this, at twenty, at thirty? Last month? I couldn't say, but I did know I was foolishly passionate about my life and I knew to save it, Polly the Pleasant would take over, even under these extreme circumstances, and I didn't want her to. I wanted to become an avenging angel. I wanted inch-long nails and a gleaming breastplate. I wanted to spring forth from my room at the Sovereign when my vigil was over and leap screaming into my own life to tear it up and start again, with or without Tom Harrison. So I lay in bed for five days and pictured him with Frankie.

For the first couple of days, I didn't even have to see her actual face next to his actual face. I could do the exercise clinically and not feel my heart being torn from my chest. All adulterous couples were the same, I decided. To study their behavior was neat and orderly, like recognizing identical cellular structures under a smeary slide. Take lingerie. There was no chance Frankie Doray wore cotton underpants with a puffy elasticized waist. She would never fold them neatly, putting them to one side before hopping into bed with my husband. They would be silk or satin and she would fling them, never minding how they fell, how they tumbled to the ground.

I busily conducted my bloodless study of two middle-aged gymnasts before things really got rolling. But by day three, I was phoning Beth not to come and calling the deli myself. It turned out at the Sovereign that this was a form of room service they honored. A freckle-faced boy brought me sandwiches named after famous golfers as my days grew deeper and darker. For I had gotten into the act by the third day. Polly Harrison had somehow entered the ménage. My name was being spoken and little snippets of conversation drifted my way as I lay still in Beth's plush velveteen bathrobe.

"We're going to wake up the whole hotel."

"And it'll be all your fault! You're incredible. Did Polly ever . . ." Frankie demurred, smiled lazily and cocked one leg girlishly as she lay on her tummy.

Bitch! I lay writhing in my bed, repulsed by her coquetry. How dare she speak my name? How could he let her touch him there? That was *my* spot. You're killing me, Tom. You are killing me and not softly either. Since I was shouting soundlessly at them, nobody paid attention to me.

"Tell me, Tom. What makes a man wander?" She traced his lips with the tip of her finger. My husband licked it languidly.

"This."

She put her whole finger in his mouth, moving it slowly back and forth. I had half the blanket on the bed wadded up in my fist as I watched.

"Was she withholding, honey?"

Tom looked blank. He was probably thinking of taxes. Frankie Doray needed to talk plain English if she was going to make herself understood.

"You know, baby. Was she a cold fish?"

He sat up in the very bed where I lay. We were all there together, only I was pushed to the outer edge.

"Polly is a wonderful mother"—I was more than that! It was my idea to rent those films when the kids were at camp. You made me stand in line to return them—"and a wonderful wife."

Frankie was moving in for the kill, I could certainly see that. Her lips were pursed for more love. But before he could have her again, he had to come clean. No talk, no action.

"But how was she in bed, honey?"

My husband wouldn't satisfy either of us. He got up out of bed and moseyed around the cruddy room, picking up ashtrays or scanning *City Pleasures*. The color drained out of the picture. It was like a play that ended too soon, before the final scene was really over. Dissatisfaction marked the rest of my stay at the Sovereign. I could take my imagination to a certain point, but no further. I felt like one of Granny Settle's cussed ponies, locking my knees and refusing to advance a single inch. It didn't matter who hit me with what, I wasn't about to push on another inch with a rider on my back.

Six

I started my car, rolling down all the windows to let in some fresh air. They were repainting the hotel and that worried me a little. The thought of a Southwestern color scheme slapped on the peeling white Sovereign put me off. The parasols were still there. The guests were still sipping under the trees and I was feeling cavalier about being fired from the most mundane job in the world. The trouble was lack of skills. Why hadn't I thought of it before? I promised myself to take one of those one-day seminars that taught you Word-Perfect. That way Lorraine would be able to send me on decent jobs. A trip to the old hotel always worked magic. I had already forgotten what Martinez looked like. I didn't feel like an avenging angel, but I felt better. The sight of Frankie Doray tenderly holding my husband's face between her hands was already going from black to gray to gone.

My beeper went off. I'd kept using it even after my volunteer career ended. Kate had the code now and promised to beep me only for emergencies. I shut it off and drove to a pay phone up the block. I pictured Toby crushed underneath a car or Granny Settle, heart-attacked into stiff surrender on my couch. Grandmother Jewel had won. That was it. Granny Settle was dead and Jewel was victorious. Kate picked up on the second ring.

"Kate! What's wrong?"

"What's wrong is I'm making my soup and she completely fucked it up."
Her voice was muffled and I knew she had dragged the phone into a closet to
talk.

"Your language is appalling."

"*She's* appalling."

"Granny Settle just wants to help out around the house. It's her way of saying thank you."

"She put meat in without even asking and ruined the whole thing. And wait
until you see the dining room."

"I'm on my way."

"My counselor wants you to come in next week."

"What's wrong?"

"I don't know. She got me out of history to tell me, though."

I shut off my beeper and pushed hard on the door to the telephone booth. It
was stuck and for a second I thought I might have to bang on the glass wall for
help.

Toby and Stewart were sitting on the front step when I got home. They were
having a contest to see who could spit the farthest. Usually they did this for
my benefit, to make me wince. Either that or to get me to drive them somewhere so the two of them would stop spitting.

"Can't you guys find anything better to do?"

"Dog crap alert. Left of center. Careful, Polly."

I stepped gingerly through the grass.

"Can I sleep over at Stewart's, Mom?"

"Only if I can come, too."

"Good one, Mom. Can I?"

It was Friday. I released him for the next twenty-four hours and went inside
to face the music. I could hear a low whirring and the steady sound of a pump-
ing pedal. The house smelled good. Whatever Granny Settle had thrown in the
soup smelled agreeable to me, if not to Kate.

"Polly Ann? Is that you?"

Two sets of overalls hung stiff and rigid on iron hangers. A couple of boxes
had been brought in from the garage. They stood in corners of the dining room
where Granny Settle labored over her sewing machine. She was like a mete-
orite, burning across a dark sky. I didn't know where my granny would even-

tually make her final landing, but I knew it would make a solid pockmark in the earth. She had taken down all the curtains in my dining room. They weren't bad curtains. In fact, I had been pretty fond of them.

"What are you up to, Gran?"

"I can't sleep a wink, light as it is in this room. I'm going to have to sacrifice my skirts. But I reckon I'll get some decent rest once they're up. I've gone and made the child mad, Polly. I put some meat in her soup because it was as thin as she is and she cussed me up and down the room."

I played innocent and sat down next to her. A ball of something sweet-smelling distended her cheek. Granny Settle continued.

"I believe she's been mad from the beginning."

"I thought she was fairly polite about it. Kids just go nutty when their environment is disturbed. I'm sorry if she didn't give you a warm enough welcome."

"I don't mean that. I mean *her* beginning. I think she came roaring out of you screaming, kicking mad and that makes her a Settle, not a Jewel. The girl doesn't know it yet, but she'll be the saddest one of all when I pass."

She muttered something I couldn't hear and went back to her sewing machine. I couldn't believe she was tearing up those skirts. They had been her finest dancing skirts, the ones she used to spread out on the floor for story shows when I was a kid. She told me every pleat held a secret inside and as soon as I was big enough to wear the skirt, I was big enough to hear the secrets. In the meantime, though, before I got to that size, she would satisfy me with stories of when she was a gal. A gal no bigger than a minute, a gal like me. Sucking on shortbread drenched with blackberry juice, I listened to tales of the rodeo, of Star and his blind eye. I'd tried to keep those stories alive in lyrics, but her words always outdid mine. Her stories outshone heaven. Her stories were like room after room of hard, bright light.

"Stop talking about death, Granny."

"And why is that?"

"It's too morbid."

"The young ones don't think so. They like my dead stories best of any of the ones they've heard so far. The girl told me that before I spoiled her soup."

Well, *I* hadn't liked them. Grandmother Jewel held my hand tight when I was twelve years old and taught me to scatter peppercorns in my front yard so nothing would come into it that wasn't welcome. I supposed that also and especially included grandmothers, so I kept my yard thoroughly peppered after

I learned Granny Settle had been dead not once, but twice. It didn't work. She just marched right over them on her way to tell my daddy somebody had been good and gypped at his bodyshop or to inform my mother that a friendship with Minah Overstreet wouldn't enhance her reputation any.

The first time Granny Settle died, all sorts of things happened. An angel entered the room where she lay covered with clouds.

"Warm clouds, Polly. There were about five piled on top of my poor, hurting body and each of them warmer than the next."

The angel was neither male nor female, but some kind of golden aura with ankles.

"The angel sat down at a table next to where I lay, crossed its ankles and —"

"Was it a man or a woman?"

"It wasn't one or the other. I said it was an angel. Stop asking questions or I won't tell you what it was like." Granny Settle lit a candle for good measure and continued.

"The angel was mighty casual, tricky, as you will soon see."

I had a lot of trouble concentrating at age twelve. Everyone noticed, too, not just my teachers at school. My mother stopped shouting at me for not doing my chores because it left her too hoarse to sing in church. Nobody told me their urgent secrets since it was clear I wasn't listening. The whole world was covered with a hard sheen and for months I could do nothing but slide along on the surface. I was supremely unmoved by all things, but this was different. A report from the netherworld was another thing entirely.

"It didn't take me any time at all to get comfortable talking to an angel. Before long, all the strangeness had worn off and the sorrow, too. I didn't miss living one bit. Being dead and talking with angels had it all over living, I'll tell you."

"Didn't you miss Mama?"

"Not one bit."

"Or Grampa Settle?"

"Even less than your mama. There I was, warmed by clouds and wrapped in mysterious beauty—"

"If the angel was beautiful it must have been a girl."

She ignored me and went on. "—when the angel stood up. We'd been talking about my life on earth with the angel doing most of the talking, and then everything changed all at once. The lights, the smells, the voice of the angel. I mean everything, Polly Ann."

My house had turned porous by this time. Sounds from the kitchen and the yard floated into my bedroom uninvited. In an instant I had gone from hearing and seeing nothing, to hearing and seeing everything. I could see my dog pushing his plastic bowl around the kitchen floor with his wet, black nose. I could hear my mother rising from a nap in the room above me, the springs of her bed creaking as she stepped into the houseshoes she kept neatly by one side of the bed. I peered at the bluejay bullying sparrows away from the entrance to the wooden birdhouse my father had assembled from a kit, cursing the catalogue for enticing him into buying something he could so easily have built from scratch. Goodbye, goodbye, goodbye I whispered to all of it. Granny Settle had brought death into my bedroom and what I could finally sense in my deaf and dumb twelfth year, I suddenly had to release. Surely death would come to me, too, since Granny Settle had thought to introduce us.

"Do you need to use the toilet? Then sit still. Well, the angel undid its wings and placed them over a hook in that room. Then I realized the angel had changed robes, even though I hadn't seen it happen. They were dark and made of wool. And scratchy. I could tell that from where I lay."

"Why didn't you get up and make a run for it?"

"Couldn't. I didn't have any bones. That's the first thing that happens when you die. Your bones slip out of your body and you just lay there like a human fish filet. Besides, child, where can you run when you're dead?"

I held my hands over my ears. It was too terrible. The room upstairs was rocking with my mother's movements.

"And then it started."

"What?"

"Why, the reckoning. The judgment. You can't just bask in your good deeds once you're dead. What's the first thing my ponies do after they wade out into cool water?"

"They wallow in the dirt."

"Amen. They lie down in the dirt. I lay there and heard my whole life said, all the dark parts. Each and every one. By that time the room was a cave as moist as the inside of your mouth. The walls squeezed out a cold sweat, the same as my body was doing while the angel recited my bad deeds. When I thought I couldn't hear another word, when I thought I would tear the ears from my head, it ended. The angel comforted me and fed me nectar to give me strength."

"Why?"

"So I could stand up for my receiving line. It was like a wedding, only there I was, naked as all get out, shaking hands with every human I had known who had passed before me. They praised me or—"

"Why do they call that heaven, Granny?"

"Who said anything about heaven? I'm telling you what it's like to be dead. I listened to all their praise and damnation and, believe me, there was plenty of both."

"What was everybody else wearing?"

"Naked. We were all naked, naked, naked. After that I came back."

Granny Settle pulled a plastic sack from a pocket of her overalls. Inside was an old stick.

"When I opened my eyes, this lay across my chest. I left the rest behind. But believe me, gal, the whole slope was littered with white flowers."

As she lay dead for the first time, having fallen from a horse into a wide gully just behind the Overstreet compound, a grove of dogwood trees burst open and shed their blossoms on my granny. Dogwood dusted the grassy ditch where she lay. As Granny Settle told it, there was such profusion, such a sumptuous flowering and falling, that after that the whole grove of dogwood trees went three straight years without ever blooming once.

I had made the candle she lit myself. As the wax dripped down one chunky red side I remembered the trouble I'd taken and the way the milk carton full of hot wax kept tipping over to one side, sabotaging all my efforts. It burned on and on; as long as it did I figured I was her prisoner. I also knew I would never sleep again. Instead I would lie awake with my hands pressed between my bony knees, watching a serpentine line of naked dead people mill around in my room.

"When I died a second time, some ten years later, there wasn't so much to-do. It wasn't anything like the first time, thanks to your Grandmother Jewel. Ask me if she forgot about our differences even though I lay dead to the world in her own yard. Ask me if my spilled blood melted her hard heart."

"Did your spilled blood—"

"Melt her hard heart? Absolutely not. Forgiveness never did matter to Elizabeth Jewel."

Grandmother Jewel's yellow stone house, grand by Granite standards, stood in the middle of a corner lot. Two important streets intersected just beyond her French lace curtains, marking her property as a crossroads both real and symbolic. One street led to the A&P grocery store and its competitor, the Circle Market. The Baptist church and the Four Winds congregation were another half a mile down the same straight road with both Denny's and Pizza Hut conveniently positioned within easy walking distance. The other road went west toward a couple of broken-down bars and a drive-in restaurant, scheduling headquarters for knife fights or car racing between warring bands of boys. To get anywhere important in Granite, you either turned left or right in front of Grandmother Jewel's house. Pedestrians marched past her house night and day, minding to keep to the sidewalks. She gardened to within an inch of her life and God help anyone who tromped on her Bermuda grass or staggered through a bed of pansies while shortcutting his way to a glass of cold beer.

"Did you visit with the very same angel?"

"What?" Her pale eyes were fastened on something inside the flickering light of the candle. I pushed at her leg with my finger.

"Granny Settle. Were you with the angels the next time you died?"

"No angels. I was lying in a pool of water, though. Under the surface and breathing, which is how I knew I was dead."

"Like a fish."

Well, it did make crazy sense, like everything Granny Settle had ever told me. If she was a human fish filet on the first go-round, it seemed fitting that she would lie under the water's edge on the second. She walked me through the land of the dead, even though I was a heavy load, a querying, wiggling weight on her memories.

"Let me tell my story, Polly. Don't ask any more questions until I'm through. Can that foot hold still if I ask it nice?"

She told me of the swirling that was water, but something else. Way beyond the thing we called water. There was a whole green spinning that was frightening and holy, shot clean through with wonder and then through the perfect stillness that followed came a voice. A deep raspy voice.

"Whose voice do you suppose I heard?"

"It must have been God."

She leaned forward and coughed so violently I thought the candle would go out. She struck her own chest several times until the gasping and sputtering was over.

"It was Jewel! Giving orders to a police officer like he was her houseboy."

Granny Settle, struggling home with two bushels of lemons from the A&P in temperatures topping 105 degrees, decided to gamble. She cut through Jewel's backyard, picking her way carefully through Jewel's Chinese waterfall, her tomato patch and the mint that came up wild around a water spigot aimed at a dozen rose bushes planted willy-nilly behind a potting shed. She was a gingerly invader, moving through enemy territory with the greatest caution.

"Did I tromp one blade of grass or break the head off one of her fool flowers? No!"

And then, a good yard from the sidewalk, Granny Settle tripped over a piece of wire strung between two poles. She landed hard, her skull hitting the sidewalk full force. There were witnesses.

"Emily Harding saw me go over. She says I didn't even have time to hold my hands out to break the fall. There I lay, my body sprawled flat on the ground, my spirit transported to that place beyond when . . ."

Jewel witnessed the whole thing from behind her French lace curtains, had watched Granny Settle's stealthy progress from one dining room window in the back to the next, so that by the time Granny Settle fell on her head, the police were already pulling up to the curb. My granny woke up dazedly from cool green depths to find an officer writing up a citation.

"She says, 'Officer, this woman is trespassing on my property and I won't have it.'"

I could imagine it. The heat, Granny Settle's ungainly sprawl with her nemesis towering above her. Grandmother Jewel had might, authority and the finest corner lot in town.

"I said, 'Jewel, dear, I've struck my head just now on the asphalt and if I'm not wrong, I was with the dead for an instant.'" Granny Settle paused and drew a deep breath, then placed both hands on my bedside table. She leaned over the candle flame and I bit the inside of my mouth. Did this news cause Elizabeth Jewel consternation and remorse? Of a sort.

" 'I should have buried you while I had the chance. Officer Reynolds, keep writing. I intend to press charges.' "

Much later I would wonder about that wire. I would wonder if Grandmother Jewel had really planted it in her yard or if Granny Settle had simply planted it in her story. But by the time I got around to wondering, I had lost the innocence it took to believe such stories in the first place and the question was never asked.

The kids sat outside on the same cracked cement step. It was the only place their bodies ever touched unless they were hitting each other or reaching for the same thing at the same time. I wondered if listening to them through the open window was as bad as reading a diary. I didn't think so. Besides I had to put on eye shadow and this was the only place I could see well enough to do it. Kate's voice was shrill. It sounded like Toby's when he was outraged.

"She's incredibly full of crap. She finds an old stick, puts it in a Baggie and makes up a huge story about being dead. Then she expects us to believe it. I mean who ever dies and comes back to tell about it?"

"Lots of people. Remember that time on Channel Three? There was a show with a guy who talks to his dead mother all the time. Bald guy, totally hairless. He said it was like phoning someone up, remember?"

"That's channeling. Lots of people do that. Being dead isn't the same at all. And besides, Channel Three only features loons. Anybody can go on that station. Anybody crazy enough."

"Okay, so forget Channel Three. But I've read about people in car accidents who've been pronounced dead. Their hearts have stopped beating and stuff, then suddenly they come alive again."

"Twice?"

All I could hear was a rhythmic sweeping sound. Surely they weren't cleaning the driveway as they chatted.

"You never believe anything anyway, Kate. You think you're so tough."

"That's not true. I believe in lots of things. What I believe right now is that the two of us are totally fucked."

The sweeping sound stopped right away.

"How come?"

"It doesn't matter whether she made it up or whether it really happened. She's institution material either way. This deal is so weird I'm not even telling my friends. You'd better not tell Stewart, either. Okay?"

"Mmmm."

"Toby, say you won't tell Stewart. Or anybody."

"Dad already knows. He doesn't think her stories are weird."

I couldn't get the eye shadow to go on right. Something had happened to my left eyelid. The inexorable march of time, probably. The other side was all right, though.

"Oh, right."

"He acts like he doesn't even know they're made up. He said he was my age when he heard about her falling into that gully. Gross, look at this leaf. It's got major acne."

And where else could I have gone with that news, if not straight to Tom? I had raced from my house to his, my chest heaving with Granny Settle's report from the world beyond, and repeated it all through the rusty mesh window screen. Tom listened solemnly, slid half a piece of Juicy Fruit under the screen, and said he knew just where the first death happened. His old bird dog howled and dropped to the ground every time they got near that place, even though the dogwoods were loaded with sparrows.

I studied my face in the mirror and wondered if maybe I had worked one eyelid more than the other and if I had, if there wasn't a better color than gray to disguise that unfortunate fact. I tried lifting the gray arch a bit. Nothing doing. Makeup wouldn't compensate for the droop, so I washed it all off and swallowed hard. Beth was right. I was withering away in my house. I hated to think so, but maybe my mother was right, too. I had to act.

Seven

*T*he air felt wonderful on my skin. Perfect, temperate air flowed in and around me in the car, making my skirt flutter up off my knees. I didn't care that it was dirty and toxic and all the rest. Disregarding the hard facts made living in Los Angeles seem luscious sometimes. It was a perfect evening to sample Paradise, a bar Beth promised only attracted the brightest and the best.

I chose my spot carefully, edging in between a silver Taurus and a blond Infiniti, my crumpled car further diminished. My conviction disintegrated as I sat in the lot. A bar was so unequivocal. I hadn't accidentally dressed up to come to Paradise and everyone in there would know it. I felt the death of innocence right there in my Pacer. I couldn't just sit in a corner and nurse a drink. I would have to talk, probably, engage with people I didn't know. Engaging was the terrifying point. There were a lot of people milling around the entrance and I gave in to an old reflex, popping open the glove compartment and grabbing a spiral notebook. I rolled down the windows and breathed deeply, scanning the crowd. A tall man with the wispy beginnings of a ponytail stood off to one side of a couple, looking every bit as uncomfortable as I felt just then. They drew him into their conversation every now and then, but he was clearly a third wheel. Maybe once he muscled his way into Paradise, he'd become part of a pair. Maybe his whole life would take a dramatic turn. I chewed on my pencil a little, feeling better. *This third wheel ain't busted, it don't need repair. This wheel's finally rolling, baby, find another spare.*

I shut my car door and pushed forward to the entrance. I would pretend I was looking for someone. That was it. A girlfriend who was on her way, a girl-friend who would wind up never coming at all. I didn't need to pretend. There was a hand on the small of my back almost as soon as I got inside the club. I decided right then that touching someone's back so intimately was not a very effective way of saying hello. I turned around to say so, but that didn't seem to bother my new friend a bit.

"Let me guess. It's your first time in Paradise."

Guys like this were rolled off a press somewhere in a dank West Los Ange-les basement. The baseball cap (Kate's were cuter), the sunglasses (Venice boardwalk at five bucks apiece) and a T-shirt from Gold's Gym were all is-sued from the same mold.

"You're right! My name's Polly."

"Tim. Tim Adams."

"Tim, I wonder if you could do me a really, really big favor?"

"Just ask."

"Take your hand off my back."

"Hey, no problem."

"Good meeting you Tim."

It really wasn't a problem. Tim was already talking as he advanced on a buxom blonde. I could see his cap bobbing frantically as he slid his hand to-ward her back. That would be fun, just watching the Tims of the world from a dark corner of Paradise. Personalities were unimportant, no's were unimpor-tant. He knew if he kept it up long enough, he would reap rewards. I looked at a glass bowl full of nuts on a black-lacquered table and thought suddenly of a petri dish. Why had it taken me this long? This was where I should have been all along. Sampling the single life, pattering, pattering to my heart's content because I, the specific me, didn't matter to anyone here. A married life didn't matter in a place like this. Nobody in Paradise cared about my stories or the songs I was writing or who was currently living in my house. This was a true laboratory, a place where cells split rapid-fire, where cultures created unset-tling new life forms. Paradise was a pastel jungle filled with painted murals of beautiful beasts. Monkeys and toucans clambered over the walls and I con-trasted this with the bars I knew, bars of a lower order. There was a time when Tom and I loved going around to honky-tonks, we couldn't get enough of them. But our passion for those old, dirty smoke holes had been about music and boozy commotion that only intensified our private connection. I shook my head hard and returned to this scene. Tim was a smash hit with the blonde. She was taller than he was and seemed ready to tip over the tops of her platform shoes, sloshing all over grateful, slurping Tim. I wondered if I could just go up to someone, anybody I pleased, and begin a conversation. Be as bold as a woman in a song. I thought I could. Everything in the whole world was up to me and me alone, just like Beth said. I felt dizzy as I moved toward a great big back that kept building until it reached a cowboy hat, just like the billboard of the Marlboro man I loved to stare at on a corner near my house. Maybe I would put my hand on his back, just to see what would happen. He was talking to a friend and the friend saw me, so I just touched his elbow slightly before he began to turn.

"Polly! What are you doing here? Hey, let me introduce you to my friend."

Russell said something about Denver and a shopping mall and I lost track of what else he said, because I was busy hiding my disappointment. I'd screwed up all my courage for an evening with Russell? Their delight in finding each other after so many years let me off the hook. I stood there smiling and fuming inside at six months scarred not by petri-like experimentation in similar joints, but by celibacy and raising kids and writing more song lyrics than ever. I felt old and tricked and terrified by my cautious, courteous life. I had never stopped being married, even after I had kicked Tom out and set my household on its ear. It wasn't loyalty to disloyal Tom that kept me locked up tight, or was it? Russell looked enormous in that hat.

"We'll talk. Give me a call Monday. Polly, pleasure meeting you." Russell's friend backed away, tossing some loose change in his pocket.

"I haven't seen the guy in five years and he pops up here, tonight. Unbelievable. We could be doing some serious business by Monday."

"I thought you were determined to stay away from malls."

"This deal may be too pretty to pass up." He took his hat off and I thought he would become plain, regular Russell once more. He knocked the brim on the side of his hip a couple of times. I tried to figure out the look crossing his face, but that was more futile than reading a weather map on the evening news with high and low pressure cells converging, swirling around and around the tip of a weatherman's pointer. "You're too pretty to pass up. Polly, may I buy you a drink?"

I ignored the slight shiver these words produced and pointed to a tall frosted glass filled with quartered limes, oranges and ice. The woman sipping it toyed with the tiny parrot on top of the swizzle stick. Russell, for all his hanging around, had never been very direct. What had he said—too pretty to pass up? Maybe I *could* banish Tom once and for all by reconsidering this neighbor of mine, part friend, part perfect stranger. He turned away from me and blew his nose long and hard. I thought of how many times I'd heard that trumpet blast from his post on the balcony. Who was I kidding?

"I'll start with one of those." I usually stuck with beer or wine, but not tonight. I hoped it was strong and sweet. If it wasn't, I'd just eat the oranges and fool around with the parrot like she was doing.

"Did you just buy that cowboy hat?"

"I've had it for a long time. You don't like it?"

"It's fine. It seems like it belongs at In Cahoots is all."

"What's wrong with that? You're the country music fan."

He handed it to me. I couldn't help laughing, thinking of how little a Western dance club in Glendale had to do with the kind of writing I was doing these days. I stared at his hair. I guessed it was the cut, but it never, ever got messed up. He wasn't prone to hat hair, like Toby, or cowlicks, like Tom. He had a very orderly appearance and I wondered what it took to break this down.

"May I ask you a question?"

He took a big gulp of beer and wiped the frothy mustache off with his forefinger. "Go ahead."

"Do you use hairspray?" He lowered his head to the table. His shoulders were shaking, so I guessed he was laughing at the question. It took a minute for him to come back up. "I mean maybe bachelors do that. Maybe they're more concerned about their appearance than married guys. Or, put it this way, concerned but in a different way."

"I never thought of all that."

He looked up at the ceiling, so I did, too. There wasn't a lot to see up there, but it kept us busy for a few minutes.

"Hey, Polly, how do you know I've never been married?"

"I guess I don't know that, but you never mentioned an ex-wife."

"Well, maybe I don't want you to know about my lousy track record."

"Why would that make any difference?"

He fumbled with a shirt button. "Maybe I'm trying to impress you."

"Don't be silly." I sounded just like a mother. I was older than Russell, but not that much older.

He started drumming on the edge of the table. "Anyway, I don't use hairspray."

I looked around the room, still curious about the best and the brightest Beth had promised I would see here. It didn't seem as if people were really meeting in Paradise. There wasn't enough surprise or apprehension for that. Reuniting seemed more like it.

"You must come here a lot, right?"

"I've been here a few times."

"For the great conversation?"

Russell grinned. "Nobody has great conversations here. Wait a minute, though. You never answered my question. What are *you* doing here?"

I thought about making something up, but realized this was someone I talked to through my hedge.

"I have no idea. Maybe seeing how the other half lives. The unmarried other half."

Paradise satisfied my own seedy curiosity, but what about his? What was Russell curious about? I could imagine the wheels turning inside his big, square head. He picked up everything he could on the table. Nut dish, napkins, salt and pepper. He didn't touch my hands, though they were folded together and well within his range.

"So, since you're the unmarried other half I'll start with you. You come here for great conversation and—"

"—You weren't listening. Good conversations don't happen here."

"Assume you try and then what happens when you don't find it? Come on. Don't be shy."

Russell cleared his throat. I saw he wished for a hat and a low brim, like the one Dwight Yoakam favored, that would hide him from me and my questions.

"Why do you look so uncomfortable? This is mere anthropology."

"You sure know how to flatter a guy."

"Will you excuse me for a second?"

"I'll save your seat." He leaned back as I got up out of the booth and slowly wiped the sweat from his glass with one finger.

The bathroom was empty and I collapsed into a rattan chair in the waiting room. I could see my head, severed from the rest of my body by a faux marble counter. It was clean and peaceful in there, with a neat stack of hand towels lying undisturbed next to the sink. Liquid soap in an amber glass dispenser and no water splattering the immaculate countertop. I sat watching myself and trying to come to my senses. Why was I clobbering Russell? I didn't have time to come up with an answer.

The buxom blonde in the platforms tripped through the door of the lounge and pressed her thighs against the countertop. She leaned into the mirror reviewing everything, eyes, lips and, yes, bustline. She opened a lizard handbag shaped like a cylinder that held more makeup than I'd ever seen in my life. She did many things to her face involving red pencils and brown lipstick, three shades of eyeshadow and, at last, blush. But the blush wasn't restricted to her cheeks. She took a golden tube out of a side compartment in her purse and pushed a button. The tube popped open into a soft, fat brush that she coated with deep pink powder and applied between her breasts. Her concentration was so intense, so pure that I'm sure she never saw me at all. She turned and took mincing steps out of the lounge.

I hadn't clung to my creed of natural allure accidentally. I had watched my mother operate for too many years to ever drop to basement level. It wouldn't have occurred to me to put makeup between my breasts. I preferred generic toothpaste and Dove soap to a dab of perfume in key locations and for years I thought Tom did, too. Once in a department store I heard a woman ask a clerk if the color of the sheets she had chosen highlighted her skin. She held them up to her face to show her. I thought about that for days afterward. At first I felt virtuous and haughty, then I wondered if she didn't have something. Why buy bedsheets that made you look sallow if you didn't have to? It was all a moot point since I hadn't even ventured into designer bed linen. Tom and I slept on white cotton sheets that I replaced when they tore and that was that.

Russell was glancing at his watch when I came out and I wondered if the kids were in bed. He looked pretty forlorn.

"Sorry I took so long. The lines were really long."

"This place is giving me a headache. Want to take a drive or something?"

"Good idea."

We left my car where it was and headed up to the hills over Hollywood in his Range Rover where we could get a look at the city and the sky. I loved being a passenger, being driven anyplace. Even though Kate and Toby usually took the bus, I put in long hours behind the wheel. Some days my ankle throbbed at the end of the day from working the clutch.

"Like the car."

"I did, too, before it got so trite. Everybody in town's got one now."

"Not really. Some of us have Pacers."

My car was a ridiculous shape and the sight of it sullied the road. Even small children recognized it. I didn't really blame them for pulling on their parents' shoulders, giggling and pointing at my car. Halloween always meant whipped cream and eggs when I forgot to cover it with a tarp I have somewhere in the garage. Ugly and misshapen as it was, the Pacer triggered thoughts of a long, eventful history and I couldn't stand the thought of selling it. I didn't think Russell's car looked trite. I thought it looked like the real thing, especially with the splash of mud on the side. He'd been way out at the edge of the Valley, helping a friend who was thinking to build on some acreage he had out there. The mud gave his Range Rover a touch of authenticity.

He slowed down and turned into an unmarked cement patch that was probably someone's private property, minus the sign.

"Should we be here?"

"It's fine. Hop out and I'll take you to the best show in town."

Russell reached underneath the seat, his arm brushing my bare leg, and pulled out a flashlight. He lit the gravel path just to the left of his car and he slid my hand through his arm. I must have looked like a mannequin with an arm and elbow locked into position, but at least I wouldn't fall down. We walked a few steps and turned into an open field, the dry grass matted down by the Caterpillar that stood at the edge of the field.

"What do you think? Worth five million dollars?"

The showy city was impossibly lit below us. Endless lights throbbed as far as I could see and past that rose a vast, unstoppable glow. I multiplied the lights by lives and the numbers seemed to range out of control.

"God."

"Great, isn't it? We're doing a ten-thousand-square-foot Tudor up here."

The lights were unbearably bright and unresponsive. They beat and blinked on and off regardless of who was gawking at them. How did people find each other in a city this size? Russell's clients must have had a much different interpretation of this view.

The flashlight switched off and I couldn't see his face in the dark. He reached for me, taking my face in his hands. Once we descended again into this alarming, frantic city, once we became neighbors again, this would just be a single, isolated moment carved out of ordinary days. A car blasted around the curve and I could see his eyes in the shock of white light. I stiffened beneath his hands. I tried to hide it, but there wasn't anything I could do. It didn't seem to matter, though, because Russell's hands stayed right where they were.

I cleared my throat. "You know something, Russell? I'm not sure how comfortable I am with this."

"With what?" He tried to kiss me but I turned my head. The kiss landed just above my ear. I had already fled the field, the view and the possibility of a kiss after such a long time. I was thinking of the particular light below that represented me and I wanted more than anything to be there, shutting it off to go to sleep.

"We're neighbors. We're friends. This doesn't . . ."

"Doesn't what, Polly?"

"It isn't very sensible." Priss. Old lady. A Jeweled life dedicated to doilies.

My eyes were getting used to the dark and I could read the expression slipping over his face. He took my hand and began to slide it to the small of his back, pulling me closer.

"This is silly. I have to go home, Russell." My maternal tone didn't bother me now. I didn't invite his hand on my back and Russell was beginning to act like the Tims of Paradise.

"You have a curfew?"

"No. I have to go home because I have two children there and a grandmother."

"So they're there and we're here. Don't be scared." He curled his hand around the back of my neck. His voice wasn't convincing and I wondered if the reminder of my children and grandmother made it as insubstantial as it sounded.

"I feel looked at and obvious and silly carrying on like this in a pasture."

"It's not a pasture, Polly. It's a construction site and I'm the contractor. It's okay that we're here." He kicked at something in the dirt, sending it into the air with the tip of his shoe. "Who's looking at you, Polly?"

"Me, I guess."

"That's not what I think. I think somebody else is watching us right now. Come on."

He held the car door open for me and I noticed it smelled wet. I wondered if the car had that odor because of a succession of wet nights or just one glorious downpour. I didn't think it was the moment to ask. Russell had let go of one wrist and reached for the other. He held my hand up just in time for the glare of headlights to strike my messy nails. Naturally no two were the same length.

"Every time I look at this hand I see a wedding band."

"That rhymes, but it's not true. I stopped wearing a wedding band months ago. What's your point, Tom? Oh, God, I didn't mean that!"

"That's my point." He turned the key in the ignition, giving me a smile. "Don't worry."

The motor started with a rumble.

"I'm still your neighbor. I'm still your friend." He sounded like Russell again. He chuckled and put his hand on my knee. "I bet you're going to think about this the next time you see me and it's going to make you blush."

He didn't look all that displeased. He put his hat on his head and drove carefully down out of the hills to take me back to Paradise.

Eight

I ran a loofah pad lightly over my skin, wondering what other kinds of makeup that woman in Paradise applied to her body and how her laundry must have been a real task, with lipstick and rouge turning up in unexpected places. I kept replaying that scene in Paradise, what a coincidence it was to bump into Russell there. I tried to scrub the small of my back with the loofah, but my arms weren't long enough.

I was still under the shower, composing, when I heard Granny Settle holler. I was off to a real good start, the hot water easing the knots out of my shoulders and brain. Very hot water was always ameliorative. And recreational. I'm the only person I know who takes baths for a hobby.

> You just had to try and tell me
> All the things you never said,
> All the girls you'd never been with,
> All the ones you'd never wed.
> Seems like all that nervous talkin
> Put ideas in my head.
> All those girls that you weren't missin
> Might be lyin in your bed.

"Polly Ann, pick up that telephone before I tear it off the wall." Her voice cut through three layers of drywall, where the continuing ring of the phone had failed. I took my time wrapping up in a towel, figuring the caller would hang up well before I was out of the bathroom. Wrong.

"It's a no-brainer, Polly. And they love you, so there's no problem with the parking validation. It is ten minutes from your house and they don't want you before twelve. Now what's to argue?"

"Golden Savings and Loan?"

"They asked for you specifically. *Polly Harrison.* You wanna know how often that happens to me? I don't need all the fingers of my hand to count. Be sweet. Say yes. I don't want to send these people riffraff."

The bank building was a sparkling white gift to the neighborhood, wrapped up in appropriate golden trim. I stood in the west tower, watching the elevator light drop from the fifteenth floor. I had already worked here five or six times, copying loan files of people who were refinancing. The work was laborious, but I didn't mind. I loved chores, repetitive tasks. I could get my mind to emulate the soothing rhythm of the machines and blotting out thoughts for a day, especially ruminative ones, struck me as more healthy than harmful. They were especially sorry about having to keep my door closed because of the noise. They had redone the elevator since I'd been there the last time. There was mauve carpet on the walls and the filtered air smelled like a lavender field. I was the only rider up to seventeen.

"Polly! Welcome back. Oh, I'm so glad we got you this time. We won't even discuss who Loretta sent us last month."

Riffraff, doubtless. Eleanor was a perky blonde who made couture copies after work and all weekend long. Around prom time, she hit high schools with her dressses and made potloads of money. Enough to send her kids to a chic private school in the Valley. I thought she was an up-and-comer in the loan department. She had so much authority over the phone and all the men brought her coffee.

"Ah, come on. Boost my ego and tell me she did a bad job."

"She lost an entire set of loan docs. Spilled coffee all over the fax machine and after three days left in the middle of a job. The machine went on the blink or somebody interrupted her one too many times. You know. She went nuts and left. Not only that . . ."

I thought this might have been called a pregnant pause. She was a great gossip, this Eleanor. She worked every tidbit as if it were a three-act play, beginning, middle and end.

"I could tell by the way she stood at the machine that she was going to come on to all the guys." She looked around for a second and, since nobody was around, rolled her skirt way up and slid the slit around to the side to show me.

"Come on."

"I'm not kidding! Collagen lips, the whole bit. She's practically doing it with the Xerox machine for all these guys. Not like you, Polly. Anyway, Greg's marriage is on the rocks, so I figure he'd be the first to fall and he didn't disappoint me."

She did the whole story, the buildup, their tryst at El Torito and the mark on his neck the following day.

"You read about the company in Orange County that won't let their employees have hickeys?" I had read the solemn article with disbelief.

"We should be so smart here. Nobody could get anything done since we were all staring at his neck the whole day. I personally haven't had one of those since junior high. To make a long story short, we're glad you're back, Polly."

"Thanks." Well, it was true. I dressed for the job with flat shoes and dark colors. Hours copying loan files hardly called for spike heels.

She spent a few minutes with me in the copy room, excusing the size of the files. Files belonging to people with real assets were killers, all right, and I probably wouldn't make any progress on the song I'd started that morning. I thought of Santoni's bank statement and flinched. Duplicate files had to be made before the loan could be processed. You had to respect the order in the file you were copying and, since all the pages looked similar, you had to pay a fair amount of attention. Such tedious work was easy enough to botch with all the interruptions. Everyone in the department needed the machine and the person copying files would always be bumped. I didn't mind, though. Most people talked to me and the frenzy was sort of refreshing. Besides, I already had all the personalities down. Which man hated his demeaning job and would therefore have me reload paper for him, just standing there watching while I was on my knees, and which woman was sweet, but ditzy and would leave her original in the machine for me to fish out of my files later, when she had looked just everywhere. Since I was only there part-time, most of it made me laugh. Incidents made the day go faster and the throbbing, noisy intimacy of that little room *did* give you things to think about, although I didn't see how anyone could do anything with the Xerox machine besides copy papers. Eleanor brought me a glass of iced tea and told me how much she liked my pants. I got to work on Stratton.

You knew instinctively which files were going to cause you trouble and which ones would be a snap. Stratton was somewhere in the middle. I flipped to the photographs of the home, to get a feel for Antelope Valley. He was a do-it-yourselfer with handwritten notes, explaining a problem he had with his ex-wife. She'd been up to no good, using a credit card to get him in a peck of trouble. Of course, that was his side of the tale. How did anybody really know what went on inside a two-bedroom house with asphalt shingle roofing in Antelope Valley? Or any house, for that matter, in any valley in the whole world? There was an orange plastic tricycle lurking in the ferns that grew at the base of a sycamore and a yellow Hyundai parked in the driveway. One of the tires looked like it could stand some air. I finished that file and reached for another, thinking of Russell's house, the way it would look if someone squeezed it into a snapshot. A bachelor would fare very well in this format, with no kiddie knickknacks to disrupt a tidy world.

I established a rhythm, gently shutting the cover of the machine upon page after page of financial detail. After three hours and three separate files, I decided people had it all wrong. There was so much power in unexpected places. I was privy to acutely personal information. Me and how many others? Tabloids were fueled by this kind of stuff. The right photo in the wrong hands could bring everything skidding to a stop. The door banged open. Don the beachcomber was one of my favorite characters.

"Hey, good-lookin'." He was out of place in an office, in a business suit. The tie rankled, the work offended and he was the first one to say so. He could never remember my name, but he handled it well.

"How are ya?"

"Good. Surf's been colossal."

That was all he ever wanted to talk about, the beach, the tide. I slid into a kind of monosyllabic rap with him every time. Big words made him very edgy.

"So how come a pretty girl like you's in a dumb job like this?"

"Bills to pay."

"Oh, right. Bills. I hear ya." He nodded his big head. He had four girls and a wife himself, big damn house in Redondo. If it weren't for that, he'd be out on a board somewhere, paddling toward the ultimate wave. I'd rented *Point Break* once with Toby. I thought that movie was the key to Don's personality. He offered me a bite of his donut and closed the door. I rubbed both hands together and reached for the next file. I was making good time.

DORAY

I dropped it. It fell right out of my hands onto the floor. It wasn't the way I've always imagined those moments. Dramatic moments are supposed to be just that, dramatic, but they aren't. They wind up dulling the senses, giving off great drafts of anesthetic. Nobody came in and I was free to stare at Frankie Doray's loan documents until I felt strong enough to pick up the heavy file. I pressed the thick folder against my chest for a moment, sorry that I'd guessed right. She was one rich woman.

My hair is long enough to cover my face if I put my head down.

"Mind if I use the machine for a sec?"

I shook my head hard, not trusting my voice. The machine whirred for a few minutes, then the door banged shut. It gave me time to figure out how much I wanted to learn. I started the copier up again, clearing additional space by the fax machine. I'd need it.

"Machine free?"

I didn't have to look up to recognize the high, squeaky voice of the ditz.

"No."

"But I'll only be a sec."

"Come back later. This is a big job."

She muttered Jeez, but left the room anyway. It *was* a big job. After all, I needed my own set of loan docs and it would take every bit of my concentration to keep everything straight. The photos showed a stylish Spanish stucco with any number of nice touches. Principal among them was my husband's showy Corvette, parked right in front of Frankie's love nest, since I could now call it that. She had other properties in Arizona and Nevada. The classy little town house was not her primary residence.

Luckily I brought an old gray sweater to work in case they had the air conditioning turned up. I wrapped my set of copies inside the sweater and smuggled them out of Golden Savings and Loan when it was quitting time.

• • •

Frankie's town house was part of a clever pair. Separate entrances were designed so deftly I felt I was looking at a single home. Mature vines rose in a delicate tracery of green and purple and the iron birds and branches that slipped over side windows seemed more decorative device than security measure. I looked at the photo in my lap and turned up the volume on a talk-radio show as I looked through the pictures, comparing them with what I saw before me.

"This is Ellen Jarre and the subject tonight is television and your children. Next caller? I'm listening."

The photo I held didn't lie. A lump of fake soil rose in the front of Frankie's lawn. A birch tree sprouted from the center. No one would ever suspect Mother Nature of doing that. I noticed none of the other neighbors went in for this kind of artifice. Just Frankie.

"Ellen? Ellen, is this really you?"

"Yes, it is. Talk to me about television and your children."

The caller broke down and sobbed. I could hear her children comforting her. An older child got on the phone and explained her mama hadn't been feeling well.

"That's okay, honey. We'll just break for a moment until your mama feels well enough to talk with us."

Classical music poured into my car and I leaned back in my seat. Frankie kept a tiny second-story window open and I wondered what was on the other side. Maybe it was just a closet window. A walk-in closet with one of those wall units for hanging shoes and a double set of clothing rods, carefully measured so that nothing would drag on the ground. Maybe Frankie had one of those doors that triggered a light as soon as it opened, so she would never have to bother with flipping a switch.

"My mom can talk to you now. Hello? Are you still there?"

"I'm here all right, honey."

"Ellen, that never used to happen." The caller had really recovered. Her voice was full, throaty and full of conspiratorial shadows. "Now then, television."

"Yes. And your children."

"I've done a little research, Ellen." The caller went into a spin, not about television and its detrimental effects, but about journalism and its sloppiness and misleading surveys.

I squinted at the vine that feathered the side of her house. It was a ficus, similar to mine, but the leaves were smaller somehow. They didn't clump or clot the way mine did. Maybe she had a gardener who paid special attention to such things as the way a vine grew and whether it became a blight or a charming complement to a stucco surface. A burgundy Seville was parked in her driveway. Her driveway. It was one of those cobbled jobs that made you think of the Old Country. It didn't even really matter which old country. They suggested refinement and elegance, not oil stains and cracks from earthquakes past. A light went on in Frankie's house. Someone was home.

"That's why, after listening to one study after another, I've gotta tell ya, Ellen, I'm ready to blow. Now, I'm a single mother and—"

"—I need to ask you to return to the subject tonight, Mrs. Ridenour. How do you think your children are being affected by the television they watch?"

"Mrs. Ridenour, that's a laugh. I've got five kids and no husband. So don't call me Mrs., Ellen. I'm Sandy Ridenour and that's that."

A light went on in me. Lovers didn't just go to bed. They ate in expensive restaurants. They drank from dusty vintage bottles. Maybe they went to the opera. They had in *Moonstruck*. They even traveled together, took trips, registered under separate names.

"I've got five undamaged, smart kids, all of them under ten years of age and with me working and with me taking care of them once I get home, what kind of time does that leave for Sandy Ridenour? I ask you, Ellen," she ran on breathlessly. "The answer is no time, except for when I can get them to all agree on one television program because, Ellen, I only have one television set and that by the grace of God. What I'm trying to say here is I've about had it with you sanctimonious people and your great jobs and your great lives telling everybody else how much they're damaging their kids. My kids aren't damaged. I am! I am!"

The phone dropped to the ground. A little girl's voice came back on the line apologizing and Ellen broke again for more classical music. It didn't soothe me like the last time. Another light went on in Frankie's house, then another as I slammed my car door shut. I watched a neighbor rip open a bag of mulch before I crossed the street to give Frankie Doray a piece of my mind. Nothing artificial there. Real mulch for a real flower bed. I walked carefully up that cobblestone driveway. If I stepped the wrong way and turned my ankle, I would find myself at Frankie's mercy, asking her for an Ace bandage or an icepack. I thought of all the things I had to say and I said them in my head, one by one, as I crept up on her house. Maybe it was fear of looking foolish or fear period, but by the time I reached her sidewalk, all my words had vanished.

As I turned around to go, I thought I caught a glimpse of her through one window, but maybe not. It didn't matter. I'd seen all I wanted. I drove home, my mind as blank and bland as a sheet of foolscap.

Nine

*N*obody remembered to draw the curtains at night, so my house was like a living theater when I pulled up. It looked inviting, but I could have been mistaken. Since Granny Settle's arrival, coming home had taken on a different dimension.

"Whas up, G?" At least I could still make them laugh. Kids like a buffoon, that's one thing I've come to understand. If you know you sound ridiculous when you mime their speech or their clothing, you will always score big. Or at least get a tight smile from them. Tonight I saw it was the tight smile, so I started again.

"So tell me a story."

Kate was watching MTV and the room was empty. I missed being able to talk to my kids without an audience; this seemed a prime moment to catch up. I stared at the group on the screen, thinking how I needed to watch television more often. A guy in a kimono, another in diapers and I couldn't quite catch the lyrics, where I'm sure everything was fully explained.

"What kind?" She didn't look up. A bag of microwave popcorn lay slashed open on the coffee table.

"I thought I told you guys not to eat in here. The kind with a happy ending."

"Here's one. An old woman descends on a family for a few days and wrecks everybody's lives because she's like a tornado or hurricane or something. But then she gets a phone call from a family member in San Francisco who invites her to come up for a few days and she accepts. Therefore, life returns to normal."

My cousin Rory owned three record shops up north and I kept promising Kate and Toby if they continued on the straight and narrow, I would take them to stay at Rory's for three days. Three days was all I could take and we both knew it. He was a famous old hippie and did land-office business with kids who craved the sixties. He had no children and attached himself to both of mine through tapes that arrived in the mail with no warning, insane tapes he mixed himself that put Kate and Toby way ahead of their peers. They turn up for no occasion with T O B Y written on the diagonal along the back of a padded envelope. He was steadfast about ignoring birthdays and Christmas, but he must have known in his old hippie heart about the doldrums. Every time the blues arrived at our house, so did a tape from my cousin to lighten our load. Rory was my favorite cousin, but he still got on my nerves.

I scooted in closer to Kate. I couldn't keep the eagerness out of my voice.

"Rory! I never thought he'd pull through like this for me. When is she going to see him?"

"She's not. You asked for a happy ending. I made it up, just like you make up your songs." She looked at me for the first time. "Tough day, Mom?"

"I guess. Sort of. I spent the afternoon at Golden Savings."

"Oh, the people who like you. The real story is Rory's on his way here. He plans to drive through the night."

"Where's he staying?"

"Here. Where else would he stay?"

I thought about my bed. I hadn't given it up so far and I wasn't about to. It seemed like the most luxurious spot on earth just then, even though it had developed a lump in the middle. From a distance it looked a bit like Frankie Doray's fake knoll.

"I think my day just got tougher."

"Sorry, Mom. Oh, *Russell* called. Is that pest starting to call now, Mom? Can't he take a hint?"

I filled my mouth with popcorn and gave her a garbled answer.

Rory arrived just as the kids were getting ready for school. It would never have occurred to my cousin to pull off the road for a minute to freshen up before greeting us. I opened the door to this vision of loveliness: hair (long as ever) matted to his head, stained shirt with second button missing and foul breath he blew in my face first thing. I always treat him like the big kid he is, though he never seems to mind.

"Hello, Rory. Take off those filthy boots, please."

He leaned over, grunting as he pulled off first one, then the other. They had been black boots once, with chains around the heel, but now they were scuffed into a kind of industrial gray.

"Polly, baby. You are looking soooooo good. How long has it been?" He didn't wait for an answer. "I gotta take a piss."

The kids called out to him from the kitchen. I'd forbidden them to chitchat until they'd wolfed down some food and made their beds. They could interview their cool sixties cousin after school.

"Uncle Rory! Did you drive down on your Harley?"

"Rory, I mixed a tape for you this time. Wait'll you hear."

Rory clomped down the hall, waving at them as he passed. I couldn't believe what happened next. It was like somebody opened a faucet full force. I didn't bother to finesse what I had to say.

"Cousin, if you plan on spending more than five minutes in my house, close the bathroom door. Rory? I mean it."

The door slammed and he continued doing his business. I don't think he had pulled over once to use the bathroom and San Francisco is a nine-hour drive. Nothing I ever say gets to him. He appeared in the kitchen minutes later with drops of water on his head. I hoped it was water. He scratched his chest and pounded each child on the back a few times.

"Damn you're huge. What does she feed you?"

Toby loved this, of course, and I had to admit as thick as Rory mostly was, he did know the hearts of children.

"I swear, the last time I saw you, you weren't the size of my little finger. Cool haircut, dude. And this one . . ."

He slid Kate's baseball cap up a bit to get a look at her face.

"Scary. It must be scary to have such a pretty daughter. I did the right thing to stay single. I couldn't live through this shit."

"Language, Rory."

"Did you eat, Uncle Rory?"

"Can we go to the Imax like the last time?"

Kate slipped two slices of bread into the toaster and Toby was pouring him juice. They would have bathed his feet if there had been time. Just looking at him made me snarl. I knew my irritation would wear off and that made me even madder. I could even absorb Rory.

"Hell yes, we'll go to the Imax."

"Kids, you're going to be late."

"So what? We never learn anything anyway."

"I don't want the phone calls. You guys make tracks. I mean it."

Toby gave Rory one of his knowing looks before finally leaving. "She *always* means it. She has never not meant it and that's her problem."

Fucking beavers, man. They are the kings of the animal kingdom! They fucking outsmart bears and shit. I knew when Rory took them to the Imax Theatre a couple of years ago that he wasn't stoned, so his druggie wonder at the beaver world bugged me. The six-story-high screen takes you in, around and through whatever is being filmed, but come on. He was drug-free for years now and sort of the high priest in his AA group in Oakland, so I never worried about him when he drove around the city with my kids. But he had retained the language and looks of those years and this made him a supreme pain in the neck. He wore the sixties like some dumb badge. And the thing is, it worked like a charm. Kids loved him and on some level, I did, too. I mean, he hadn't driven down here to see me and the kids or to savor L.A. He had come to pay his weird respects to Granny Settle.

"So . . ." He turned to me and this time his breath was improved. I smelled my baking soda toothpaste and just bet he had used my brush. "How's she doing? I told her she could crash at my place, but she seems content here."

"She's old, Rory. Why would an old woman want to 'crash' at your place? Granny Settle doesn't know what a futon is, so wake up. No, this seems to be my ordeal."

"Why is she here?"

"To give stuff away before she dies, except she's not in a hurry to go anywhere."

"Wish I could help you, Polly."

"I do, too. Will you stop doing that? Let me get you a toothpick or something."

"Where is she anyway?"

"With Mr. Feldman, most likely."

"Fill me in. Who's this Feldman?"

"Her friend. They play horseshoes together. They also walk before breakfast and she tells me he's after her to do water aerobics at the YMCA."

"Holy Jesus."

"I know what you mean."

Here we were, two hapless singles whose ancient grandmother seemed to be pulling off what we couldn't manage. She had company and conversation mere weeks after hitting town. I was looking at seven months of physical and emotional celibacy. As for poor Rory, he looked whipped by my news. After all, the guy had just been rejected by the television show *Studs*. It wasn't that the girl hadn't picked him. They wouldn't even let him go on the show. The sixties didn't work for absolutely everyone.

"This is heavy, Polly. Really heavy. I mean Grampa's not even cold yet."

"He's good and cold and so far the only thing she's done is play horseshoes and ruin my grass doing it. Our grandfather's death isn't what's bugging you. It's her vitality." I had barely gotten this out when Rory started doing the chicken thing. He was up and flapping, bwawk, bwawking all over my kitchen, because Granny Settle had just come inside. He did a very passable chicken imitation.

"Come give your old granny some love."

He lifted her up off the ground. Granny Settle had favorite grandchildren, and no qualms about saying so. Rory was still the light of her life, even though she chose to stay with me. I looked at the two of them, going silly over each other, and turned away to do the breakfast dishes. Rory had loved her rodeo stories best, plus he wanted to touch everything she mentioned in her stories. She had to tell them with a cardboard box full of props (her preferred set of spurs and a bodice she'd worn as a young girl, now yellowed and tender, the rusty curry comb she'd used on Star), otherwise he would give her no peace. He wouldn't believe her tales unless she provided proof that they were true. Rory was an easy boy for her to love, pulling on her skirts and wanting proof from distant times. She praised his hard mind. I, on the other hand, was a sap. I believed every word the woman said until I discovered boys for the first time. Boy. Around the time when friendship with Tom expanded into romance, I began reexamining everything, even Granny Settle. If I had known so little about someone I'd known forever, then life was full of hidden peril and pleasure, concealed under a surface I thought I knew by heart.

"Granny, seems like I'm the one who got old, not you."

"Polly Ann spoils me so."

Well, that was new. I kept scrubbing, half pretending I didn't hear. It was sweet, Rory flirting with her and Granny flirting straight back, pretending she was just a helpless little thing. I wondered if it would last the whole visit.

"I hear I got some competition."

"Who says?"

"Polly. She tells me you've got a beau."

She was wearing a starched flannel shirt under her overalls. It looked like the stiff collar could slice off her head. She giggled and covered her mouth with her hand. Then, sly and smiling, she reached inside her overalls and brought out a single white carnation. Its leaves were lightly tinged with brown, but that clearly didn't matter to her.

"That fool! He wants me to marry him."

Well, I stepped back fast and so did Rory. We met hard in the middle of my kitchen and apologized at the same time.

"So, what are you going to do?"

"There's nothing to do. I don't like that little beret of his. When he asked me to marry him, I just pretended I didn't hear. We were about to play a game of cards and I suggested he deal."

I thought of Mr. Feldman, earnest, anxious Mr. Feldman who walked his daughter's three dogs at the same time. The widower was a religious man; I saw him walking to temple each Saturday. He nodded to me on our street, but once I stopped in a kosher deli on Fairfax and found myself standing next to Mr. Feldman. He wouldn't speak to me and after a few clumsy efforts at conversation, I let it go, figuring we were street acquaintances and nothing more. I couldn't believe he'd fallen for my grandmother on such short notice. Rory kept after it.

"What made you fall for Mr. Feldman?"

"Didn't say I did."

"Didn't say you didn't, either. What did it, Granny? I'm serious now."

People can always surprise you, no matter how well you think you know them. This tough old bird suddenly went pink as a petunia. She tried to turn her head, so he wouldn't see.

"Something I happened to see. That's all."

"You want to tell us?"

"Partly. Partly I want to keep it all for myself." She wandered over to a window and started messing with the curtains she'd made. She pulled this way and that, pretending to adjust the way they fell. Then she stared out the window, the way she must have stood when she saw it the first time. She was seeing it again and decided to share it with us. Rory was careful not to move or talk. He knew once *telling* was upon her, there was no turning back for her or anyone listening.

"These California streets don't take much to people, now do they? You folks got all the sidewalks in the world. They don't have scraggles of grass growing in the cracks or old hopscotch games drawn on them. It might be that they're just too pretty to walk on, so folks don't. Anyways, I was up early, way before the rest of the house. The birds were yammering at that hour. The trees were thick with them."

She stuck both her hands in outside pockets and started rooting around inside, searching for something. She found it, a candy she took her time unwrapping. It smelled ferny, like the inside of the forest, but sweet at the same time. She sucked hard for a few moments and recommenced.

"My legs hurt me, so I thought I'd try to walk some. I thought walking would do me some good and I came to the window more to look if the sun had risen than for any other reason. I knew nobody was walking down those pretty sidewalks, but I was wrong."

My shoulder bumped against Rory's and I left it there. I wanted to see what she saw, but I didn't want to do it alone. I was glad my cousin had come.

"Even though it was barely light out, I still saw everything that happened. I heard a car coming down the street and saw Mr. Feldman at the same time. I didn't know his name then, but I saw the man and saw the beret he wore. In that light it didn't look silly. It looked like God had just tapped him on the top of the head and left a little something there so he'd never forget it."

She turned and stared at us both for a second. She must have seen the correct expression, because she turned to the window again and nodded her head.

"I noticed how he walked. He'd walk a ways and stop. Walk and stop, looking every which way when he did. I wondered if he was a defective."

"What do you mean by that?"

"Well, it was a walk, not a field trip. I had just about decided that a man like that would make miserable company, walking, stopping, walking, stopping on the way to anyplace, when I started listening to the birds again. Only there was only one singing now. It was a solo performance. And beautiful! Why, I never heard the likes before in my life." She stopped talking to button her collar. "Then that bird dropped dead. It just fell out of the tree like a stone. Maybe it was sick and just happened to pick that moment to die, but here came Mr. Feldman on his field trip. Well, he stopped all right. He knelt down to look at the bird and I could see from where I was standing how hard that was for him. He's as old and achy as me. Anyways, he took that bird up in his bare hands, without a handkerchief or anything and slipped it in his pocket. He took the thing home and buried it in his yard." She squinted her eyes at Rory. "Yes, there's a white marker in his yard and no, I don't have it with me, so don't even bother to ask."

Granny Settle came away from the window and looked at herself in a small oval mirror I have hung with a piece of velvet ribbon. She talked to herself, not us.

"I hadn't seen such an act of fool kindness in eighty-two years of living. I've never thought twice about animals. They either did what I wanted or caught hell if they didn't. Horses were for working or riding and rabbits were for eating. Dogs did nothing but get underfoot, and cats? I used to fill up my barn with them to kill mice. But I never so much as gave them a bowl of milk." She stroked the brown ribbon with one finger. "That's a nice touch, Polly Ann. After that I couldn't stop thinking about what I'd seen."

Somebody had to break the spell, so Rory did.

"Sounds like love at first sight, Gran."

"Somebody who'd behave so crazy over a dead bird is crazy period. I wasn't a bit surprised when he asked me to marry him."

The spell was broken all right. Rory asked if he could crash on the couch and didn't wait for a yes or no. Granny Settle slapped a piece of meat in her pan and turned the flame up high. She started to sing, a sign she'd done enough telling for one day.

Ten

"*D*ad called." Kate's voice was matter-of-fact.

I had just that moment thought of him. It was a cool, neutral thought, for once. I wasn't good in department stores. As soon as I was inside, I longed to be out. The lights, the smells, the zeal or indifference of salespeople made me want to scream. But Tom would push through a revolving door, stride through a shoe department and bloom like cactus in a desert spring. Stores were his element and he made the whole thing festive. He would make me try things on, things that looked droopy or ludicrous on a hanger, and most of the time his instincts were right. How many men want to go in a dressing room with their wives? I was remembering a particular day and a particular party dress I had to squeeze into with Tom's help, the hush in the crowded dressing rooms because I had smuggled a man into a woman's territory. The party had been boring, but I'd been the smash hit because of my great dress. Maybe the thought wasn't all that neutral.

"Yeah? What'd he have to say?"

"Not much. I'm making dinner for him on Sunday if that's okay. Is that okay, Mom?"

"Sure. Do you need a ride to his place?"

"Actually, he's coming here. His kitchen has ants. Plus he only has that one big pot and no hot pads or anything."

Kate was shaving her legs in my bathroom. That was good and bad. She'd stopped shaving for a few months, then decided to take it up again and there was an assortment of cold wax, shaving cream and Nair messing up the only room in my house with a lock on the door. On the other hand, she talked to me as she tested products. She had taken off her baseball cap and it was nice seeing her without skating paraphernalia.

"You can come, too. I mean, if you want."

"Sounds serious."

"It's kinda like my weekend project. We'll have to go to the store and stuff." She looked solemnly at her legs. "They look like an endangered species."

"I think they look pretty." I understood hating body parts at her age, but I didn't condone it. Part of me thought Kate should shed her baggy pants in favor of shorts and skirts that showed off her legs. The other part of me, the forty-year-old part, was content with the less-complicated status quo.

She twisted her hair into a knot and tied it still against the nape of her neck.

"*God,* Mom. You don't get anything. I mean they look naked and vulnerable. My legs don't have any hair on them and this is not a self-esteem issue. You have one way of looking at everything in the world."

"Doesn't everybody?"

"No. Everybody doesn't. Some people can get themselves out of the big fat picture. I believe that's what they mean by thinking. I am trying to become a person who thinks and in this house, that's like declaring war."

Well. I sat down on the edge of the tub.

"Kate, with all your dad and I have been through, I sometimes—"

"—you always. And that's the point. I don't have one friend and I mean one, whose dad or mom haven't split up, so get real. By the time most kids are my age, if the parents haven't busted up, they're about to and kids are ready for it. Toby and me are the norm. It's not my frame of reference and I wish you'd get that."

"Boy, you make us sound pretty trivial."

"Well, you are. I mean, I don't mean that *you* are trivial. But divorce or separation or whatever you guys are happens all the time."

"We're separated, Kate."

"Doesn't matter. Nobody even talks about that kind of stuff. It's like, so what's new? Anyway, I keep my nose out of everybody's business. That's how I like to do it."

"How come Marshal doesn't come around anymore or Megan? Or Dinah? I like those kids."

"They're boring. Pass me that moisture stuff, please."

She was buffing her legs like crazy. Simonizing them with a white wash-cloth until they gleamed. I wondered if I dared a compliment, if that would be all right.

"You have such great legs."

"I hate them. My knees turn in and one ankle's bigger than the other." She threw the washcloth at me and grinned. "But I'm supposed to hate them, right? I'm a teenager."

"So how come those kids don't come around anymore?" *How come none of your old friends come around anymore, Kate?* I wanted to ask and couldn't.

"Because they don't skate and they basically make me sick. And I don't want to talk about it. Remember about Sunday, okay? I gotta go. Rory's taking me to Get Ripped. Don't look like that. Mom, I need new trucks."

The skateboard store de luxe was so sinister. It was like a bumpy trip to the end of the world. Mothers were not welcome, but I got to sit there without abuse because I'd learned to keep my mouth shut. Woe to the mom who got into it with the owner. He was a surly guy who thrived on insult. He drew signs to answer questions he didn't want to fool with. I DON'T SELL ROLLER BLADES. THERE ARE NO DRESSING ROOMS. DOES THIS PLACE LOOK LIKE THE CHAMBER OF COMMERCE? Get Ripped was five blocks from the beach and he got his share of out-of-towners asking for directions.

"I don't mind driving you."

"That's all right. I'll just go with him." She patted my forehead, frowned at her own and untied her hair, then threw it all over her head, shook it a few times and smashed it under the cap.

"D'ya think Dad would like that wild rice stuffing I know how to do?"

"I know he would."

" 'Cause I was thinking that would be good, plus I might do chicken with it."

"I already can't wait."

"Do you think . . . never mind."

"Finish your sentence."

Her voice dropped to a whisper. "Do you think Granny Settle will be here?"

"Where else would she be?"

"I just thought maybe she could have dinner with Mr. Feldman or something. Or maybe the two of you could go . . . I don't know, Mom. Forget it! Rory's taking me to the beach later, so we'll probably be late."

She was gone by the time I got to Rinse the Sink or How About Putting This Stuff Away. Or even this, I will get out of the house and so will Granny Settle, if I have to hog-tie her. And you, beautiful, beautiful Kate can cook for your daddy with no noise from the peanut gallery. She had danced for years until skating took over. She would be alarmed to know how much those years at the barre still clung to her, how she dropped the classes and the nerdy tutus, but not the grace that charmed the way she walked and held her body. Pirouettes, those swift, sudden turns that left you breathless, even invaded her speech. Talk, shave, rant, rave, then boom. Clobber your mother with a throwaway line that's not as disposable as you think, Kate. So kids are ready for it? Ready for the world to blow apart into a thousand bits of shrapnel? Ready to ask permission for your own father to come to dinner? I sat on the edge of the tub for a long time, wishing she hadn't run away.

> I used to be in training for trouble
> Shadowboxing with my destiny
> Life was getting harder and harder
> Doing everything to bring me to my knees.
>
> Incidents became my new attraction
> Accidents were just my cup of tea
> I always chose the closest seat to heartbreak
> I didn't care who wound up next to me.

There was something unsettling about appropriating my own child's unhappiness, but I didn't let it stop me. I wrote fast, fueled by one of Tully's jellyrolls. My pen flew over the legal pad. I thought about it all night: legions of children girded for tragedy and the only way I could get rid of this image was to trap and transform it into a song.

> Never guessed defeat would feel this way
> A moment of pure bliss
> Before I knew it, I was down
> Knocked out with just one kiss.

"This is good. I'm not sure about the defeat part, though. A kiss isn't exactly a defeat. Although you might be right to use it there."

"God! You scared me, Tully."

"You know what? Go on and keep it."

He held a pot of boiling water in his hand and before I could say anything, he handed it to a passing busboy and sat down heavily. He lay his pudgy hands on top of the table.

"So what happens now?"

"Well, I go home and fuss with it some more. Play with it until I get it right."

"Yeah. Then?"

"I put it in a drawer along with my other stuff. Where is this conversation going?"

"I'll tell you where it should be going. It should be packing a suitcase and getting the hell to Branson."

"Branson! Tully, what an insult!"

"Make it Nashville, then. Listen, guys like me are important. We're the ones who listen to the radio *all day long*. I'd go off the deep end if I didn't have decent music to keep me going, so don't dismiss what I have to say, Polly. This—"

He stabbed at my paper with a fat finger.

"—is full of heart or soul or whatever you wanna call it. Somebody oughta be singing it. Enough said."

He didn't go anyplace. He just clung to the edge of the table until his fingers turned white and bloodless.

"But you gotta get moving. You gotta go to them. Go to the stars! They're dyin' to sing real words written by real people. It happens every day, so why can't it happen to you, Polly Harrison?"

His breathlessness was contagious. I was suddenly hemmed in by Tully's, suffocating in this cramped corner of the world. The bus roared by and I could see people outside coughing and covering their eyes with their hands as it pulled up a carpet of dirt and soot from the sidewalk.

"Would it calm you to know that I have an appointment with a very hot agent this afternoon at two o'clock? And, Tully, that I met him here?"

Tully's grin affected the whole restaurant. A busboy stopped what he was doing to watch, then a waitress who fiddled with her hairnet as she waited for an order. They stared at him expectantly.

"No foolin'. Here?"

"This very booth."

"So it's kinda like I had a direct hand in things."

"You absolutely did."

"Just remember this when you meet him, Polly. I could walk right into this song and make myself at home. And there's a world full of Tullys out there. We listen and we care. Tell him that. Now get outta here. This is on me."

He tore up the ticket and hopped up out of the booth to greet a little knot of people who stood by the register. I ate what was left of my jellyroll and checked my watch. There was just enough time to pick up the vest Beth had borrowed and never returned.

The thin black stripes on either side of my hood were peeling. Sap did it I supposed, rubbing my hand over the scraggly mess before I got in my car to leave.

"Hi!"

I could envision the exclamation point as the man marched toward me. The man had on a black, disappointed suit that made his cheery greeting a lie. He looked like a Jehovah's Witness or a pollster of some kind.

"Hi there! May I have just a moment of your time?"

Times like this made me wish for a blanket approach to all strangers. A line, just one, that I could produce for any unwanted occasion to make it go away. I didn't have one and, besides, he had me and he knew it. He had something bad on his face, near his nose, and I could see that he'd been tinkering with it.

"Make it fast."

"Oh, you're in a hurry? Of course you are. I could sense that, ha! I know this will seem strange, but . . ."

I had my car door open and looked around for a parking lot attendant. He was behind the wheel of a big Lincoln.

"Ma'am, this will just take a second."

"Look, I don't want my windshield washed and I don't want to sign any initiatives today. I do not have one dime to give you. Not one."

He was standing too close to me. He had a hand on my car; he was touching the stripes.

"You've got a problem here, lady. That's the trouble today. See, if these stripes had been painted on, they could have lasted forever. I would not hesitate to take this in to the dealer. Make them fix this. You can, you know. Make them. Oh, please don't do that!"

I was in my car and looking for my keys. Stupid, stupid. They were usually tucked in the side pocket, but not today.

"You have kids, right? One, probably two. Oh, a little boy! There's his baseball cap. Bet he's got a thousand of those, am I right?"

It was Kate's, but I didn't correct him. I was digging for keys and if I didn't find them in two seconds, I would start honking. I would make a scene and Tully would come rushing out and the attendant and people who sat by the window eating eggs and fried potatoes with garlic salt if that's how they wanted them prepared. My face was slick and hot.

"So, here's my question and I know it's odd, but you look like such a nice lady. Notice I said 'lady' and 'ma'am' because you have manners. I saw that rightaways, rightaways. How much does it cost to have somebody like you? I mean with kids and everything, how much does somebody like you cost every year? A lot, huh."

I felt cold metal, finally. I'd gotten my door locked and the window rolled up on his last words, but I could still hear them. Hear the words that kept coming through at me, even as I started the engine up.

"Because I need to know exactly how much it costs before I take the plunge, see. I bet you don't come cheap, ladies never do, but I really want to know before I make a—"

I pulled out fast and nearly rammed an Oldsmobile that was waiting for my space with the blinker on. There was nobody in front of me, so I sped out of the lot, past the puzzled attendant just then coming to ask me for money or my validated ticket. I thought about driving to the police station or even stopping and going in to tell Tully. But tell what? That some nut was bugging me and I didn't have the sense to shut him off before he could get started. Dope. I looked in my rearview mirror before I swung out into the street. The man in the sad suit was writing something down on the palm of his hand.

Eleven

*H*ow much does it cost to have somebody like you? The palms of my hands sweat as I drove and thought about that question. I kept checking the rearview mirror, but the man in the parking lot seemed to have stayed where he was. His question was the only thing following me now. It was startling to think that even though I traveled around town in a foolish-looking car and wore clothing haphazardly purchased, I somehow gave the impression of being an expensive woman. I ran my fingers over the top of my hair, reminding myself that this assumption came from a crazy man.

Money. When we were first married we tried to train ourselves not to want much because there wasn't much we could buy. We told ourselves we were good lookers. Every store was a museum: admire, don't acquire. That wasn't always so easy. The strongest lyrics I was about to pitch were rooted in that time. A time when Tom had been less prosperous, less sure, well before The Wafer had been developed. The Wafer, that little cookie, had certainly transformed our world. He hadn't always been a sales manager. There hadn't always been a Corvette parked in our driveway. Once upon a time Tom had been a simple salesman, struggling with dozens of products, each harder to push than the next. Most of our fights were about money then. All of them had a beginning, middle and an end.

The house was still when I pulled up
The kids were tucked in bed
The silence just reminded me
Of all the things we'd said.

I started for the kitchen
As those words echoed in my head
Instead of our old argument
Here's what Annie said:

Why that moon's just made for swooning.
Look how full it is tonight.
All I'm trying to do here
Is to make up for our fight.
There's something I forgot to say,
I thought just now I might.
It's not what you're doing wrong that counts,
It's what you're doing right.

After twenty years of listening to
My crazy, mixed-up plans
Annie's gotta figure
I'm a crazy, mixed-up man.

Failed dreams crawled in to fight her words,
The schemes that never went my way
Until Annie leaned against me
And softly said my name.

Joe, that moon's just made for swooning,
The way it shimmers caught my eye
It's an ornament for all of us
That God hung in the sky.
Come and stand beside me
Share a little of the light. Hey,
It's not what you're doing wrong that counts,
It's what you're doing right.

It's not what you're doing wrong that counts, It's what you're doing right. Unembarrassed relationship songs, Shel. Those are the songs people want to listen to. I repeated that to myself in the car and patted the worn dollar bill inside my bra for good measure. Another washed dollar bill had turned up in the pocket of my jacket and that had to mean something. I counted on the worn bill to protect me against evil and bring me a measure of luck. Since it had gone through the washing machine, it was soft enough to put right next to my heart. I locked the doors of my car and headed into Shel's office building. The gloomy structure had no windows and looked as sinister as the squat, brown Friars Club I had just passed on Santa Monica Boulevard.

I corrected my posture in the mirrored elevator. The brown leather pouch that held my songs was not quite a briefcase, but it did look serious. Long skirt, the short vest I'd retrieved after a six-month loan, lizard skin boots I'd had for years . . . with my shoulders pulled back, I looked every bit like an up-and-coming country lyricist. I checked my lipstick as the elevator doors moaned open to water.

Water slid over red stone walls into a phony gully that squared off the room. The narrow ditch was assiduously constructed, with occasional rocks jutting up out of the water streaming past and thick moss planted on its banks. From there it flowed into a central pool fronting the receptionist's desk. I stepped carefully over the floors, which shone with an icy, black gloss, watching every step, and sidestepped a plant that looked as if it could effortlessly lower a solid green branch and roll me up inside. I tiptoed across the wide space toward the receptionist. She was bent over an appointment calendar, inelegantly blowing her nose. It sounded like a trumpet blasting off key.

"Hi. I'm here to see Shel Elliot."

She swiped at her nose and sniffed. "Name?"

"Polly Harrison."

She continued swabbing the end of her nose.

"Shel told me to mention we met in Tully's Coffee Shop."

"Would you take a seat, please? I'll just let Shelly know you're here." She turned away from me and sneezed hard, bending double as she did it.

"Bless you."

"Thanks. It's so humid in here. It's just so damp. I practically live on extra-strength Contac." She rose heavily and struck off for a door behind her. She motioned to a bowl of mints on the coffee table. "Help yourself."

I hesitated, unwrapping one of the sticky candies I hoped would dissolve right away. I couldn't pitch my lyrics with a wad of candy in my mouth. The candy ate away at me, burning the roof of my mouth with a concentrated strain of menthol. The fumes filled my head and I relaxed into the deep leather chair, daring to touch the thick leaf of another strange plant next to me. It was spongy and sprang back from my fingers as soon as I lifted them from the quilted green surface.

"Straight from *The Little Shop of Horrors,* if you ask me."

I peeked around the edge of the plant to see a young woman in transparent knee socks and Mary Jane shoes. The thin, pink shell she wore was transparent, too. I could see a silver ring glinting at the tip of her breast. Her hair stood up in silver shocks and it looked as if she had a black eye. I didn't know where to look.

"So, how'd you meet Shelly?" She stroked her tummy when she said his name and I pulled my leather pouch onto my lap, just to have something to hang on to.

"Oh, me? I was in a coffee shop, writing, and he asked me what I was up to."

"Did you tell him?"

"Not specifically. I mean, he knows I write lyrics. But that's about it."

She rubbed her stomach harder as she spoke. I picked up the candy bowl in desperation and held it out to her.

"Oh, yes!" She stuck about five candies in a pouch that hung from her shoulder. "Yum, I'd rather eat candy than do anything else in the world. Well, that was good that you did that. Because I know Shelly. And I know he loves surprises." Her hand slipped down to her hip. "The more surprising, the better he likes it. Honest."

I heard the heavy click of heels and turned to the closed door. There was a muffled shout and then the door pushed open.

"He'll see you now." The receptionist waved to me, then frowned when she saw the girl in the knee socks. The candy still throbbed in my mouth, though it was nothing more than a transparent disc. It was as potent as anything Granny Settle had ever dug up out of her dusty overalls. The dollar bill tickled my breast as I walked through the door.

The receptionist's hair swung suddenly to one side as she turned her head to me. "Did you help yourself to a candy?"

"Yes, thanks."

"Good. Shel's pretty neurotic about bad breath. You didn't talk to that kid, did you?"

Water was the only constant. Niches, lit from above, each held a fresh interpretation of water. It dribbled over a stone construction in dark blues and greens, or sprayed straight up in a single black jet. The receptionist pinched the end of her nose to stop a sneeze.

"This water. I get sick just looking at it. You *did* talk to her, didn't you."

"A little. But she's way too weird for me."

The receptionist stopped walking and turned to face me. "Oh, thank you! I am so glad you said that." She slipped off her jacket suddenly and showed it to me. "Butterick's. I *sew* the minute I leave this office. Honest, I don't take phone calls from anyone except my boyfriend or my daughter who lives with my ex back in Des Moines, because I run for my old Singer the minute I leave this office. After I've lined a jacket or put in darts that are completely perfect, I can relax and fix something to eat."

We'd definitely come to the end of the hall and my throat should have been closing because of nerves, but it wasn't. I didn't know how to sew, but I could certainly understand how a rickety Singer machine might usher in the precious, ordinary world that sometimes got lost in this business. She must have sensed that I understood because she squeezed my shoulder in a fervent goodwill gesture.

"Good luck, kid." She knocked twice on the door, paused, then knocked again. Harder.

"Entrez, entrez."

Shel Elliot was talking on the phone, but took the time to wink and look me up and down before pointing to a chair by the window. He held a cigar as if it were a writing pen.

"You heard me right. Fuck him, fuck her, then go fuck yourself." He didn't slam the phone down the way you'd think. He slipped it softly, lovingly back into the cradle. He pursed his lips, thinking of something private and intense. I waited a few beats before speaking.

"Mr. Elliot, maybe I've come at a bad time."

"Call me Shelly. Oh, no. You've come at a wonderful time. I've had the same nasty conversation with this guy for seven weeks. Calls me the same time every afternoon, begging for it. He loves it. No. Change that. We both love it. What're you wearing, Polly?"

He stood up and came over to the window. *Come and stand beside me. Share a little of the light.* I remembered why I'd come and felt my chest warm.

"You mean these?" I lifted my skirt a bit and admired the way the skin glistened in the sun. "Lizard skin boots I bought in Oklahoma."

"Where?"

"Outside of Granite, the place I grew up. I bought them on a whim."

"What sort of whim?"

I shifted in my seat. The sun was warm and it was making me a little too comfortable. Shel sat so close our knees touched. I reached down and touched my leather pouch. I still had the taste of menthol in my mouth. "Probably the same kind of whim that makes me get up to write song lyrics at two o'clock in the morning."

"Nice transition, Polly. Very smooth."

I wondered suddenly if there was much difference between the ring that girl had attached to her nipple and the piece of money I had placed over my heart. Maybe everything in this business was about enchantment and wild hope, or warding off evil.

"Show me your stuff, baby. Give it to old Shelly."

I cleared my throat and started describing the story behind the words, the night and the way the moon intruded on me, unfastening memories until I had to write the words I was saying, spewing, swinging before him hoping he would lunge for them. Figuratively lunge. I had reached the chorus, *It's not what you're doing wrong that counts, It's what you're doing right,* when Shel's hands started to shake. The whole length of my neck was probably bright red. I hadn't dreamed I'd get such a fervent response.

"Read me the others. The others!"

I dug into my leather pouch, praying the order was right. I'd thought hard about how they should be read. Which themes, which words would fuse nicely. Lyrics were as combustible as any other kind of writing. I remembered the sweat on his lip from the coffee shop, the way he had begun to glisten in the middle of our conversation. Shel was so passionate. I sighed and crossed my legs as he hunched over my work.

He grabbed the unlit cigar from his pocket and rolled it along the side of his face as he read, then licked the tip and stuck it back inside his jacket. I noticed his teeth were clenched when he raised his head.

"So, this is what you do, Polly. This is how you spend your time. You got kids, right?"

"Yes."

"How many?"

"Two."

Shel passed a handkerchief over his lip. Sweat had broken out on his forehead, too. "Kids. Shoulda guessed." I heard something fall over outside the door, but Shel continued, unaffected.

"So did Melissa and Roy Wheeler."

He really had my attention then. The couple had produced some of the most poignant lyrics in country, lyrics lanced with pure poetry.

"Oh, yeah. Babies. They wheeled them in here and turned them loose in my office. Does this place look like Raging Waters to you, Polly? Does it?"

I tried to envision children splashing and playing in Shel's offices as the Wheelers talked business. I couldn't.

"You people don't get it. I hate country music. The Wheelers talked their way in here just like you did. So did Ty Brown. All you people do is write unimportant little stories about tears and beers and broken dreams. You people write about *family* in a time when *family* doesn't exist."

"Families do exist. They may be bleeding. They may be bleating like lost sheep, but they exist. We need writing about important things and what's more important than family?"

"'Bleating like lost sheep.' You talk like you write." He wiped the side of his mouth. "You're wasting my time, Polly, and I don't like when people waste my time."

Shel looked as if he wanted to get out of his chair, but couldn't. He was getting more and more agitated. "Lemme put it this way, Polly. I'm a visionary and you country people are stuck in the past." He stopped to get his breath, then went on excitedly. "Ever hear of the word 'opus'?"

"Sure."

"And you know what it means?"

"Of course."

"Good. Then let me share this with you. My opus, Shel Elliot's personal opus, is millennium music. Call it my gift to the world."

I thought of the sales clerk at Tower Records. He'd been evasive about Cactus and Ivy, mentioning something about an acoustic sound and how he had to go because of a customer. He hadn't said a word about millennium music.

"On January 1, of the year 2000, the day we flip our calendars to the first day of the new order, trumpets aren't gonna blast, baby. Shel Elliot's music's gonna rock the world! You see that kid out there? Eden Again, remember her name and remember where you first saw her. That kid with the black eye is where music's headed. The world is ending, Polly, and music's gonna lead the way there. Lemme put it to you this way . . . I don't do boot music, Polly. I know you've got a partner out there, somebody who'll set this crap to music, but it won't be Shel Elliot who participates. No deal, baby."

My lyrics slipped off my lap and Shel watched as the papers floated to the ground. He took his cigar from the pocket and licked it again. He grinned slowly and I saw gold glinting at the back of his mouth.

"Can I tell you a secret, Shel?"

He looked like an inquisitive little bird, the way he cocked his head. "Whad'ya say?"

"I said I want to tell you a secret. When I met you in the coffee shop, I knew I'd met a gentleman. A man who knew something about courtesy. Taste, manners, all of that."

He didn't like where this was heading. He started eyeing his desk, his busy-ness, his way out. Before he exited completely, I continued talking.

"And I'm still sure of that. But sometimes this gentleman must get a little shy, a little too timid to emerge on his own. Somebody, maybe a total stranger, has to understand he's there in the first place and then invite him to come on out."

The little bird opened his mouth to squawk, but could produce no protest song. Shel had to get down on all fours to pick up my papers. One of my songs had slipped under his desk. He bumped his head as he retrieved every piece of paper and glared at me darkly, thrusting them into my hands.

"Here. Gentleman, huh? You're conning me, Polly. Don't think I don't know. You probably pull this shit with your kids when they misbehave. Gentleman . . ."

Even though he shook his head in disgust, I could tell the notion pleased him. The thought of a better self beneath all the nasty, bullying Shels seemed to touch him for one slender moment. Then Shel Elliot moved out of the sunlight and began to rub his belly. Eden Again entered the room without knocking and I don't think he heard me say goodbye.

Twelve

Country music wasn't unimportant—Shel Elliot was. Puttering around in the garden rinsed him from my life. I watered until puddles formed around every mature plant just to make sure. A patch of mint had sprung up in one predictable corner and I gathered a few sprigs before going indoors. Then I pulled on the kitchen door to fall backward into the handrail with the doorknob in my hand.

"Shit, shit, shit." Tom had installed the deadbolt lock, the brassy knob and the brand-new door. Now, a few major rainstorms later, the door had fallen apart because he mistakenly bought an interior door and the knob twisted off effortlessly. I was lucky the handrail held. He'd built that for me, too, right before he left for a long tour of the Western region. A very long tour of the Western region. I rubbed my back and took a good look at Russell's house where clocks ticked on time, doors held, where anything that buckled or bent or broke received immediate attention. He was always after me to let him fix something. Well, maybe I just would. I went around to the front of the house and banged hard. Toby let me in and looked at the knob I held in my hand.

"Great." His eyes were red-rimmed.

"It came right off. Do you believe it?"

"I'd believe anything that happened in this house. Give it to me, Mom."

"Did you have a snack, hon?"

He looked down at the ground, shifted his weight heavily and gave the floor a short, stubby kick with the ball of his foot.

"You know, that's a really boring question. You ask me the same thing every single day. Either that or 'Hi, hon. Have a good day?' Think about it, Mom. Think about hearing the same question day after day for six years. Did you do that to Dad when he used to come home from work? I bet you did. I bet you said exactly the same thing to him, with your voice just like that. All peppy, like you think everybody's life is so happy. I bet that's just what happened."

He marched down the hall to his room, dragging his dirty hand along the wall, just daring me to bring that up. He turned on the Stones and started rummaging around in his tool kit. They were having their nineteenth nervous breakdown.

"You came very close this time, Toby."

He turned the music up and I knew he couldn't hear me above Mick, who had just brought up a good point. *Oh, who's to blame?*

"You're not the only one who has bad days and bad moods, you know. You're not the only one who gets sick and tired of the same things repeated day in, day out. That's what families are about, Toby. Monotony and love, better get used to it, buddy. By the way, your dad didn't leave me. I kicked him out."

Neither child had demanded an explanation, so Tom and I glided over why we were breaking up, making do with some banality about growing apart. Maybe this was the aftermath. Maybe Toby really believed marriages broke up because of cheery, repetitious greetings at the end of every day.

I knew his red-rimmed eyes meant trouble in school, trouble on the bus, but trouble was everywhere and couldn't a kid still be nice to his mother occasionally? I wanted to cry in front of him. I wanted him to walk out of his room and see his mother breaking down, no more peppy questions you could count on her asking every day, no more solid, sexless, eternally on-site mother. I wanted my son to feel sorry for me right then. I had the good sense to return to the kitchen, because why else do you tape pictures and poems on the wall, if not for moments like this?

I looked at the artwork all over the kitchen, all the poems and citations and devilry that filled my life. Here was an old note from his principal summarizing behavior that defied categorization. But then, right next to it, was a poem about a boy who turned into a tree that shaded a whole town and fed it, too, raining it with apples and pears and meat, because this was a multipurpose tree created by a six-year-old boy who could imagine such hybrids and draw them, too. Big steaks fell from leafy branches into open arms. The pictures were up there to save his life and mine. You looked at them, read the lines from an old story or poem and you fell in love all over again. And that was what kept families afloat . . . having your heart break again and again and setting things up so that could happen. By the time Toby marched through with his toolbox, I wasn't one hundred percent, but I was better. I knew, because I'd stood there reading and rereading it, that he loved me "verry, verry much."

Toby strolled over to the phone to continue a conversation he must have started in another room.

"So, you wanna hang on for a second while I take a look at it? Can you, Dad?"

He lay the phone down casually on the counter and headed over to the door, a book on household repairs tucked under his arm. He hunched over the broken doorknob and I could see Tom as he must have waited on the other end of the line, the phone caught between his shoulder and neck, writing a memo or reading a sales report, hanging on for his son's next question. Toby returned to the phone.

"Dad, I'm not sure what kind of screw I should use."

"How about a finishing nail, honey?" I brought up the only kind of hardware I could name. Toby turned his head woefully toward me. His eyes told me everything I needed to know about my role in this operation. My input wasn't correct or even interesting.

"Yeah. Yeah, okay. I'll call you back if I need to." He shifted his weight suddenly to the other foot. "I love you, too."

He hung the phone up and returned to his toolbox. He began whistling.

"What are we having for dinner?"

"Are you asking that because you want to pick a fight or because you really want to know?"

"That's not funny, Mom."

"You know something? If I depended on you and Kate for a good opinion of myself, I'd be a zero. I'd be a smudge, a stain, something no one would ever order in a restaurant."

The knob was back on, but I wondered if it would really open and close my warped and rotting door.

"I think I'm smart. I think I'm pretty." My voice sounded so thin. Toby still didn't look up.

"I do, too."

"Gee. You do?"

He looked up then, and pushed a strand of long hair behind his ear. He looked more like his dad every day. Up until about ten years old, he could have been anyone's sandy-haired boy. But then he started to change, each feature slowly recast as a younger Tom Harrison. He had the same great single dimple and round, wondering eyes.

"Know what?"

"No. What?"

"Stewart does, too. He gave you a ten."

There was nothing casual in his face and I decided not to be flippant. I definitely thought flippant would be a mistake.

"That was sweet of him. I didn't know women my age could still be tens."

His shoulders relaxed slowly and he looked at Russell's house, ran his eyes slowly up and down the side of the stucco.

"Why'd he make it so huge?"

"So he can make more money when he sells it. That's called speculation."

"It still looks stupid. So what're we having again?"

"Granny Settle is cooking. And Rory."

"Great."

That was my second disparaging "great" and it was only four-thirty in the afternoon.

Granny Settle fanned the flames in the hibachi until they leaped wildly from the bed of coals. She had dismantled her bun and as she fed the fire, I imagined her straggly, thin hair as a burning halo of light.

"You're standing too close to the heat."

Granny Settle as a living, leaping flame. The lurid thought made me jump back from the fire. We probably shouldn't have tried to barbecue in such close quarters. The hibachi was too close to the hedge, too close to Russell's house. He was probably fretting away inside, just smelling the smoke.

"I was making campfires before you were a mote in your mother's eye."

I thought the expression went "gleam in your mother's eye," but I didn't want to quibble. She was so intent on getting the fire going. Russell peered down from on high, but I ignored him for the moment. I had enough on my hands. She'd been talking for days about building a genuine campfire and naturally Rory egged her on, but I begged off. I didn't want the scorched ashen circles I remembered from her Granite garden to reappear in mine. I didn't want the iron stakes set into the ground with an iron bar balanced between them, I didn't want her old gouch hook hanging from the whole construction which would support a kettle full of stringy stew. Her chuck wagon skills belonged to another time and place, Granite and even further beyond. How could I explain Granny Settle's cooking methods to the Los Angeles fire department?

"I made campfires and a whole lot else, Polly Ann."

"What do you mean by that?"

She stood on the other side of the fire and her teary eyes were fixed on me. A gentle breeze was sending the smoke her way.

"I mean I've been alive one hell of a long time. I've looked death in the eye twice. I've been kicked and bitten by so many fool horses, goats and mules, I finally learned how to kick back. I've roped mules and men, but no one's ever put a rope around my neck, Polly. Never!"

Maybe it was my comment about standing too close to the fire. We'd gotten into it a couple of times in the kitchen, about where the dishwashing soap ought to be kept and that sort of thing. Was this a turf war about how to manage a barbecue grill? I rubbed my hands on a dishtowel I had hooked in my belt and she accelerated.

"If that woman thinks she can force me to go where I don't want to go or do what I don't want to do, she's got another think coming. And I don't care how much money she's dangling in front of me."

"When did Mother call?"

"Today while you were out."

She took a few steps back, finally satisfied with the height of the flames. Russell was a wreck. He abandoned discretion and stood in his window with his hands on his hips. The flames leaned toward his house, not mine, as the breeze gained strength. Maybe this wasn't the perfect night for a cookout.

"She doesn't love that fairy Denario. She loves his money."

"Bobby Denario is no fairy, Granny. And I'd much rather you didn't use that expression."

"I'll use whatever expression I please. He's not an Indian, is he?"

"Not that I know of."

"Well then, *you* tell me why he's wearing so much turquoise jewelry if he's not one or the other."

My mother and Bobby had taken their cruise to Mazatlán and I hadn't tried to get in touch with her since their return. I thought I'd wait for the effects of those weeks at sea to wear off first. Some of our worst conversations had taken place after my mother had gone port-hopping with her husband. Water just wasn't her element; the desert suited them perfectly. Those shocking blasts of heat as they leaped from Bobby's luxury cars to their glistening white compound, built low and level as a string of boxcars, jolted them into passion. They came out at night to lie on the throbbing deck around the pool and let the heat soak into their skins before going to bed. My mother said desert heat "inflamed" her libido. She had always told me much more about her marriage than I ever wanted to know and the new one with Bobby was no exception.

"What does she want you to do that you don't want to do?"

"Live with her. With them. In that godforsaken place."

"Actually Palm Springs isn't all that bad."

"Mind the fire, Polly Ann."

I could hear her clanging her skillets and aluminum camping equipment around in the kitchen. I wondered what my mother had proposed specifically and why. She hadn't shown an interest in my grandmother for years. When Granny Settle turned down her third invitation to visit, my mother got her feelings hurt and said so, cuddling closer to Bobby as she did. "I may come from Granite, Oklahoma, but I'm no rock. Isn't that right, Bobby?" Bobby lapped this up, of course. He was a big, burly fellow and my mother had carved a niche out of his solid physique. She snuggled into her more or less permanent nesting place at his shoulder and sighed contentedly. I disagreed with Granny Settle; my mother loved Bobby. I also think she got tired of be-ing chased with tire irons or whatever my father had handy. One day my mother stopped watching Minah Overstreet have all the fun. She decided to have some of her own and for that I didn't blame her.

She was calling to Rory for help, a sign she lumped me and my mother to-gether as one disagreeable package. I could see Kate inside, circling her room with the phone at her ear. She pulled on the extension cord and wrapped it around her wrist like a bracelet. She waved at me and tapped at her wristwatch, which meant she was starving. She stuck the phone under her arm and leaned out the window. "So no dinner?"

"Granny Settle and Rory are cooking."

"Great."

Monotony and love. The window dropped shut and she went back to her conversation. Rory wandered out clutching a book to his chest.

"What're you reading, Rory?"

"Book on antique firearms."

I scowled at him.

"Wanta look at it, at least?"

"Why does everyone make such a fuss over those things?"

"You're joking, Polly. You can fire these without reloading. Can you imagine what a Winchester meant in Oklahoma in 1873? No fear, Polly."

No Fear. The phrase had surfaced in stickers that graced bumpers all over town and here was a fresh context. Not that it mattered to me . . . I still hated guns. Everyone had them in Granite. I don't think we were more murderous than any other community, but owning guns was common. Just thinking of them made my skin crawl. On bad nights in Granite, I used to take a thick blanket into my father's card room where a case full of guns was prominently displayed. It was a wonder to me that he never stormed into that room, demanding the key that I hid in the folds of that blanket where I lay curled with the flea-bitten dogs. I had contingency plans by the time I was eight years old. If he tried to bust open the glass front to get a gun, I would bite his ankle like I'd seen one of his collies do. If that didn't work, I'd throw the Bible at him to remind him that shooting your wife meant eternal damnation. The worn red Bible lay open to the Psalms on a table next to the guns. The Good Book would stop him if I couldn't.

Rory was holding his gun book a little too reverently.

"I'm fine with most of the stuff you bring into this house. But get that out of here."

He hugged his book closer and went back inside to hide it.

We played Rory's tape over and over as we ate. The theme song from *Rawhide* had come back into fashion. He laced it with Hendrix and the Grateful Dead so the kids could save face when they asked for the tape, but he was sure that the reason everybody bought it was some very real craving for the Old West.

"Uncle Rory, listening to the theme from *Rawhide* is just another way of being alternative. It's like watching *The Brady Bunch*."

"There is no alternative to music, Kate. Another thing." Rory talked with his mouth full. I could see that by the light of the full moon. "The kids who come to my store are earnest. They don't buy music to laugh at it, they really listen to it." Rory dug in his pocket and pulled out a black and white pin. "They get this with every purchase. If they've already got one, I make 'em take another. It's my campaign slogan in case I ever run for mayor."

Kate giggled and pinned it to her floppy T-shirt. IRONY SUCKS . . . I wondered if enough of those pins would get him elected.

Granny Settle had us all sitting in the grass because the table wobbled too much. She even made me turn off the strand of white lights, saying the moon was light enough.

"Food always tastes better when you eat it on the ground, doesn't it?" She waited for an answer. "I asked you children a question."

"Yeah."

"Kate?"

It took all of Kate's resolve, but she did eat, chewing carefully, as if her teeth weren't up to the task. Beans and corn Granny Settle served cradled in blackened husks. She even swallowed a little forbidden meat to try to rise to the occasion.

"Mmm."

"Speak up."

"It's like camp food."

"What would you know about camp food, girl?" She reached into a side pocket and rubbed a little dirt between her fingers, sniffed at it a couple of times and carefully put it back in her pocket. "I'd like to hear all about that."

Kate pulled the bill down on her baseball cap and looked into the center of the circle. "We used to camp out with my dad."

"That so? Now where would that be?"

"At Big Bear. Here, too. Not here, exactly, but over there where Mom planted that orange tree. He taught me how to pitch a tent and build a fire. That kind of stuff."

"I remember that! What were those cookie sandwiches we used to make?"

"S'mores."

"We always ran out of chocolate. Remember how we never had enough?"

117

Kate rested her chin on her knees. Toby would always eat supper by the fire they built and fuss about making the tent. They'd all crowd inside and Toby would slide into my bed toward midnight or so, having heard "sounds." Kate had been impervious to bugs and fear and squashed living quarters. She would have lived forever in trees or the tent we still had somewhere in the basement. Those were lush nights and I remember all of them. I felt as complete and cared for as my own children, watching the three of them stab marshmallows with sticks by soft firelight.

"Did your father teach you to make boggy top pie or the secret to making good pooch?"

The baseball cap lifted almost imperceptibly. "What's pooch, Granny Settle?"

"Nothing to it but stewed tomatoes, sugar and a little leftover biscuit. Those cowboys took canned tomatoes everywhere, child. They helped cut the thirst on dry rides. Did your daddy teach you to calm a spooked longhorn steer by singing a song?"

"No ma'am."

Ma'am? From my son? I looked at Rory, but he was already riding the range with Granny Settle. He pushed the stop button on the cassette player, cutting all further interference.

"Your great-grandfather taught me, bless his heart. Bless his fool heart. I guess I didn't love animals any too much, seeing that they were my competition. Oh, he didn't love another gal after he'd made up his mind to marry me over Eveline Parker. But oh, did he love those old cow ponies of his. Don't ever marry a real cowboy, Kate, because you'll just wind up frustrated. No, you've got to take what you can get from a cowboy and be grateful. I had him in my bed at night and at my table the next morning. The rest of the time, he belonged to those old spotted ponies and cattle. I got whatever he didn't give them. Wasn't that the truth, Polly Ann?"

I remember that defiant trek to the Granite library on a summer day so hot the librarian wept as she shuffled back and forth between the dusty stacks and the reference desk. She cried a little as I asked her where I could find out everything about cattle drives and the Chisholm Trail, vaqueros and horns that measured seven feet across. She begged me to come back in the fall. She said I had a good mind and curiosity that was worthy of weather that would let her think straight. I let the top of an olive green book bag fall open accidentally to reveal a pack of cigarettes as she pulled on her red nose with a handkerchief.

She saw those cigarettes and got my message. If I couldn't learn about the most romantic twenty-year period of our nation's history, I would descend into smoking and Lord knew what else. That research project, conducted in the middle of a ruthless heatwave that had windshields bursting all over town, freed me from being sad forever. I knew my grandmother had made her strange peace with a failed rodeo and a two-bit riding ring outside of town by appropriating history. If she could own that time, that stretched back to days when she wasn't even alive, then I could, too. I listened to her stories with a deeper faith and attention. My grandmother's tales were pure in essence, if garbled in detail. That summer they belonged to me more than any other time of my life.

"Those nights, oh those nights. It was like sleeping with a newborn, the way he'd wake at midnight when he knew the cows were turning in their sleep."

"What cows, Granny?" Toby's eyes danced. He tried to keep the eagerness out of his voice.

"Why the cows he spent years minding on those drives up through Texas and Oklahoma. He was a night herder back then, used to put tobacco in his eyes to keep awake so he could sing to his cattle toward midnight. They'd always wake up to turn, see. It was an instinct, child, and I can't think of anything as moving or fearful as the sight of three thousand head of cattle rustling and about to turn on their other side on a full-moon night. About then, anything will spook them. The sound of dry brush crackling, why one wheel turning'll cause the whole lot of them to stampede. For that reason, your great-grandfather and some other cowboys would circle the herd slow and easy, singing as they went, crooning love songs and cradle songs to lull them back to sleep until daybreak. Well, he kept on hearing those cattle stir long after he'd left the trail."

"The trail to what?"

"The trail to the railroads in Kansas." She grabbed my knee with one hand and turned to me vengefully. "Polly. It takes more than food and shelter to nourish a child. Why haven't you been *telling?*"

"I don't know, Granny. Our lives are so busy, we never have—"

"That's no excuse. Look here, the ground's getting cold. Rory, help me up."

He did better than that. My crazy sixties cousin lifted our grandmother up off the ground and held her in his arms like she was a child.

"Time for bed, Granny."

"I'll go to bed when I damn well please."

"Think of it as beauty sleep."

"I'm too old to be beautiful."

Rory jostled her gently and laughed. "I think Mr. Feldman would disagree."

"Mr. Feldman? Never heard of him." She was sound asleep by the time they got to the back door.

Thirteen

*R*ory took Granny Settle and Toby out so Kate could make dinner for her dad. His gear stood by the door; he was leaving tomorrow morning and he wanted to get an early start. I was trying to get ready to leave myself and with Kate calling me to the kitchen every five minutes, it wasn't simple. A magazine lay open to several step-by-step guides on how to tie a scarf, but I wasn't having much luck. The room was heating up and by the time I got the cotton scarf properly knotted, I was dripping wet. I turned up the collar on my blouse but it didn't give me that natty look I was searching for.

"What are you doing, Mom?"

"I'm trying to revive this shirt and it isn't working."

"That scarf looks incredibly stupid."

"Thanks, hon."

"I mean unless you're going to a square dance or a costume party or something. Where exactly are you going?"

"In Cahoots."

"I don't believe this. I do not believe this. My friends go there, Mom."

"Really? I didn't know it attracted a young crowd."

"They go there to laugh." She stretched and started to yawn. "I also don't believe you're going with *him*. It's bad enough that he lives next door."

"I'm just meeting him there."

"Is that it?"

The smell of chicken was all over the house. Ordinarily I would have found that fragrant and comforting. Tonight it made my stomach turn. All of a sudden I couldn't remember what Russell looked like.

"After that we'll decide what to do. Maybe go see a movie or something."

"So how come you're not driving there together?"

"He's going there straight from work. Kate, tell me the truth. Do I look stupid?"

"No, Mom. You look worried. Are you worried?"

She was wearing my apron and even though she'd asked what a basting bulb was and whether sauté was higher or lower than simmer, she looked like a young woman in complete command of the situation. I didn't. I couldn't get a scarf to stop looking like a noose. Plus I couldn't get Granny Settle's evil sentence to quit echoing in my mind. *I'm too old to be beautiful.*

"I wouldn't say I'm worried. Perplexed would probably do it, though."

Kate sat down on my bed and tugged at my waist.

"Don't highrise. You're perplexed about what?"

"The single life is a little weird."

"Yeah?"

"It makes me feel as tentative as someone your age." I got rid of the scarf and started rubbing at my lips with a tissue. "I'm too old for this nonsense."

"You don't have to go out, Mom."

"I'm afraid I do. The alternative is to stay in the house and rot."

She sat with her elbows on her knees, tapping her foot to some beat in her own head.

"Are you actually thinking of sleeping with him?"

"Kate!"

"See? That's your problem. If you are, just go on and get it over with. Once you sleep with him and it's either good or bad, you won't worry about scarves. You won't keep pulling on your collar, either. Plus, if it's bad, maybe he'll stop calling and knocking and *looking* at us all the time."

I wanted to cancel everything. I wanted to stay inside my house forever and raise my children, keeping them young as long as I could. Her eyes were too cool, too gray. Maybe I could still reach Russell on his car phone. I could plead a daughter whose level suggestion that I hop into bed to get it over with gave me goosebumps. I sat down beside her and she sighed.

"Here we go."

"Tell me something, Kate."

"*No,* I am not sexually active. Anyway, if I was, they have condoms in the nurse's office and all you have to do is help yourself. If I'm anything, I'm probably a lesbian. I'm probably some loser lesbian who'll never have a date, ever."

"That wasn't my question."

"Oh, no? Then what was it?"

"I guess my question is do you really think that? I mean about just closing your eyes and doing it?"

"Sure. Anything you're scared of doing you've got to just do."

"That line of reasoning could get you in a lot of trouble."

"Hasn't so far. Anyway, skating is like that. I have to bite the inside of my cheek before I do most of my tricks. I bite it hard, too. Otherwise I'd just settle for easy or safe and I'd never get better."

I finally got the knot right on the scarf and she went off to see about her dinner. I kept getting it wrong with her. Maybe she was riding that board the way I had ridden a horse, sliding down dry hillsides clinging to the flimsy loop on a bareback pad. All of it just to kick up dust, to slip and scramble down an incline, scaring lizards from their stuporous spot in the sun. All of it just to see what it felt like to land in one shaking piece at the bottom of a dry gulch. Maybe flying off a curb on a sheer, flat wooden deck was like that. Maybe landing a kick-flip was like that or rail-sliding with the music shrieking in your ears. Maybe it was all about putting your body in a scary, empty space. I didn't really dismount until Tom got his driver's license, and maybe Kate wouldn't either. Maybe there had to be a boy to break the spell, a boy who invited you to perform more daring stunts still and acts of free, fathomless joy.

"Bye, Kate. Smells awfully good."

"Want a taste?"

The rice fell apart in dry, delicate bits inside my mouth.

"I think it's perfect. Your dad will swoon. I think I hear his car."

His Corvette was shinier than ever, with the interior glistening and probably deodorized. A clean car was a point of honor to him. It even changed the way he drove. When it got dirty, he was more likely to run red lights and park haphazardly in a crowded lot. Tom was coming up the path with roses for Kate. I looked at the tight yellow buds, wondering whether they would burst apart all at once in a loud blast of glory or whether they would open gently, slowly.

The doorbell sounded more shrill since he'd fixed it. He had fixed it, too, the same afternoon I spent at Golden Savings and Loan. It was a good start, but not exactly what I had in mind.

"Hey, Polly. You having dinner with us?"

I smiled and brushed past him with the keys in my hand. "Can't. I'm going out."

"Ah. Have a nice time."

"You too. Oh, while I'm thinking of it . . ." I dug in my purse for my inventory of broken things. "I've got a handyman coming over next week. If there's anything you think should be added to the list, let me know. He's sending the bill to your office."

"Those guys charge an arm and a leg, Polly. I can take care of this stuff." He looked at the list and put his hand in a back pocket. "What the hell is scribing?"

The scarf was beginning to itch. I took it off and mopped at the back of my neck. "I took a good look around, Tom. All the things that have been stuck or broken for years I put on the list. Then I added a few eyesores and not even all the eyesores and that's what the handyman is coming here to repair. You look gaunt."

Just a few pounds on or off showed up immediately under his chin. I didn't have to try to remember his features. His nose, his eyes and full lips were part of a constant, familiar topography that included our two children and even me. Over the past seven months, I have sometimes stared into the mirror to find not my image gazing back at me, but his.

"I've been down with the flu. This is a pretty expensive list, Polly."

"So are wine lists."

He looked puzzled, at first, then less so as I went on.

"Perfume. Now there's something that's gotten outrageous. Flowers, too. The simplest arrangement is just a fortune, don't you think? And jewelry, all those little gold knickknacks people exchange without thinking—"

"I never bought her expensive gifts, Polly. It wasn't like that."

"You mean *we* never bought her expensive gifts. Whatever money you spent came out of your family's hide and I don't know why it's taken me so long to get that."

It had grown hotter outside or I had. I felt a drop of perspiration roll between my breasts.

"While we're on the subject of home repairs, let me ask you this. Did you fix stuff for her, too? Were you the one who built that stupid fake hill in her front yard?"

I probably had a rash around my neck. I would take a circuitous route to In Cahoots. I would roll down all the windows, do some deep breathing until things settled back down.

"All those trips, Tom. All those fucking trips. You weren't alone, were you?"

He was standing in the light, right there where I could see him. I thought he was on the verge of a smile, but I must have imagined that.

"I was alone on those trips, Polly. Trust me. I've been alone for years."

He stood on the front porch for a moment, watching as I got into my car. He lifted his free hand up as I drove away, looking as solemn as a stranger. The other hand held roses, yellow roses. Tom was finally bringing flowers to the right address.

In Cahoots was a faint heartbeat in a dying strip mall on Glendale Avenue. Sees, Angelo's Deli, Clothestime. Letters were missing from colorless signs, as if someone had tried to rub out any trace of business. None of that was enough to dissuade a dancing fool. I looked around at the jammed parking lot and went over the steps to the Cowboy Cha Cha in my head, then joined the powdered, painted crowd that streamed into the club.

From the entrance, I could see a dark hall filled with pool tables. It was empty except for a couple practicing free swings and complicated steps in one corner. A larger central room was mostly made up of dance floor. Surrounding seating made me think of a corral where you could watch cattle-roping competitions or barrel racing. Tonight the women seemed to be doing all the roping.

Truly ladies' night, In Cahoots just about clobbered me with hairdos. The biggest hair seemed to be centered at the bar behind me, while shorter, more modest cuts whirled around the dance floor. A disc jockey managed things from a cracked leather armchair that sat on a raised platform. There was no sign of Russell so I turned my back on the dance floor. A painting of an enormous bottle of Jack Daniel's took up the wall behind the bar, but I resisted and ordered myself a Coors.

"Light?"

"No, just regular Coors." I liked the bartenders here. They looked like they were all in college or saving up for it. I settled in to watch things. My guess had been that In Cahoots would be a one-night flirtation with the two-step for most people. Clearly I hadn't done any research on the place.

There were teachers for the uninitiated and I watched as beginners struggled with the Horseshoe and the El Paso. An older crowd did the West Coast Swing. These were the really passionate dancers, the ones who must have performed at county fairs and local benefits to cure disease. They brought costume changes to In Cahoots and women hurried to the bathroom with pastel skirts flung over their arms.

I peered down the hall for a minute to find it swirling with gossip and heat rollers, tubes of pink lipstick and dated entertainment magazines promising intimate interviews with Johnny Cash and Willie Nelson. Bare shoulders were de rigueur and there were any number of white eyelet blouses held in puffy place with elasticized necklines. The young and the hip wore skin-tight jeans, lots and lots of visible lingerie, and Guess ankle boots made up the second, subtler kind of costume you found there. I was taken in tow at once by a woman named Toni who worked for the phone company. She looked me up and down as I stood by the doorway and put her hands on her hips to study me.

"Now I can't believe a pretty thing like you would be out there dancing with strange partners."

"Oh, I'm supposed to be meeting someone."

"Can he dance at all?"

"I'm going to find out."

"Do that. If you can find yourself a man who can dance, honey, don't let him out of your sight. That's the secret to a happy life and you can quote me."

It was nine o'clock and the evening was really warming up. I knew meeting my neighbor at In Cahoots would hardly lead me forward. This was not what Beth would have hoped for me and, to be honest, it wasn't what I hoped for myself. I would leave here without a single line in my head because there was no inspiration in a place like this. I needed to concentrate on lyrics that were fresh and crisp, with kicky takes on the stuff of modern living. Maybe Shel, for all his unkindness, had done me a favor. Maybe family was out as a subject. Maybe I ought to write about depression and weight loss, some of the urban strains that had everybody worn to the nub. Marty Stewart was blasting the room, a room increasingly filled with the fumes of Aqua Net. My mother still used the stuff, though her hair stylist begged her not to. I jiggled my foot and decided I would give Russell another ten minutes.

"Smile."

I hate this kind of line. It is not only intrusive, but frighteningly unoriginal, plus it reminded me of high school. I turned around viciously and was about to say so.

"You know, I hate—"

"What do you hate, Polly?"

"Drinking alone. Where have you been?"

I was surprised at how happy I was to see Russell. He was nice in a time when nice was underrated. He looked happy to be here, happier than I was, and though the hat was back, it didn't look as foolish as it had the night we met in Paradise. He ordered a beer for himself and another for me.

"You just look great."

"Yeah? Kate didn't think so."

"It's her job not to think so. That's what kids are supposed to do."

"What do you know about kids?"

"I was one, once. I've got nephews and I've picked up a lot of info just standing around in my backyard, to tell you the truth."

I took a long drink of beer, wishing he hadn't said that.

"You oughta look at that skateboarding business, Polly."

"Meaning?" The disc jockey was crowing about the Tractors, a hot group out of Tulsa. I *had* looked at the skateboarding business.

"I wonder why she would choose something like that to do. Something that brands her as an outsider."

"Get to the point, Russell."

"Now, don't get mad. I'm just saying it pegs her as a troublemaker. I gotta tell ya, Polly, from a contractor's point of view, it's a pretty sorry sport. They damage property, they injure pedestrians. I hate to see them come near a construction site. I'm concerned about her, Polly. But hey, I brought you here to dance, not to lecture you on how you raise your kids."

He leaned down and kissed me, then went right on talking. It was so matter-of-fact and natural, I didn't feel like objecting. I didn't feel anything other than queasy comfort. It was exactly like the first time Tom told me he loved me. I was sixteen and he was making a left turn in his car, explaining how I needed to drop a waterski, how that would lead straight to being able to slalom; when I started to object, he continued the turn, wedging his declaration in quietly as if he were still explaining how to get me up on one ski.

"—so now I have to pay a security guard to chase them off."

"That was very smooth, Russell."

"Thanks."

The music was getting louder as the disc jockey, still comfy in his rustic living room, announced that the rest of the evening would be Sadie Hawkins night. *Attention, ladies, this is the chance of a lifetime.*

"So. Aren't you going to ask me for a dance?"

It could have been the beer, but it seemed to me the crowd parted for us. It was lovely to be by his side. I folded my arms over my chest.

"How good are you? This lady in the bathroom suggested I find out."

"Good doesn't begin to describe it."

I wondered if Russell actually worked on his own construction sites or if he was just born big. He had a broad chest and not one of those artificial chests, either, the ones that come from hours of grunting under dumbbells. I saw raw envy in the eyes of several women and it wasn't pretty. A little number in a leather skirt tried to cut in.

"Have this dance?"

"He's taken, hon."

I took a giant step forward and landed on the upturned toe of her cowboy boot. Luckily, she was wearing the real thing. Her boots were made to cut across a dusty corral and I didn't really hurt her. She muttered something and stepped back into the throng of people.

"This place is so hokey."

"I thought you wrote song lyrics. Country music, country dancing." Russell swung me out on his arm and pulled me back in.

"There's country music and then there's country music. This is pretty generic stuff. You know, the kind of old-timey tunes tour buses roll into Branson to hear. I've got a lot to teach you, Russell."

"Sounds good. When do we start class?"

His hand tightened around my waist and we completed another turn. Russell really knew how to lead. He took me around and around the floor and I didn't stumble once. One sugar push just seemed to naturally follow another. A golden rhinestone vision whirled by, clasped tightly in the arms of a man half her size, leaving Russell and me blinking and momentarily blinded. *You caught me when I wasn't listening. What was that joke that you told? I just had a glimpse of my future and destiny's decked out in gold.* I took one last turn on the dance floor with Russell, thinking about all my misconceptions. . . . In Cahoots did provide its own quirky form of inspiration. I wondered what else I could have been wrong about.

I waited in the driveway, thinking Russell would pull up any minute. I needed to thank him for the nice evening. I'd lost track of him on Wilshire, in the corridor west of Beverly Hills that turned into a nighttime speedway full of college and high school kids. I sat looking at his entry, his landscaping, his solid contractor's sense of what should follow next. There was no tumble of things at Russell's doorway, there was logic and order. I brushed the lint from a breath mint I found at the bottom of my purse and popped it in my mouth. It had melted down to a flimsy shard by the time I realized Russell wasn't coming home.

I bumped my leg hard getting out of the car and said the worst word I could think of out loud. It would probably be bright blue in two days. When I opened my front door I could still smell Kate's dinner lingering in the air, but her light was off and I'd have to hear about it tomorrow. Why was the aftermath of food sickening, when the same smells filling the air before food was eaten delighted the senses? I didn't know, but the odors accosted me and I hoped they weren't in my bedroom, too. My door was closed, but low, flickering lights spilled out under the door. Someone had left the television on without sound. It wasn't Rory. He slept inside a messy white mound on the couch. I tiptoed past the closed doors of the dining room where my grandmother slept, getting madder all the while. How much longer was I going to have to tiptoe through my own house?

"Toby! What are you doing up? It's way past your bedtime."

"Look who's talking."

I wouldn't jump into this. I wouldn't make any snap decisions right now. My judgment wasn't what it usually was; however, Toby's bare-chested presence in my bed did invite comment. He turned my bedside clock around to face me in one painfully slow movement.

"One-twenty. What have you been *doing* all this time?"

"Dancing and talking."

"For so many hours? You don't know that many words."

He looked like a pint-sized judge, the way he held his arms crossed over his bony chest.

"How come he didn't come to the house to talk? He lives right next door."

"I wanted to give Kate and your dad time to themselves, that's why."

"They had it. They had plenty of time. I couldn't sleep after Dad left. I couldn't fall asleep and school's gonna be terrible tomorrow and I'm gonna get screamed at because I'll be too tired to pay attention. Thirty-five thousand children were murdered last year and guess what? Their parents weren't home when they were murdered."

"Toby, you made that up."

"I read it and you just feel guilty."

I thought his growth spurt would happen soon and then the rest of it would follow. The shadow on the lip, the chipped and broken voice, the belligerent boy would break through to man in time and the time was coming. I could see it moving at me like a dust spiral on the open plain.

"And anyway, forget that Kate and me could have died."

"You have two adults in the house."

"They're not my mom. They're not my dad!" His voice was quaking. "You're not telling me the truth about tonight, about just dancing and talking with dumb Russell! *I don't believe you.*"

The tingling started at the back of my knees. It rushed up from there, pressing flashes of heat up ahead of its progress to my face. I could have done anything right then, broken any rule about raising my children in a split-second. Self-righteousness always started at the back of my knees. He looked like such a punk just then, such a tired, disappointed and frightened punk.

"I'm going to say a lot of things to you right now and you're not going to interrupt me while I'm saying them."

One thing about Toby. He knew when to back off. He knew exactly how long my line was and when it was about to break.

"You, Mr. Statistic, are going to start knocking on my door before you plow in here with some fact or figure on child murder. You're also going to stop crawling in my bed whenever you damn well please. You're too big and I'm too old. You're going to stop insulting me and asking questions that are none of your business. Nobody likes a wiseass kid, Toby."

"You're my mother. You have to like me."

"I love you and I don't like your behavior. Why aren't you wearing pajamas?"

"They're too small."

"I'll get new ones. You're also going to stop running around in your boxers."

We sat fuming as the clock ticked on toward a terrible hour. I didn't know how to straighten our crooked limbs and mend our broken hearts in a single conversation, but like anyone who has finally seen the light, I wanted to try.

"You're becoming a man, Toby. And I know it's hard to do in a house full of women, believe me, I do know. But I think we could all use more privacy. More courtesy, too."

"Right. With my great-grandmother living in our dining room and your cousin asleep on the couch. You make me sick, Mom. You make this whole thing my fault and Kate's. You do it every time. You made Dad go away and then you complain about what happens because he's not here. I hate your face when you look like that and your voice when you decide you're going to be this tough mom all of a sudden. You make me puke. But I'm not the only one."

"What do you mean, Toby? Say what you mean."

"I'm trying to."

The chicken smell had gotten all over my room. It was probably inside my drawers, searching for a permanent arrangement inside. I thought about air freshener, but a floral scent spread on top of everything would just make it worse.

"Stupid Kate. Brags about how she's such a great cook and then pukes it all up once Dad leaves."

"She threw up?"

"Lots of times."

"Why didn't you beep me? I told you guys to beep me if anything is ever wrong."

He couldn't have been more effective if he'd held a gavel in his hand. The pint-sized judge rose gravely from my bed to hit the sack in his own chambers.

"Everything is wrong, Mom. We've *been* beeping you and you just haven't heard."

I looked out my window and saw treetops waving slowly in the moving air. In my room, the television turned everything gray, but not the good gray of the moon-stroked backyard. This gray was ghastly. This gray punished everything in its path.

Fourteen

My grandmother's kitchen equipment lay heaped upside down in a clean mound, the form I'd come to recognize. For some reason she wouldn't put them in my cupboards, claiming she didn't want to mix her cooking things in with mine. What if that mound grew to become a mountain, squeezing us out of our own kitchen? A note taped to the frying pan stated the obvious: I AM OUT.

"Who wouldn't throw up after what she told me?"

The next morning I sat at the table with Kate and searched her face for clues. She was a poor liar and I was glad for this basic incompetence. Her eyes went haywire when she lied, scooting right and left. Her whole face squirmed, in fact. If she had to tell a story that wasn't strictly true, Kate generally turned to face a blank wall.

"Mom, you need to seriously consider our situation here. Yeah, I vomited after what she said and you would have, too."

I saw it all unfold in my mind's eye and wished fervently that I could repackage the whole scene in a neat, tidy box like the ones you got with take-out food. If I could do that, I could send the whole thing back where it came from. Kate, washing up the dishes from a successful chicken dinner involving love and labor, turned to watch her wild-eyed great-grandmother flail the warm air and launch a discourse on chickens and blood and their horrible shit which got everywhere, everywhere.

"You'll never believe what she called me."

"Let me guess. Chickenshit sonofabitch."

"Hey, how'd you know that?"

"Intuition, honey. Come here."

She finished the rest of the story by muttering it into my hair and shoulders, the tops of my arms. She left a little wet square right where I might have positioned a Paloma Picasso brooch, if I'd had the money to buy one.

"Oh, Kate. I'm so sorry. You worked hard on that dinner."

"She probably ruined everything for him, too."

"I doubt it. Your dad knows all her stories by heart."

"I don't care! Mom, she screws everything up."

"She's old, honey. She's incredibly old and we have to give her a little latitude because of that. Those memories of Minah Overstreet are as vivid to her as if they happened yesterday. The Overstreets ruined her farm. The stink of those chickens made her move into town from a life she loved and then Minah stole her daughter."

"I don't care. I hate her." More snuffling on my shirt, but there was a new attentiveness. "Was she a kidnapper?"

"It might have been better if she had been. She was a huge influence on my mom, honey, from grade school days on. Granny Settle feels like she lost the battle over my mother's soul to Minah Overstreet and she's probably right."

"She destroyed my dinner. She talked about smashing chicken heads with mallets and using their entrails to tell fortunes. Then she and Daddy went outside to talk and he left without hanging that picture up in my room."

"Think of it as an initiation rite, pumpkin."

"Don't call me that. What do you mean?"

"Once you've been called a chickenshit sonofabitch by your great-grandmother, you're really a Settle. Last night was a watershed experience, Katherine. Here, blow your nose."

She did. I buttered a muffin and passed it to her.

"Besides, I'm relieved to hear that's all that happened. Toby had me scared for a minute."

"Why?"

"Well, the thought of you vomiting up your dinner made me think maybe you . . ."

Her face began to set and harden against me. Against mothers who said the worst possible thing after the worst possible night.

"That maybe I was one of those bulimic girls who eats five packs of cookies and three bags of chips and then vomits and hides the vomit in jars until she can dispose of them? You forget, Mom. We watched that show together."

"What did I say?"

"Nothing. Nothing at all." She stood up to leave, but it was as if she was already outside, on her skateboard, sailing away from all of us. I could see her body hit that odd, tense slouch in preparation for the welcome jolt that would send it into the air.

"Kate, don't leave me like this. What did I say?"

"You said a lot, actually. You said that if I was a professional puker, you'd be worried about me. You said if I had some secret disorder, you'd take care of me. You said what happened last night was nothing. Someone has to stick fingers down their throat to get your attention. Someone has to die in this house before you do anything. I'm skating after school."

The door slammed and I watched her drift away, still graceful even with an angry, resenting back and a polished slice of wood under her arm. Bleary-eyed Toby waited for her on the driveway where he was eating a breakfast of dry cereal and Gatorade under the trees. Two voices had become a shout and the shout seemed to say TAKE CARE OF US! I picked at the edge of my sweater and slowly opened the note Rory had left on the table.

Hey, Cuz!

I'm probably in Oakland now, but maybe I'm not. Maybe I pulled over to stretch my legs and as I did, just as I did, there was my one true love, waiting for me in Buellton with a bowl of that famous pea soup or San Simeon with a pass to tour the castle. It's a long way from L.A. to Oakland and anything can happen. I leave your home full of family love and hungry for some of my own. Picture it. I did this morning at 4:45.

Toby tells me you've been writing lyrics. Why didn't you show me? Afraid cousin Rory would pirate same? Shame on you.

With love nonetheless,
Rory

A joint was taped to the inside of the note. I unrolled it and sniffed before flushing it down the drain. It was the real thing, if I could still recognize the real thing after so many years. Rory was gone, then, and life could return to normal. No, life could return to what it had been before. That was probably more accurate.

I picked up the phone and called Tom at the office.

"Mr. Harrison won't be in until later this afternoon. May I ask who's calling?"

There were handprints by the wall phone. I grabbed a sponge and started scrubbing. How many times had I told Toby not to put his dirty hands all over the wall?

"This is Polly Harrison."

She sputtered something about his not feeling well. Was this urgent? Did I have his home phone number? She must have been a temp. God, maybe she came from Professional World. I scrubbed harder, trying to get the marks off the wall. Dirt had apparently become indelible.

Tom finally picked up on the sixth ring.

"It's me. Did you fire Lily?" She had worked for him for years and I'd even driven to her home once for a Tupperware party. Lily was the *only* person I'd go to a Tupperware party for.

"Her husband's getting transferred and she's training a new girl this week. What'd you think of her?"

"Kind of a ditz, actually."

He sounded a little under the weather.

"You're not sick because of dinner last night, are you?"

"Why would I be sick because of that?"

"I hear Granny Settle was carrying on about chickens."

"Oh, she was in rare form. No, it's not that."

I plucked at a thread on my sleeve. This was the last silk knit anything I would bring home. They were ridiculously fragile, running as easily as sheer pantyhose.

"Last month's physical checked out fine, I feel a little sluggish is all. I'm gonna go run pretty soon. That should help." He sighed and I could hear him shift his weight. He must have been sitting in his great armchair, the one I made him take when he left. I wondered if he had a touch of what I'd been through months before. A traveler could stay naked and drunk, too, as long as he sobered up enough to make that inevitable flight out of town. Who would check up on Tom, since he lived alone? "You know, the more I think about it, the more I think it's a good thing for Kate to learn about . . ."

Old people. Oklahoma. We talked for twenty-five minutes about the children, all the quantifiable things like grades and school and friendships that held or disappeared overnight. Tom was kind and for twenty-five minutes he assured me I was doing a great job raising the kids.

"I used to know that."

"What do you mean?"

"When you volunteer all the time, when you're at the school every living minute of the day, you've got tangible proof that you're doing a good job."

"I don't get it. Who has tangible proof?"

"Everybody at the school."

"That's what I mean, Polly. The school has proof. The other parents have proof, but I wonder if the kids get as much from that stuff as you think. All they care about is your love once they get home. And that's never changed, even if you're not in charge of a committee. You're a wonderful mother, Polly."

"Beat it!"

"Pol?"

Who let her in here? This was my home and a conversation that was strictly none of her business. Yet Frankie Doray now floated on the rim of my consciousness, just as before in the Sovereign. The imagined scene reopened before me, but this time I heard only Tom's words, not hers. *Polly is a wonderful mother . . . and a wonderful wife.*

"Was I?"

"Who else is in the room with you? Polly, are you talking to Babe?"

"Tom, listen to me."

"I'm trying to."

"Say I'm a wonderful mother."

"I just did."

"No, what I mean is say I accept that I was and still am a wonderful mother." Everyone was leaving, it seemed. Our mailman had accepted a transfer and a woman had taken his route. She looked carefree despite the shoulder bag that must have weighed a ton. I watched her hop over a snail on our sidewalk. "But was I a wonderful wife?"

Frankie Doray receded and dimmed as a long pause lengthened. I didn't hear Tom breathe or move or fiddle with the morning paper. I felt slow and sleepy. I could have curled inside that quiet space as if it were a warm bed.

"I was the one who screwed up. I did it. Well, Polly . . ."

He couldn't answer my question or finish his sentence and this time the space between the words was so deep I was scared I would fall in headfirst. We both said goodbye at the same time.

Our new mailwoman had charm, I could tell by the way she walked. Widowers would probably offer her cool drinks on scorching days and adolescent boys would watch her unload junk mail through parted venetian blinds. I opened my package right there on the porch. My mother's note was exuberant. Her words seemed shot full of helium, floating just over my head. Black-and-white aerial shots of the property that now belonged to Bobby Denario and my mother had very little to do with memories, mine anyway. The pictures showed nothing but dark patches of vegetation and a careless series of hills, one long row of buildings anyone could tell was in shambles. Most of the roof had caved in, you could see that from the air. One picture showed a flat piece of land that contained the faint outline of a circle. The place where the old riding ring had been looked like a gaping mouth. I flipped through the pictures again. Where was the timbered barn, the one shamelessly showy building on the place?

Dear Polly,

I don't know about you, but I'll tell you what I see here, though it's not for the faint of heart. I see me, me, me buried in the dead flat middle of that awful circle. I love the rodeo like nobody's business, but any fool can see there's no rodeo here, there never was. We've opened an account out here in her name. Bobby's thinking of donating the land to the conservation people although I can't see a single thing worth conserving. Can you?

Yours,
Carla

I didn't start a load of laundry or straighten the house or return Beth's call after I read that. I looked at the Nevada postmark and plunked down to scribble out a rough draft on a notepad. What if my mother *had* stayed in Granite?

I doubted anyone could have buried my mother under a second-rate riding ring. I looked up just then to see a raggedy-looking stranger pull up a chair and sit down. He was in a big hurry to tell his story, breathlessly insisting it be told from his point of view.

> He took some loose change from his pocket
> Lots of quarters and some dimes
> He lined them up the day she left him
> So they'd form a broken line.
> He wrote a note to tell the story
> With the words he couldn't say
> All the things he planned to buy her
> The second job he took today.
>
> He would have bought her Cadillacs
> He would have purchased gold
> He would have had a second home
> For them when they got old.
> He didn't have a chance to buy
> That gold or a Seville
> She went and found her heart's desire
> She met her Dollar Bill.

If Bobby hadn't owned a string of motels and sold them for a fortune, would she have loved him anyway? I thought about her fans back in Granite, most of them small businessmen, some of them even smaller businessmen than my father. Her flirtations had run the gamut, it seemed, from grocers to growers to mechanics who competed with my dad. Yet it was true that when she finally settled down, "wore herself out with all the running around," as Dad put it, she settled happily into the arms of a very rich man.

> People saw them stepping out
> They liked to dance till dawn
> She told Bill she liked her gifts
> With all the price tags on.
> His note said when she'd used him up
> Spent Dollar Bill's last dime

> He'd be waiting patiently
> Cause all he had was time.

I looked at it hard and bit into some melba toast. I could hear these words sung, if not on the radio stations I listened to now. I'd finish it and file it away anyhow—this ballad was for me. I stared at the word "patiently." What kind of guy would sit around waiting for his gold-digging wife to hang up her pick and come back to him? Nobody I knew. That kind of forgiveness was too implausible. I was about to get rid of that last verse when the phone rang.

"Get down!"

It was my father, shouting at his dogs.

"Polly, hold the phone a minute. Damn these dogs."

I heard boot heels striking cement and clatter, a terrible clatter at the other end. It sounded like a whole china cabinet going over. My father was at the shop and I tried not to imagine what all the commotion meant.

"Pop? Are you there?"

"I'm here."

"You're not hurting the dogs, are you?"

"Nah. I bought 'em some toys is all. They don't give me a moment's peace without their toys."

I pictured a dog pound full of ghoulish diversions for pups. Neighbors had called Granite Community Services a few years ago complaining that he didn't keep his dogs quiet and when he did, they couldn't stomach his methods. The accounts made me blush for my father. He would wind up becoming one of those features in the *National Enquirer*: "Oklahoma Man's Dog Toys Don't Play in Granite!" I didn't know how bad it had really gotten, but I didn't think it should be up to me to go back to Granite just to free the dogs. I had to delegate my father and I had long ago delegated him to his own mother, Grandmother Jewel.

"Lemme just ask you this." He cleared his throat and I heard paper rustling at the other end of the line. "What do you make of a woman who lives the life of a movie star or Arabian princess and *still* isn't happy?"

"I'd say she was either spoiled rotten or a fool."

"I'd say both, though I've gotta tell you, Polly. There's still only one woman who makes my heart beat and that's your mother."

I looked at my last stanza. Maybe I'd leave it the way it was.

"I got this letter here I've wanted to read to you for a long time. Written from the deck of the *Sun Connection.* Says that here in small print."

Oh, she was a case. My mother needed to give up ocean cruises and my father needed to give up pets. They didn't have the temperament for either enterprise. Had she gotten so bored with the cruise and undiluted Bobby that she needed to write my father love letters?

"I don't get it, Dad."

"Get what, baby?"

"Why you would even want to hear her name spoken. Why you keep acting like this about a woman who tormented you as long as you two were married."

"Hell, I did my share of tormenting, too. Besides, baby, I told you. Your mother's the only woman who can really make my heart beat."

"Even when she's standing out in the yard in her nightgown?" I was probably eleven years old. I saw the outline of her body under the sheer nylon nightgown. Everything had turned sickly and yellow because of the colored light bulb my parents used on the porch, but I still managed to see everything from my bedroom window.

"Oh, you mean that time I locked her out of the house? It was worth it once I let her back in . . ." My father chuckled softly and I kicked a cupboard door shut with my foot. ". . . Bet your mother'd agree. Now right here she just starts out talking, it's the damndest thing. Doesn't say 'dear' or anything. She just goes full throttle about how she's had time to think out there on the sea."

"You two wrote the book on dysfunctional. If you want to call me to tell me about a tornado touching down or who won the Miss Granite title or what you especially liked about last week's *Law and Order,* it's fine by me. But I will not listen to this."

"You don't have to listen, Polly, but I've got to tell."

It was endemic to our family. We told but didn't talk. We sent word after word up into the air, most of them smarting when they landed. But we sure didn't talk. Not the way all the self-help books say families ought to talk if they're going to survive. Not flourish or prosper, but survive.

"You better pay some attention to this, Polly. If your mother embarrasses you, I'm the first one to understand. But there's something here that concerns you. Something you ought to know."

"You can read that."

"It goes, 'I need to help poor Polly. On top of all her troubles, she's got Mother out there living in her dining room of all places! How can she entertain with her grandmother in the middle of everything? Honestly! She won't be any trouble to us here. Bobby and I are building guest quarters for her. Or for any guest that might come into town. Even guests from as far as Granite, hint, hint! It will be alabaster white, too. Like the white in the Old Testament.'"

"That's enough, Dad."

"You've got the picture? Get off the customer's lap, you damn mutt!"

The phone fell out of his hands and I hung up. I had the picture and it wasn't just an aerial shot. My mother had decided to renew her membership in the family for some reason and I didn't quite know why. It wasn't out of genuine concern for me and my dinner parties, that I was sure about. It wasn't that she longed for Granny Settle's company, either. What was my mother up to? One thing was certain, though. I would fight my mother tooth and nail. The rush of granny love that swept over me when my father read about those plans to park her in swanky white guest quarters was stronger than anything I'd felt in a long time.

Fifteen

I didn't have to speculate about my mother's motives for long. Her voice was low and rich. It flowed over the telephone.

"I'll let you in on a secret if you promise not to tell."

"Promise."

"Bobby's mother is moving in with us this week! Your grandmother and Edith Denario are going to be just adorable together."

I understood everything then. My mother's selfishness was breathtaking until you got used to it. Then it was reassuring, the one sign on a long highway that would never blow over from high winds or high waters.

"What makes you think she'll go for this?"

"Well, she'll have her own money, for one thing. And I'm not talking about those puny Social Security checks, either. Bobby paid twenty thousand dollars for that landfill, can you imagine?"

I did the math as she talked about how Granny Settle's own Palm Springs bank account would give her a sense of independence. The sum worked out to five hundred dollars an acre. I wondered if that was the going price.

"Forget money for the moment. They're made for each other. They even look alike! Those two are going to be the talk of the town."

"No, Mother. You'll be the talk of the town."

"You've got *that* right! I can't wait to take them to lunch at the club. It's going to be perfect."

Another line rang and she asked if she could put me on hold. When she came back, she had other things on her mind. Granny Settle's future was a fait accompli.

"I'm back. And so is Johnny Day."

I thought of that long-ago line of Johnny Day Jewels, the dinky fake sapphire ring my mother once ordered from a television ad. She held it up to the light when it arrived and found it wouldn't shine. The disappointing stone even fell out of the setting after she wore it for a month or two, but it never stopped her from listening to his music. Over the years she'd fall in and out of love with Merle Haggard and Buck Owens, getting mad at them because of a song or a haircut she didn't like, but she always remained doggedly faithful to Johnny Day.

"Guess how I know he's making his comeback, even though he's never really been gone?"

"Tell."

"He contacted all of us. Every single former fan club member."

"You were never just a member."

"Of course not. That's why I got a *telegram* from Daybreak Village saying he'd be playing Palm Springs next month. I called up the newspaper and they aren't even releasing his schedule to the public yet."

The former president of the Johnny Day Fan Club, Oklahoma chapter, accelerated into a high-pitched whir. Her voice sounded like one of the engines cranked up high in my dad's shop, operating at a deafening roar and going nowhere. A long series of bells went off in her house. I could hear them echo down the long marble corridor.

"That must be the lamps. I told my designer all about Mama coming and his imagination just went wild! Hold on a minute."

I waited and thought of the lamp man, standing in the blazing heat with a delivery order and the lamps that would successfully trivialize everything my grandmother loved the best. I imagined a rawhide shade and miniature metal horses galloping under a hundred watts. My mother's plan was about interior decoration. Granny Settle and Edith Denario would be little more than an adorable set of matching old ladies.

"I'm back. Anyway, the reason I'm calling is to let you know Johnny's coming to Los Angeles! He'll be doing a concert at the Williamson and the really big news is that he'll be at Fanfest in Pomona. That's where you'll snare him."

"Not interested."

"Polly." There was genuine despair in her voice. "Wake up. Get going. You need to get those lyrics of yours to Johnny."

"Nobody listens to him. He's old-hat in Nashville and probably even in Branson."

She took a long moment to answer. "Old hats wear very well in country music. And anyway, Johnny sings even sweeter now that he's matured."

"The only audience the man's got left is his mom. Forget it." The singer's well-publicized relationship with Ruth Day was legendary. Every Mother's Day outing my father ever planned was nixed because Johnny Day was doing a television special honoring his mama.

"What have you done with that song of yours, the one about the rodeo?"

"Oh, I'm still polishing it."

"Uh huh. Well, you just keep right on polishing and in the meantime, new lyricists are being discovered right and left. Keep right on rubbing away on those songs of yours, Polly."

"That's very mean."

"The truth always stings some, like Mama says. I'm faxing you his schedule and—"

"—You know I don't have a fax machine."

"Then I'll mail it, for heaven's sake. I'm telling you that I can hear Johnny's voice right now, singing the song you wrote about the old cowboy and if you so much as tell him Carla sends regards, he'll pluck you out of the crowd at the fairground . . . anything is likely to happen. Of course, you'll have to flirt a bit."

"Not interested, Mother."

"Not interested or not able? Get moving before it's too late. Watch old movies if you don't know how to do it, they're a wonderful resource. Curl your hair for once in your life. I'm not leading you wrong on this."

I thought of Frankie Doray's appearances with a pang. Even though she seemed to come and go as she pleased, I knew her existence was based on my volition as much as anything. Visions only appeared to the people willing to see them. The line went dead, but my mother's voice seemed to go on and on. I couldn't have shut it off if I'd tried.

• • •

"Smile, Polly Ann. Mama likes little girls who smile."

She was sitting in the living room, leaving a ring on the top of the coffee table with a glass of cold tea. It was stifling even with three fans rotating in the small, tight room. I was grateful for their noise because otherwise she would have heard me snap my fingers behind my back. I was trying to snap them the way she did when she had an idea. The sound she made was crisp and dry, like biting open the shell of a nut. I still hadn't gotten it right, though I practiced all the time.

"Come see if I'm dry."

I went around to the back of the sofa to check the pincurls in the back. She wore it long, like Minah Overstreet, except for the top, which she had cut short so it wouldn't fall in her eyes when she danced. I pulled gently at the bobby pin to loosen one of the curls.

"Still damp."

"Oh, I swear. Move the fan over here. I'm gonna lose my mind if I don't get out of this house."

I pointed one of the fans at her head and sat down across from her. She was the prettiest woman in Granite, Oklahoma. She never went anyplace without turning heads. She kicked a cushion off the sofa with her foot.

"What are you looking at, Polly Ann?"

"You."

"And do you like what you see?"

"Yes ma'am."

"I guess that's good."

She pulled a magazine off the top of a stack she had on the floor under the table. Johnny Day's baby face stared at both of us from the cover. She let it fall open and started flipping pages fast.

"That's it. I'm dry."

She slid each bobby pin off of the careful curls, then bent forward to shake her hair loose. I reached for her hairbrush and pulled out the hair that was caught in the bristles. She washed the brush religiously each night in ammonia.

"Can I style it, Mama?"

"I guess. Watch how you do the top though."

My mother's hair had once been complicated, a shiny mix of gold and brown with white blond near her face in the summer when she went to the river each day to sunbathe. Now her hair was a single color, Overstreet Blond, as I called it, for the shade matched the woman's in the photograph on her desk. I put the finishing touches on her hair, lifting the ends just the way she liked them.

"How about a picnic at Moon Bird Creek?"

"All right, Mama."

I'd said no once, but that had gotten me a ringing slap on the cheek I still remembered. *What kind of little girl says no to a picnic with her mama?* So I didn't say no anymore. I didn't say no to anything my mother suggested.

"Go find us some bananas to go with the sandwiches. And Coca-Colas, too. Would *that* make you smile?"

I nodded, the knot in my stomach growing tighter, and arranged our lunch the way she liked it, tied inside starched white napkins and knotted so we could put sticks through them and pretend to be hoboes. I didn't like playing hobo. Those men who slept under the bridge scared me. I didn't like how they looked at me and I thought they spoiled Moon Bird Creek. People said they'd leave town in time, but I didn't believe that. I imagined them living under the bridge forever, playing cards and smoking cigarettes, lighting fires at night that threw shadows on their sharp, dark faces.

"I like riding in the car, don't you?"

I nodded. When she got up speed outside the Granite city limits, the air felt fine. Not hot and oppressive, the way it did inside our house.

"Having fun?"

"Yes, Mama."

"You could have fooled me. Might be those braids that make you look so serious. I'm going to cut your hair. Yep, that's just what I'm going to do."

She pulled the car right up to the banks of the creek. It was the only car there, for no one ate outdoors on such a hot day. But my mother and the hoboes knew the secret of Moon Bird Creek. They knew that under the bridge ran a steady updraft of cool, renewing air. They knew the creek water ran crisp and cold in three spots under the wide bridge, that if you stood there long enough you'd have to clench your teeth to keep them from chattering. That's how cold it was. One of the spots was always taken by the men. They kept their cans and bottles there, chilled them until they were ready to drink in the sun. My mother was the first to leave the car. She slammed her door shut and bent her body over and up like a cat's jaw opening in a wide yawn.

"What are you waiting for, Polly?"

I was waiting for a fire truck, the way I always did. That's how I guessed salvation would happen. If I turned my head I would see a fire truck heading for Moon Bird Creek, heading for me. Men in bright yellow coats would rush to my rescue and speed me away from danger. I never imagined their faces, only their immense bodies sheathed in clothing that would protect them from fire and enormous feet in heavy boots that could kick down a door and save a child from a house in flames.

"Suit yourself."

She was on her way down to the cool spot, laughing as she slipped on the steep trail to the bottom. She didn't look like a hobo. She looked like a pretty present for somebody's birthday in her polka-dotted sundress that tied in a bow at the back of her neck. Carrying lunch on a stick wrecked her balance. She stumbled again and motioned for me to get out of the car.

There were three men watching her progress and mine. They shared a cigarette, each one taking a puff and passing it on. The hoboes had never said a word to either my mother or me. But they watched us. They watched everything we did.

She shrieked when she hit the cool currents, holding her dress up high. I sat down to guard our lunches and look at stones by the side of the creek. I always managed to return with a pocketful of nice rocks. I didn't blindly collect them. Each rock in my room held something in place. A paper or a picture I'd made that I didn't want to lose in case a strong wind blew. I was in charge of cleaning my room and those rocks made it a longer chore than it could have been. I looked down and found that water sprinkled my blouse in places. She was splashing me, inviting me to enter the current.

"Come on in! The water's fine."

No it wasn't. It wasn't fine at all with three men looking on and saying nothing. One of the men shifted his position where he lay, turning on his side so he could be more comfortable. They weren't far away, yet she acted as if they were. She acted like my friend Candy, who had the lead in the school play, turning and pivoting with acute self-consciousness before a packed house.

"Stop being such a stick in the mud, Polly Ann. Now come on in here before I get angry."

I decided to make my body a stick, a rigid stick that wouldn't be dislodged. I sat right where I was, inside a nice draft of air, getting stronger by the minute and watching her face redden because of the men who smiled at a stick daughter with long, serious braids.

"I'm counting. One, two . . ."

I opened my napkin and bit fiercely into a sandwich. The ends of her hair were getting wet, the ends I'd worked so hard on.

"You're going to be sorry, young lady."

I didn't need firemen, after all. I thought of Granny Settle and made my way out of a burning house, using her words to guide me through the smoke and flame. *Don't let anybody call you a young lady. You're a young girl and there's time enough to be the other thing. Anybody who calls you a young lady is up to something the way I see it.* I watched as my mother sloshed her angry way toward me. For once I was ready for her. One of the men on the opposite bank pulled hard on a long-necked bottle and pushed his hat to the back of his head. I spoke before my mother did.

"Mama?"

She stood over me with sand clinging to her wet feet.

"What would Granny Settle say if she knew we came here for picnics?"

The wind seemed to sigh. In fact the whole scene seemed to change like when my friend Candy stood on stage with a sword in her hand and all of a sudden a hand-painted screen dropped down in back of her bringing a pale dawn.

"I don't know that she'd say anything at all."

"I think she wouldn't like it. I think she wouldn't like it one bit."

There was a long moment of silence. Then my mother spoke.

"You've got mustard on your mouth. Go wash up in the creek. Think you can manage that?"

I knew my father couldn't tame her. When they fought she welcomed the battle. The more he threatened her, the more he chased her with whatever he had in his hand at the time, the worse she got. But she feared my grandmother, a woman who had died twice and lived to tell about it. I watched her eat her food. I enjoyed it that day, knowing we wouldn't come to Moon Bird Creek again. She ate each bite of food with as much flair as she could muster. The wind blew at her hair like a man's breath and her bare shoulders gleamed under the bridge. She peeled her fruit slowly, taking her time with every bite while the men moaned so that we could hear. When she washed her lips in the water with the edge of the skirt, one of them called out to her in a hoarse voice. I don't know if she ever went back to taunt them.

She flipped on the radio driving home and finally settled on a station playing Johnny Day. She loved his rusty voice, especially when it was paired with a background fiddle.

Linda Phillips Ashour

"I must be the only mother in America whose kid doesn't like to play."

She was right about that. I didn't like to play my mother's games. I curled my knees up to my chest as we flew over the roads to Granite, but I wasn't afraid anymore. I knew we would make it there in one piece.

Sixteen

The first thing to do was line up an ally. I always shopped with someone who knew the ropes, who could flip through a rack of rayon and silk and linen with prowess, knowing what was ultimately a stinker and what was not. Alone, I made phone calls and drifted along in the zone between designer sportswear and young misses. Without an ally, I hemmed, hawed and got hungry for lunch by ten-thirty.

"So we're on. Listen, thanks."

"No problem. I'm only slightly offended."

"Beth? By what?"

"Shopping with you used to be Tom's job. I was so jealous of that, Stan wouldn't be caught dead in a woman's dressing room. So what if I'm a stand-in, what the hell. Bring me a picture of this Johnny Day. That way I can dress you to suit him."

"Now, hang on just a—"

"—Polly. We have to at least agree on this much. You are dressing to catch somebody's eye. And if he's as old as I think he is, we're going to have to really pour it on."

She barked at me and slammed down the phone: I'll pick you up at two don't even think of canceling bye. She knew the owner of a terrific store in Beverly Hills and, better yet, she knew me.

. . .

The woman hadn't heard of Johnny Day and glanced cursorily at his head shot, sent courtesy of my mother. "I get the picture. Williamson Theatre, sure. The place that looks like a pancake parlor. We want a warm look. We want a sensual look."

Beth cut her off right there. "We want sex. In a certain context, of course. But we want sex."

"Gotcha." The owner scurried away, leaving us seated on two satin ottomans, defeated over the years by curvy bottoms and feet too swollen and tired to move another inch.

"She always talks about redecorating this place. Never does." Beth's ponytail swung as she spoke. It wasn't lank and thin, like mine if I let it grow too long. She folded one leg neatly under her bottom. A bottom quite different, I imagined, from the ones that habitually landed here.

I tried to whisper, but it didn't really matter. The store was long and deep, cushioned in disorder, and we were on the second floor. The owner scurried around below us. "Why'd you suggest this place?"

"You'll see. Trust me. Aren't you going to undress, Pol?"

I shook my head no. I could wait for the tirade that always came when we shopped together. I didn't go to the gym, hers or any other. It was true, I had no hunger for "definition" or "upper body strength" or any of the other things that brought her clients and brought her praise. Her muscle tone was chic now, the body type of the moment. That I pulled on my size six Speedo only occasionally or walked when I felt like it irked Beth beyond measure. I hadn't earned my shape particularly and it drove her mad.

We heard the shop owner on the stairs. She huffed along, then pushed through the door using one solid thigh.

"I'm back and just wait'll you girls see what I've got here. If this doesn't knock his eyes out, he needs glasses. Baboom, am I correct?" The thing on the hanger was pastel beyond belief. My face must have revealed all. "Tie it this way and don't you dare pull it up. I see a little fox under that sheep's clothing—come downstairs when you've got it on. Beth, I have something for you. Follow, follow, follow," she sang a few bars and smiled. Her small, dim teeth gave me courage and I pulled on the dress as soon as they left.

It clung. It cleaved. It changed what I saw every day under a spray of hot water or in the wavy reflection of a flea market mirror. I ran a finger to the top of my breasts and stopped. The dress gave me a sort of cleavage. A warm draft of air suddenly lifted the bottom of the dress.

"I like it, I like it very much." Frankie Doray appeared next to me and I gasped, pulling my hand away. She was wearing a Pancho Sánchez bathrobe. I always shuddered at both the price tag and Pancho's vivid color sense. This one was iridescent purple and gold. The colors rose and fell in the same erratic waves that crossed my television screen when I needed to call a technician. "It's high time we talked."

"What makes you think I'd want to talk to you?"

"You'll have to if you want to get well."

"I'm not sick."

"You're heartsick. And that's the worst affliction of all." I kept my eyes focused on me, so that she was off to my right. That way, she was like a silly sidecar, belonging to another era. Mistress. What man these days had a mistress? Yet that was irrefutably what Frankie Doray was. I spotted a pincurl just in front of her left ear and out of the corner of my eye, I watched her light up a cigarette.

"No way. Throw that out."

"Polly, loosen up. I'm a specter." She took a deep pull on the thin cigarette and watched me squirm inside my dress. "Very nice. Shows off your curves, for a change. You *have* curves, Polly."

"And you've got a lot of fucking nerve."

Oh, a smile that I knew, apparition or not. A come-hither smile I had seen a thousand times on my own mother's face. "That I do. Dressed like this, Johnny Day will notice you for sure. Make yourself appetizing and he'll gobble up every word you write."

Was that what sweet-sucking Eden Again had done to Shel? Made herself a confection he couldn't turn away? The reflection in the mirror was getting as wavy as the one I saw back home. I heard Beth talking downstairs, but she was too far away to hear or help.

"Do you suggest I tuck my song lyrics here, Frankie?" I stuck my hand down the front of the dress. My skin had gotten sticky, like I was wrapped in cotton candy. I drew my hand back quickly and motioned to a side slit. "Or maybe a little word or two here?"

Frankie Doray seemed to expand. Pancho's purple and gold fabric filled every inch of that tiny dressing room, sliding over the two dilapidated ottomans, sidling down fat, upholstered walls to the floor. She crowded a space too small, too intimate to begin with, pushing me until my back was against the mirror. There was cinnamon on her breath and I thought I spotted telltale brown sprinkles where neck melted to snow white chest.

"You're finally getting somewhere, Polly. Men just love to play!"

I must be the only mother in America whose kid doesn't like to play. Where was the playground now? In a tumbledown clothing shop in Beverly Hills or a creek streaming along outside Granite, Oklahoma? Whirling to face Frankie, I found she completely encircled me in an image that turned up everywhere I looked.

"You two are just alike!"

Oh, she was coy. Frankie Doray looked like she didn't understand a thing I was saying. I slapped at the air a couple of times, but she didn't budge.

"You and my mother. Always playing breathless pinup girl for the gas station attendant or the school bus driver or the bums who live under a bridge. It's just like both of you to assume I'll get what I want if I wiggle it a little for Johnny Day. Know what I think? I think there's a time to play and a time to give it a rest, for God's sake, I don't care whether a person's trying to pitch song lyrics or, or . . ."

I wasn't about to spell it out for her. I wasn't about to tell her Tom didn't need Pancho Sánchez bathrobes and pouty little lips and a dash of cinnamon. I wasn't about to tell her a bar of Dove soap worked beautifully.

". . . Continue, Polly."

"I'm finished."

"Shouldn't be. Shouldn't ever be finished playing." She dug into the pocket of her robe and brought a cookie to her lips, taking the first tiny nibble. Not just any cookie, either. It was The Wafer, the protein snack that had changed Tom's life and mine. What was *she* doing with The Wafer?

"Bye, bye, Polly." She was less than before and thinning. Thinning into sky blue vapor. I snatched at her, snatched at what she was eating.

"Wait a minute, you bitch! You hold on." But it was me who was holding on, just barely and just in time to hit one of the ottomans as the dressing room door swung open.

"Cleavage! Polly, you never told me you had cleavage."

"I didn't mean to disgrace you."

"You didn't. She knew the pink was a long shot. Still, it looked great on you."

I hugged the department store bag tighter. It held a slightly zippier version of everything already hanging in my closet. I would be comfortable, confident and the dress I'd chosen and Beth had settled for would be ideal both in Pomona and a theater that looked like a pancake parlor.

"I just don't like artificial cleavage is all."

"Help out on that one?" She drove with great style, the way Lana Turner would have if she'd leased a Lexus. Beth turned the kind of heads, male and female, that combined highlights and mousse. I found it a toxic blend, but she reveled in the attention.

"I mean ordinary breasts don't look that way without serious engineering."

"Yeah, so?"

We turned into the parking lot of the gym where she taught her aerobics class. She needed to pick something up before dropping me off.

"The key word is artificial."

"Shit, Polly, the sixties are over. I feel like I've just spent the day with your cousin."

"Unfair. Besides, this has nothing to do with the sixties."

"Think about it. This is Roryspeak, with or without the 'fuck, man.' We burned our bras, Polly. We did that already." She punched the ticket machine a little too forcefully and plowed into the speed bump. "I wish I could convince Stan that artifice is fun. In, out, in out for years. God, I'm sick of boring sex."

I was fond of her husband and always felt like a traitor when she started in on their troubles. She got this tell-all habit from the magazines. She only started talking so freely after a school magazine drive a few years ago. *Cosmopolitan* and *Redbook* kind of loosened her tongue.

"Let's go in. Don't worry, Polly. I won't make you get on a StairMaster."

I put my hand on her knee. "You have a wonderful life."

Her eyes shot wide open. "I have a comfortable life. Passion is serious, Polly. People try to dismiss it, but if you ask me, it's the secret ruler of everything. You can try to cover it up with busyness and children and best friends, but in the end, it's going to take over."

A gaggle of women in leotards passed in front of the car; Beth grinned and waved.

"Stan and I used to talk about how connected you guys were. For years, you two were like this incredibly high standard. But even you and Tom were vulnerable. All of a sudden, passion came at your house with a ball and chain. Didn't it?"

She wasn't being unkind on purpose. My best friend sat there, pert, hard and cross-legged, tearing at my heart with her question.

"No."

"What was your breakup about if it wasn't about uncontrollable passion?"

Her questions made me so tired, it was probably all the shopping, all the heaving and hoing, squeezing into dresses that were thoroughly wrong.

"If I ever knew what happened I've begun to forget."

"Come on, Polly. You can do better than that. This is your *marriage* I'm talking about." Her voice carried clear to the sidewalk. The gaggle of women in leotards stared at me as they hit the door, not Beth.

"Stop yelling. Now that I'm over the initial shock, I've begun to forget why I kicked Tom out and that's exactly why I think I'm being visited by a phantom. So I won't forget what has happened to this family."

"To the two of you."

I took a gulp of air and continued. "So I won't turn this into something inconsequential, because that's what I'm good at. I'm good at walking with a limp, I'm good at sweeping things under the rug. I'm good at accommodating ancient grandmothers and annoying cousins and living with kids who have to kick me in the teeth to get me to recognize they're in terrible trouble."

There were tears rolling down my cheeks before I could stop them. I glared at those women who didn't want to exercise at all. They just wanted to stand around in leotards and eavesdrop. Finally they entered the building.

Beth cleared her throat delicately and wiped my cheek with the back of her hand.

"Look what I've done. Here, take a tissue. Better?"

I nodded, keeping my head low.

"Let's go inside and you can tell me all about that phantom."

I waited for her upstairs, leaning against the rail over a snake pit of men and machines. Besides getting me to be a successful dater, Beth wanted so badly to convert me to this: row after row of flashing metal, the stink of human sweat and the anguished cry of a middle-aged CPA or lawyer pressing more weight than he should.

"Why are we here? This is like an officeworker going back to stare at her computer on a day off."

"They wanted this insurance form signed today. I don't mind, it's like my home away from home. Anyway, I had an ulterior motive. There are really cute guys here when you stop wasting your time with Russell."

"He's fun. I like him."

"The boy next door. I get it. Slept with him yet?"

"Will you let up? You sound like my daughter."

Beth winked at a passing muscleman, his shirt stamped with the slogan GOTTA HAVE IT. She carried on wildly with strangers, only to say no with genuine surprise when they took her seriously.

"Have you?"

"None of your business."

"Hurry up and do it, then tell me about it. I'm going to be forty-five next month and it looks like I will have had the same partner for twenty of those forty-five years. And my partner doesn't care for artifice."

"Uuuuuuungh." The low bellow came from the center of the room below. It issued from a clump of guys who all had the same marine crew cut and shabby sweatpants. They weren't the silly bodybuilders who pranced around in Lycra eating and drinking Zeemie products, the same bodybuilders you sensed would flee at the first sign of real trouble. These guys were just here on some day pass from lives of military maneuvers and high school equivalency exams. They were the real thing like Russell was the real thing. Big by birth or trade.

"Beth, you're full of crap. You and Stan have a lovely time when the lights go out. It's on you. It shows."

"Sometimes. Okay, most of the time. But monogamy is monogamy. You wonder about things. Anyway, I wonder about things and you could be my research library."

We listened to the groaning for a little while, then Beth slipped her hand inside mine.

"Don't get mad at me for suggesting this, but you need help with this thing. Having visions is serious, don't you think?"

"She doesn't interfere with anything. I can still concentrate. I can write and think and raise my kids."

"See, right there, Pol. You don't refer to the experience. You refer to her. She's real for you."

The Santa Monica Mountains filled the front window. They didn't look noble or mean or particularly high right then. They looked manageable and strangely domesticated, like a cougar you could summon with a whistle.

"I can take care of this on my own. Don't worry about me."

"Toby, are you trying to cure that piece of beef or just salt it? If you'd get out of that soft bed of yours at a decent morning hour, you'd taste real meat. Yes, meat, Katherine. A nice big hunk of blood-red beef thundering over the plate. You can smell the trail from my frying pan."

I had mean thoughts all through dinner. Mean thoughts about having a house to myself, no children, no grandmother, no long, looping detour in the trail I was traveling. I dreamed of a silent house filled with noise that I made.

"What are you looking at, Polly Ann? I guess you prefer that view to this one here."

"View? I'm looking at a whole lot of empty."

"My mother the living lyric. She sees dumb Russell's house with dumb Russell in it. Don't you, Mom?"

"Leave Mom alone."

"Oh, Toby the defender."

Fists were beginning to clench under the table, even though I couldn't see them.

"Dinner's dismissed."

"You can't dismiss dinner, Mom. This isn't a class."

"I'm not so sure. If you leave right now, you won't have to do the dishes."

The thundering wasn't on the plate, it was on the linoleum floor. They crashed through the doorway together and Toby grabbed the hat off her head, running down the hall to the bathroom. Doors slammed in unison.

"Why do they do that, Granny?"

"Because there's no range for them to roam. You don't have any cows for them to rope, Polly Ann, so there's no flesh to brand but their own." My granny's eyes drifted to the window and I guess she agreed with me. "Mighty dark nights you people have in Los Angeles. No matter how many lights turn on, it doesn't seem to change."

I washed the dishes and longed for chores to do before bed. Not jobs, but chores, the kind that wore you out to a point past exhaustion. To a point where the body didn't sleep, it disappeared into a slumber with walls so thick no sound could intrude.

I didn't find the chore I was seeking or that inviolable chamber. I walked around without waking anyone up. Granny Settle turned heavily in her sleep and called out something I couldn't understand, but otherwise the rooms were dark and still. I dialed Tom's number without turning on any lights. He picked up the phone right away but took a minute to answer. He cleared his throat heavily and I could just see him switching on a light and squinting at the cheap traveling clock he bought on sale. It went everywhere with him, I suppose, folded shut and ticking away until he sprung it from a black case.

"Yeah?"

"Tom, it's me."

"Oh, hi, Polly. What's wrong."

"Nothing. Well, everything, but it's not about the kids. It's about me."

I wondered for a horrible moment if he were alone. Because maybe Frankie Doray wasn't just a vision who appeared to me. Maybe she was as real as she ever was, lying warm and heavy beside him. My hands were shaking.

"Are you alone, Tom?"

"Are you?"

That was fair and I hadn't thought about it until right then.

"I want to ask you something and I want you to be awake enough to answer. So can you wake up?"

"Okay. Yeah, go on."

"After I found you two at the Sovereign I was too busy wanting to kill you to ask why you did it. And then it got too hard to ask, the longer I waited. But I want to know why. I do."

"Right now? It's one-fifteen in the morning, Polly. Is this a dream or is this you?"

"It's me."

The sheets on his bed rustled and he took a drink from a glass of water. The cup was probably plastic. The kids told me he didn't trust glass and china anymore.

"I did it because I was scared."

"Scared of what?"

"Scared I was turning into this guy who just pulled up to a house every day and since everybody knew he was going to pull up, either that or go out of town and pull up after that, it felt like no big deal to actually be this guy. I mean, nobody exactly rushed to the windows to see if it was me in the driveway. That's the ordinary part of what happened, I think."

"Now tell me the extraordinary part of why you started seeing Frankie."

"It doesn't sound extraordinary when I say it, only when I think it."

"I still want to know."

He paused and I heard something clatter to the ground and then it was quiet where he was. "Because I missed you, Polly."

I hung up the telephone and stood there in the dark for a while. Maybe I stood there for two minutes or twenty. I don't know. I thought about missing the person you ate breakfast with and shared toothpaste with and made children with. I thought about missing the one person you could always count on to get your jokes, the person you listened to at night when you couldn't fall asleep. When I couldn't stand it any longer, I switched on the light to look for a pencil.

> I'm testing the waters without you
> Wond'ring how deep it is here
> Feeling my way to the bottom
> While I still cling to the pier
> All this I hope will show me
> What it is I really fear
> How you can sink without swimming
> How you can be gone and still here.

Seventeen

*I*t isn't a rocky ledge, the kind I know from old Western movies, the kind dappled with dusty sunlight and a clear mountain stream bubbling nearby, but my garage serves as a fine hideout all the same. The shabby square provides peace, quiet and solitude. Sunlight streams through the roof in spots and a million dust particles dance in each yellow ray. The ceiling rises to a pitch in the center and that creates the illusion of space. Tom used to dream of repairing the roof and painting the interior white, even laying down carpet. He would have liked a skylight installed, but I was always wary of tampering with such familiar shelter. Granny Settle's things stood together like a group of strangers at a party. I pushed past them and lugged three boxes of mail into a corner and sat down, thinking of Lorraine's phone message: "Nothing fancy, you bring the work home, call me back, sweetheart." She had finally stopped mentioning the monkeys who could do the jobs she offered me, leaving our exchanges brief and clear. I liked the formality and often found myself saying yes to her jobs without the old resistance.

I picked up the first card from the pile. My job was to pick seven hundred names, then put them on a computer disc and it wasn't a task I took lightly. I'd typed up contestant entries several times and I knew the ropes by now. Sometimes contestants put messages on their entries.

I have been eating Country Crunch for thirty-two years, way before it became so popular. It's not that I don't like what you people say about it on the box, it's that I have something to add: IT KEEPS YOU REGULAR! Of course how would you tell people something like that. Sign me, A Devoted Fan.

My job was to type. But if you had any kind of mind at all, you thought about these people. You imagined their lives. Sometimes these imaginings gave rise to a song or two. Mostly they didn't. I picked up a handful of cards and letters when Russell's cat started mewling to get in. The stray had turned up recently, lingering in the yard until Russell broke down, self-consciously setting a bowl of milk outside before driving off to work one morning. The cat had stuck around ever since. I sighed and got up to open the side door to the garage.

"Come on in."

I wasn't a cat fan, but this animal was something else. So gutsy, so entitled to everything. He jumped up on my lap right away and started purring. I kneaded his neck for a second and felt him go limp.

"Did Russell feed you this morning?"

He turned his fine head to me and stared, then lolled again, begging for more massage. I wondered if he was as demanding with Russell. Did he drape himself over his legs, the way he was doing to me now? I scratched him under his chin and he turned the purring up louder. He rolled off my lap when he'd had enough and I went into high gear, typing up my lists and trying not to daydream about the names on the cards. The phone rang in the kitchen. I kept the back door open so I could hear it from where I worked. Granny Settle had announced she was going to Oxnard to visit some "Oklahoma people" and that this would take most of the day. I felt like a truant in my own home and this truancy felt terrific. I even loved having to get the phone.

"You sound out of breath."

"I was working in the garage. Good thing you called. Your cat appears to be starving to death."

"He's not mine."

"Is it such a big deal to look after a stray cat? Russell, he's hungry."

I looked out my window and saw him standing in an enormous kitchen that suddenly made me mad. So what if Russell's responsibilities now included a single cat? The window box was angled so that he could see me if he leaned way forward, pressing his stomach into the sink, which was exactly what he was doing. A bird shot straight up from the hedge between us.

"Bring the cat over in twenty minutes. I'm going to feed both of you."

"Really?"

"Oh, bring me a lemon, if you've got one. I hate to use that concentrate stuff."

I hung up the phone and watched Russell pull away from the window. The boy next door. Beth kept wanting updates and I didn't have any. I wasn't soaring or worried or even preoccupied. I was just going along, happy to hear his voice on the phone or spot his car idling in the driveway as he waited for the electric garage door to open. If he wasn't exactly invading my dreams at night, he was a frank, familiar daytime feature. Russell's cat slid in through the open door and banged hard against me, purring and doing his figure-eights through my legs with a vengeance.

"I'll get him to feed you, now cut it out." I tugged on his tail and weighed a fast shower versus more typing; the shower won hands down.

I lopped off a branch full of camellia blossoms and headed next door, the cat in my arms. His claws opened and closed, but a thick sweatshirt saved my skin. I thought about the new dress hanging in my closet and how dressing up for this impromptu lunch would have made Russell laugh.

His front door stood open and I could see him from the landing, standing in the kitchen just beyond a sweeping entrance he had dreamed up during an airport layover in Denver. I watched him stirring something over the stove—a dishtowel stuck out of his back pocket. He didn't have any idea how charming it was to watch a man frown over a steaming pot, taste and stir some more, adding a pinch of something from a bowl. Or did he? I knocked on the open door and the cat leaped out of my arms.

"Hi, come on in. Did you happen to bring that lemon?" He ran his hand through his hair, bringing it straight up like a stand of stiff field brush, and mopped his forehead with that dishtowel.

"Here you go." I handed him the lemon and lay the flowered branch on his kitchen counter. His grin spread until it took over his whole face.

He leaned down and kissed the top of my head, then rooted around in a cabinet for a vase. The only one he had was square with glass that looked like a shattered windshield. The branch fell awkwardly to one side.

"Pretty ugly."

"Let's just clip the blossoms and float them in a bowl."

"Good idea."

I peered at what he was stirring. I hadn't suspected sophistication. It smelled complicated, full of spices I probably didn't even have in my worka-day kitchen. This was no guy stew, no meat-and-potato medley. A lopsided white square floated to the surface of the soup.

"Fish?"

"Yeah, fresh coriander and that lemon you brought. Buncha things. I call it Russell's Bouillabaisse."

"I am really impressed."

"Don't be. I only know how to cook five things and this is one of them."

"Will I get a chance to try the four others?"

Russell stopped stirring and stared at me through the vapor. "Polly, you get to taste anything you want."

I cleared my throat and started looking around for the cat's bowl. "Why don't I feed him so he'll give us some peace?"

I would have ordered his soup in a restaurant. Russell's Bouillabaisse was served from a piece of chipped pottery that didn't match the napkins.

"What's the occasion for all this?"

He crossed his legs and knocked the table, so that soup sloshed over the side of my bowl.

"Oops. I like to cook. There's that."

"Yeah. Well, I like to eat. What a happy coincidence."

I ate and so did he. There was bread to tear apart, wine to uncork, camellias floating in Pier One blue bowls, but precious little conversation. I bit the edge of my lip, flabbergasted at having nothing to say. I had never had nothing to say to Russell.

"What were you up to in the garage?"

"Typing job. Dull, really."

"Working, then."

"Right. Speaking of work, why are you home in the middle of the day?"

I had never eaten with a man who stuck his napkin in his collar. I'd seen that in European movies where big families gathered around a heaving table and wore napkins as naturally as babies wore bibs. Today was definitely a first.

"Took a day off. I do that. I play hooky sometimes. Part of the pleasure of being self-employed." He pulled the napkin away and wiped the corner of his mouth. "For better or worse, I like pleasure. A whole lot, as a matter of fact."

"Well. This has been a real treat. A pleasure, like you say."

"Coffee, Polly?" The grin was long gone, but he obviously found something funny.

"You look like you're thinking of a joke. Are you?"

"I'm thinking of how easy it is to make you blush. I love doing it, see that? There it goes. That's why you're so charming, Polly. You're the exact shade of that flower and I haven't said anything at all. What's on your mind to make you turn so pink?"

His house was so still, as empty as I often wished mine was. The world outside was noisy, filled with sirens and birdsongs, collisions of every sort and radios turned up far too loud. In Russell's house, right then, I heard nothing at all.

"I'm wondering something."

"Wonder out loud." He folded his hands over his stomach.

"I'm curious about what my house looks like from your balcony."

"Right this way."

The cat was folded into a downy cushion on the couch. His tail twitched a couple of times, though his eyes were closed. I followed Russell up a spiral staircase I already knew. I'd prowled through his house just before it was completely done, sitting in that fabulous sunken tub as I imagined water bursting from ten Jacuzzi jets, water that stayed piping hot no matter who flushed the toilet. My heart was beating so hard. Maybe Beth was right. Maybe I should have taken out a gym membership somewhere.

His bedroom was almost all bed. I poked my head through the open door. It seemed oddly depersonalized, but maybe that was only Russell's nonchalance. The clunky vase was the tip of the iceberg. He had taken care of all kinds of expensive, high-tech built-ins, but he seemed to have accessorized the place at a garage sale.

"Who are these guys?"

Two framed photos stood on sharp metal night tables. Somebody had made these frames, arranging stones, sequins and seashells to contain two mop-headed boys of about the same age and wiry build. Same wide eyes, same *I'll punch you if you take one step closer* slouch.

"Those are the nephews I told you about. They lived with me for a couple of years when their father skipped town. Being around a man seemed to help some. They were too much for my sister to handle."

"Your sister's a lucky woman."

I thought of Toby, his fits of missing Tom that drove him to sleep with a piece of his father's unwashed clothing. I couldn't seem to rid myself of the occasional T-shirt or old bathrobe of Tom's that would turn up when Toby yearned for his dad.

It wasn't much of a balcony, more like a lookout. Russell could mark sunsets up here, though, and look out on his private waterfall. I could hear it when I sat in my garden at night, that was the only time he turned it on. Seen from his balcony, it emerged from a cluster of ferns, fronds and the same lacy green growth composing the inside of a damp forest.

"Lovely."

I turned away from that view to another far less lyrical. Everything was visible from up here. I could count every hole in the garage roof, every spot where the sprinklers didn't reach and every bare stucco patch begging for paint. My backyard looked as if it had hosted a ground war.

"Who lives over there? Squatters, probably."

Russell reached for the back of my arm, turning me slightly to look at the pavilion. "The only thing I would change is that."

"What?"

"Last shingle roof left in Los Angeles and I promise you, Polly, it's a real fire hazard. You're begging for a lawsuit with the floor in the shape that it is. Somebody trips and falls and you're out big bucks."

"But I love it out there!" The pavilion had been the reason Tom and I bought the house in the first place. It put a spell on both of us the first time we saw it and we imagined ourselves in middle age and beyond, with the kids growing and gone. Stringing up those Christmas lights had been Tom's idea, the trellis and the flaming orange trumpet vine had been mine.

"It's sweet, but it's deadly. I can get rid of it for you."

He still had his hand on my arm. I turned around and his hand stayed in the same position, sweeping across my ribs.

"I can have it torn down and hauled away for free. Even the busted floor. Some guys I know owe me a favor. You can plant all kinds of things back there. You like my waterfall? You could do something like that in the empty space."

"Why are you so eager to tear that down? Is it that ugly?"

"It's dangerous. Nothing on your property is ugly, Polly. I've told you that a million times. I like what I see from here."

He remained where he was, even though it was time to go inside. I stood still, too, my whole self straining for one touch of him. I felt like a bird dog, trembling at the border hedge that stood between us, fixed on the bird hidden inside the brush. Every single one of my senses had turned toward him.

"I know I'm repeating myself, Polly. But I've gotta ask what's on your mind."

"Not much. Not a whole lot, actually."

He ran his hand under my hair. "Doesn't seem like that to me. Seems like you've got more on your mind than you can handle at the moment."

I had forgotten how to kiss. This shocked me so much I stopped what we were doing and took a couple of steps back. How could I have forgotten how to kiss? Everything was creaky and locked, I felt like the Tin Man in *The Wizard of Oz*.

"I don't know what to do."

"Then don't do a thing."

I stood in the middle of his bedroom while he pulled shades and threw off the bedspread. He took off his shirt the same way, sort of tearing it from his back and up over his head. Maybe the haste was supposed to suggest passion.

"Come over here, Polly."

I wished we could start over again. I walked over to his bed and dropped down beside him.

"You don't get it. I *really* don't know what to do. I've never done this before."

Russell laughed and looked away for a minute. He was younger than me. Maybe by a lot. He drew a deep breath and the movement came from his chest, not his stomach. I watched it swell and deflate, settling back down to its natural size.

"You're saying you're a virgin, Polly?"

What were you if you'd only slept with one man your whole life and that one man was your husband? Still your husband, in fact, since legal documents hadn't been drawn up. Did that make me an adulteress? What did that make me, exactly?

"Kind of. An old virgin, by the way."

He was slipping my sweatshirt over my head, only not peeling it off like he'd done with his. He was careful, solicitous and suddenly not in a hurry.

"Would you mind not looking at me so hard?"

"I would mind that very much. You're beautiful, Polly."

It sounded new the way he said it, even though I knew it wasn't. I was his next-door neighbor, after all, and he had told me all those stories, though I couldn't remember details now. His eyes ran all along my body; I felt them burning a path into my skin.

"So since you don't know what to do, since you're thoroughly baffled, I'll tell you. Step by step."

"The voice of experience." I made myself go ahead, contemplating all the old girlfriends I knew about and imagining the ones too insignificant to be considered old girlfriends. "Don't you think we should . . ."

"I definitely think we should."

I put my hand on his shoulder and left it there.

"I didn't bring anything. Any, oh whatever they're called."

"Don't worry, Polly."

He turned away and fumbled with something in the drawer. Then he fumbled with me. There was no passion to sink into, the incontrollable kind Beth described or any other. There was just my mind, which wouldn't let go of my body. I looked over his shoulder at the nephews, their eyes blazing out of the photographs. I listened to Russell's voice and hoped it would smooth over everything, even me, so something else, something wilder and wiser could take over.

"Maybe . . ."

"Yeah? What, Polly?"

I'd managed to look a condom in the eye, another first, though I looked away when he put it on. His face was so close to mine I couldn't see him. I could smell him, though, or what little remained after mingling with my skin. Mostly it was my scent that came back to me now.

"Maybe if we didn't talk anymore. Let's not, all right."

"Beautiful." His voice sounded muffled, as if it were dripping through a screen. Russell seemed to be having an okay time. He sat up and I could see him. I could also see myself as I lay in his bed, whiter than bone and too bare, too raw. I felt a great and distant sadness for this body, detailed and glaring in the cold light.

He pulled me toward him, encouraged by my suggestion, made bolder. He moved me here and there, shaping my position to his own liking. Sitting up as I was, free as I seemed to be, I caught sight of the two of us in a mirror. Without Russell's voice, the room seemed to produce its own set of sounds, sharp and distinct as a baby's first cry. Then I heard singing. It was far off and right by my side. It was my grandmother singing and wailing old, known songs in my backyard. Her voice could pierce a thousand walls. Her songs could pierce intentions that took months to grow.

"Katherine, now don't you—"

I strained to hear and see them as they were below me. There was Toby's voice, high-pitched and taut with unhappiness. I could single out my son.

"I have to go. My family's . . ."

But I didn't go anywhere. I listened to Russell's breathing raking down my back. His breath grew louder than anything else inside this room or out. His breathing blotted out Toby's voice and finally blotted out me.

"Go for a walk. Take the side door and go around the block. A walk right now would be the best thing to do."

He looked so complete standing there. Nothing could have been added or subtracted to Russell at the moment. He could go to a meeting like that or a Dodger game and no one would suppose anything out of the ordinary.

"Next time's going to be very different, Polly."

I had on tennis shoes, that was good. I hadn't known Russell had a side door.

"What do you mean?"

"We'll plan things better. You know."

He made sure the street was empty and I walked out that side door fast, as fast as I could. I didn't kiss him goodbye.

The air was hardly pristine, but I could still make out the tops of the Santa Monica Mountains. My tennis shoes were new and a blister rose behind my left heel, but I bet I could still scale those mountains if I kept walking. I could scurry over those hills and keep on going, my heel getting tougher every day I kept up the march. I could just ease out of my own life, slip away like people did when they had too much on their minds. Then Tom could come home, our kids would get their father back and Russell . . . well, Russell would do whatever bachelors did. Move to greener pastures. For the moment, though, no one was going anyplace. Mr. Feldman stood at a corner a few blocks from my house. I shouted out my hello, thinking maybe he hadn't heard all my other greetings. He stumbled forward, smashing one of his dog's paws, and frowned when he recognized me as Granny Settle's kin.

"Mr. Feldman, how do you do? I'm—"

"I know *exactly* who you are."

The dog whose paw he stepped on stiffened in response to his voice and let out a low growl.

"That's all right, that's all right. You see, a dog instantly knows who is his friend and who is not. You are related to someone who is not."

"Your friend?"

"At all, though she had me fooled for the past several weeks. Is it true she has friends in Oxnard?"

"Yes. Look, I didn't know about them either."

"You look like a kind-enough girl, so tell me, why don't you?"

"What, Mr. Feldman?"

"Arnold. Why I get this treatment from her for nothing. We're walking nearly every day, taking sun, taking pleasure from talking. We are such different people, there is always something to talk about. What do I know about a horse and, frankly, what do I care? But the way your grandmother talks, she makes it all seem so appealing. So possible. Like tomorrow, Arnold Feldman, if he wished, could sell off his house and his belongings, leave all his troubles behind and ride off into the sunset like one of those fellas in a Western picture. As for your grandmother . . ."

He gazed right and left, forgetting I was there. Feldman was on one of his field trips. After a minute, one of the dogs broke his reverie. Splayed-legged and shivering, he tried to pee. A piteous dribble fell between its legs. The dog seemed older than Feldman.

"Couldn't it wait? Yes. Your grandmother. This," he said, touching the top of his yarmulke, "she calls my beret. Charming, ignorant girl. Okay, so she doesn't want to marry me, Polly. It's Polly, isn't it?"

I shook my head yes, but didn't speak.

"She doesn't want that, fine. She doesn't want to spend so much time with me, that's her priority. But this silent treatment is worse than unkind. It's unnecessary. I'm an educated man, Polly. An educated man takes bad news more gracefully than your ordinary dunce, yet she's treating me like one. Now, if your grandmother deigns to walk with me, she does so with a very damaging silence. Did she dry up? Is she so dead inside? Arnold Feldman deserves better."

He continued walking, his march little more than a wounded limp. I moved off in the opposite direction, weighing possibilities. Was she consciously preparing for death, casting off people as well as possessions in her trudging journey to the grave? Maybe the truth lay laminated in the top drawer of my desk. Old newspaper accounts of my granny's daring on horseback showed a crowd-pleasing cowgirl who shot at imaginary Indians while lying flat on her horse's back. The same girl could dip down to pick up a fallen hat at a high-speed gallop. Later photos taken in town showed a second Settle with a broomstick clenched in her fist. Those cold, glassy eyes would have killed any conversation before it was born. Had this Settle emerged to cut Feldman off at the pass? I was lost in the thought, so lost that my heel hurt remotely, almost as if my pain belonged to someone else, though I turned toward home with a limp as pronounced as Feldman's.

Eighteen

"*H*i!"

I didn't recognize him right away. The man from Tully's parking lot was wearing a straw boater and white suit. Pudgy hands were wrapped around the steering wheel of a tiny cream-colored Rambler with blue and red stripes. Hand-painted, cursive writing was just under the door handle. I strained to read what it said, but he covered it quickly with his hand.

"It's me. I'm the guy from the other morning. Listen . . . " He pulled the Rambler to my side of the street, the left side, and rolled along beside me as I limped faster. ". . . about the other day. I bet I sounded callous, am I correct? Like having a woman and children is all about money and nothing else. I've got to work on that. I've got to work on first impressions because in a town like Los Angeles what do we ever go on besides first impressions? I look at a lady and it's either a yes or no, right away. You look at a guy, you size him up in about two seconds flat, and if he doesn't succeed in two seconds, you're gonna discard him before he even opens his mouth. Tell me I'm wrong. Ha! You can't."

He swerved around a parked car and returned to my side, his tire bumping the curb. My hands were shaking, so I kept them inside my pants pockets. I still had some power, though I didn't know how to use it. Did you try to second-guess a lunatic? I didn't think so. I think you just tried to save your skin any way you could. But if I bolted now, ran up to the door of any house, what would I gain? He would have won this round, by making me afraid. This was still accidental. The fact of this man on a street near my home was pure, though unpleasant coincidence.

"Nasty limp. May I offer you a lift in my automobile?"

He feigned an English accent and twirled a flower he had stuck in his lapel. I hadn't seen it before. I stopped walking and took off my sunglasses.

"I'm going to say this once, so listen very closely. If you keep bothering me, I'll go to the police."

He tipped the hat to the back of his head. "The police, really?" He started to giggle and sunlight struck his shining face. He was sweating like a pig. Water rolled off his face onto the shoulders of his white suit. "But what have I done?"

I walked through my discomfort, it had returned to claim me, really stomped on it, and turned up a street that wasn't my own. I was ready now. I would scale a backyard fence, push through an open window to get away from him. I could see activity about three houses up. A man was working in his garage and the door was up. I heard the reassuring roar of a power saw and I walked faster.

"I mean this is not like I'm some stalker, is it? You act like I'm threatening you or something crazy like that. The only crime I can see is that you're not looking close enough at my new car and that's a shame because you'd see something really special if you'd just take a look. Here, here, right where I can touch it!"

His voice ran on and on. There was a nasty edge to his voice and I could see the face of the man in the garage now, I was that close to safety. I turned my head to look at his car as I moved up the incline, and saw *Polly*, written in pretty red cursive letters. The two L's in my name tickled the edge of his elbow.

I blurted out something to my neighbor in his garage. He bolted up the street after the Rambler, his safety glasses banging against his chest, but he couldn't reach the car in time. There was no license plate and so there was no number I could give to the police. The only thing I could say and did, in a voice not completely my own, was that someone in this city knew my name. He had taken it and painted it in trembly letters across the side of his car.

. . .

"Here, Mom, drink this. God."

One child wanted to put a bandage on my heel, the other wanted me to grow strong and sure again with fresh lemonade. I was shaking so badly by the time I reached the house, I could barely open the door. Granny Settle was rooting through a box in the dining room, searching for something she said would calm my nerves.

"He drove off, did he, Polly Ann?"

"Yes, thank God."

I could hear her muttering about Tom, about what he would do when he got hold of that chickenshit sonofabitch.

"So what'd the police say, Mom?"

"Not much. I gave them a description of him and his car over the phone. He's got my license plate number, but I don't have his. That must have been what he was writing down in the parking lot. You guys would never give out your names to strangers, would you?"

They wouldn't stoop to answer that. Of course they wouldn't, their jutting chins said.

"Or mine."

"Why?"

"Nothing. Just making sure, is all. Actually, this is probably a good thing. We ought to renew this safety discussion every now and then."

"Don't try to turn this into a good thing. It's a bad thing, it's a really bad thing."

I looked at Toby, my twelve-year-old son who had to be twelve and forty, boy and man of the house all at once. He was right. He was having a lousy childhood.

"I'm gonna check all the windows. Make sure they're all locked."

"Good idea."

Kate rewrote the emergency numbers so everyone could read them easier. Toby was in his room, digging around for a second neighborhood watch sign he would put in the kitchen window, just in case the first one wasn't visible enough. I thought of my father's dogs, how nice it would be to have a pack of furry, snarling animals swirling underfoot, leaping at the door with claws exposed every time they sniffed out a stranger. Funny that Russell didn't have guard dogs. I pulled back the curtain with one hand and stared outdoors. As concerned as he was with protection, it was downright odd. It seemed like Russell would have a pair of shiny Dobermans patrolling the property. Of course, Dobermans would eliminate stray cats as well as intruders. I sighed and let the curtain drop back into place. I twisted the cap on a bottle of aspirin, trying to get it off.

Toby peeled the back from the sign and pressed it into place. "Hey, Mom. Do you always take walks when we're at school?" He smoothed every wrinkle out of the sign and looked at me over his shoulder. His eyes drifted down to my mouth and I swiped at it hard with the back of my hand.

"Because if you do, maybe you shouldn't for a while. Because maybe this guy knows just what you do every day when we're at school. You should probably mix things up for a while."

The moment seemed right for a statistic, but Toby didn't produce one when he spoke.

"Mom? Do you work on songs the *whole* day when we're at school?"

Maybe whatever Granny Settle was mixing up at the sink would stop my head and heel from hurting. Then again, maybe not. I would take an aspirin just in case.

"Could you get this stupid thing off for me?"

He popped off the plastic cap with his thumb and shook a pill into the palm of my hand. He watched me swallow it and went back to work on the decal, his fingers stiffening as he smoothed out every crease he could find.

The phone rang for the eighth time that morning. I was ready to heave it out the window, but didn't. It was Beth.

"You're shaken up."

"I'm not, I'm telling you—"

"—Why don't you and the kids come stay with us for a little while? Or, better yet, why not have your friend come camp out on the couch?"

"No!"

"Well, have Tom sleep over for a while, that way we'll all get some peace. Polly, if he's not calling you about this, he's calling me."

"We're just fine." I looked at the area rug, sure if I looked at it closely enough I'd find Tom's footprints. He'd been over three times so far with another question or another answer. He circled the rug as I talked, giving him yet another description of the guy or one more detail I'd left out the last time he came over.

"Doesn't seem like you're fine. You let everybody stay in your house except the very person who should be there."

"What do you mean by that?"

"Talk to you later."

I bit into an apple. Three days had passed since the incident and I really wanted to beat this alone. I thought Beth's suggestions were hysterical and hysteria wasn't what my kids needed right now. Russell was on red alert in his house. He poured all his frenzy into plans for tearing up my backyard, calling with a new idea or coming by to take another measurement. After his last visit, he casually left a personal-attack alarm on my kitchen table, a little yellow box that shrieked once you pulled the pin. I'd talked to several people on the street and given them a description of the man. I had phone numbers pasted up all over and keyed locks on every window in the house. I didn't want to live with fear closing my throat all the time. I'd taken reasonable precautions and the rest was discipline. Mental discipline would get me through this.

"Ssssh. You guys leave if you can't be quiet."

Toby filled his mouth with popcorn and Kate turned her head toward Granny Settle, who had begun to snore from her seat in the corner.

I turned up the volume on the television set. Dick Clark was hosting a show on Johnny Day and I tried to pay attention. His concert at the Williamson Theatre was a week away. Clark's voice punctuated an old film of vintage Johnny Day. I wouldn't have recognized the singer's face, but his voice enveloped cloudy memories of agonizing Sunday drives and scratchy, uncomfortable picnics.

"—until Johnny Day gave country a new dimension."

Johnny in 1959 was a modest number, a young man barely twenty carefully dressed in a business suit. Girls were fainting in the film. The cameraman didn't seem to know what to do, photograph the girls who were dropping like flies or fix the camera on Johnny, who sang his way softly through all the screams and cries. Johnny Day was about nuance and suggestion. He seemed a shy and boyish object of desire, at least in the first part of the film. I kneaded the back of my neck and watched his eyes, the most important thing about him besides his voice, which began to carry me away slowly, like water swirling insistently around a wooden boat. I thought real hard about that boat, that water, just traveling with the current for a while and stepping out on fresh soil, wherever the wooden boat landed. I blinked a few times and tried to pay attention to the television. That was Johnny's magic, I guessed. His voice could have you drift off in your mind so far you would never come back.

Dick Clark talked through what must have been Johnny's dry period, the time of fake jewels and mail-order belts. He described Johnny's hardships: the breakup of his first marriage and his mother's illness. In fact, Ruth Day's bout with hepatitis took us right up to Johnny's thirty-fourth gold record. He'd written the song by her bedside, convinced that it would be the last thing he would ever sing to his beloved mama. Toby squirmed and sang his own rendition of Johnny Day's tunes. Kate threw a handful of popcorn at him and I stood up.

"All right, out. Both of you, beat it."

"No, we like it. We're going to write you a country song, Mom. What rhymes with Mama besides llama?"

Kate picked popcorn off the floor and swung her head toward me. "Drama. Trauma. Mom, I'm scared for you."

They both came over and hugged me until my neck hurt. Kate was the first to let go. They quieted down; Johnny Day did have stage presence. There was something muted and surprisingly erotic about his singing style that Dick Clark wasn't about to discuss.

The public went wild for "I'd Sooner He Took Me than You" and Ruth Day shortly rose from her deathbed and sailed for England. Footage continued as Johnny steered his mother's wheelchair past Big Ben and Westminster Abbey. Ruth's hands fussed incessantly with her lap robe as her son gave a command performance for the Queen of England. Again, the cameraman seemed schizophrenic, flitting back and forth between Johnny Day's public reincarnation and Ruth Day, pale but victorious in a box seat surrounded by the Royal Family. With the Beatles creating such a stir, Johnny probably had no choice but to drop the drab business apparel. He emerged from behind a royal blue curtain in red and gold with a twelve-inch leather fringe dangling from the backs of his solid arms. Our doorbell rang just as Johnny bent forward in a bow.

"Check through the peephole before you open it."

Toby ran for the door.

"It's okay. It's Beth." He opened the door a crack. "We don't want any."

"Oh, yes you do."

"She's watching this thing on TV."

"I'll keep quiet."

She saw Granny Settle asleep in the chair and slipped off her shoes, then tiptoed over to the couch. I poured her a glass of lemonade; she was still flushed from class.

Red and gold would be his signature colors for the next twenty years. His lyrics and soothing voice had developed quite an edge by the end of the film short. He would become his own sun, his own red-hot horizon to the delight of his business manager and new wife, Lola. Dick Clark didn't mention that Lola was all of fifteen when Johnny met her, but I remembered it as I sat there. Granny Settle stirred in the chair, coming back to life. She stared at the screen and rubbed her eyes.

"What? Is he singing again? Well, I know somebody who's bound to be happy."

I remembered how my mother cracked a china saucer as she slammed a coffee cup down one morning listening to the news of his remarriage. Minah Overstreet was visiting and the two were examining every angle they could think of. How ancient he'd be when their kid graduated high school, for young Lola was showing, her belly bulging firm and round under white lace, in all the photographs they'd seen of the marriage. How Lola's parents reacted to Johnny Day, since he was older than they were and, of course, whether or not Ruth Day had lit into him for such a demeaning marriage. My mother and Minah were in complete agreement regarding Ruth: they thought she was the cat's meow. Dick wrapped up the performer's career, calling him country music's very own Sun King.

"So that's it?"

"Yeah, show's over." I got up to turn it off.

"No, but I mean this is the Johnny Day we went shopping for."

"Right. And I'm going to his concert next week and I'll try to see him backstage."

"Your mama did that. Your mama did that lots of times." Granny Settle sat forward in her chair. "What else are you fixin' to do, Polly Ann?"

The kids were still. Kate was watching her great-grandmother closely, waiting to see how Minah Overstreet and my mother, chickens and Johnny Day converged.

"I'm going to show him a song I've written. Try to get him interested in singing it. Look, he's not exactly Garth Brooks, but he does have kind of a following."

Beth pointed her toes in impatience. Movement was in her blood, just like it was in Kate's. I watched her foot slide along, hugging the floor until the very last moment, then the arch rose grandly, strained and collapsed. She repeated the motion and began talking. "Sure isn't very systematic."

"Songwriting isn't. Neither is trying to get it sung. I mean, if I were living in Nashville, things would be different. In Nashville there's Music Row, there are places like the Bluebird Cafe, places you go to make things happen."

"You're saying you have to live in Nashville to have a song published?"

"No, but it sure helps. Talk about systematic . . . well, down there you network in clubs and stuff."

"Polly, you don't go to clubs."

I wondered if Paradise counted. "I probably would if I lived in Nashville."

I was beginning to lose the audience right here in my living room. Granny Settle was humming to herself and the kids stared at the black screen. "In Los Angeles you make it up as you go."

"But aren't there guilds you can try to get into or contests you can enter?"

"Songwriting contests, Beth? You've got to be kidding."

"You might win one, Mom."

"Yeah. You might even get some money."

They looked so hopeful. They looked more like Tom than ever before.

"You guys, songwriting isn't like a sales contest. The best way to break into the business is to get somebody's attention."

"Your mama spent her whole life doing just that." Granny Settle was up out of her chair. She had her hands on her hips. "Yep, she had all the attention a woman could want and all it did was make her hungry for more."

"That's different."

"Doesn't sound like it to me. Of course I'm old. Too old to do all this talking. I'm going to bed."

Kate watched her cut across the floor and whispered something to Beth. The doors closed behind her. Beth smiled and scratched her head.

"Is that her way of saying good night?"

I nodded.

"Think about what I said, Polly. There's got to be a better way of going about this."

"Yeah, Mom." Toby yawned and continued. "You could write songs half the day and try to sell them in the other half of the day. Ask Dad. He knows how to sell *everything*."

He'd stopped wearing that St. Christopher medal. It was probably lost or else he'd broken the chain wrestling with Stewart. Or maybe he'd found it too precious to risk wearing, hiding it instead inside a sock or a shoebox. It hurt me to look at him right then. The hope I'd seen earlier still hadn't left his face.

Nineteen

"What is it about this place?"

Tom's bout with the flu had passed and he was fighting those extra ten pounds again. He tugged on his belt a couple of times and paced as we waited for Toby's principal to call us. When he put on weight, he never let out his belt or bought fat pants, the way I did. He believed discomfort was part of the cure.

"Probably reminds you of Mr. Moore's office." The geography teacher's paddle had been notorious in Granite. All the popular boys had known its solid whack. Tom had been very popular in tenth grade.

"You're right. No wonder I'm a wreck." He looked at his watch another time. "You sure he said two, Polly?"

The principal's voice on the answering machine had been testy. It wasn't a request that Tom and I drop into his office at two o'clock, but a command. I watched a surly kid with a piece of paper wadded up in his hand and another mother who was talking to herself in a low, comforting murmur. The boy hopped up off the bench as soon as we arrived and slammed his back against a wall to wait. He kept his eyes on Tom.

"Mr. and Mrs. Harrison."

He used an intercom from his office to call waiting visitors. There was no one in the front office besides someone I recognized from the PTA who was making phone calls from a corner. I realized with a start that whole regimes had risen and fallen since I'd been active at the school. We walked down the hall toward the principal's closed door; I didn't know who would be shaking my hand today. In our meetings over the past couple of years, I'd always thought a little humor was welcome and appropriate. I didn't have that sense today.

"Sit, please sit." His pants drooped a bit in the back. The skin on his face hung down loosely and I missed the old chunky authority right away. Tom hovered in the doorway.

"Coffee?" He motioned to the two chairs in front of his desk and sat down slowly.

"Not for me, thanks."

Tom shook his head no.

"I hope Toby hasn't done something awful."

He leaned back in his chair and rubbed his closed eyes with the heel of his hand.

"May I impose on the two of you for a moment?"

Tom finally sat down, his watch emitting little beeps.

"Did you notice the boy out there? The one next to you on the bench?"

"He looks furious."

"Furious isn't the word. He's lost. He's gone. Last week he was in here because he slashed the tires on his teacher's car, then he came in here and threatened me. The end of our meeting, he looks at me, sits up straight in his chair after I've called his mother at work, and asks me how my baby is doing. Quiet, steady voice. My newborn baby just three weeks out of the hospital. I'm expelling him today. After my meeting with you, I'm going to sit him down in that chair," he pointed to Tom's chair, "and expel him from school. Fourth grade. Can you imagine what his life will be in five years?"

"What did he do?"

"He poisoned Mrs. Victor's rabbits. We found pellets in the cage, the same ones we found in the pocket of his jacket. Take this."

He handed me a box of Kleenex. Tears welled up out of nowhere. Every kid who had come through this school loved those rabbits. Toby had brought them home several times. They were a little tipsy and stupefied after years of being handled by children, but the lop-eared grays had survived and even managed to multiply over the last few years. I couldn't get hold of this news. It was like an equation I didn't understand no matter how long I studied it.

"Lucky the other children didn't see them. Mrs. Victor happened to come in early from recess. So today I'm expelling this boy and you want to know what I feel?"

Tom slid to one side of his chair, looking more and more agitated.

"Fear. This kid's got older brothers and cousins that make him look like a cherub. I want to pack up and leave. I'm afraid for my baby and my wife. I've been around children for years, loved them, punished them. Despaired over them. But this year for the first time . . ."

He plucked a Kleenex from the box and dabbed the back of his neck.

". . . There's something different out there. Something I can't put my finger on. This is unforgivable. I don't mean to burden you with this, but . . ."

We both waited for a few moments. Out of respect for the horror, which at that moment seemed so present and enormous, filling the whole room with its loud pulse. I forgot why I was sitting there. I happened to look up and find the principal staring at me intently.

"My wife and I are thinking of moving to Oregon. She's been offered a position there."

"I'm sorry."

"We're only thinking of it."

"You know how to work with the parents and the kids respect you. Even Toby, with all his misbehavior."

"Oh, yes. Toby."

We could have been seated in a giant cup and saucer, spinning away at Disneyland, the way that room seemed to tilt and veer in one erratic direction after another.

"Toby. I wanted to speak to you about him."

His eyes lowered and lighted on my hands, then fixed on my left hand. I had stopped wearing my wedding band. The principal handed Tom a stack of standards, single sentences written hundreds of times, and I leaned over to read the sloppy handwriting. *I will not spit at my teacher.*

"He didn't tell me about this. He spit at Mr. Cloaker?"

"Repeatedly. Used some pretty creative language, too."

"Are you putting Toby and that boy outside in the same category?"

He shook his head. "You're seeing me on a very bad day, Mrs. Harrison, so I may as well tell you that Cloaker makes me want to spit, too. But Toby can't do this. He can't keep writing standards, either."

"No."

No to all of it. No to the boy on the bench outside, no to my son's rotten behavior and to writer's cramp and standards. No to the madness that made children and adults rage out of control. I pictured Toby's hand, the blister that would swell on his middle finger from writing all those standards. It filled out as I watched, fattening into the pudgy hand of a stranger, every finger lightly touching the letters in my name.

"I'm sick of this."

"Of course you are."

"I can't do this anymore. I can't be called here anymore and I can't make jokes on the phone and try to pretend things are settled after we've hung up."

"Polly."

"I can't! Tom, I'm exhausted."

There was a little row of porcelain ducks marching across the edge of his desk. The ducks started minute and grew, until the duck at the end of the line was sleek and fat with solemn black eyes.

"I don't know you well, Mrs. Harrison, but I know you love your boy. Don't you?"

I nodded heavily.

"Mr. Harrison, you must know what you represent to your son. Cloaker, even at his angriest, says Toby draws beautifully. You drive a sports car, I believe?"

"How did you know?"

"He spends time drawing it at recess. Your son's class is studying Rome and it seems he's turned your sports car into a chariot."

Tom looked at the ground and shook his head.

"That boy outside is lost, but your son isn't. Toby is sad. He carries sadness with him day after day. What I am suggesting may sound illogical, but it isn't really. Give your son what he wants most. I'll keep giving him standards until you do, even though it won't change his behavior. I don't know what's missing in his life, but you must. Give him the greatest gift you can think of. Here, Mrs. Harrison, take a Kleenex. Why don't you take the whole box?"

I waited until we got outside the school. We stood under a shade tree that had been planted forty years ago when the school was built. I'd written speeches using the tree as the one reliable symbol any parent could understand.

"I should never have followed you out here! If we had stayed in Granite—"

"—Ah, come off it, Polly."

"All right, Tulsa or Oklahoma City, then. You heard what he said and you saw that kid on the bench just the same as I did. They play by different rules out here. This would never have happened back home. And don't give me that look."

He was trying to look uncomprehending. What was so complicated about what I'd just said?

"You brought up Moore's class so why don't we talk about that for a minute? I didn't give a rat's ass about geography, that's what all the screwing around was about. I sat in the back of the class and made trouble while you were in the front row, just drinking in those relief maps. You were the one who couldn't wait to leave Oklahoma, Polly. You couldn't stop thinking about a getaway, even when you were in grade school."

His voice trembled and I looked away.

"You know damn well our problems don't have anything to do with geography, so don't try to stick me with that. Want to hear something else, Polly? You're not the only one who's exhausted. Other people get worn down, too."

He turned away abruptly and headed to his car, jamming his fists in his pockets. I rested in the shade as he drove off, my back scratching up against the rough bark. I thought about Toby's artwork, his chariots and town-saving trees. I spent a minute imagining the steaks and fruit that rained down on anyone ready to receive such gifts.

I glared at the entrance to the coffee shop, then stomped on the ground, thinking Tully's new doors would open automatically. I stomped harder. Nothing moved. He stood on the other side, waving at me to come forward. I pushed hard and the partially automated door opened the rest of the way on its own. He gave me a big smile when I finally crashed straight into his arms.

"Careful, honey."

"Why the hell did you change the door?"

"To make it easier to get in here."

Nothing was secure. Not a rabbit hutch or a newborn baby. I pictured the principal's face, the way his eyes skittered across the desk as he talked about Mrs. Victor's rabbits. *There's something different out there.* There sure was. It had even found its way into my neighborhood.

As he led me to a table near the back, I felt calmed for an instant, as if Tully would lead me through his restaurant not just to a booth but to a wide, permanently safe place. He sat down on the edge of the seat in front of me. His big legs stuck out into the aisle; waitresses glowered at him as they hopped over his legs with scalding plates.

"What's eating you, Polly?"

"I've got to get some work done."

"You will. First talk."

"I'm having a lousy day."

"Yeah. And?"

I took a sip of coffee. "Tell me something, you've got two grown kids, right?"

"Yeah."

"Are they happy?"

"In general or with me?"

"Both."

"Not especially. They say I was too hard on them growing up. That I robbed them of their childhoods. It wasn't my fault, Polly. What should I have done—lied? They shared a room, see. That was before I bought this place and things were pretty tight. They shared a room and my son says to me one night when I'm making them say prayers, 'Daddy, is there a Santa Claus?' I said no and the girl from her bed says in the dark 'Or an Easter Bunny?' Boom, two down and one to go. They both said together 'There's no tooth fairy, either!' And then they cried and I couldn't get anybody to say prayers. Does honesty make me bad? Is that what they mean when they say I robbed them of a childhood?"

He pushed a menu toward me, jabbing at a new insert.

"See what I gotta do? One whole cholesterol-free page, for cryin' out loud. Fat-free this, fat-free that until I could scream, but I gotta please my customers. I'll tell you something, Polly. I wasn't unhappy that night. To tell you the truth, I felt lighter, a thousand pounds lighter. No more Santa, no more Bunny. No more sliding dollars under their sleeping heads and holding my breath so they wouldn't hear me. I figured life would be easier with fewer secrets. So shoot me. I never told anyone that before. Your turn. You tell me something big."

Something big? Something bad? I could tell him plenty from both categories, but I knew where that would get me. Someone is *following* you? A guy you saw here in *my* parking lot? Tom, Russell, Tully . . . three hysterical men in my lifeboat would make it sink. I glanced at the clock and started looking for my pen.

He pushed himself up to his feet and patted my shoulder.

"Fine, don't talk. I'm glad to see you're at it again. Something told me after our last conversation I'd gone a little too far. You know, spoken out of place and all that. It's not like you wanted career advice from the king of hash browns. You're not mad at me then?"

"Of course not."

"So how'd the meeting with the agent go?"

"Would you stop?"

Tully looked like a big puppy who'd just been swatted with a rolled-up newspaper.

"I didn't mean to jump on you. Forget the meeting, Tully. I have. There'll be other Shels, believe me. All it takes is one person to say yes. One syllable can change history."

He looked appeased. "Work. That's the trick to everything. Work is the only thing I feel entitled to, when you get down to it. I couldn't please a single one of my wives and my grown kids tell me I stole their childhoods. So I work. Speaking of which, I better let you do yours. Don't order any of that, okay? An egg white omelet . . . makes me sick thinking about it."

I chewed for a little while, thinking things out. What could I really do for Toby? I knew what he wanted most. He didn't just want his father back. He wanted the two of us together. Toby, his face buried in Tom's old clothes, was like a hound following a trail growing colder every day. He didn't want traces of his dad. He wanted the real thing, day after day. If Tully had ended childhood abruptly, what had I done? What had we done? Everything turned to a sickening paste in my mouth as I thought of something Frankie had said. If it was true, if I was heartsick, how long until I got well?

The restaurant started to fill up and as it did, my problems seemed to recede and get smaller and smaller, until I could almost scoop them up and slide them into my pocket. Something else was growing, though. An image was pushing its way into my mind with a word or two, then several. I worked it out imprecisely on some loose papers I had folded up in my purse; I'd left my notepad at home. The papers were kind of spread out over the table. I scribbled some lines and read as I worked along. I'd picked up a tabloid featuring stories on great country stars. Skinny columns of smudged print provided life snippets, little vignettes about each singer's hardships and hard-luck stories that almost undermined my right to write. I hadn't been born in a boxcar and I was no child of rape. But the stories I'd lived myself fed me words I wrote and rewrote, trying to clear out the weeds choking the flower. I thought hard about the girl who couldn't wait to leave Granite and the woman who couldn't seem to leave it behind. I thought, too, about the boy she persuaded to come along for the ride.

I'll buy the gas and pump up the tires
I'll talk to you all night long.
When you're too tired to drive anymore
I'll keep you awake with a song.
Hurry, Jimmy, get your things
Don't make me wait too long.

First Tulsa, then Texas, then New Mexico
We'll pass them as quick as we can.
Maybe we'll go to where seagulls cry
Do they let people walk on that sand?
I've had my fill of the life that I know
You might say the road is my plan.

She smiled as she sat there beside him
We two were just meant to go
Please promise me that I'll never see
Another damned rodeo.

She talked and Jimmy listened
As her words blew around in the air
When all he felt was desert heat
He reached out to touch her hair.
He thought she'd be looking for what lay ahead
But he found her head bent in a prayer.

She smiled as she sat there beside him
We two were just meant to go
Please promise me that I'll never see
Another damned rodeo.

That prayer. I wondered if she had an inkling of the trials ahead, the danger out on the road. And I wondered if the woman in my song was me, my mother, or both of us. Certainly the driver of that car was Tom.

Twenty

I thought of double-spacing my cover letter to Johnny Day. That way he could comfortably read between the lines. Dear Mr. Day, I'm sure you will remember my mother, Carla Settle. Sandwiched inside those careful words lay the real message: *Dear Johnny, Think back to your first big performance at the Oklahoma City Rodeo, 1960 . . . remember how the crowds pushed to get near you and the cloudburst that followed your song? My mother pushed harder than anyone else and I was with her that day.* Mr. Day, I've enclosed my song lyrics, which I believe are right for you. *Johnny, I've written you a song about that rodeo and I'm Carla's girl. I'm Carla's girl.*

I took Sepulveda Boulevard as far as I could, anticipating the top of the pass. For a time I was the lone car on a lonely stretch of road and I imagined Johnny's worries as he fretted backstage. I imagined him fussing, turning this way and that in front of a mirror, then calling out to his wife right before show-time. Damn it, Lola, I know you love me, but will they? I took a deep breath, welcoming the sight of the soupy basin below, weighted down under the blanket of smog. That blanket felt snug tonight. Of course they would love him. The Valley would welcome Johnny Day who would, in turn, welcome me.

I held the leather envelope under my arm as I made my way up the sloped steps of the Williamson Theatre. The wide porch was decorated with potted palms and the occasional lectern loaded with handbills and programs. The

Williamson featured gospel programs and Scientologists, dance companies from Central America and motivational speakers who couldn't quite finance an infomercial. I plucked a stray hair from my new dress, thinking about what the owner of the dress shop had said. The friendly white clapboard structure did suggest a stack of hotcakes would arrive any minute. No one would guess the homey old building hosted such eclectic performers.

An usher showed me to the center of the old theater. Somebody I didn't know waved and I waved back. I imagined an auditorium filled with cousins and uncles and row after row of an extended family so large and close that nobody would need an introduction. In this extended family everyone had been given the loan or treatment program they needed and the reunion spread out merrily over a lakefront, beach or public park with an empty seat and barbecue for everyone. I bet this theater, stuffed full of people waiting for Johnny Day to sing, was tranquil enough to have calmed old warriors like Granny Settle and Grandmother Jewel. Old warriors like my mother and father. I eased into my seat and put the leather case in my lap.

> Say, mister, excuse me for asking
> I sure oughta know by now
> There was a time when I knew it by heart
> But I've lost my way there somehow.
>
> Get me up near to the grit and the noise
> The heat and the dust don't offend
> I'm not afraid of commotion
> I'm looking for my old friend.

My mother licked her way to the top of Johnny Day's Fan Club. Literally. She didn't use sponges the way other women did when they sent out newsletters about Johnny's comings and goings. She preferred to use her own tongue as a symbol of her devotion, she said. She held a stamp out to me on the tip of her finger. Want to help me, Polly? Then what are you looking at? She said once she was president everything was going to be different. For the longest time that was what president meant to me: change. You could president something away that you didn't like. You could president a bully from the schoolyard and president your way to a straight-A report card. You could even president your mother if you licked enough stamps.

How do I find that old rodeo?
The one filled with broncos and steers?
All I want now is a seat near the front
Is there anything close to that here?

He walks funny and can't speak directly
He's liable to look at the ground
He's an old cowboy who grows kinda shy
The minute a woman's around.

If you see him just tell him a lady
Decided to let him know
She loved him for years without saying
The things that he needed to know.

How do I find that old rodeo?
The one filled with broncos and steers?
All I want now is a seat near the front
Is there anything close to that here?

After returning from Oklahoma City, my mother discovered her yardstick, the one she used to wag at Granny Settle. She couldn't resist comparing the Settle Ring with the rodeo her parents had lost and the one she discovered in 1960, complete with riders who were national champions and marching bands and Johnny Day. That cloudburst turned into a deluge and we barely made it back to Granite. The car smoked under the hood and the rubber on one of the windshield wipers came off, but the real danger wasn't the engine. It was my mother and her temper. The car stalled three miles from our house and she grabbed my hand and pulled me along in the cold rain. Your father the mechanic. Mr. Take My Car. I'll show him. As for my father, he wanted to know where her crimson scarf had gone, the one I saw her slip into the pocket that buttoned over Johnny Day's heart. I slept under the bed that night and the night that followed. I didn't pray to God, I prayed to Granny Settle and sure enough, when someone's hand finally reached under the bed to get me, it was hers.

The crowd oohed and aahed. Curtains lifted on a full-scale replica of the kitchen where Johnny had penned his first ballad. The rough wooden surfaces and peeling paint, tattered curtains hanging above a windowpane taped up against the winter cold . . . it was all just as it should have been for a poor country boy bound for glory. Except for one thing, the one thing that kept recurring in scene after scene of Johnny's early life. In the middle of the rickety table that tilted precariously to one side stood a proud English teapot. It was a piece of Spode; I knew the classic pattern. His mother could buy a piece of pricey porcelain, but couldn't replace a broken window. Ruth Day's affectation was everywhere and I thought about Johnny and his mother as a golden wand of light fell on the singer's fine head. Traditional country music was long on humility and patriotism, but Ruth never bought into either of those things. Johnny's fans all knew his mother was an Anglophile; it was my mother's reporting that made it known. Once she was president, she conducted telephone interviews with Johnny for her "circulars." They were no longer called newsletters after my mother became president.

"Good evening."

People cried out loud when they heard his voice. The whole auditorium rustled with welcome and excitement, even if they didn't call out his name directly.

"Welcome home."

Applause rang out and Johnny bowed his head over his guitar and waited for the last voice to die out. He hadn't played in a decent place in years. His unctuous voice rolled on about his childhood and a second set lit up, a reproduction of Johnny's very own bedroom.

A gilded portrait of an English king hung over young Johnny's bed, yet the view from his room was dismal. Tires were mounded outside. They weren't even arranged in straight rubber columns, which could have contained some romance. These tires were just thrown every kind of way over the front yard. Tires and coffee cans. There must have been fifty dented coffee cans just lying around that nobody cared about picking up.

"But that wasn't all I saw from my window, friends. I saw the night sky. And it looked to me like it was full of good things, so I took to calling everything I saw, every bright, shiny star, a hope stone. Hope stones shone down on me then, just the way they do now."

He opened with a song he composed when he was Toby's age, when he'd seen Jesus drop out of the heavens, his hands full of hope stones. I expected the song to be maudlin and it was, but it also summed up a young boy who looked out at a dismal view and past it to a deep, impassive sky.

His voice was steady and low. The microphone seemed almost unnecessary, as Johnny's voice carried to every seat in the house. His music appealed and appeased; there was a soothing quality to his performance that I didn't remember. Had the years rounded off every raw edge? He sang for over an hour, prefacing most of the music with the story behind the song, the agony or ease that went into its making. He praised his musicians and the technical crew at the Williamson. He paid homage to the veterans in the audience, even bringing a few of them up on stage before he broke for intermission.

"Courage. It's a mighty big word, but it's still just a sound in my mouth. I'd like to bring a few friends up here on stage right now who know courage first-hand."

Privates, sergeants, lieutenants gathered around Johnny as he called them by name. The wand of light grew broader and brighter, expanding to enclose the assembly on stage.

"Come on up here, Melvin Carpenter. We need you here, sir."

He sang to them and for them in a song that brought back the rough edge. While the words honored bravery and sacrifice, the melody was sharp and unsettling. Johnny's voice changed, bringing back the raw edge I remembered. There was a lot of movement in my row. Legs crossed and skirts rustled and were rearranged. Several men slipped off their jackets—the heat in the auditorium rose as Johnny sang. In the thunderous applause that followed there was anger and tribute, protest and praise. The whole theater went dark at the end of the song, and when the lights came back on, the stage was empty. I sat where I was during intermission, making notes on what I wanted to say to Johnny once I got backstage.

The tempo swerved in the second half of the show. Songs were hard and fast, venturing far from traditional Johnny Day. These songs embraced issues and the lyrics felt oddly faceless, bogged down in big ideas. The stories Johnny told about their composition didn't sound right or even particularly true. Long, uncomfortable pauses marked his speech and something was even off about his costume change. The white suit he wore seemed designed for someone bigger. I dug around in my purse for my magnifying glasses. I read the program through again, looking at the acknowledgments.

The family reunion was breaking up before the pie was served—half of my row left in the middle of a song about rape. A man next to me broke open a box of Red Vines in the middle of the dolorous refrain, making a lot of noise getting it undone. He finally got the paper off the box of candy and stuck one quickly into his mouth, then turned and offered me one, too.

"Thanks."

"These songs suck. I know Johnny Day and this ain't Johnny Day. This is some Hollywood body snatcher thing."

"Sssssh!"

He sunk lower into his seat and focused on his Red Vines. Johnny finished singing and the man next to me threw his empty box on the ground, sighing deeply. Applause was light at the end of the song. The lighting on stage shifted one last time, softening on the view from Johnny's window. They had added something to the scene during intermission. The tires and cans were still lying around, but the tree outside Johnny's room had burst open. Arms filled with white blossoms seemed to open in front of his window.

"These are cold times, my friends, and I want to thank you for letting me sing about them. Sometimes I wonder if the world has turned so cold that the tree you see outside my house will stop blooming, stop bearing sweet fruit."

The man next to me sat up straighter. The body snatchers had vanished, leaving the real Johnny on stage.

"Cold times never last, my friends. But while we're waiting for them to pass, we need to live warm and well. We need to take shelter in a house of love."

I thought Lola would surely appear to stand by his side in the center of all that light, but Johnny sang his love song solo, even a cappella in the end as his musicians lay their instruments down and walked quietly off the stage. It worked. Just as tears of appreciation began to fall, at the very moment that the crowd begged for the encore that wouldn't follow, a panel slid open overhead. Instead of hope stones glinting above, all I could see were sheets of white paper floating down from on high. I caught one before it fell to the ground. It was a songsheet, containing words and lyrics to one of Johnny's hits. The ground was littered with sheets of paper and people gathered them up quietly, lining pockets and purses with words carved from a long career. I looked around for the lyrics from the second half of the show, but there didn't seem to be any of those. These were only Johnny's hit songs from the past.

The backstage area was drafty. Everyone I passed slapped at the tops of their arms, complaining. There were no throngs of well-wishers here. Maybe they were discouraged by Johnny's refusal to do an encore. Or maybe the backstage freeze was meant to turn away fans sniffing out Johnny's autograph. There were several corridors to choose from, all badly lit, smelling either of dust or incense. I chose incense, even though it gave me a splitting headache. I walked faster down the corridor, then rounded a corner and slowed down to a mincing walk. There was a security guard parked in a chair and a Johnny Day fan trying hard not to look like one. There were no stars in his eyes, no delight at finally being so close to Johnny Day. His expression was grim and self-absorbed.

I'd spent the lucky dollar bill after my episode with Shel Elliot, so I was armed with only my lyrics and a cover letter so understated it was practically a lie. The man I saw dead ahead was young, probably early twenties, and was dressed in long denim shorts and a patchwork vest over a white T-shirt. He carried a briefcase, while I carried a mere envelope, and he scowled at me the closer I got. The security guard wore a shirt that said TRAIN YOUR BRAIN. He was buried in an Elmore Leonard paperback and didn't even look up as his walkie-talkie squealed instructions.

The young man held a song that had fallen from Johnny Day's sky. I could hear Johnny's voice behind a closed door and being so close to the singer had a dizzying effect on me. Since I took the man in denim shorts for a fellow songwriter, I supposed the evening worked on him in the same way. I could read the title of the song from where I stood.

"Amazing." I expected him to verify this, but he didn't. Light frown lines between his blue eyes deepened into a couple of gashes.

"I don't know what you're talking about."

The security guard turned a page and didn't look up.

"Are you a friend of Johnny's? Or a fan?"

"Neither!" He hugged the shabby fake leather case tightly to his chest and eyed me like I was a member of the KGB.

"You write songs, don't you? Because I do, too, and I love that he let his lyrics drop down like that at the end of the show. What a tribute to songwriters."

"As if Johnny Day gives a shit about songwriters!" He chortled and looked at the security guard, then stuffed the lyrics in his pocket.

I looked at the floor and ran over my introduction one more time in my mind. I was midway through when the door to Johnny's dressing room opened. I could see Johnny in the background, soaking his feet in a bucket, white pants rolled up to his knees. A big bear of a man wearing a Hawaiian shirt peered around the edge of the door. My man in denim pulled on a strand of hair and cried out in a voice different from the one I'd just heard.

"Hey! I know you."

"Should I know you, son?"

"I'm not your son. I'm Kid Wonder. And you're Randy Nelson!" There was accusation in the last line and Randy Nelson wiped his face with the back of his hand.

I didn't pretend not to listen or look. Randy Nelson was very cool, but things were changing and changing quickly. He eyed the security guard, who cast Elmore aside and put on dark glasses. TRAIN YOUR BRAIN seemed to expand and move across his wide chest. He pressed a button on the walkie-talkie and muttered something I couldn't hear.

"You have a home in Butte and you hang out with heavy metal people in your spare time and you don't really care who you manage as long as they make you money. You'd sign an ax murderer if you thought he'd sell you records. I know about you. I know about the young girls, too. There's nobody in Nashville who doesn't!"

"Get your facts straight, friend. It's Missoula. I have a home in Missoula."

The songwriter was disintegrating. His voice scraped on and on hysterically.

"You and Johnny called me backstage in Nashville and don't pretend you didn't. I showed you my lyrics and you—"

Randy Nelson looked at me suddenly. The security guard was waiting for a signal.

"—We what, son?" Nelson opened and closed one hand, holding the other behind his back. "That's an old story by now. Courts ended that story for us, didn't they?"

Kid Wonder flinched, his face crumbling suddenly. He looked as if he would cry. "I gave up a lucrative career writing jingles because you gave me hope. You gave me false hope. I am living in a ten-year-old Chevrolet at the moment, Randy, while you are busy flying in and out of Nashville with your scumbucket teenage girlfriends. Take my calls, why don't you, it's the least you can do." He looked completely sapped by his tirade and leaned limply against the wall. He didn't seem to have the strength to turn his head.

The security guard lay a hand on his shoulder. "Afraid we have to ask you to leave, sir."

"Give me a minute. You can give me a minute, can't you, Randy, after everything you've taken from me?"

Kid slid down the wall until he was in a sitting position, then set his briefcase on his knees. The guard began to reach for a billy club and Randy Nelson grabbed his hand. It's okay, he mouthed.

The writer rooted around in the mess I could see inside the briefcase. Wadded-up papers and pencil stubs, torn magazines and crumpled newspapers, plus a packet of Fig Newtons. He finally found a fresh piece of paper and began scribbling furiously.

"Wind it up, son." Randy Nelson had both hands behind his back now.

"One second." He finished and snapped the briefcase shut. Then Kid Wonder turned to me. "You saw me write this, so you're a witness. Nobody wrote this but me." He pressed the paper in my hand and squeezed my fist over it tightly.

"Let me show you outside, sir."

They headed down the hall, making it just Randy Nelson and me. So far Johnny Day hadn't ventured out of his dressing room.

I gave Randy Nelson my best smile and stuck my hand out for a shake. He didn't look frazzled, he looked bigger. Unfortunately, he noticed what I held under my arm.

"I know this is poor timing, but—" I felt his hand slip away.

"Let me tell you a story about that man you just saw. Memphis, not Nashville the way he tells it, he comes backstage after a concert to pitch a song. Well, both Johnny and me listen, we're gracious. Nobody's rude. Months later, Johnny writes and records 'Twin Pines,' which goes to the top overnight and guess who shows up again? Kid Wonder, saying Johnny copped the lyrics. Suddenly we're in court. Now naturally we won but it wasn't something we'd want to repeat ever. Would we, Johnny?"

Even though his feet were soaking and cold times were clearly upon him, Johnny Day understood gravity and grandeur, how they can be easily confused. He removed his feet from the tub, one at a time, shaking them both over a purple towel. He turned to look at me and his mouth dropped open slightly. Randy Nelson moved in front of the door, blocking my view.

"If I could just have a word with—"

"Oh, you'll get to have more than a word if you drive out to Pomona next weekend." Randy Nelson was hustling me out of there. He wasn't being unkind, but he wasn't exactly avuncular. "Come on out to Fanfest next weekend and I'll make sure you get more than just a word. You'll get a photograph of Johnny and a handshake from Johnny and . . ."

He walked me down the icy corridor until we could both read the exit sign, then lowered his voice and thanked me for being faithful to Johnny. I told him being faithful to Johnny Day was a family tradition. Randy looked skeptical for a minute, then handed me his business card.

It wasn't until I got to my car that I opened my fist to see what Kid Wonder had written. The fierce penmanship was hard to read, but I could make it out. Had Kid, the aggrieved party, decided to turn around and steal Johnny's stuff? I held his lyrics under the faint light of the glove compartment.

> Hope stones are raining on the ground
> They're falling on our heads
> Old Johnny Day'll get his way
> When all the songwriters are dead.

Twenty-one

"Mom."

"I'm on the phone."

"I think you should get off."

I waved him to one side and finished my conversation with Lorraine. A shipping company had an absurd deadline to meet and everybody was frantic. I promised I could type at the speed of light for fifteen dollars an hour.

"Now, Toby. What's so important that couldn't wait?"

"Russell backed a truck into *our* driveway and he's unloading guys, that's what. Four guys with tools are headed for our backyard." He pointed at the police telephone number I'd taped to the wall after spotting the man from Tully's.

"Honey, it's okay." I anticipated a headache. I had the soft buzz in the ear that meant a bad one was coming on and all I needed was the catalyst. I'd forgotten today was demolition day.

"Nothing's okay! He didn't even ring the doorbell. He didn't ask permission. What's he doing here, Mom?" Toby's voice had changed ranges, rising to a high petulance.

"He and those men are going to get rid of the pavilion once and for all."

"I like our backyard the way it is."

"So do I, honey, but it's dangerous. It's a fire hazard. Someone could get hurt."

He glared at me, working his jaw. He was too mad to risk speech and spun around to leave the kitchen, hitting the doorway with his shoulder.

I stepped outside into a vast chalk blueprint sketched all over my driveway. Russell was bent over the finishing touches. I frowned and tried to make sense of the scrawled yellow diagrams. A rendition of my pavilion had a big red X through the middle. Wavy lines ran on either side of it.

"Polly, this is Augustine and these are the three brothers."

Augustine and the three brothers sparkled in the sun. Even though I'd beaten my scare alone, I'd noticed a new love of commotion since that man and that car with my name on it had turned up. I didn't mind their presence one bit. The brothers were dressed in white undershirts and wide cotton pants that slapped their legs in the breeze. Augustine wore a necktie and a Stetson. His white shirt had the sleeves rolled up above his biceps.

"This is coming down." Russell pointed at the rendition of my pavilion. "From that busted shingle roof to those cracked concrete slabs. This old mess is coming out to make way for the new."

I fought my headache off at the pass. It had started at the base of my skull, the pounding which would put me completely out of commission if I let it. I wouldn't let it. I would corner it there with enough concentration. Headaches were just as manageable as fear.

Granny Settle came out of the garage and took a slice of lemon from her overalls. She offered a slice to Augustine and the brothers. Augustine covered his heart with his hat and looked off into the tangle of telephone wires and rubber tree limbs that marked the end of my property; I supposed that meant no. She began to chew on that lemon, her head studying the chalk blueprint at a cocky angle.

"What do you think of our plan, Mrs. Settle?" Oh, Russell. He was wearing his baseball cap backward and my grandmother narrowed her eyes to study him. Her reply was slow and steady, issued in the tired tone she used to address very small children, too small to be of any real interest.

"What plan would you be speaking of?"

"I've finally talked Polly into letting me get rid of this rickety old eyesore."

"And what are you putting up in its place?"

"Granny, we thought—"

"—I didn't ask you, Polly Ann. I'm asking this gentleman what he's planning to build, since he's aiming to tear down what's already here."

"Matter of fact, Mrs. Settle, we hadn't really gotten that far. You could say we're just in phase one."

"If it was me paying for work to be done, I'd make sure I had myself a phase two."

Was he paying for this? He reached out to touch her arm, describing his vision, now that she mentioned it, of phase two, but she pulled away before his hand brushed her elbow. I had cornered my headache. It was only operating in one spot now. I stared at the pavilion, disturbed and delighted as always by its odd outgrowths and fierce, wrecked shape. It belonged to this backyard as much as it belonged to me. And to Tom. We'd spent our first night as property owners not inside the house, but under its tumbledown roof. The cement floor hadn't buckled back then. We'd slept perfectly well by the light of the moon, feeling protected as children. As our own children, the children we designed that very night in whispers under a pile of army surplus blankets. One boy, one girl. Your eyes, my hair. Oh, God, what if they get my teeth and your allergies.

"Polly Ann! Where are you?"

"Here." We'd had those children. That night was years ago. Russell turned his baseball cap around the right way and he folded his arms over his chest. He scratched his elbow and smiled at me. Probably nobody else would have noticed, it happened that fast.

"What do you say?"

What could I say? This was a good, pragmatic decision and I didn't care what he was or wasn't paying these workers. "Yes, do it."

Her eyes darkened and settled on the garage. I thought of the stepladder of shapes that took up a corner of the garage. I'd long understood that Granny Settle's strange freight was strictly off limits and my curiosity about it had waned until now. Did she fear Russell's team would turn on the garage and whatever she'd hauled out to California?

I looked at my house, the things I hadn't added to the list for the handyman. A rusty gutter hung at a crazy slant along the back of the house. One good rainstorm would bring it clattering down. Toby stood in his window watching. Finally something daunted him. He didn't dare tangle with Russell, let alone the four men he'd brought along today.

"Ready, boys." Russell's smile was frank now, right there in the open for everyone to see. He'd gotten what he wanted all along. I ran my hand underneath my hair and looked up at his balcony.

Augustine loosened his necktie and put his fingers to his lips and let out an ear-splitting whistle. They lifted lariats from a mound of tools and burlap sacks lying all over the grass and positioned themselves in front of the four posts that supported the sagging pavilion.

Augustine led off, twirling his lariat ceremoniously over his head and waiting for each of the brothers to fall in. One by one, each man joined the movement, whipping the air into swirling sounds overhead. Just as the last brother joined them, completing two or three circles with the others, Augustine called out.

"Now!"

The ropes sliced through space and fell exactly on top of each post. In a second, the ropes were taut, the men leaning back with heels dug into the soil and teeth bared. I imagined the stiff-backed jolt of the longhorn as the ropes fell. Forget stampedes and drownings. How had those animals survived round-up day on the range and, later, roping exhibitions in Granny Settle's penny-ante rodeo?

Russell came to stand next to me and I was glad he was there. What was the shallow platform to me? Nothing but shattered concrete and a few memories. It was a wonder earthquakes and aftershocks hadn't done it in already. I thought about asking the men to be careful of the little turrets on top of the posts, but decided not to. They were silly and out of fashion. The ropes pulled tighter and tighter and one of the brothers shouted a Spanish word I couldn't understand. I stared at their backs and arms, perfectly brown and muscled under the sun. It made me ashamed for sports club memberships the world over. It made me ashamed for Tom, for how he spent all his energies, his year after year after year. This was how we were meant to get strength and what we'd done instead seemed a frail substitute. Could any of those guys at the gym pull down a building? Lat pulldowns, however faithfully performed, could never lead to this more honorable effort.

Augustine's post was the first to fall. Another brother, so encouraged, gave his rope a hard yank and with that a second post was pulled from under the cracked and shaking shingles.

The last posts slid out simultaneously and the whole thing shattered and collapsed with a great groan. A cloud of dust and dirt lifted above the wreck and drifted over us and rosy heads of cosmos. Lavender spikes were spectators to the whole dismal mess. They seemed to droop, but maybe I imagined that. I looked at my watch. It was noon in Granite, but only ten o'clock here. It had taken six minutes to sink my pleasure ship. I sniffed at the dust and Russell handed me a crisp white handkerchief. I blew my nose and stuffed it in a back pocket.

"Thanks. I'll wash this and give it back."

His eyes were shaded by the baseball cap. That smile returned.

"Keep it."

That's what my mother had said, in that little-girl voice she had long outgrown. Keep it. She'd nattered on afterward about how he would always have her crimson red scarf, downpour or no downpour, girlfriends or no girlfriends, and nothing could change the little bit of her she had given to Johnny Day. I watched as Russell's smile disappeared.

"What is this, Polly?"

Toby was hanging around in the doorway, whistling and watching his father from a safe distance. Had he spelled things out on the phone or just told Lily's replacement it was an emergency, that he needed his father right away? Tom had on new sunglasses—they looked indestructible. He didn't look at Russell or at me, he looked straight ahead at the rubble and the dust.

"Whose idea was this?"

I waited a beat. "Mine."

Nobody spoke, but Tom seemed to be listening to something. He shook his head, as if he disagreed with whatever it was he heard. He took off his sunglasses and began carefully polishing each lens. They left deep red dents on either side of his nose. When Russell spoke, he glanced up in surprise, he seemed to have just noticed Russell was standing there.

"Tom, I'll be straight with you."

"Shoo!" Granny Settle snorted and slapped at a fat black bee.

Russell cleared his throat and started again. "I encouraged Polly to go ahead with this. I've seen too many expensive lawsuits that could have been avoided."

"Lawsuits over what?"

"Personal injury. That pavilion was an accident waiting to happen."

The dark glasses were back in place. The longer I looked at them, the more it seemed they were made for Tom's face. Pretty soon I probably wouldn't be able to recognize him without them.

"And I suppose I'll be getting a bill for this."

"Oh, no. This is on me."

Granny Settle backed away, humming "The Tennessee Waltz" under her breath. I heard the familiar lyrics to the song in my head: *I was dancing with my baby to the Tennessee Waltz.* She started inspecting the mess for herself, with the tip of her shoe or a loose board she pulled from the top of the pile. She must have thought she could salvage something.

"Big of you. You pay for the permit, too?"

"Tom."

His hands were in his pocket and if they weren't, I wondered where else they would have been. I'd watched my father's dogs enough times to know exactly when ragged growls erupted into snapping jaws and torn flesh. Tom started to shift his weight back and forth, jiggle his keys.

"Stay out of this, Polly."

Russell tugged on the brim of his baseball cap. "I was looking to do your family a favor, okay? In my opinion, you had a dangerous situation going on here—"

"—have a dangerous situation, if I'm not wrong. You just brought up lawsuits, do you carry workman's comp for these guys? Because I don't and yet they're working on my property, Russell."

"Look." That conciliatory tone was the worst one to use with Tom. He always got it mixed up with being patronized. "You may have a point."

"I have several."

"Maybe I acted without thinking. But you're not getting a bill for anything, Tom. These guys owe me and they're working it off this way. No, I didn't get a permit from the city. And, no, I don't carry workman's comp for these guys and if you've got a real problem with that, why don't we talk privately for a minute?"

"Good idea."

They walked down to the end of the driveway and I watched as Tom paced and Russell talked, drawing wide circles in the air with one hand. As long as Tom kept moving, things would even out. It was when he stopped that everything threatened to explode. Tom was acting the way he did in high school, right before a key game, and I didn't like the way he had of not looking Russell directly in the eye. It meant he was focused on something, what I didn't know, and he was holding himself in that strange, intense contraction I hadn't seen for years. Russell looked out of place on the driveway, unremarkable as a drifter whose face you wouldn't recognize tomorrow. Even though he was a bigger man than Tom, he didn't look it now. I was probably looking pretty forgettable myself, staring at the two of them with a slack jaw. I turned my attention back to what was real, what I could hear and see directly.

The brothers set upon the concrete with mallets. I wondered how much those heavy heads weighed. They crashed onto the concrete and sent quivers along the flesh of the brothers' arms and along mine. I had envisioned jackhammers, at the very least. I never dreamed tearing something down could be so simple. I grinned and thought of one more simple thing.

"Wildflowers in a can."

"Say what?" Granny Settle stabbed something into her bun.

"We're going to have so much space. We could do a real lawn, an old-fashioned lawn where we could string up a volleyball net or we could forget grass altogether and have a rock garden. We could always work the soil and plant those wildflower seeds that come in a can."

"That's just the trouble, if you ask me. You people live too much in your cans and your jars. I say we go with corn."

"Babe's right."

I could hear the truck start up in the driveway. Russell was backing it up slowly, paying more attention to my lawn than the hedge we shared. He looked younger than ever as he peered over his shoulder.

"I say we go with corn. Doesn't it take about seventy-five days to mature?" Tom watched Russell as he spoke.

"If conditions are good."

"Conditions are good." Whatever Tom had arranged at the bottom of the driveway certainly seemed to suit him. *We* go with corn. What did that mean?

"Just a minute. Who's going to harvest the corn? It doesn't just take care of itself." How well I knew that. Granny Settle's kitchen garden had been my responsibility as a kid, my chore and my pleasure at day's end. I used to eat it raw, without waiting for boiling water. As soon as I was shrewd enough, I enlisted others to help me pluck the ears when they were ready and search for sow bugs underneath the silky leaves. Whoever helped me work the garden got to keep half of what they collected. Tom had begged off with summer jobs of his own. Why the belated interest?

"Is this about lost youth?"

"They're not lost. But it wouldn't hurt them to take care of something besides themselves. Working a patch of corn might be good for them, Polly. Look out." He whistled contentedly as Russell hopped out of the truck, his face looking tight and pinched as he slid on work gloves. Augustine stared at him for a minute, then handed him a shovel.

"You got yourself one hell of a neighbor, Polly."

"Tom, what's going on?"

"Nothing, now that I understand what he's up to." Tom's sunglasses turned toward the balcony. "He just wants to clean up this site so he can sell his terrific house and his terrific view. He was hoping he could talk you into waterfalls and vistas. He's gonna get a view all right. Of some Okies and their patch of corn."

"I'm not so sure I like this idea."

He took those sunglasses off and when he did, I saw exactly what I was getting. It had nothing to do with fancy landscaping.

"You managed this whole thing without consulting me. If Toby hadn't called me this morning yelling and screaming, I wouldn't have known for days. Would you have just mentioned this little detail in passing?" He bit down on the stem of his sunglasses. They'd wind up like all the others, with little bite marks nicking the surface.

"Any other little details you keep to yourself, Polly?"

I didn't like how he looked at me. He wasn't about to get an answer from me, with that look on his face.

"I think I ought to have a vote here, Polly, and I vote for corn. Bye, Babe."

He bent down and kissed my grandmother's cheek. He looked at me and scratched the corner of his mouth. "I'll be back day after tomorrow, Polly. Toby's got my number."

It must have been fallout from that guy from Tully's, but for a very solid second, an ultimatum felt good. Even an ultimatum as simple in its significance as a row of corn.

"Toby yelled and screamed on the phone?"

"Yeah."

"And then what?" They must have talked for a long time, gone from one subject to another. What other things did Toby talk about to his dad?

"Then I canceled an appointment, spent about fifteen minutes looking for my keys and drove over as soon as I found them. Then this."

His words meant the whole dire scene. Well, demolition was dire, but who cared, if what followed was better, more beautiful, safer? I can live with it, I wanted to yell at him and didn't.

· · ·

The work went on most of the afternoon, the crash of stone and cement echoing on the metal floor of the truck. I ran food and drinks out at intervals and found Augustine the most voluble of all the workers. He talked about helping his mother plant beans in Mexico over his Christmas holiday. He showed me a scar on his neck he'd gotten diving for abalone. It was Russell who worked in angry or thoughtful silence, I couldn't tell which since he wasn't talking to me. And Russell who lingered after the truck carried away its load for the third and last time.

"Well, looks like that's about it."

"I should have done that a long time ago. Thank you."

I knew he was lonely in his Mediterranean-style villa and, if I let him, Russell would be in my house all the time, listening to the kids carry on or the whir of my grandmother's sewing machine or any of the general din that seemed to start where there were pots and pans. A bachelor's house probably didn't have a decent human hum, but that wasn't my problem. The way I felt now, if I had one more thing to worry about, I would splinter into five million pieces. Little bits of Polly Harrison would be found all over Los Angeles.

"Tell me something, Polly."

"What's that?"

"Were you high school sweethearts?"

"Yup."

"Knew it. I fucking knew that."

We stood a little longer looking at the ravaged, empty space. Then I thanked him one more time and went inside to look for a little company, a bit of conversation. Everybody's door was shut. No radio played and the television wasn't turned on. For a desperate second, I felt like Russell, starving to death for a healthy dose of noise.

Twenty-two

*T*wo days later I found Russell standing on my front porch, right there next to dirty baseball cleats and a fern crying out for water. He barely looked up from the newspaper he was reading when I pulled up. I wondered if looking so casual was a struggle for him. He'd been in the sun too long, even the tops of his earlobes were sunburned and peeling. As soon as I saw him, my heart did that funny little thing. It was either a double beat or a missed beat. Either way, it fluttered uncomfortably in my chest.

"Did the kids hear the bell?"

"Your son's not too eager to see me at the moment."

"You came here to see Toby?"

"Yeah and that other kid. That buddy of his with the Coke-bottle glasses. What's his name?"

"Stewart. Stewart! Toby! Why don't you guys open the door?"

The window was open a crack and I knew they could hear me, wherever they were. I listed to myself what I usually found lying all over the entrance as I slid the key into the lock. Dirty socks were de rigueur, then there would be one backpack certainly and perhaps two right in front of the door blocking the way. The kitchen was routinely disastrous at this hour. Crumbs and knives smeared with mustard or jam, dirty dishes that only occasionally landed in the sink. But Russell had lived with nephews for a while and probably knew it all by heart. Pushing open my door was just as tricky as pushing open Tully's. I gasped as we stepped over the threshold. The odor was unbearable.

"Oh, God. There must be a plumbing problem or something."

He looked pretty composed despite the noxious smell.

"Kate! Toby! What's going on here?"

The living room was empty and there was no mess on the coffee table, no grass-stained socks in the foyer. The doors to the dining room were standing open and the edges of Granny Settle's bedspread were tucked tight as a box. I reached for Russell's hand instinctively.

"My house is too quiet. Something's wrong."

"Nothing's wrong. They're hiding from me. Come on."

"What did they do?"

"I'll let them tell you their side of the story first."

He led me down my own hall. He was the kind of guy who took charge of things immediately. No confusion about roles here. Even though it was my house, he was taking the lead. Maybe this visit would do it. Maybe Russell would finally stick. Maybe I would start dreaming about him, days and nights, thinking of him when a certain song played on the radio or, better still, watching him stride right into the lyrics I wrote myself. The smell thickened the closer we moved to the back of the house. We were walking down the middle of my mother's old floor runner, the one she'd had draped over the stairs in our Granite house forever. It was a deep red field of birds and beasts, woven together as if a cardinal perched on the back of a lamb was a natural marriage. I studied the prints in the hall, pulling on Russell's hand as we walked. The flea market finds usually pleased me, but not now. Those gilded frames were a serious mistake. Maybe that smell was toxic . . . I felt ready to keel over.

"You let him stick this on the door?"

A lewd sticker for Trashy Lingerie now graced Toby's door. Everything was going to hell. Had it happened when I blinked, while I slept, as I idled at a red light in a car that children tarred and feathered every Halloween? Exactly how long had it taken? Years or six and a half minutes, as an ugly pavilion sunk to ground zero? Russell was already knocking, testing the lock. He jiggled the knob hard and knocked again. "Hey, open up in there." Maybe he thought a strong male voice would do it. I had an unfortunate moment imagining him doing that door-breaking routine you saw in old movies. That familiar scene where to save a lady the guy puts his shoulder to a locked door and bursts into the room. It always seemed silly and painful to me, plus I didn't think it would work.

"Let's try Kate's room." I rapped hard. No answer. "Kate."

Luckily there was no lock on Kate's door. She was under a quilt and a Walkman with her nose in a book. The end of her nose was pinched together by a set of orange rubber plugs. I rapped gently on the back of her book and she looked up.

She eased the headsets off and left the plugs where they were. Her voice was soft. Unfortunately, not soft enough.

"Oh, so you let him in."

"Kate, where are your manners?"

"You *told* us never to open the door to strangers. We were just doing what you *told* us."

"Since when is Russell a stranger?"

"Ask him. Be sure and ask him what he called Toby."

"How about calling off the war, Kate? Truce?" Russell's voice sounded so formal.

He stuck out his hand and she looked as if it were dipped in something unspeakable. She buried her own hands under that quilt.

"Up to you. Want to know what that smell is, I bet."

"Yes! And where it's coming from. I had a terrible thought. That maybe you and Toby were— "

"Dead? Stinking up the house by decomposing? Sorry to disappoint you."

"I don't want to wait for Toby's side of the story."

"Toby or Hector?"

"Or 'little bastard'?" Kate pulled the quilt up to her chin, countering Russell's question with one of her own.

"You two tell me what happened."

I looked at my daughter, then at my neighbor or friend or whatever he was to me. "I'm very confused."

Russell's face now matched his earlobes. He wasn't peeling, but he was bright red. "Your son and his friend decided to go into the house-painting business. I caught them just as they were putting on the finishing touches. Toby tagged my house and his nom de plume is Hector."

I spotted a suitcase in the corner. No, two suitcases. There was a smaller one, mine, standing right in back of her big Samsonite.

"What you smell is fertilizer and that's my stuff. I'm going to Dad's for a while."

The mind is so tricky. Maybe it wasn't such a bad thing to stop thinking every now and then. I was numb from head to toe. Not a single thing occurred to me right then, no panic, no flying off the handle. I was dumb and slow as a slug.

"For how long?"

"I don't know. But I'm not staying in this asylum a day longer than I have to."

Russell had wandered to the window and was peeping through the slats in her closed blinds.

"That grandmother of yours is too much."

I joined him at the window. Augustine was working the raw earth, tilling it with a machine that churned it up and tore it into hefty blocks of soil. The three brothers followed, grinding the clay down with simpler tools. Every now and then, one of the men would stop and examine something he found, some treasure, some artifact and either stuff it carefully into a pocket or chuck it into a garbage can. They came to the edge of the fence and set their tools against the sagging wood, then carted shovels to the back of Granny Settle's truck, which held a thick, level layer of raw fertilizer. If I could have just listened to the sound of it, things would have been pleasant enough. They worked in a steady rhythm and the scrape of the shovel against the metal truck calmed my nerves. And yes, there was my grandmother stretched out in a plastic lounge chair, the kind you bought for under ten dollars at drugstores, the kind that wouldn't last a full summer. There was a straw hat covering her face and a bag of red dirt lying on top of her belly.

"What on earth is going on here?" I didn't leave the back porch to shout this and she didn't remove her hat. Russell stayed behind in the kitchen, coughing politely.

"Why that's easy, Polly. I met some nice folks who've come all the way out here from Porter."

Porter peaches. They appeared briefly in supermarkets throughout Oklahoma, signaling summer. The sizzling sun beat down on dark, muddy ponds until they receded, gradually shrinking back toward their still centers, the sticky air scorching our throats as we threw ourselves into play, whatever wet play we could create with hoses and sprinklers when ponds seemed too precious, too fragile to use. But it wasn't even that sun that meant summer had dropped down on the land. The keen flavor of the fruit rose in my mouth, sudden as sweat soaking the bangs I'd worn then to hide my forehead. The disappearance of the sweet fruit meant hope, an eventual autumn we could dream of throughout awful heat and taste just as vividly as those vanished peaches.

"That's right, a whole band of them's come out here, only now they're retired people living with family and what not and in their free time they work a little old plot of city land out by the airport. They donated this manure to our project. The smell shouldn't go on past a few days."

A familiar blend of voices chattered for a minute or two, then stopped dead. "I think I hear Toby in front."

Russell followed me back through the house. He walked so close behind me that if I'd stopped suddenly, he would have run me down. My house felt smaller with him inside.

"You know, maybe I should talk to him before you say what you need to say. Mind?"

"I'll just wait here."

He put a hand hesitantly on the kitchen table. All around him were pictures of the kids, pictures of me and Tom. He'd seen them all many times, but his interest seemed sharper today than before.

"Great."

Toby stood at the front door with mud up the side of his legs. He had leaves in his hair and tears had left a track down the left side of his face. Stewart stood beside him with his fists clenched at his side. Something bulged from Stewart's pocket.

"What's going on, guys?"

"Perhaps we should be asking you that question, Polly." Stewart glowered at me.

Who made these solemn boys anyway? How did they become such fierce little judges, so ready to damn the women who raised them? Stewart treated me the way he treated his own mother, foolish, beaten-down June. He won the right to go off from time to time like a stinkbomb because of his purported intellect. It made him difficult, according to dopey, awestruck June.

"Meaning, Stewart?"

"Meaning your son thought he was a goner so he ran out of the house to escape."

"Mom, did you hear what Russell called me?" Toby's voice was still shaky

"Yes and I also heard what you did. Did you think you wouldn't get caught? What did you think you were *doing?*"

I walked around to the driveway to check the damage myself.

HECTOR

It was scrawled way, way up, all over the side of the house, the side that faced our kitchen window, our garage and the whole miserable spectacle that was our life at the moment. My life. I stroked my shoulder; it was sore for some reason, as sore as if I'd been lifting weights in some weird spasm of fitness. What did I think *I* was doing? I stared up at the balcony, thinking they could have shimmied up there, for a look inside since they were so adept at high-wire acts. They could have done that anytime. Maybe they had, maybe Toby had, on a day when I was least expecting it. HECTOR, HECTOR, HECTOR! It scrambled all over the side of Russell's house, wildly legible in black and red paint. It screamed for attention, howling its horrible lesson about families and ignorant, ignorant love. What did I think I was doing? I didn't have any idea, no more idea about what I was doing than Toby. Or Tom. The heart can't think, it's just a poor, helpless organ and here was the black and red proof. Russell had intruded on Toby's property and he, unlikely man of the house, had struck back in stupid defense.

Stewart had gotten taller since I'd seen him last. He towered over Toby now and maybe that fostered this new protectiveness. I'd never seen it before.

"He should have left when nobody came to the door. Why did he hang around like that on your porch? Toby practically killed himself using back-yards to get to my house." Stewart reached into his pocket and brought out the rock that was making his pants bulge.

"See? We were gonna let him have it. Right on the back of the head, too."

The fear they felt had clearly overtaken the crime they'd committed. I knew Russell had raised nephews and therefore seen it all. But I wondered if they'd ever tried to stone him.

"Toby, if you were really scared you could have gone to Augustine and the brothers."

"Like he speaks Spanish, Polly."

"Granny Settle is here, for heaven's sake."

"An old woman can't fight a killer. He called him a little bastard and he was banging down the door. Toby had to come and get me."

213

They'd tagged Russell's house and run to their separate homes, lying low until Toby panicked. Hearing Russell at the door, the man of the house had tears in his eyes for the second time today. I knew it was taking every bit of self-control for him to keep calm. He gave me a little shove, for Stewart's sake, and pushed by me to his room. He stormed past Russell, who heard us from his exile in the kitchen and was just then coming around the corner.

"Toby! You could at least apologize."

He didn't say a word to Russell or to me. He made a fast retreat to his room and closed the door with a tight snap.

"It's all right, Polly. Once things settle down we'll have ourselves a workday."

"Oh, you mean like gang members?"

I felt like spanking Stewart. The silly thought didn't even make me smile. Wise guy. Wise guys.

"Would you rather I called the police? Remember, you boys hadn't quite finished your work of art when I arrived. I'm going to come and talk to your mother about this, but for now you can go home."

Russell was working hard to find the right tone; he didn't seem comfortable with the one he adopted.

"No one's there. No one's ever there."

"Go home anyway."

His eyes narrowed behind the thick glasses and he studied Russell skeptically. Then he wheeled around, tossing the rock into the hedge as he did. He mumbled something as he did.

"What?"

"Nothing."

Russell put his hand on my back. I knew he meant well, but it didn't feel right. Nothing felt right. We were too new for a moment like this. It was like releasing a fledgling in the Grand Canyon. There might be a frenzy of flapping wings and bird cries, then an optimistic up and down resembling flight. But ultimately that young bird would go down in a red-rock earth scar a mile deep and a billion years in the making.

"I'll call you later, Polly. Or should I?"

"Should you what?"

"Call you."

Russell seemed to recede, even though he hadn't gone anyplace. He looked puzzled when I didn't answer, though he gave me a very tender, very brazen kiss goodbye. Maybe he thought this incident meant the two of us had taken some kind of weird step forward. I wanted to crawl inside Kate's blanket and join her in obliterating the senses. No peaches, no sweet, sweating long-gone summer. Nose plugs, earphones . . . that was the way to go. It was the first time we'd kissed since I'd been to his house for that lunch.

"That's right. Your soil's pitiful and I'm fixing to get it back into shape."

She was washing her hands and her arms. They were like knotted bundles of sticks, the way the cords stood out under her flesh. She scrubbed hard at her forearms at the utility sink and then used my kitchen sponge on her elbows.

"Used to use cow chips back in Granite. Lucky I had a tetanus shot before I left. Why think of it . . . I didn't have any idea about what I was going to do before I did it. God's at work in the world all right, Polly Ann."

She started singing as she rubbed her arms with a pink hand towel. An old sad tune about the sun going down. How it set so low in the sky, a little boy thought it drowned in the river and there would be no more heat to warm the earth. I'd never asked her where she got all those songs and broken melodies, but I'd heard them all my life.

"Children are leaving, I expect."

I was cutting onions, weeping openly over a gouged-out wooden board. It was the first time I'd welcomed the chore. Onions beat back the raunchy smell in my house. Which, God help Polly Harrison, I found I was getting used to.

"I expect they'll be staying with Tom for a time."

"When did they tell you?"

"Didn't. I've been seeing it come."

I tipped my head up so the tears could just slide out without a fuss. One had trembled on the tip of my nose before falling with a plop. Granny Settle stood at the back door, looking outside.

"Now it's not like me to ask a question that could make a person uncomfortable."

"No, that was never your style."

"Because most things I generally sort out myself."

"Yep." I scraped the knife over the top of the board and some of the onions missed the pan, landing all over my bare feet.

"But one thing I never could figure was why it is exactly Tom's not living here. Polly, he's like one of my own. It pains me to see him not living where he ought to be living."

What a smelly day it had been. What a hard smelly day. What a successful single parent I was not with onions on my feet and my grandmother there, not leaving until she had turned my garden into some cornfield she'd imagined in a senile daydream. I thought of this week's *Cosmopolitan* with a roar inside my throat and grabbed the handle of the knife. Smiling from the protection of the glossy cover was a full-bosomed, cleavaged creature with big hair grinning about "Sex After Forty" and "Satisfy His Appetite with Your Own . . . Secret Recipes!" I looked up at Russell's house through the window. I had even ruined that recipe, staggering next door for a little of Russell's bouillabaisse, which now seemed to have spilled all over my lap. Everything was so messy. My kitchen, even my dining room. Was I supposed to eat cramped at my kitchen table for the rest of my life? Maybe my mother was right. I couldn't have a decent dinner party with my grandmother here! Dinner parties for ten or twenty or two, romantic dinner parties with candles, fine china, food that fainted in your mouth . . . it was all completely out of the question. My dining room had become as disorienting as the one I remembered in Granite, piled high with Johnny Day bulletins and my mother licking stamps, turning her head to stare at me with scary, glinting eyes. I stabbed the cutting board with the knife and spun around to face my granny.

"Tom's not here because he was carrying on with another woman and I caught them red-handed."

Her hands were burrowing in deep pockets. I had no idea what they would pull out next, a bag of dirt or a sweet.

"When?"

"About eight months ago."

"So he's been gone eight months on account of stepping out on you and the children."

"On me."

"When a man is unfaithful, it's both." She weighed the sentence, her fingers fishing wildly for something. "All right, then. As I see it, it's time Tom came home."

The roar in my throat hadn't gone away and I wondered if it ever would. Maybe I wasn't meant to be gracious Polly Ann with golden hair. Maybe I was a wild woman toting a Winchester loaded with words.

"Granny Settle?"

"I'm listening."

"I think your visit has come to an end."

She turned away from the window and found what she was hunting for. She frowned as she unwrapped the gooey candy and popped it in her mouth.

"It won't be long." Her mouth was full of chocolate sop and it was hard to understand her. "That thief called me this morning."

"Thief?"

"Bobby Denario. She didn't have the courage to get on the phone. So he was the one told me about the final heist. Twenty thousand dollars for my land. Chickenshit chickenfeed's more like it. Those two are closing in on me."

I turned around to find both kids standing in the doorway. Their faces were wet and red as the day they were born. Babies were made to protect and cherish, just like the children and adults they would become.

"How long have you been standing there?"

"A long time, Mom."

"Come here. God, come here."

I found out my arms could get around both of them if I stood a certain way. It was night. Finally it was night and I held them both until the darkness swallowed us all.

Twenty-three

I helped Toby pack his things. I studied what he chose to take and what he chose to leave behind, seeing much more laid out on his bed than just a radio and some underwear, an array of T-shirts that suddenly looked tattered to me. What kind of a mother would let her son dress like that? His baseball card collection, the basketball that Magic had once held in his immense hands and signed, slingshots and Swiss Army knives, the only weaponry he was permitted . . . it all stayed in the big metal box in his closet. I hung around his room all morning, getting underfoot, wondering whether he chose to leave such terribly important things in his room to comfort me. I finally got up off his bed to leave for Pomona. Johnny Day would be signing autographs at two and I didn't want to be late.

"You're leaving now?"

"Got to. Hey, I'm following your advice. Half the day writing songs, half the day trying to sell them. You should be flattered."

He tossed a baseball into the air and snapped at it with a mitt, then let it roll to the ground. "Yeah, well. Good luck."

"Thank you, honey."

"Here, take this. Maybe he likes baseball."

I didn't know much about those cards, but the careful way he scooped this one up indicated its value. His generosity always shocked me. It was sudden, sometimes excessive and it wasn't a trait that came from me. Strangeness has shivered down my back as I've watched Toby empty his pockets to a street musician or hand over the very last ice cream sandwich to a friend. Toby or Tom? Tom or Toby? Here, take it, Tom had said when he was Toby's age, handing me the Tootsie Pop at that crucial moment when the red sheen gave way to the hidden chocolate core, the very point of all that hard candy. And I had taken it all right, without any ambivalence at all. Had I thanked him? Had that stringy sun-browned kid who was me even thanked him?

"Thank you, honey. This just may work."

I reached for him, but he dodged my arms and tossed his head back, his hair all tangled up with his eyelashes.

"You need a haircut. Get your dad to take you."

"How long am I staying there anyway?"

I didn't want to talk about it. If I talked about change, developed an attitude and a plan to manage it, it might harden into permanence.

"Camp's coming up and you should spend as much time with your dad as you can."

"He's always traveling."

"He's slowing down for the next month so he can be with you."

"Are you doing this because of *him?*" He tipped his head due south.

"Because of Russell?"

"Who else would I be talking about? Because if you think this is punishment for what I did to his house, it's not gonna work. I'm gonna still hate him. I'm gonna still think he's a creep who stares through the bushes at us."

"Toby, this has nothing to do with that. You did something foolish and something wrong, but I would never send you away to punish you."

"That's what you did to Dad."

I looked at that locked metal box, the sharp chiseled edges and padlock that secured just about everything my son owned to defend himself.

"What are you doing?"

I was putting that box on a high shelf, that's what I was doing. The corners were really unforgiving and if someone stumbled around in here with the lights off . . . I was saving shins, that's what I was doing, mine and everybody else's. "Somebody could clobber themselves on this thing. I'll call you tonight to make sure you guys are settled in."

· · ·

I found my way to the county fairgrounds in Pomona with no problem. Traffic was light on the freeways even when I reached the exit I needed. I followed an aged Volkswagen van through the gates to the parking lot, latching on to those plates from Nebraska even after we got inside. A bright orange van that had traveled the world would be easier to find in the enormous graveled lot than my squat Pacer. Memorabilia from trips decorated the van and I tried to imagine the drives to Ottawa, Tucson and Charleston as I pulled in alongside them. Assorted children dressed in shorts and tank tops tumbled out the back. I stared at the mother who hopped down, tucking her blouse into a peasant skirt and adjusting the belt. Two clean, polished teenage girls were the last to emerge from that miracle van. No one was sullen or fighting and they must have all listened to country music, for there were no manacles in sight. I followed them inside, slightly spellbound, and bought a Fanfest program and my entry ticket, then sat down on the edge of a low wall. What exactly was "California's Premier Country Lifestyle Event"? I tried to find an answer by leafing through the glossy magazine filled with ads for Western clothing and accessories, dance clubs and steakhouses, and feature articles about established country singers or "rising new stars." The fan festival was just that. A fairground event with continuous country music, dance contests and autograph booths with celebrity signings throughout the three-day affair. I smelled popcorn and cotton candy, the elements that always signaled a real jamboree.

Johnny Day was signing at two. That was all I had to remember. Johnny Day was my job, nothing else. I shook my head. That was why I had come in the first place, to hand him my name, my connection to him and his past, followed by the sweetest gift of all—my song lyrics. It wasn't complicated and yet it was. I sat surrounded by so much that had never, ever changed even though I was in California. This was California, wasn't it? And I was a forty-year-old woman, wasn't I? Not a girl, mysteriously gliding along on high heels, my arm brushing Tom's inside a crowd that had grown way beyond what Granite could provide. Towns all along that stretch of Oklahoma highway were starved not for food, not for drink, but for entertainment. Oh, Lord, someplace to go! Someplace where we could stare and be stared at, drink beer furtively from paper cups because we were underage at any age back there. Too young, Tom and I were always too young. But not at the fair, not at the county fair. It was a place to gobble corn dogs and wear short shorts, yelping at the red-hot vinyl seats and loving that burn which was so close to another burn, a different burn I might feel driving back home over dark, empty roads, that burn I might feel and give in to. My mother didn't matter, my father didn't matter, their wars and their worries. What mattered most was that burn I felt in a hundred ways as I lined up for it all: roller coasters and ferris wheels, candy apples, shoes without a strap in the back, shoes that showed everything, shoes that stayed on my feet through some miracle of construction as we watched taut, blue-ribbon pigs and people we'd never seen before and would surely never see again, so we could laugh and point and think hard about that long drive home.

"Ma'am?"

I scowled at the man dragging me back to the present, dressed in a chef's white hat and apron, looking as if he'd escaped from a backyard barbecue.

"Care for a chili sample?"

He held a little white cup out to me and I noticed his stand for the first time. Long, silver handles and stacks of paper boats stood ready to serve the masses.

"It's extra spicy."

I downed the chili and made appreciative noises, then moved on to find the Wherehouse Building, the spot where Johnny would be signing in about twenty minutes. I squared my shoulders and made my way toward the crowded building named after the chain of music and video stores.

"Two thousand people waited to get his autograph. Do you believe it?"

"I was one of them! I stood for hours to get this. Tim McGraw is such a honey."

A couple of women leaned against the front of the building, fanning their faces in the shade. One woman cradled a cowboy hat, looking down at a signature scrawled on the brim, and the other hugged a guitar, stroking the shoulder strap with one hand as if it were a pet or a fitful child. What kind of crowd would Johnny Day draw? A line curled around the outside of the building and I asked a man in a wheelchair what he was waiting to see. He looked as if I was speaking a foreign language so I bent my knees, lowering myself a bit, and repeated the question. Wrong move.

"I'm not deaf. I'm dumbfounded. You asking if you can cut in line?"

"Mr. Cowl and I haven't moved from this spot for over an hour."

Mr. Cowl's nurse looked me up and down.

"I just want to make sure I line up for the right person."

"If Johnny Day's your man, you're in the right place." This comment came from someone closer to the door. A woman in a white crop top and white leather skirt called out at the front of the line, but there was no camaraderie in her voice. The family reunion at the Williamson had scattered to the winds.

I followed the line around the building, the leather pouch growing heavier. I gave up counting at three hundred and found another entrance to the building near the back. The Wherehouse Building held more than the promise of an autograph from Johnny Day. I wandered the aisles, studying contest requirements to win a free living trust, stopping at a booth selling curly ponytails. Several people tried them on as I watched, settling them onto the top of a French twist or trying them out with a baseball cap. Guitars were for sale and leather boots and belts, everything in the building sported a six-inch fringe. An announcement was preceded by a few seconds of ear-shattering static.

"Whoa! Sorry, folks. Johnny Day will be signing autographs at booth A, located in the southwest corner of the building. Johnny Day in five minutes, ladies and gentlemen."

Signs soundlessly shouted their news along the center aisle: FAST GUN! THE SINGING COWBOY. SANDY STORM—NO ONE CAN STOP THE STORM. I gritted my teeth and headed down that aisle, transfixed by the spectacle there. Aspiring singers and songwriters rented space here and the further I wandered, the harder it was to speak or smile at the hopeful faces. The building was a high-ceilinged cavern, but by the time I reached Ardell Blithe, the walls seemed to be squeezing toward me. Ardell was losing one set of false eyelashes, but it didn't disturb her vision. Her big green eyes were fixed on my leather pouch.

"Are you an agent?"

"Sorry, I'm not."

She sighed and smiled at me, then handed me her mailing list, while I fished around for a pen. There was one other signature.

"Here, this writes good. Care to listen to my demo tape?"

I put the earphones on. Ardell's voice was high and pure and her songs ran continuously, with no beginning and no end. It was a lovely voice, singing about it being the "prime time for love."

"Is this your first time at Fanfest?"

Ardell offered me a single rose, barely alive thanks to a plastic tube of water attached at one end. She laughed and her voice dropped to a stagey whisper. "Heavens no. I've been at it for years, even when they had it down in Nashville. You do whatcha gotta do."

I thanked her for the rose and promised to look her up if I ever got to

Needles. I hurried toward booth A, where an assembly line of people had begun moving past Johnny Day. I stood behind a stand that sold videotapes on training young horses. Brochures promised foolproof reining and performance tips and I leafed through them, feigning interest. It was a perfect lookout: Johnny glowed resplendent in his red and gold uniform. Fans merely wanting to peek at him were kept constantly moving and a second line forked to the left. Those were the people wanting a photo or signature. Flashbulbs kept the area bright and three policemen worked the crowds, gently insisting the time was up. Sorry, but that's your minute, miss. I would try the blond cop who kept breaking rank to talk to a woman dazzling him with a purchase I'd watched her make. She flipped her curly platinum ponytail back and forth, pressing his arm with long fingertips. I checked my watch . . . Johnny's time was almost up.

A Fanfest official pressed his way through a curtain and put his hand on Johnny's elbow. They had a short conversation and the man took down some notes on a clipboard, then disappeared behind the same curtain. I took a deep breath and one last look at Ardell and the others for fortitude. It was either sink or swim. I had to interrupt the cop and the platinum blonde, ducking as the ponytail swung in my direction.

"Excuse me, can I speak with you a moment, officer?"

"Help you?"

"You sure can. I'm an old friend of Mr. Day's and I was wondering if you could just slip him this note while I wait here."

He walked the note over to Johnny, who was locked between two older women for a snapshot. Both women shrieked as he kissed them on the cheek. He read my note as the women backed away, then turned that huge, furry head in my direction. His hair was still wonderful. My mother and Minah had always gone on about that, how he always let it fall free, not waxing it into place like other country stars. Johnny nodded his head slowly and tucked the note in a back pocket. The cop waved me over and belligerent eyes watched me step behind the velvet rope. The signing was over and not everyone had gotten that signature or that precious photo.

"Whatzat woman doing?"

"Hey!"

I was ushered behind that curtain into a large room divided into several partitioned sections. A bucket full of suds sat next to a director's chair. I kept my attention focused there and tried not to read a terrible omen into that frothy surface. Shel Elliot had been a water lover, too, and Johnny Day felt like a last chance. Without him, lyrics would probably pile up inside drawers for the rest of my life, unsung, unrecorded. My mother's voice haunted me. You just keep on rubbing, Polly.

"You're her image."

"Mr. Day—"

"—J.D. Your mama used to call me J.D. Polly, is it?"

For a strained moment I really was Carla's girl as his eyes swept over me in a quick survey. I crossed my legs, glad I'd left the pink behind in Beverly Hills.

"Has your mama handed you the Holy Grail?" His eyes skimmed over me once more and I nudged a stray bit of hair back into place. He studied my forehead for a moment, then licked his lips. "You the new president of the Johnny Day Fan Club?"

"In a way, yes." I gamboled on from there, his comeback, the comeback we'd been waiting for and the concert at the Williamson, Randy Nelson's close encounter. Me.

"That's where I saw you then."

"Yes, that was me in the hall."

"Funny. I thought I was losing my mind that night, seeing Carla like that. Seeing you, I mean."

Johnny groaned and I thought my mother's memory was painful for just about everyone. But it wasn't actually Carla who was causing fresh pain. I watched as he slid off his boots, grunting as he bent over to pull them off. A boyish expression still graced his face, but his body belonged to an aging man. His knees creaked as he peeled off one sock at a time. He set his feet down into the pail and massaged his ankles.

"Mama's happy. I finally made Mama happy by making her believe she's in England, even though she's in the middle of Tennessee. Built her a little bitty white cottage all covered with flowers, the way they do over there. Every day I ask her how she likes Cornwall and she tells me she likes it real fine. They get to a certain age and . . . it's got so bad we sometimes find her in the pool trying to swim the Channel."

"What about Johnny Day?"

"What about him?"

"Is he happy?"

"For a while he was. Hell, for a while he was on top of the world. Ten years ago, I didn't think it got any better. You know what I mean? That was the time of my last gold record. Those boys in town were falling all over me with offers. I didn't think I'd have to sing at another county fair. I really believed I had it made. Had a beautiful wife, beautiful life. Songs came to me in my sleep. No foolin'! I'd wake up and transcribe them just the way they came to me in my dreams.

"Then something happened, haven't figured out what. But my luck just dried up, seemed like. Now I'm making deals with cereal companies to pay the upkeep on my place. I live upstairs in my own house! I turned the bottom part over to fans. Hell, this Fanfest is nothing. I find fans in my kitchen back home."

He cracked his knuckles loudly and it seemed to bring him into a new reality. He bit his lip and grunted.

"Now it's time I met you, Polly. This makes two times you've come to see me." He slid forward in his chair, his legs falling wider apart at the knee. "Why would a pretty thing like you go to all this trouble for an old coot like me?"

I lay the leather case on my knee and cleared my throat. Frankie Doray's words contained as much life as the words I held on my lap. Men just love to play. I saw they did, this one at least. I cleared my throat and began, thinking of Frankie's sage and sickening advice. Advice that was nothing more, nothing less than my mother's motto. He listened and I hoped I didn't sound as desperate as I felt.

"Hell, Polly. You're wasting your time."

"I am?" I held my eyes open wide as I could. If I blinked once, tears would come tumbling down.

"I'm used up. I'm sure you write wonderful lyrics and you're a wonderful girl, but I'm nothing but an old man singing for his supper. You heard me at that concert! You saw how I lost 'em. The minute I try to sing those damn issue songs, my people go to sleep on me. Hell, everybody's leaving me. I can't even keep a woman anymore."

It was Johnny's turn to cry. He sniffed and rubbed his nose with the back of his hand, his feet sloshing water out of the bucket.

"Lola ran off with somebody last spring. Ran off, now there's a funny way to put it. She didn't run anywhere. She walked out the door in one of those business suits newspaper reporters wear. That bitch was wearing gloves when she left me. Said she was late for an appointment." He pulled one of his feet out of the bucket with both hands and I leaned forward to look. It was covered with furious red blisters. He toweled it dry tenderly and hoisted the other one out.

"New boots, I guess."

"New heartache. I went to Europe for a change of scene. Made a point of walking everywhere to see things. Thought exhaustion and a change of scene might help me forget."

I felt so bad about his feet. I thought of the blister on the back of my heel, what I'd been trying to run from myself. I knew it didn't work and I knew how badly it hurt.

"Egypt, France, Spain. Hell, I even went to Morocco to forget her. I'm back and all I really want is for her little feet to walk through the door again."

"She'll be back. Once she remembers just who it is she's lost." I summoned up every ghost I knew. Every single one. And with the help of all assembled, I took a big leap forward into empty space. I crossed my legs one last time and leaned forward toward Johnny Day. I put my hand on top of his and squeezed gently. Carla Settle, Frankie Doray, lend me some of your bravado. I prayed to every unholy ghost in my life.

"Johnny, I want you to give me one hour." I held my hand over his. "I'm going to leave you these lyrics to read and I'm going to go write you a hit song."

His laughter rocked the thin walls of the room. "Are you now?"

"I am and I need one hour to do it. Shall I meet you here?"

"Well, that'd be just fine, Carla. You are Carla, aren't you, coming back to haunt me one more time? She used to boss me up one side of the wall and down the other. J.D. do this. J.D. do that. And now I've gotta listen to you doing the same thing."

I fled the building and put my back up against a tree to work, a cup of beer beside me. I thought of Johnny tramping up and down the cobblestoned streets of Europe, hard at work on forgetting. I knew something about the insistence of memory, the futility of obliterating the past. I spilled beer all over the paper and nervously mopped it up. I wrote and rewrote, scratching out words until a song crowded its way onto the page. I wrote hard and long, fearing that center aisle in the Wherehouse Building, the demo tapes there terrorizing me into a song to fit Johnny Day's circumstances. This song felt like a lot more than a last chance. When I finished, I placed Toby's prize baseball card on top of all those words. I would offer Johnny a guided tour of his own emotions.

> I took my troubles to a buddy
> Who had just got back from Rome

He said the way to solve my problems
Was to get away from home.
He claimed I'd find my cure
In Old Mexico or France
Put some miles on your mind, my friend,
Travelin's your only chance.

I crossed one ocean, then another
Put my feet on foreign soil
Started walking toward a monument
Until the darkness fell.
Booked myself a single room
In a fine upscale hotel
Stared across a cold white bed
Into a face I knew so well.

It took three weeks to discover
What I already knew
There's no currency to buy me
A guided tour of you.
I ran away to ruins,
I passed through golden doors
And I found out that forgetting you
Just made me love you more.

Well I'm back but I'm not better
Though I'm now a cultured man
Every culture I encountered
Welcomed one real lonely man.
If you've ever thought of coming back
If I've just once crossed your mind,
I'd wade through a dozen oceans
To try my luck a second time.

It took three weeks to discover
What I already knew

There's no currency to buy me
A guided tour of you.
I ran away to ruins,
I passed through golden doors
And I found out that forgetting you
Just made me love you more.

Twenty-four

I had promised to recap my meeting, but that wasn't really what my mother wanted. She cut me off when I began to describe how I'd cranked out those lyrics in an hour's time and the song itself, how I imagined it would affect Johnny, touching his feelings about missing Lola.

"Did he ask about me, Polly?"

I watched my grandmother through the bedroom window. She inspected something in the ground, then used the spade she held in her hand to bury it, dead or alive.

"Polly, you didn't tell him about me and Bobby, did you?"

"Why would I do that?"

I could have hinted that there was a world beyond Carla, shocking as that would have sounded to my mother, but contentiousness took too much energy from me today, so I agreed to speak in her strange foreign tongue. When my resistance was low, I slipped on her point of view for practical reasons, and my resistance, as I watched shadows select my backyard at the end of this day, felt very, very low. I could hear my grandmother singing a fruitless melody. There were no words to her song, it was just empty humming.

"Because part of Johnny Day never wanted to believe I was a married woman. Not then, not now. I took off my wedding ring when I had dinner with him. I took off my wedding ring and drove straight over to . . ."

She described her evening with Johnny after he'd played Palm Springs and I asked why she hadn't told him about her songwriting daughter. Why did Carla's girl come as such a surprise to the singer?

"We just had so much old business to cover. Why, time got away and . . ."

And why hadn't Johnny mentioned their dinner together to me? I thought of everything that old business might incorporate. I wondered when my mother slipped off her wedding ring, the exact moment that all those carats tumbled into a black velvet handbag. All those carats she'd never had in Granite.

"And did Bobby order take-out food?"

I could hear grinding in that long pause. She was getting ready to move to a different speed, shifting like the gears of the crabby old trucks my dad repaired.

"Ready or not, here we come."

"What is that supposed to mean?"

"That Bobby and I are driving out to get your grandmother in a few weeks. She knows."

"She hasn't mentioned it to me."

"She's in denial. Believe me, Polly, she knows. We are getting ready to set you free."

I considered my freedom once we got off the phone, the freedom my mother assumed she was about to offer. Freedom was already here, stalking my empty house. My nearly empty house. I kept the doors to the children's rooms closed. I had what I thought I wanted all along, quiet, tidy rooms that were the mark of an orderly world. Music no longer blared, rude lyrics no longer insinuated a dark and gnarled landscape where angry children roamed. But the new neatness was silent and bare. I found myself longing for fallen chewing gum wrappers or my missing hairbrush, the one I would find on the floor in Kate's room. No, everything from makeup to mail was exactly where I left it. Granny Settle stuck closer and closer to her dining room encampment and so many locked doors made a grim and lightless house. I opened things up again, pretending as I did I would see Kate with the phone cord wrapped around her wrist three times or Toby lying on his bed, sliding dirty shoes off the side as he heard my footsteps coming down the hall. I didn't see either of those things and I missed both desperately, as cheery, unconvincing phone calls flew back and forth between Tom's home and mine.

• • •

I was reading a book and felt someone breathing above me. Granny Settle held a straw market basket in one hand and a battered vinyl pocketbook in the other. She looked as self-conscious as a kid about to break curfew.

"Going out?"

"The Porter people are coming for me."

"What's in the straw basket?"

"My things. They don't like to drive after it gets dark."

"So you're having a sleepover."

She tested a window lock, then scowled at me as a horn blared out front. "You'll be all right here alone?"

"No problem." At my age I hoped it wasn't a problem.

She put her hand over her stomach and pushed. "I suppose I'll go, then."

"Have a wonderful time."

She looked as unconvinced as I felt. I heard her footsteps on the sidewalk. She went a little ways and stopped, then the steps sounded again on the brick, growing fainter and fainter.

A house to myself. What I'd longed for since Granny Settle had arrived, two and a half months ago. I turned several pages of the book, a biography I'd picked up in a used-book sale, and realized I couldn't keep my mind on Hank Williams right then. I looked at my watch. I didn't feel like calling Beth or making any kind of plan at all.

I'd just be planless. I would just revel in having no particular thing on my mind. A light meal that I would eat in front of the television, paying no attention to the time. That in itself would be new. I would do whatever I didn't do ordinarily.

The top shelf of the refrigerator was tragic. There was expired milk and a little bit of coffee, just enough for tomorrow morning. Granny Settle's things were arranged in a tight little group on the second shelf. Her honey and dates, mysterious grains and seeds, her bran and some barbecue sauce with the label peeled off made the notion of dinner melancholy. There were two brown eggs, that was good. So I would scramble them, no, I'd do an omelet.

I thought I heard the cat in the backyard. He sometimes turned up there this time of the evening, betwixt and between our two houses. I needed to turn the back porch light on anyway, the one Russell kept insisting I change to a motion detector. I had too much movement in my house for one of those things; I knew a motion detector would drive me wild, flickering on and off all night.

No cat. But the light shone on the square below the basketball net and I stood looking at it for a while, thinking that I shouldn't have been so strict with Toby and Stewart over their games. I should have let them just work things out on that cracked, makeshift court, instead of insisting they quiet down. That gag order probably didn't make men out of boys. Maybe it just taught them how to fake it, how to patch things up artificially. Maybe yelling and screaming was what it took to achieve real peace. I thought of calling Toby and telling him, but that conversation would start others and this was my night off. I didn't have any duties at all.

Maybe the cat was around the other side of the garage. I went outside to check, smelling the dirt the way it was tonight. The sharp edge of that fertilizer had worn away and the odor was thick and full of promise. Little wonder my grandmother carried her favorite kind around with her. Its perfume was stronger than any other I knew. From the back porch light, I could see how it rose in long waves, all the corn plants cradled there, that would spring up out of infancy. I stretched my arms up over my head. It was a good night to be alone.

"Pretty quiet over there."

Russell sat in the dark up on his balcony. A little of my porch light sneaked up there, just showing the outline of his body.

"Spying on us?"

"You must be pretty lonesome with those kids gone."

"Not at all. I'm enjoying the peace and quiet."

Could you be baked inside silence? It felt like heat, like someone had just shot the oven up to five hundred degrees. And all of that just because two people couldn't find anything to say to each other.

"Well, I'm lonesome. I'd like you to come over here to have a drink with me." Will you do that for me, Polly? I thought I heard him say that, but his voice was as dusky as the place where he sat way up there. Clever Russell, a drink would turn down this hot silence.

"Sure."

I pinched a little of that dirt under my nose before I left. Rubbing it released even more of its smell, it was like rolling a spike of lavender between my fingertips for a stronger dose. I had begun to come around to Tom's way of thinking, though for different reasons. I could see our children standing there, looking out at both of us from underneath a green canopy. What I saw had nothing to do with chores.

I washed my hands before going over for that drink, listening to the clunk of pipes that started up once anyone wanted water from that sink. Now the noise felt like company. I splashed some of Kate's cologne on my neck, wanting to cool down even more before I had that drink. It was a fresh scent, a young scent. I thought about her perfumes and mine, which ones we could share if we were on an even more severe budget, then grabbed my purse and headed out the door. I made sure to lock up, even though I was just going next door.

Russell had music turned on. He never played music in his house, at least not that I'd heard. I thought about that door in his house, the one I hadn't known existed. My stomach growled as I knocked on his door and I wished I'd eaten something, if only to make it quiet down.

He had on a stupid shirt, the sort of thing you'd buy in Hawaii and wished you could return once you got back home.

"You look different tonight, Polly."

"Good different or bad different? Never mind, I don't want to find out." I hoped this wasn't going to be one of those times when nothing we said came out right. I watched as he worked all the locks on the door. "How about that drink?"

"Yeah, good. I've got . . . you know what I've got."

It was a night for gin and I was glad to see it, among the bottles that made up his bar.

"Shouldn't a bachelor have a wet bar? God, whatever happened to wet bars? You never see them anymore." Tom and I had made friends years back with a couple we met on the beach. We tanned together the whole summer long, feeling that mixture of sun and wind on our skins, talking in an intermittent way with people we'd just begun to know. Wonder of wonders, this couple had a wet bar in their condo. We stared at it, madly in love with our new life, truly drunk on California.

"They're around, they're just discreet." Russell opened doors I'd never thought about and revealed a wet and barren bar. He kept his hodgepodge of bottles in a kitchen cupboard.

Russell had a lime for my gin and tonic. I held the cold drink to my cheek and thought how different our houses were, no matter who was there and who wasn't. I would never just have a lime around. He watched me drink without fixing anything for himself.

"Where's yours?"

He pointed at the coffee table in front of the couch and we moved together to sit down. He twisted the top off the beer and sat rubbing the back of his neck.

"Long day, Russell?"

"The longest day."

"I loved that movie."

He looked at me blankly.

"*The Longest Day*. It's an old war movie." It was awfully old, now that I thought of it. The back of my neck had begun to feel stiff. Maybe the long day he'd had was contagious. Plus my eyes burned. I wished both of us were sitting in soft, dusky shadows. I blinked a few times, making a show of things.

"I feel like I'm in a display case."

"I can do something about that." He got up to dim the lights, another bachelor feature along with wet bars, I guessed. His shirt was hiked up in the back and I slapped at it as he sat back down. The light was better, artificial but better all the same. He scratched his head and shifted around on the couch.

"Better?"

"Oh, much."

I drank faster, really thirsty now. He had covered his front windows with expensive shutters since the last time I'd been here. They looked as if they were solid oak, not just some veneer that let light fall in or out. No, these were thoroughly masculine. The real McCoy. Once Granny Settle left, I would fold away those dingy skirts, the old stories they held, and put something similar in my dining room. A little privacy, a touch of style, now wouldn't that be nice?

He wasn't drinking. He was looking at my purse by the door.

"You heading out tonight, Polly?"

"Matter of fact, yeah. Not right away. I can still stay a little while."

I'd brought the purse with me out of habit, but I was grateful to have a getaway plan, if I needed one. I could leave, just go driving somewhere, after I finished this drink. A long drive, maybe to Malibu. That was something I'd never think of doing ordinarily.

"Something the matter, Russell? You seem—"

"—I'm a little preoccupied. Long day, like I said." He laughed and squirmed, the couch squeaking behind his back. "Where've you been, Polly?"

"Where I've always been."

"That's not what I'm asking. I want to know why you're working so hard to avoid me."

"I'm not. I've just been busy."

"Everybody's busy, Polly. You must be lying low for a reason."

I looked down at his shirt. It was a weird landscape, all right. With the lights dimmed, my eyes didn't burn anymore. But I couldn't tell if those loud splashes of color all over his chest were meant to be flowers, exotic animals or abstract designs that meant nothing at all. I touched one of them in the center.

"Tell me where you got this."

He held on to my hand and moved it to his face. "Like it?"

His face was rough. Maybe he didn't shave on Saturdays. Tom didn't. He would have gone entire weekends if I hadn't complained by Saturday night. Sometimes I would do it for him if he was feeling too lazy. It was one of the scariest pleasures we had. The razor blade in my hand, I would glide it over his cheeks just to get him started, then make him do the rest on his own.

"It's very colorful."

We weren't going upstairs tonight. There were faster, more furious things to do right where we sat. I should have eaten. I thought this as if someone else were thinking it for me, knowing only a drink on an empty stomach could produce such strange echoes. I was thinking of things in a rush and tumble, letting everything go out of order. The order I'd sought in my house, the same order I'd achieved that had me frightened not just for tonight, but for the rest of my nights . . . I let that all melt away. I would sample something else willingly, something I sensed as my head knocked into a hard corner, something you would never guess lay under such a plush sofa.

"You okay?"

"Fine."

"Oh, Polly."

His voice was caught by a sentiment, a surprise. I held my breath for a moment, feeling something familiar rush over me, something so familiar I'd pretended for months it wasn't there at all. I hadn't known what to do with this feeling, so I'd buried it, just like my granny had done in the garden with one determined metal jab. I opened my eyes for a look at what had been stowed underground for so long.

I saw me, then the two of us worked our way into the picture. Though the lights in that room were low, the sight grew sharper and brighter as I stared down intently from some high, perilous perch. That had to be my pale skin and round arms curved and clutching like nobody else's. My hair fanned out over the pillow on the sofa, moving slow as seaweed under the pull of the tide.

And over me lay Tom, not Russell. He stretched over me like an unthinkably beautiful blanket and under his warmth and the one human landscape I knew by heart, every whim was still permitted. And every pleasure. I wasn't sleeping with a stranger. I was making love to a partner I'd held in my heart and my arms forever. Tom's face, white and smooth as the moon, was suspended in front of me. For a while the two of us were happy and astonished and whole, hungry again for the same satisfactions of body and mind. Then Russell's voice shattered the reverie. It wasn't any voice I recognized.

"Didn't I tell you?"

I tried not to stop what we were doing, but instead of swimming in new and wonderfully familiar memories, I felt the pinch of a zipper, the knock of a hardwood frame. Russell's skin now tore and abraded my own.

"Tell me what?"

"Here, put this under you. That the next time would be really different."

He was younger than ever, all hope was in his eyes. But what exactly did a bachelor hope for?

"Oh, Russell, I am so . . . I've got to get up."

"What's going on? Polly, we just had the greatest—"

"—Right, we did. But it was all wrong. I mean, you've got the wrong idea about what was going on here."

"It wasn't great for you? You sure had me fooled."

I was so naked. No one had ever been so naked as I, except my own grandmother, flanked by androgynous angels, those golden auras with ankles. I was that undressed, that bare, and everyone was filing by with a personal complaint to lodge against me. I was the harshest judge of all. I had to get off that couch before it snapped over me like an angry set of jaws. Stupid! I was trying to put on Russell's jeans.

Now I heard his voice. It was the same voice my son had heard, the one that sent him scuttling out the window, to arm himself with a rock and a pal. Russell was naked, too, but he didn't care. The same sound in his voice marked his rigid body.

"Is this because of your kids?"

"Not at all."

"Did they go to Tom's because of me? Is that what's wrong? Look at me, Polly."

"I am."

I wasn't free. I was the most burdened single mother on the face of the earth. I couldn't even have a night to myself without the encumbrance of memory, desire and something that wouldn't go away, no matter how much I wanted it to. I tucked my shirt into my jeans (and they were mine this time), but even that didn't help.

"I'm a mess."

I couldn't figure out all the locks on his door. Here I thought I could just grab my purse and run. There were lots of complicated things to do before I could leave and I waited as he did them for me, so hot it was as if I'd never had that drink in the first place.

I backed out of the driveway too fast, narrowly missing the garbage can poised on the curb. Even though I had the locks down on my car, each time I rolled to a stop I felt unnerved. As if someone would squeeze through the slightly opened windows. What a dumb thought. But it kept me off the Pacific Coast Highway. Malibu seemed too far, too much of a risk to take on a night like this. So far freedom wasn't going well at all.

I thought about Kate and Toby, when they were really little. Every fall, every scrape had been properly iodined or bandaged, either that or kissed and erased. The most important thing was the noting, the remarking that some small, aching tragedy had occurred. Minute disasters were recorded and that was the thing that healed the pain. Someone was looking on, someone who cared. Figuring that out, as I rounded one of those corners in Tom's neighborhood, one of those corners that looked identical to every other corner, that made you despair of ever finding your way home again, I had a crazy longing for Frankie Doray. I wished she were here now, telling me something to prove she'd been a witness to painful events. I wouldn't have minded if she'd shimmered into my open windows and just sat there beside me with nothing to say. The saying didn't matter at the moment, the seeing did. But why her, of all people? Why did I want her to cluck her tongue and shake her head sorrowfully, putting me back together with the gesture as she did.

"I'm losing my mind."

Because look where I'd wound up, a tourist in a terrible country. This place seemed to my sore, smarting eyes more terrible than charred hills ravaged by flames or the rubble left from riots and earthquakes. This country was filled with outcasts. I could tell from the flags that flew in the visitors' parking lot. The flags were not patriot symbols, they triggered no loyalty. They were just red and green rayon pennants with a fake coat of arms in the middle. They announced a transient community of corporate apartments, filled with stainless steel forks and spoons, linen and china suggesting home and taunting residents with a thorough absence of intimacy and warmth. Month to month, inhabitants of this country pledged their allegiance without passion or hope. A sign pointed me toward 200 E.

I stabbed the lock down on the car, slamming the door shut. I couldn't even manage a decent night out. What was I doing here, visiting my children on my one night off? I should have been in Paradise, trying my luck again. My jeans were uncomfortable, too tight or something. I poked at my hair, wondering what I looked like. I hadn't gone to the bathroom to put myself back together. I was still a mess. I looked around in my purse for some chewing gum, but couldn't find anything.

The path curved in and around phony green islands. Couldn't landscapers do a decent job of making things look like they just appeared? Why did everything in these complexes look so well planned? Somebody didn't know how desultory and dispiriting neatness without end could be.

Tom's apartment was easy to get to and I suddenly didn't like that. Anybody could come striding up the path . . . why just look who did. I jabbed at my bangs, sweeping them off my forehead. There was no security gate here, probably no guards roaming around either. This country was in a recession. Tom should have thought about that when he said yes to Kate's request. If he wanted to put himself at risk, that was one thing. But did his kids have to be sacrificed, too? This was no place for kids and I would tell him so. I banged hard on the door to 200 E. Tom took a long time to open. I saw his eye in the peephole. The dark pupil widened and the door swung open fast.

"Are you all right? Polly, what's wrong?"

"You always ask me that."

"I just wasn't expecting you."

An old smell, a musty smell rolled out on an invisible cloud. Maybe his place was too dirty, maybe that was why he didn't take me by the arm and drag me inside, out of the dark night. His shirt wasn't buttoned all the way and he didn't have any socks on.

"The kids are asleep."

"Were you?"

He hadn't been reading. He didn't have those oval prints on each side of his nose his glasses left. He hadn't been asleep, either. He spoke too clearly. Why didn't he open the door? I squinted, looking at his mouth. He'd been having a midnight snack. Golden crumbs had collected in one corner of his mouth. Cookie crumbs or something else? Maybe he'd been nibbling on The Wafer at this hour, then on to a few crunches before bed.

"What's wrong with your face, Polly?" He slipped his hand in a side pocket of his jeans and frowned. "It's all red."

You really couldn't run away. Things pursued you, caught you when you weren't paying attention. I stood taller, pulling my legs together.

"Heat rash."

A different look crossed Tom's face, one of disbelief, then slow, slow understanding. An understanding that slopped over boundaries, leaping from one person to another. I saw what he saw, a rumpled, tousled woman standing outside in the middle of the night. Upset for reasons that were unclear, looking red-faced and rushed. I wanted to put my hand on the side of my face and press. Just push hard until there was no color, no night like this. No stupid, thoughtless night. Something was building, some new provocation, a threat of a different order. This night was risky, retaliatory. Dumb. But what had his been out there on the road? My face was red, but his should have been redder. I took a step away from him, stumbling slightly. I felt as if I were growing webbed feet that would never know their own power. There was no water here, no free, wet push as I swept along. I would never walk with grace again, never walk at all without this new restriction.

"Let me go!"

"Who's holding you back?"

"You are and Granite is and my grandmother is. I am sick to death of all of you, but mostly you, Tom Harrison. How dare you look at me like that."

"That heat rash is making you pretty edgy, Polly. You drove all the way over just to criticize the way I'm looking at you?"

"No. I came to make sure my children are all right."

"Our children are fine. Our children are asleep."

He still hadn't invited me in. And where was Frankie Doray? She'd missed a wonderful opportunity to taunt somebody who was slightly, temporarily down and out. Maybe because she was busy elsewhere. Maybe there was an epidemic of couches tonight. I tried to peek around the edge of the door.

"I wouldn't put it past you!"

"Put what past me?"

"Anything."

I had never touched Tom in anger. It had never even been an impulse. But I

239

wished my limp arms were hard and muscled. I wished in one mad minute that I could just stand here, flexing my triceps and my biceps, my what have you, making it clear without saying so that Polly Harrison was nobody you could mess with. But instead of doing that, I marched off, angry and nervous about what I looked like as I marched. I was not free, had never been free. There was no such thing as liberty in a country like this. I was a hopeless prisoner, wishing as I stomped off that Tom would catch me from behind and never let me go. I realized this was the second time I'd wished he would follow me. And this was the second time he hadn't.

Twenty-five

*B*ull's-eye. I plowed into the garbage can, wincing at the crash it made. Sacks tumbled out of the container and if it hadn't been for the ravenous cat, I would have just left them there, dirty and defiant. But because of the cat, be-cause I, for one, was a responsible person, I piled them back into the can and smashed the lid on top. This time I didn't mind the noise. The porch light blinked a couple of times and blew out with a little pop as I walked up the path. Just perfect. I'd managed to put this moment out of my mind. My kids were gone and now a dark house, a dark porch was waiting for me. I staggered blindly up the steps. The geraniums had been moved to the wrong side of the doormat and I stubbed my toe on the edge of the clay pot. It was a gin night all right. I imagined Russell's house watching me as I stooped down to move my flowerpot. I fumbled around in the dark, waiting for my eyes to adjust. I struggled to get my key in the lock without a porch light.

"Hey, ho. Hey, ho. Hey, ho."

His voice poured down my back. It was ingratiating and smooth, sticky as syrup. Panic circled my neck with damp fingers as I looked at the street. There were no insomniacs, no midnight dog-walkers, no foolish joggers having a run before bed. Houses all along the street looked sealed and snug. The whole world was bedded down except for the two of us. I stabbed at the door and got the key in the lock, but it wouldn't turn. Everything was in slow motion, especially my thoughts. It was the wrong key. I tried another, without turning around. His voice was closer, thicker. I thought I smelled him, but maybe not.

"I've been waiting and waiting. I didn't want you to come home to an empty house. Honey. That would have been just awful."

Honey. He spat the word out. I turned around then, for I had all the time in the world. Every moment seemed slow and blurred at the edges as the thick hedge by my side bent and broke. I watched by the dim light of the streetlamp; he emerged wrapped in a drop cloth, maybe the one I kept in the garage. He peered out from the center of a whitish mass that cupped his head like a cowl, and my skin prickled as I felt his eyes on me. Something tingled at my breast, a sensation, a reminder that I didn't have a lucky dollar tucked away. There was nothing to rely on, nobody to call for help. Vulnerability fed me a mouthful of words that came out in a rush.

"Well, hey . . ." Empty house. Maybe he was bluffing. "Listen, we need to keep it down. My husband's asleep and I'd hate like anything to—"

"—You don't have a husband anymore. I checked on that. Oh, I've been checking for the longest time. You're all by yourself tonight and I couldn't bear to leave you alone. Sweetheart."

He drew out the syllables, exaggerating the length, the importance of that word. I remembered something Kate said in an ode to vegetables and almost cried out loud. *If we ever saw the animals we ate, we'd never have the courage to kill them.* I had to make this man see me. I would do that with telling, the kind of telling I'd heard all my life from Granny Settle.

"Boy, I am just tired out tonight. Do you ever get the feeling there is too much to get done in a day? Well, I do. At least I sure did today. There was all this stuff I had to take care of and it was taking me away from the things I really love, the things I consider the real business of life and *that's* the paradox."

"Shut up, Polly." He didn't move any closer to me, but I could smell him now. His skin had a stink. It had a sharp, acid stink. "I tried to talk to you. Once in the parking lot at that coffee shop and then right here in your neighborhood, but you didn't want to talk to me. And I found out you're really ordinary, not like I thought in the beginning. In the beginning I thought you were a lady, someone special.

"But you're like every other woman I know. Always rushing someplace taking care of stuff, like you said, and when I found that out, I painted over your name on the car so now there's no Polly written there, it's just plain paint, and nobody will ever know I thought you might have been different. Nobody will ever know anything because I painted over you."

"Where did you get that drop cloth?"

It slipped off his head and fell to his shoulders in folds. I was drenched with sweat. I fought to keep my voice steady, though there was a dry-mouthed thickness that I couldn't disguise.

"Did you find that in the garage, because I've been looking for that forever. I paint, too, and I have a project in mind that'll probably take me years, but if you love what you're doing, who cares how much time it takes?"

He took a step closer to me, his arms rustling the cover of the cloth.

"Take what I'm doing now, this writing. Oh, it takes forever and it tries my patience, but I do have this sense that if I just—"

"—Polly, Polly, Polly. Why don't you ever ask who *I am? I'm Barney.*"

Slowly, slowly, he opened the drop cloth and stepped out of its center. All I could see was the flow of cloth that was sliding to the ground. He seemed almost to have forgotten me, forgotten us. He knelt down, smoothing the edges of the cloth. I ran my fingers over another key and the chain rattled.

"This looks like a picnic. Not that I ever had a picnic, not even when I was little. What kind of a picnic would that have been anyway with just Mother and me? See? I didn't want you to get dirty, Polly. You turned out to be ordinary, but I'm not."

I remembered picnics with *my* mother and panic almost swept me away from this moment. Almost. I knew something about danger, but I also knew about strength, buried deep and extreme as a river current.

"Two people can have a perfectly good picnic, Barney. Why don't we have one right here?"

He stood up suddenly, jerking his hands at his side as he spoke. I was too frightened to pray.

"You must really think I'm stupid, don't you, Polly? Oh, perfect, a picnic on your doorstep!" His voice was raw and exposed. "Wonderful, Polly. Well, guess what? It's me who's finally going to get the drumstick."

I cleared my throat hard, hoping the sound would muffle the click of the key. I turned it slowly, every muscle tensed with the scene I was preparing in my mind. I would slip in, one motion. Slam the door. Another motion. He pulled the drop cloth back over his head.

"I'll help!"

He butted me out of the way with his shoulder and moved where I was supposed to move. Inside my home. One motion. He got inside where it was dark as an animal's eye except for the folds of cloth that contained him. His hand slipped slightly on my arm as he pulled me along with him. His hand was wet and slick.

"Show me, Polly. Show me where you live and how you live and who you talk to when you're lonely. Barney wants to know everything, every, every thing, large and small!"

His voice had lost something and gained something. It was different and I didn't know who had the power now. It was boyish. He was inside my house, yet was still asking permission for something. I tried to think and conclude and plan, but things seemed flung out on the floor. Pick-Up-Sticks, that game. Every thought was a scattered stick in a remote corner too far for me to reach.

"Would you like to see pictures, Barney?"

"Oh, yes!"

Who you talk to when you're lonely, Polly, he had spoken those words. It could get me to a phone if I could keep him like he was now. Eager, complaisant, hugging himself under a stiff layer of cloth. I started to move to the kitchen, the phone. Maybe I could dial Beth. Maybe he would love to listen to a phone call between women. He was rancid with fear and craziness. His smell followed me along with his voice. Would it ever leave? Or would it take hold of the house like skunk spray?

"Let's turn on a few lights so we can—"

"—No! No lights."

"I've got pictures in the kitchen."

"Of the children?"

My chest was tight as I groped my way through Granny Settle's room. I passed my hands over the maze of boxes and trunks she had covered with stained, faded quilts, mysterious shapes and forms that calmed me as I ran my hand over their smooth edges. I stopped in front of the window, tugging on the edge of one of her old skirts, begging a story, a comforting whisper out of its fold. I could feel the outline of his body behind me, the hard, unremitting fact of his body under the shapeless cloth. Too close. My flesh prickled and burned with him so near. His body bumped against mine, demanding a response.

I turned and reached out to shove him away. He grabbed both my hands as I did and twisted them enough to hurt. I could feel his warm breath travel up the side of my face.

"Why does it always have to be this way? Why does it always have to turn out ugly when you try to get a sweetheart? All I want is a sweetheart."

"This isn't the way to get a sweetheart, Barney."

He closed his mouth suddenly and began grinding his teeth. He could have crushed anything with the strength of his jaws.

"Then what is?" His voice twisted into a whine. A petulant, dangerous boy wanted answers and wanted them now.

"You have to talk to a woman the right way. We're so thrilled and surprised when a man will really talk to us." I hesitated, then continued. "That's all women want. Forget how much money it takes to have a woman, Barney. Let's go look at those pictures."

His hands let go of mine briefly and I turned around, my back to him again. He took hold of my wrists after I turned, his hands a gentle manacle behind my back. I spoke faster and faster. I was ready to move if he decided to let me go.

"Imagine a man who gives a woman about two minutes before he turns the conversation back to himself. How does that make a woman feel? Terrible! Like nothing she says has any value."

"All right." He still held on to me, but his body started to sway loosely. As if there was melody locked inside him. "So I listen for more than two minutes. A lot more, say. I spend a whole hour listening to her.

"And then we don't have any more things to tell each other and it's late and she's hungry and I'm hungry, only not for the same things. My mother used to say men and women are always hungry, but not for the same things. Isn't that right, Polly? Isn't that right, Polly, liar, liar? You made it all up so I'd forget everything in my plan. You thought I'd forget why I came here in the first place."

I curled my body away from him, accommodating the now-mounting pain in my wrists. He yanked them once hard, then began pulling me closer to him. I locked my knees and stiffened, then he jerked my head back. This was the devastation I always felt was on its way; the walls of my own home were finally falling in on me.

"No!"

My shout seemed as raw and wild as his animal stink. The cry lured another shape toward us, a shape I could recognize even in those slow shadows. Nothing moved at the right pace. Not my thoughts, not my words or what I saw, what I hoped I saw.

"You're hurting me!"

Russell knocked me into the wall. My shoulder hit first, then the side of my head. I hit something sharp, the side of the window frame maybe. Free. I was free and pain proved it. I didn't mind my wrist, which I couldn't move once I was thrown from Barney's tight grip. My wrist dangled like an injured paw and I held it against my chest and ran toward the kitchen and the telephone numbers I'd taped to the wall. I heard something crash to the floor behind me, then words. Cursing like I'd never heard in my life, filthy oaths promising slaughter, devastation, the end of the world. I tried to shut my ears to this millennium music, but couldn't. I had to shout over the phone, screaming my address twice so it would be heard. When Barney's raving stopped, I was still shouting for help. There was no one on the line and I continued to yell at the top of my lungs.

"It's okay, Polly. I got him down."

I snapped a light on with my good hand and shielded my eyes from the brightness and the sight of what was on my wooden floor. Russell was on top of him, with Barney's chin caught in one hand, Barney's hands in another. Wetness seeped out of him, it curled around him in a horrible yellow pool. I squeezed my eyes shut, then pressed my forehead inside the curve of my arms and breathed the swift, lapping breath of labor, thinking of Kate, thinking of Toby. They were safe. They were away. Hearing Russell's voice meant I was safe, too.

"That wasn't a nice thing to do now, was it? Scaring Polly like that. Shouldn't do that." I heard Barney let out a little cry. Maybe Russell had pulled his chin farther back. I couldn't have said for sure.

I decided to lie down for a while. I just needed to go to sleep right away, that was all. I would thank Russell once I woke up, but right then, oh, right then . . . I was sinking down or the floor was rising up, it was all the same. I heard Barney say he only wanted a sweetheart. My wrist throbbed and I hoped it would throb hard and long until the pain made me stop hearing him cry. Barney kept saying all he ever wanted was a sweetheart. I heard sirens, all the sirens of the city it seemed, just to take one crying man away. I think someone put a head under my pillow then, but I could have been wrong. The next thing I remember was Tom.

"Try."

My throat was too raw. I wanted to open my mouth for some of the soup in the spoon he held in front of me, but I didn't think I could unlock my jaw. I was too worn out.

"Polly, just a little something now and we'll try again later. It's only broth. Try for me and for the kids."

"Mommy, hi. Mommy, we love you."

"Mom, they say you're lucky. That guy is really crazy. They even got his mother to come and say so. That way they could lock him up."

Kate's eyes were teary. "Mommy, we love you. It's true. They're going to put him in an institution and no one will ever try to hurt you again."

They both tried to crawl in bed beside me.

"Hey, you two. Your mom's been through enough. Let's let her rest."

He left the bowl of soup by my bedside and led the kids away. The sun was hard yellow and bright and someone called Barney would never follow me again in a car with my name painted on it and things were probably pushing up outside, insisting their way out of the ground through black soil. I wondered how much time had passed. Flowers were growing stale in a vase by my window. Daylilies would soon leave that telltale smudge of gold dust on a passing sleeve or the tablecloth under the vase as a signal that their finest hour was over. Someone had sent candy and my vanity was covered with a crowd of noisy greeting cards, standing wide-armed to welcome me back from wherever I'd been. I had no notes from that place I had visited. The only thing I knew was that I was exhausted and, for the moment, my condition couldn't be turned into a country song. I looked down at my chest. Someone had slipped me inside the silk pajamas Beth had given me at the Sovereign.

I must have been asleep. Tom's voice came in around the edges of a dream I'd been having. I had just entered a chilly stone hall split by long tables filled with revelers. Though there was an enormous fire at the end of the room that roared and spat as another log was added to the blaze, it did nothing to warm the place I was in. Everybody stopped talking as I peeked into the room and raised their silver goblets in a toast. I didn't have time to find out whether I was a real hero or just a celebrated guest, for there was Tom's soft voice curling up the contour of my dream. It frizzled and blackened, as if it were a photograph slowly starting to burn.

"—and if they can do it, we can. I know we can."

"Tom?" His name left its taste on my tongue. That night had left my mouth so vacant and dry. His head was resting on my leg. I could feel its heavy weight and opened my eyes partially just to make sure. I reached out to prove the new face was his. He hadn't shaved in a long while, it seemed.

"How long have you been awake, Polly?"

"I'm not sure."

He cupped my chin in his hands. "Want me to call the kids?"

"Not yet." My tongue stuck to the roof of my mouth and I was afraid more talking would rip up the palate, the way it felt. I pointed to a carafe of water by the window and he tripped over a wicker trunk at the end of the bed trying to get it.

"Damn, sorry." He apologized to my trunk and poured nervously. I had no sense of time or sequence. Had this already happened to us? It all felt so familiar, as if we were going through these motions for a second time. I'd already seen him miss the hand-painted cup with the stream of water, had already noticed his unironed shirt and his chapped lips. When he brought the glass to my lips, I'd tasted it much sooner. I drank big gulps and saved the roof of my mouth. I wanted to talk.

"Is this what they mean by 'under medication'? Because I feel real different. I don't want to see the kids quite yet."

He rubbed his hands back and forth over his knees.

"It's okay. I'm okay. I'm back, I think." I assured him, going back to that long, drafty room for a second and thought about being the hero returning from some adventure. Did survival make you a hero? Hero, hero. Where was Russell? Questions started flooding in, all kinds. My head was clearing. My mind felt as peeled and clean as a hardboiled egg. I looked at my bedside table, filled with tiny bottles. Great tiny bottles, that let you hear and think and speak after days of deep sleep.

"I must have fainted that night."

"You did. That's part of the reason you got so banged up. You've got a broken wrist and a lump on the back of your head from the fall. Your shoulder's all bruised up. I'm surprised he didn't break a few ribs, the way he threw you into the wall."

"Barney threw me into the wall?"

"Russell did."

Tom looked awful and sounded worse than he looked. It wasn't just the shadow on his face.

"Russell saved my life. Or did I get that part wrong?"

"He could've sent you flying through the front window, the way he described it afterward. He didn't have to do the whole storm trooper routine. That's what I'm saying."

"The way that creep Barney was holding me in front of him, Russell *had* to shove me out of the way."

"So, you're saying I should thank him for hurting you?"

"I'm saying we should thank him for saving me."

I looked around at my room. It seemed complete with Tom and me inside. It didn't even matter that the kids weren't standing around. The bedroom felt stocked, filled to the brim. How could I safeguard a room like this?

"Has he been over?"

"Who?" Tom's voice cracked.

"Russell. To see how I am."

"No, but he telephoned. I got him on the third call."

"Who got him on the first two?"

"Toby. He forgot to tell me he called."

"Right."

I smiled and wished I hadn't. Tom cocked his head.

"He's usually real good about giving messages. Seems funny he'd just forget like that."

I looked at those sympathy cards across the room and wondered how long well-wishers would feel those empathetic pangs.

"I guess he got really upset over that whole demolition thing."

"Maybe." His shoulders sagged, as if just thinking about it wore him down. "You know what gets to me the most?"

He brushed my bangs from my forehead, then let his palm rest there, feeling for fever.

"If I had brought you into the apartment for a real talk that night, or if we'd left a note for the kids and walked around outside to talk things over, I mean, I saw you were upset . . . I saw you were upset about something, and if I had done that instead of just thought about doing it, none of this would have happened."

I imagined his hands circling my waist the way they might have touched me that night, the warmth from the flat of his hands, how they would have held me still for moments or hours.

"He would have lurked around and figured you were out for the whole night. It would never have happened if I'd . . ." He squeezed his hands shut. ". . . you know something funny, Polly?"

I didn't know anything funny. I shook my head.

"I never used to think of myself as an asshole. Not when I was Toby's age or when I got to high school or even when we first came out here."

"Because you weren't."

He winced when I said that, almost as if I'd given him a little poke. "I wasn't, was I? Back then I never doubted myself. And after a while, I don't know, I just got to a certain moment where all I did was doubt myself."

That wasn't funny at all. Tom had never questioned himself, *we'd* never questioned ourselves. So when did it start and where was I when it did? I had never known this Doubting Thomas. "That's in the Bible."

"Huh?"

My broken wrist was under the covers and I wiggled my fingers and tried to raise my arm. It was surprisingly light. I pulled it out and found my cast pretty and pink.

"Pretty glamorous."

"Kate chose it for you. She thought you'd like that. Glows in the dark, too." He paused and shook his head slowly. He looked as if he wanted to say something more.

I wanted to smooth his hair, but shook his shoulder a little instead. "You're supposed to be comforting me. What's going on here?"

"I'm supposed to have done lots of things." He picked up one of the bottles from the tray, rattled it and put it back down. "Only I haven't."

I thought it was safe to go back over that night in my mind and I did that for a few minutes, pretending it hadn't been me. I moved players around on a wide checkered board until I figured it out. I watched the wall in front of me as I did, startled by the game developing there. One thing didn't work.

"If Russell was such a storm trooper, how come I didn't hear him break a window?"

"That's not how he got in the house."

"He broke down the kitchen door? I just had that handyman fix the knob and add a deadbolt."

"He didn't have to break a thing. He heard something, the garbage cans or something and he was prowling around outdoors when he heard you shout. You left the back door wide open."

250

"Oh."

I stuck my hand back under the covers, still staring at the wall. One more move had been completed on the chessboard and this one was likely to bring on a very different sort of rash, a creeping rash of shame. Just what could I have been thinking of that night?

"I feel like I've been lying here forever."

"More like a couple of days. You'd sleep and we'd feed you, then you'd sleep again. You wouldn't talk to us."

"You were here the whole time?"

He nodded.

"What did you do the whole time?"

"I watched television in the kitchen."

"I don't have a television in the kitchen."

"I bought one and put it in there."

"Hey, you know I don't—"

"It's tiny, Pol. A small-screen Sony, black-and-white. I had it going night and day and I found out something while I was waiting for you to wake up. Those talk shows, here I thought they were all so stupid. They're not."

"Go on."

He gave me some more water and watched me drink.

"Maybe we should talk about this some other time."

"This is the perfect time." Now lying there listening was like being recharged. One limb at a time had started to tingle. If this continued, my whole body would be zapped with new strength. Maybe the shock of this business had sent my body into a higher dimension. Maybe once I got out of this bed I would do triathlons to give my new strength someplace to go.

"Two days ago, are you listening? Two days ago there was this guy on Montel."

"You're watching Montel now?"

"He's all right. Anyhow, he has this show dedicated to couples who've divorced and remarried."

"Big deal."

"No, Polly. Divorced and remarried to the same partner. Some more than twice, even."

It was working. Everything felt alive and well now, I bet my wrist would heal in no time.

"The thing is, he didn't just have truck drivers on the show. He had a restaurant owner from West Palm Beach and a marketing guy from Brooklyn . . ."

I turned one arm over slowly and stretched it up over my head. It didn't hurt, nothing hurt.

"What are you doing? So they start talking about their affairs, Polly, because that's why all these couples broke up in the first place. And I found out—"

"What?"

"Mostly that *it's all the same.* I mean, not the people because all the people were different, but the way they felt was all the same. Polly, please put your arm down."

"What is your revelation exactly?"

"That it's not impossible. People can forgive each other and get on with their lives."

"Oh. Even after they've cheated and lied and trampled on someone they were supposed to love?"

"Yes."

I heard the struggle to keep his voice even, but I didn't care. "Interesting. Thanks for sharing, hon."

I looked past him out my window. It was a view I loved no matter what. No matter who shouted what, no matter who loved or stopped loving whom, I would always cherish this scene. The most wildly different greens in the world all nodded leafy heads outside my window. Opening my eyes only slightly revealed a world as rich and near as the tangle of trees outside my room.

"They did it, Polly. They patched up their lives and went on."

"Patched up. Like with plaster and Super Glue?"

"Don't make fun of me, Polly. I'm trying to get at something."

"So am I. Those stupid shows don't tell anyone *how* to forgive. People come on with their big, moist cow eyes, all lovey-dovey, and tell you everything's patched up, just like you said, without any explanation of the miracle. What do you think, Tom, that you're the first person in this house to watch talk shows? People like that are a dime a dozen. Tell me something I don't know instead of everything I do."

I hoped Mary-Chapin Carpenter would forgive me. It was her line, but it sure fit. I was all right, then. I was back, the same as before. But my arm itched under the cast.

That night was beginning to return full-strength and it wasn't any design I could keep on the wall. I felt afraid and glanced at the army of little bottles on the stand, wondering if there was something I might swallow now.

I was shaking and Tom made me drink again, one last time. He said he was sorry, more sorry than I could know, and then I stopped listening to what he said. I didn't hear his footsteps when he left the room, but he did leave. I thought I was all alone when I woke up next. I was wrong.

Twenty-six

"Granny Settle, is that you?"

"Yes and no."

I reached for the edge of the blanket and pulled it up to my chin. It was her voice all right, but the overalls were gone and in their place was a long divided skirt and high-heeled boots, a crisp white shirt with shimmery embroidered details along the closed throat and yoke. All of it was held in place by an enormous gold belt cinched so tight it forced my granny's belly into a painful-looking mound. The hat she wore seemed to have had many lives. Most of the brown had been rubbed away on one side. She walked to my bed slowly and leaned down to kiss my cheek.

"You're all right then."

"I'm all right."

She had dressed up to honor me. The costume was her way of expressing regret and concern. I knew the cowgirl ensemble was the most effusive gesture she could make. Stories would follow, the same stories I was offered as a girl to fix whatever feuds and fears drove me to sleep under beds, to hide out where no one would be able to find me except her. Stories then had generally meant I am sorry as hell this happened, Polly Ann, and they meant the same thing now.

My head filled up with the smell of talcum powder.

"I wore this before you were born, Polly. Even before your mama was born. This was how I looked the day they named me Queen of the Cowgirls in the last Ponca City Roundup. Young as I was, you couldn't tell me a thing I hadn't already figured out."

She cackled to herself and I curled my toes under the blanket, watching her face under the hat. She smoothed out a wrinkle in her skirt with the flat of her hand.

"A lot of girls were in the business just so they could be discovered. They made it tough on the rest of us. All they did was snuggle up to the crowd on horseback, hoping somebody would put them in a picture. They didn't give a hang for tradition. Half of them didn't even know where the rodeo'd come from. They were just going along for the ride. But it was a wilder ride than any of those girls knew."

I didn't have to beg this time. Didn't have to pull on those skirts now hanging in my dining room, begging a story out of every pleat they held. She had turned generous in her eighty-second year. Granny Settle was giving away her stories while she could.

"Tell me the one about Star."

"You know that one, Polly."

"I want to hear it again." It was good to listen to her and pretend that my life was pierced by a line as straight as the one that ran through all her stories. There was nothing messy or haphazard in Granny Settle's tales. Mistakes became hard lessons and that was that.

"Suit yourself." She shook her head, wondering why I wanted to hear about the savage old pinto. "Should have put a bullet in that animal's head on day one, but I got attached to the sorry mess."

I looked at the carafe of water, but decided against reaching for it. I didn't want to break her concentration.

"All right then. We heard about the animal first in Bliss, Oklahoma, back in . . . I don't fully remember what the year was. But it was after your grandfather and me had our rodeo going good. We were booked into every town in Oklahoma and Texas that was worth anything. It was late summer we heard about that dang horse. I remember goldenrod was in bloom. Can't recall who was president, but the fields were full of yellow."

She unsnapped a little pocketbook and took out a chunk of lemon rind, bit into it and sighed with satisfaction.

"Some old fella comes hobblin' up to the office where your granddad and I was doing our paperwork at the end of the day. We'd had a real good afternoon and I guess that made us especially gullible to the story. Said he had a horse called Star that would make our show a cut above all the other rodeos. A real Wild West show. Told us with a retired cow pony like Star, we could double our receipts. Wouldn't have to do anything more than saddle him up with something fancy and let him dance around the ring for folks to get a look at."

Her hands drifted over the brim of her hat, pulling it down a bit over her eyes.

"John Purdy, he called himself. Said he'd ridden the horse up to Montana from Texas a dozen times at least in the days when it was still wild. You know. Before chuck wagons were even on the trail. Of course, your granddad and I knew it was a fat lie. We were business people, or at least that's what we thought then. And this old codger's arithmetic didn't make any sense. His Star couldn't have got to be that old, but we just let him go on with his stories about . . ."

She was offering up a revised version for a more sophisticated audience. She hadn't mentioned any faulty arithmetic when I was seven or twelve. Star had been a cow pony, plain and simple, straight off the trail and I had uncovered the time warp in that hot Granite library all on my own.

"Hhhmph. You know cowboys. More or less stuck to those saddles and once they attached themselves to a horse, they were attached for the rest of their lives. Said Star was something, more surefooted than a goat and beautiful to look at, which was a rare thing. Purdy taught him to do tricks, too. How to kneel for his saddle and open up his fool mouth for the bit, like he was expecting a carrot. Star could dance a sidestep and ladies in town all ganged around, wanting to have a closer look. You see how having a horse like that would enhance a cowboy's reputation some. All right, then. Here's what happened next."

I wished she would let that belt out. I could see her ribs, that's how hard it pressed along the middle.

"Purdy got so he didn't want to leave Texas anymore. Anything north of Laredo gave him a nervous conniption the older he got, so he got himself a little ranch down near the Mexican border and a wife to go with it. Pretty thing, it seemed. A little Indian gal who thought Purdy hung the moon. They settled right in, put in a garden and set up steady business with some of the better ranches who fed their hands more than meat and sourdough bread. Not that cowboys would drink from Purdy's cows, but there was a school down there that took it for the kids. No cowboy I ever knew would drink milk. They just wouldn't have it in their coffee or on their breath."

Granny Settle scratched a spot behind her knee and stretched her leg out as far as it would go.

"And then the troubles started. That cow pony got itself a jealous bone. Nobody had ever seen the like. That Indian bride would set a pie on the sill to cool and the horse would knock it off and set a hoof smack inside. She'd hang her wash out on the line and Star would come galloping in out of nowhere to tear it off. He'd chew up her new curtains and then when she'd make a fuss, he'd get after her with his ears clamped flat to his skull. Seemed like the animal had just gone wild. Oh, he was sweet as ever to Purdy. The two of them got thick as thieves and that's what drove the Indian gal to her knees. Purdy didn't take her side in the affair. He wouldn't get rid of the jealous horse. In fact, the way it was told to your grandfather and me, all he ever did was laugh. Drove his wife straight out of her head. You know what happened next."

"I want to hear it again."

She rubbed her shoulder, then sucked the inside of her cheek for a minute. "Purdy's up at dawn, mending some fence that was down around the bean patch. That's when he hears Star pawing the ground with his hoof and making all kinds of commotion out in the little barn."

I wonder if Kate knew, if Toby had been told. If they'd heard Granny Settle's dead stories, it was likely they'd heard this one, too.

"Well, in the night that woman went and put out the pony's eye. Blinded the poor animal. At least that's what we were told."

My heart almost heaved through my chest. I could see it all so clearly, the sky lifting to morning, the cowboy's tilted walk to the barn to see about those cries and then the horror of the disfigured horse.

"He was gone by noon. Both him and the horse. Didn't say a word to the woman, didn't lay a hand on her. Got a vet out to tend to the miserable horse and saddled him up to go. Now here was Purdy before us, broke and crippled up with arthritis, needing to sell his horse. That's how the story was told to your grandfather and me and there was something in it that pulled out the stop on our common sense. STAR, THE LOVESICK COW PONY, we could sure see that on a handbill. We took the day's receipts and put them in a stranger's pocket. And that, Polly Ann, was the beginning of the end."

Not for me, it wasn't. That's when the story really began. The story of my granny's irrational fondness for an animal she had no business loving. I never saw her warm to an animal, except in these stories about the temperamental pinto.

"Go on."

"You always did like this part. The part about how your grandmother came to be such a damn fool."

As she continued talking, a familiar expression of disappointment and disbelief returned to her face. That she and my grandfather fell for a fancy story about a blind horse sixty years earlier still astonished her.

"Of course when he delivered the goods, I knew we'd been had. There wasn't a way in hell that your grandfather or I could have turned that fleabag into anything presentable. I tried for a time. Did I tell you, Polly Ann, that I made the animal a beautiful patch to go over that eye? Beadwork and I don't know what all. I did? And I suppose I did mention that I tried every handling trick in the book to get the horse to take to women? It never did figure out I was one, the way I dressed in overalls and such to groom him. Hair was always stuck up inside some kind of hat. But he'd get mad once he saw anything in a skirt. And you can't do much with an animal like that. It wouldn't have won our show any friends, having some woman stomped to death by an insane pinto. Oh, I sure should of shot the thing."

"But you couldn't."

"Nope. I couldn't."

She rose up off my bed and took a quiet stroll around my room. Was she living it again, like she had then? Figuring the price of oats and hay to keep a nuisance alive? She stopped by the window, but I was resolute. I kept my gaze level, aimed at what I could reach out and touch. What waited for me out there wasn't going anyplace. Bed rest, that was what the doctors had said.

"It was the first thing your grandfather and I failed at. If we'd had any sense, we would have taken it as the sign it was. But we kept on and it seems like after that horse, the two of us couldn't do anything right."

"Granny, it was the Depression. Staying alive at all was a victory."

She grabbed the hat off her head and marched over to the side of my bed. She gave one of my pillows a whack. I think she was aiming at me and missed.

"We could've done it! If we hadn't listened to that snake in the grass, that buzzard in a green suit, we could have still had ourselves a rodeo, instead of a second-rate riding ring in Granite, Polly Ann. But I listened to that advance man. And I listened to your grandfather."

The story darkened like it always did. Her voice changed to a low rumble as she muttered about Public Relations. Advance Men the World Over.

"Said he'd do the booking for our little show. Said leave everything to him, he'd take care of things. So we did, until it was too late. Any fool could have seen what he was doing. Booking us into deadbeat towns further and further west, crisscrossing that desert until we were bankrupt. Polly Ann, he was being paid by another rodeo to break our backs and your grandfather wouldn't hear about it. He was blind as the cow pony we just bought and not a *whole* lot better-looking."

"Granny Settle!"

"I never said that before, but I'm glad it's off my chest. I wouldn't want to die keeping that thought company."

"Stop talking about dying."

At last. She started to loosen her belt, a young woman no longer.

"Why not talk about dying? It's my biggest project so far and I was never one to do something halfway. Let me talk while I can, girl."

She lay the belt on my lap in a kind of surrender and her stomach relaxed. I was sorry for that, sorry I hadn't let her go on full-tilt about anything she pleased. She needed to talk before it was too late.

"So anyways, you know where the advance man landed the two of us. We finally ran out of steam with freight costs overrunning our profits. That viper booked our last show into a little town just outside of Bakersfield. Right there in the San Joaquin Valley was where it all finally fell apart. People were too poor to buy a ticket to the show, so we opened the gates to everybody and gave away our final performance. That was a bitter day." She reached into a pocket for a sugary antidote to that memory. "Wasn't anything but Okies out there. Running from the dustbowl landed those people in a worse mess than the one they left. Nearly broke my heart the way our rodeo ended. The show ended and we paid people what we could, sold off the animals right then and there."

"Except for Star."

"Yes, may the good Lord help me. Except for Star."

The horse would live on and on, way past when his living was a welcome thing. Star warmed to my granny unexpectedly the year he died. He became a nuzzler, whinnying when he saw her approach, and would even tip his nasty head for a scratch between the ears. He followed her around like a house pet.

"He didn't die noble or even mean. He was a plain nuisance when he finally went."

"But you loved him."

"Against my better judgment. I loved that worthless horse *and* your grand-father."

We were both satisfied, I thought. But there was something else. She fussed with the hatband, trying to scoot it around to a different position. I thought for a minute she had to go to the bathroom, but needed to be reminded of that. She opened her pocketbook a second time and took out a pink notecard she'd folded into a tiny square half the size of her finger. I put the light on, hoping she would read it aloud.

"This came yesterday. That mailgirl of yours and I've gotten friendly. I told her to tear up anything from Palm Springs, but I guess she forgot. She must've had a lot of mail to carry that day."

She handed me the soiled little paper. It looked like somebody had actually rubbed dirt into one side.

The Friendship Circle
12 Laramore Place
Palm Springs, Ca.

Dear Mrs. Settle,

I feel we've already met! Your daughter has such wonderful things to say about you. I'm just writing to say for myself and for the little community I represent how much we are looking forward to your arrival. There's never a dull moment for members of the Friendship Circle, our activities chairperson sees to that! I've taken the liberty of enclosing an "interest index." If you would just take the time to check off the activities you prefer, it would help us extend you the welcome you deserve. (We have a lively storytelling circle that meets on Friday afternoons.)

I'm looking forward to meeting you, Mrs. Settle. If you permit, I shall address further correspondence to "Babe." Your charming mother tells me this was your professional name during the Golden Age of Rodeo. How anxious we are to hear all about that!

Most Sincerely,
Mildred Adams
Secretary

I couldn't think of a single thing to say about that letter. Neither could she, I guess. She stuffed the letter back into the pocketbook and gave me a hard look.

"You look better already, Polly Ann."

She didn't seem delighted by this discovery. But maybe she was just angry at my mother's tactics.

"Matter of fact, you look better than poor Tom."

"Poor Tom? I'm the one who nearly got killed!" Fury released a rush of warmth. I lay there pulsing, watching as her face changed into the same expression I'd seen as she worked salve into an animal's hide. She cursed the stupidity of the horse who crashed through the barbed wire of the Settle Ring trying to make a break for freedom. But she was still there, on hand with medicine and melody, to patch up the wounds when the horse finally hobbled home.

Twenty-seven

*T*he smell of fresh paint, not hot coffee, woke me the next day. I clumsily knotted the belt on my bathrobe to follow the odor. Learning to function with a cast would take some getting used to. My legs felt steady enough, but my head was as light and detached as a helium balloon.

"Did you quit your job?"

Tom was on top of a ladder by the window. It would be hard work to match up the paint with the vintage white in the rest of the house, but I guessed he'd considered that.

"You're not supposed to be up. Edwards wanted you to have one more day of bed rest."

"I'm better, Tom."

He seemed doubtful on top of that ladder and the paint was dripping off the roller the way he held it.

"I'm glad you put something over the floor."

We both glanced down and, as I did, my head seemed to float and bob above the whole scene. But what lay on the ground wasn't the drop cloth from the garage. It hadn't held a lunatic stranger inside. This was sheer and disposable. We could strip this piece of plastic up off the ground when the paint job was done, wad it into a ball and get rid of it. Pretty soon, we'd even get rid of what remained of that night, too. Eventually I'd be able to pass through this room with equanimity. Soon, I hoped. I looked at the spot where Russell had thrown me into the wall and felt a quiver of what I'd felt that night. Tom teetered a bit from where he stood on top of the ladder, on display for anyone who cared to look through the window.

"Seriously. Aren't they going crazy at work?"

"I'm the one who's going crazy, I think." He sat down on a rung of the ladder and handed me the paint roller. "I can't stand to be in the office and I can't stand to be on the road. And every day I fake it. The problem is, you can't fake it forever."

I felt the weight of his head on my leg again, as if I were still in bed, still complaining that it was me who needed looking after. You look better than poor Tom. Granny Settle's words didn't get the same kind of rise out of me this time. Tom looked thoughtful and abstracted, the way he did when he was chasing down a concept just barely out of reach.

"I can't do anything. I can think of reasons to do things, but I can't actually get them done. First time in my life, too. I'll make us some coffee."

"That's doing something. So is painting. Why are you painting, by the way?"

He scratched the back of his head and was quiet for a moment. "I guess I'm trying to cover up what happened here."

A little creepiness oozed into the room. Barney had painted, too, masterfully covering up my name in a grim scheme that ended here.

"Polly, what'd I say? I said the wrong thing, didn't I? Look, I—"

His hand swung out and over the top of the paint can. Down it fell, and as it fell, we both stood stuck in place just watching it go. Paint splattered everywhere. Granny Settle's curtains, the mirror, windows. I couldn't move, but I could still manage a wisecrack.

"Well, you got your wish. This room will never look the same."

Then I noticed Tom was crying on top of the ladder, crying in the shitty way men do. Tears squeezed out of his eyes. He didn't gasp or shudder or go through any of the theatrical delirium that brought me relief. He held it all inside until sadness just leaked out of him. I put my good hand on his back as he came down off the ladder.

"Tom, it doesn't matter. Look, water-soluble, says so right there on the can."

He wiped at his face with the back of his arm.

"Incredible. No matter what I try to do . . ."

We got the worst of it up with rags and paper towels. Then I followed him into the kitchen. It seemed as if I'd been away forever, turning it over to a happy band of invaders. So much was new . . . kinds of fruit I never bought were arranged in a bowl. Notes for the children in Tom's hand, reminding them of things I didn't have the energy to mention anymore. A small television stood in the windowbox over the sink and all my sun-loving plants were pushed to one side to accommodate it. It was turned on, the volume low, even though nobody was watching. I snapped it off and on, then watched as Tom measured coffee into a filter. He whistled softly, fitting the carafe inside the machine. He watched the coffee begin to drip, then looked at me, taking one of my hands in his to study my nails.

"Good color." He dabbed at my arm. "I can't believe you're already up and around."

"It's time."

For wasn't that a point of honor in my family? To get right back on the horse after a fall. To be at least as strong as they were as they circled the deadening ring, never dropping in their tracks, never yielding to the heat that throbbed and pulsed while they stumbled through their paces. He tilted his head slightly and I felt my cheeks redden as he studied me. There was something new in his expression, something I'd never seen before.

"What's the matter?"

"Aah, nothing. Nothing important."

"What, Tom? Come on."

He took a deep breath and rubbed the side of his face. His hand left a splotch of white over his cheekbone.

"It's stupid. It's nothing. I had this dumb fantasy of coming in and fixing everything."

"You are. Fresh paint was a great idea."

"No. I meant fixing everything else. Us." He made a noise with his mouth. "Why do so many things sound right before you say them and stupid the minute they're out of your mouth? Here, coffee's ready."

I lay my broken wrist down gently on the table. Nothing for the next few weeks would go unnoticed. The smallest things, the things I never paid attention to would demand a new, necessary consciousness.

I drank my coffee too fast and burned my tongue. He watched me do it and flinched, pushing a pitcher of cream across the table. Right then, in that single gesture, something quietly widened like a ring of water on a lake until it held us both inside. I didn't fear it or fight it. I just let myself be swept up inside its insistent pull.

"Tom?"

I turned to the wall for a moment, an old habit. I didn't want him to see my face since I couldn't imagine what emotions were racing across it. Gladness rose inside me. It was pushing against my skull and my chest; it was like not breathing, but in a good way. Tom took my face in his hands and made me look at him.

"Say it, Polly."

"It's a question."

"Then ask it."

My question felt too ardent, too overheated, but I pushed myself to go on with it anyway. "What would you think about coming home?"

"You mean that, Polly?"

"Yes." I cleared my throat. "What would you think about it?"

"I think that's the greatest question I've ever heard you ask."

"I don't know where you'll sleep."

"Anywhere. It doesn't matter where."

I went back over horse handling and came up with the first thing Granny Settle taught me before I could enter the ring. The sound of my voice must never let on uncertainty or fear. In fact, it was Granny Settle who trained true condition out of my voice. If it worked with horses, maybe it would work with men.

"Well then. I guess that's that."

Tom's mouth tightened and he stared at me a second before looking down into his empty cup. "Kinda sounds like a business deal the way you say it."

I squirmed, wishing speaking was like writing. That way you could scratch out what was awkward or foolish or dead wrong. You could scratch it out and polish it, again and again, until it was exactly the way you wanted it. And no one would see all the mess and the labor and the mistakes.

"A family isn't a corporation, Polly, or anything close to it. When it *feels* like that, everything can get confused. That's when people make terrible mistakes."

Chairman of Children, CEO of Kitchen and Bedroom. Was that me? Was he talking about me?

"Of course I'll come home, Polly. I've been trying to come home forever."

When did forever begin? Which year, which sales trip, when was it exactly that Tom started trying to get home?

"Now do me a favor and get back into bed. You don't look so hot."

He was right. I did need to get back to bed. My head was loaded with questions so heavy the only option left was to lay it carefully on a pillow.

I ventured outside the next morning. I flapped my arms for a minute or two; I wanted to swim through the warm air. My senses opened in a simple burst. Everybody was back home. My grandmother stood by Kate's window; the two of them whispered through the screen. I noticed Granny Settle had trampled some of her own plants, the better to hear Kate's secrets, whatever they were.

Granny Settle wasn't wearing overalls. She had on an old-lady dress and old-lady shoes designed not for stirrups or rugged terrain, but for fallen arches. She had on support stockings, the especially awful kind that look like sausage casing. She didn't look like Granny Settle anymore. She was a dead ringer for Jewel. She looked at me briefly, then turned away from Kate.

"Hi there."

"Hi yourself."

The soil had recovered from Augustine's onslaught. The old familiar color had returned, but everything else seemed radically rearranged. It was alive, terribly alive, churning with earthworms and seeds springing to life. The baby plants didn't look tender to me. They looked as if they were a tiny conscription army on the march. Their upward thrust hinted at a merciless takeover of the bare earth. I pictured a rowdy future of butterflies and bees, hordes of noisy birds drawn to all the action. I looked at the hedge out of the corner of my eye. There *was* action here and all kinds of living things had been drawn to this scene, including birds, bees and bachelors. Russell was outdoors less and less these days. I almost never sensed his presence on the other side of this leafy wall.

"You broke down and planted flowers. Tell me what everything is."

"I can't."

"What do you mean, you can't?"

"I mean I can't. It's time for my nap." She was as petulant as a child, pouting at the word "nap."

I thought of Jewel again, who had begun napping the day she turned sixty-five to save what mind she had left. She'd actually told me this, putting down a piece of embroidery in the middle of a stitch as she did so, and pointing to her head. I wondered for a moment if Granny Settle had taken a fall or some medication. Or maybe a call from Palm Springs.

"Did Mother phone?"

"Didn't need to. Had her henchman do it for her."

"Bobby?"

"The very one. They're driving over to get me soon."

I put my arm through hers gently. That was it then. It was probably my imagination, but her arm felt weightless. It was as if I held the fragile wing of a sparrow.

"Come on now. I need to know what all this is going to be."

"I'm tired, Polly Ann."

"It won't take two minutes."

She scowled at me but began walking, pulling at me to look this way and that. "This here I put in for the young ones. It'll be up to Toby and Kate to water it and watch for pests."

"It's going to look like a rainbow when it's mature."

"I meant it to."

The arcs of color were separated by gravel, so that each curved arm of color would hold the eye without confusion. The red spears of salvia plants stood guard, rising above the fanfare in a long row. I held on to her arm even though she forgot about being enfeebled as we made our way around the backyard. Occasionally she would see something that wasn't right and would kneel down to tear out a vine snaking its way where it had no business being. She threw a rock at a bluejay digging around for sunflower seeds and pulled at the collar on her dress.

"Damn this thing. A person can't breathe in a getup like this. My idea over here was to have some wisteria crawl right up this old trellis I brought you."

The sheets were coming off one by one. I had loved that iron trellis as a little girl . . . it stood in her backyard, a thorough anomaly, looking like pictures of other places, pretty other places where flowers curled up and over your head, flowers that hadn't a thing to do with heat and dust and domestic war. I felt a sudden rush of understanding for Ruth Day. This trellis was my England. Now it stood in my backyard.

"A bench underneath seemed the right thing to do."

"I remember this! You used to make me sit on this to change into those horrible rubber boots before I fed the horses. I carved my initials underneath." I reached under the old bench until I found the deep furrows. They were still there, carved out with the same curved metal hook she used to clean mud from the horses' hooves.

"Yard-long beans and snap over on the left and this here is Indian corn."

I didn't care what Rory got. I felt like her favored grandchild. The gleam, not the mote in her eye. The regimented order stretching plant after plant down long rows promised a new and sumptuous beginning. She had provided for everything and the disappearance of the old pavilion didn't alarm me any-more. There was food for the belly and the eye. Even a cool place to sit to take it all in. Granny Settle had considered everything.

"It's wonderful."

"Don't gush. I can't abide gush." She waved me away, fearing an outburst, and went around to the door of the garage, reaching for a key in her pocket.

"I thought you wanted to take a nap."

She stiffened and looked at me darkly. "Who has time for a nap? Those two will be here any day now."

Better, perhaps, not to give the enemy a name. Carla and Bobby were head-ing our way and it was true, there was very little time remaining. She turned the key in the lock and twisted it with both hands. When the sticky old door wouldn't open, she gave it a good kick and snapped it shut behind her.

Twenty-eight

 *B*eth came over all the time with presents and gossip. Today she was concerned about the circles under my eyes.

"I'm not wearing makeup. And don't exaggerate things."

"So do you think about him all the time?"

I looked at Russell's house through the window, then realized she didn't mean him. There was so much to think about now. Much more than I'd ever imagined.

"Less every day. Think how it would have been if Barney just kept turning up in the neighborhood from time to time."

"You have an interesting mind. Perverse, but interesting. So you think it's a good thing he showed up here."

"No! I just mean he's locked away and that every day I'm further away from it."

"All right. That much I get."

Today she brought me an assortment of soaps and bath oils. I suspected collusion. Toby and Kate had built me a wooden planter that held a half dozen soap plants. They were in flower and stood to the side of the tub. Indians had discovered the plants long ago and they still grew wild in the hills above the ocean. Beth's array of soaps and oils would fill the étagère next to my old tub.

I uncorked one of the heavy blue bottles. The odor that floated out was wild and not too sweet.

"Sage?"

"I don't know. I bought it for the bottle." She lifted one edge of the curtain and peeked outside. "Boy, everything looks pretty great around here. Kind of makes you want to jump out of your clothes and get back to nature."

"I thought the sixties were over."

"They are. But speaking of jumping out of your clothes—"

"Oh, you're clever."

She gave me a big grin.

"How's it going, Polly?"

It was going oddly. It was a strange breed of dog hobbling along on three legs and I didn't feel like talking about it. So far I couldn't imagine a way out of miasma. We all gathered at meal times and walked about the house on the thin soles of our bare feet. Most of my energy was spent in being careful. Even Granny Settle was careful. Preoccupied and careful.

"This must be the sound of one hand clapping." She pulled a compact out of her purse and checked her teeth. "My shrink always used to say that to me. I never understood what she meant, but it did make me talk."

She waited, then dug around in her purse for her car keys. "Have it your way. But you know who to call when you feel like talking. We don't even have to talk. Just call, blurt out a little news, and hang up. I'll pretend it never happened."

I didn't really want visitors, though I never told her. It was all too confusing. The dining room was chaos. Granny Settle was getting ready to leave and this meant more boxes for some reason, boxes to the ceiling in two corners. She left the sewing machine at my door and I thought that meant the card table would soon be folded and returned to the garage, but I was wrong. It meant increased secrecy, with an old quilt draped over whatever she was working on now. The closed doors were, more and more, nonnegotiable. Strange odors floated through the house and Granny Settle's lights burned late into the night.

The roomy pantry revealed another screwball landscape. For in the middle of the airy storage space, home to canned tomatoes and corn, earthquake survival kits and water bottled somewhere up near Lake Arrowhead, stood an army cot completely filled with Tom. It was the only room left in this crowded hotel. A lamp sat on a milk crate turned on its side. The bed was made with hospital corners and a small Book of Common Prayer shared space with the lamp.

My first visit to the pantry didn't go too well. I brought a carton of milk along with me. It was late, about eleven-thirty, and he was reading with such concentration he didn't hear me come in. He would probably go blind if he kept reading by such poor light.

"It says here it's a criminal offense to take those milk crates and use them for anything other than hauling milk."

I was standing in back of him and he lifted his chin way up in the air and looked at me through the bars of the bed. He was unrecognizable upside down.

"Are you going to report me?"

"Don't be silly. I'm just saying if they catch you—"

"—the milk police?"

Hotel guests were getting edgy, I saw. It occurred to me as I stared down into his nostrils that maybe I'd made a mistake to let him come back home. Things weren't as easy or simple as I'd imagined and the old question I'd put to him was being asked in a myriad of ways. How does forgiveness happen? It hadn't happened yet. The cot in the pantry felt like a pity bulletin tacked up in the middle of our lives and that wasn't helping. I wrestled with telling him this when I noticed the milk carton was leaking. I backed out of the pantry toward the sink. Sticky milk was all over my hands.

"Why are you sleeping in there?"

"Where would you suggest I sleep, Polly? With Toby? That would be great. Then we could be like buddies. Me in a bag on the floor and ghost stories all night. Or maybe I could shack up with Babe in the dining room. Come on."

I decided to tape the milk carton. That way no milk would leak. Ever. It could sit on the top shelf near the back until it went sour and I would make sure it would never lose one drop.

"There *is* the living room."

"Which is the only normal room in the house. I thought we'd keep it that way. It might help us avoid going berserk."

He had turned by then and was recognizably Tom, not just a pair of dark nostrils. Something else occurred to me.

"Brushing up on the Ten Commandments, Tom?"

My question was sardonic, but there was no matching expression of irony on his face. Tom looked dead serious. He didn't answer my question.

His foot dangled over the edge of the bed and I tried to imagine how he did it. What elaborate physical geometry it took to fit his frame into the small space. I was having my own struggle with geometry. The pantry was welcoming, though cramped. I lowered myself to a partial crouch and reached for a jar of tomatoes. Soon the cupboard would be crowded with real preserved tomatoes and corn. I would have to figure out paraffin and mason jars, if Granny Settle's prediction about garden surplus was true.

"Smells like cinnamon in here. Maybe a lid's loose or something."

I wondered all of a sudden if those smells had soaked into Tom's skin. If the pantry alchemy had enveloped him. There was a bruise on the inside of his forearm and it was healing, going light yellow in the middle. If I lay my mouth over that scant blue mark, would I savor plums or blueberries?

"Anything wrong, Polly?"

"Uh, no."

"Well, you look white as a ghost."

It was midnight. Visiting hours were suddenly over. Tom didn't know it, but ghosts and specters came in all the colors of the rainbow. In Los Angeles, they were even turning up in Technicolor. Maybe that bruise wasn't as innocent as it looked. Maybe I was a real chump, wondering idly about the taste of my husband's skin, while another woman *knew*. I thought of one hand clapping, just what it would take to surmount the old difficulty, then pinched myself hard to get the words out.

"Are you still seeing her? Just tell me."

"Of course not."

"When did you stop?"

"The day you found us at the Sovereign."

"The very day?"

"Would details help us, Polly? If you think they would, I'll give you as many as you want."

I kept pinching, because I had more questions to ask. But the pinch didn't work. I had to get out of there before the room swallowed me up.

"Good night, Tom."

"You don't have to go."

"Oh, yes I do. I'm going to take a bath."

"Now?"

"Puts me to sleep." I was in such a rush to get out of that storage space, I crashed into the corner of a milk crate.

"Shit." I would have a whole bruise there. One day I'd learn to look where I was going.

I looked at my tub, thinking I'd really missed an opportunity. I should have had Russell draw me a bath in that tub of his. Even the words *draw me a bath* implied a handful of short change, the something less I had come away with. My contact with him had been so rushed, so fraught with guilt. I should have lolled in that tub, letting ten Jacuzzi jets strike me at different angles, and studied that view of the airport while I could. I thought of calling Russell with an apology. No, not an apology. An explanation, although how in the hell would I explain what was going on here?

A hot bath was still my idea of absolute luxury. Beth's bath salts made my skin tingle and I liked having those soap plants so near. Those white flowers made it seem as if a larger world was right at hand, pushing its way inside. I thought of writing that down as I soaked in the hot water. Lyrics still occurred to me, but they stayed locked in my head. I couldn't seem to pick up a pencil and there was no good paper in the house. Fatuous excuses aside, I couldn't concentrate on anything but my pantry and Tom in it with a prayer book for company.

"*La vie sentimentale.* It *is* confusing. Not that I'm often confused, but sometimes, just sometimes, there's a little nuance missing. So I turn to that ancient love culture for illumination. France always works like a charm."

I slid lower into the bathtub and covered myself with both arms. I was appalled. Frankie stood there in skintight blue jeans and a black-and-white-checkered shirt tied into a knot underneath her breasts. She had on black high heels and cradled the poodle I'd seen once before. She was wearing my sunglasses. I would have ripped them from her face if I hadn't been so naked.

"I'll give you a for instance: boudoir. Consider that *bouder* is the verb for pout."

I found my voice, though once I used it I wasn't so sure I wanted to claim it for my own.

"Get out."

"Now, now. I don't want us to squabble today. After all . . ." She gave the gray poodle a kiss on its ear. ". . . this will be the last time you see me. May I continue?"

She fingered the soap plant and smiled. I hugged myself tighter still and stared. If what she said was true, if she was really not bound to return, I decided to pay attention. It was hard enough to remember what was real, let alone what was fantastic and shimmering about two feet above my bathroom tiles.

"Good girl. Now, back to *bouder*. Terrific concept. A bedroom where a woman could attend to her toilette, catch up on her beauty sleep and even pout for days on end. Don't you love it? Those were the days when women could be capricious if they wanted to be. You naughty thing!"

The poodle wanted down. He squirmed and snarled at her once and I thought maybe the dog was my agent. Maybe the poodle would give her the good bite she deserved.

"I'm not pouting, Frankie. I'm stuck!"

Not that I'd known that before blurting it out to her. She pushed some towels out of the way and hopped up on my étagère. She shoved my sunglasses up to the bridge of her nose and pursed her lips.

"Oh, that. That's just choreography. Tom will have to move out of that silly pantry into your bedroom. That's a snap compared to what you have to do now."

She examined her fingernails, then reached for some of my polish and began touching them up, blowing each one dry as she delicately pulled the brush over each tip.

"And just what do you think I have to do now?"

"You said yourself that you're stuck. Well, Polly, that's because of me. I'm the only obstacle left in your path."

"So why don't you give me a break and get lost?"

"I will. But before I do, you've got to forgive me."

Forgive Frankie Doray? I slapped at the water, tempted to go all the way under. Surely she wouldn't pursue me to the bottom of the tub.

"I've lost the best man I ever had and here I am trying to give a few pointers to the woman he always loved better than me. *I lost him.* I've gone to a lot of trouble to get here, Polly, and I won't be able to come back again. The least you can do is try."

Her nails were done and she took my sunglasses off thoughtfully and laid them on top of a towel. Her eyes changed colors as she looked at me. They bled from light green to blue. The blue of some uncharted sea home to coral and buried treasures. Kind, plankton-fed fish swam under the surface of her eyes.

"You're sort of at a disadvantage like that. I don't want you to be at a disadvantage anymore, Polly."

Her clothing fell off her body, one piece at a time, and she came to sit beside me, next to the soap plant and the wooden planter my children had made to speed up the healing process, next to the set of bath oils Beth hoped would do the same. Instead of recoiling, instead of trying to hide under a tiny piece of wet terrycloth, I sat up straighter.

"See? It was you he wanted all along."

For I stared at my own body. Her voice, her face and self topped my body with all its inglorious topography. I squinted, looking closer at what I thought had been a spray of tantalizing cinnamon sprinkles splashed over her chest. They were sunspots, my own eloquent warning, much louder than words, to Kate and Toby about sunbathing. I even recognized the same pouch of flesh that pool laps would never diminish. Frankie shared the same dark stripe up the stomach that meant children, the stripe that was supposed to fade away but didn't. It was my sound, middle-aged body.

"I didn't know you had children."

"Surprise."

She picked up a bottle of oil, sniffed and wrinkled her nose. I repeated the question because I didn't think she'd heard me. She seemed to be listening to someone or something else. For the first time it was Frankie who looked worried. She set my sunglasses over my eyes with a funny expression on her face and whistled for her poodle.

"Good luck, Polly. I mean it."

The lenses in my sunglasses grew darker and darker, and soon it was impossible to see anything at all. The water in the tub began to rise in waves, each one striking my chest and slapping at the sides of the tub. I locked my knees, imagining that I could somehow steady the water by the strength in my legs. But I couldn't. The water raged on as angry gusts of hot air blew the hair back from my face. By the time the lenses lightened and the water stood in a silent pool, Frankie Doray had come and gone for the very last time.

Twenty-nine

I wasn't sleeping well, I had lied to Beth, and the puffy little crescents under my eyes seemed like fortune cookies to me. I didn't like the messages they sealed inside: YOU WILL HEAR A STRANGER'S FOOTFALL AT DUSK. YOU WILL WAKE ON A PILLOW SOAKED WITH TEARS. Even though I knew Barney was locked away, a little of him had settled into my days. I'd find myself imagining that Rambler, the uneven tilt of the letters in my name. Or I'd hear his voice again, his grating voice insisting that all he wanted was a sweetheart. I was jumpier than I cared to be, looking over my shoulder when there was nothing more to see. The whole world was slightly suspect and memory was as obdurate as ever. That wasn't all, of course.

"Tom, I'm not sure I can pull it off."

He crossed the living room with drinks in his hands. They weren't crammed with fresh fruit and parrots weren't perched on top of swizzle sticks, but happy hour in my dilapidated living room was exactly where I wanted to be right now.

"Of course you can, Polly."

"But I was never good at these functions in the first place. And now, with all the . . . with everything that's happened to us."

Tomorrow night was the Zeemie awards banquet. It was just a big dinner party, really, with bodybuilders and salespeople congratulating one another, and the president's presentation, an unvarying and humorless ode to good health. It was easy to tell who was who. You were either muscle-bound or you weren't. That wasn't what bothered me. What I dreaded was facing people I hadn't seen in a year.

"Do you have a plan, Polly?"

"I'm going to have my hair trimmed. I'm going to wear a black dress and one of those awful frozen smiles."

"That's not the kind of plan I mean."

I was crunching ice and this made me stop. The whole world had a blurry, pleasant feel to it except for the ice cube I held in my mouth.

"Which plan are you talking about?"

"The plan about how this is going to work. How we are going to work."

"You mean a plan like a marketing plan? You're the one who doesn't want family and business confused."

"Okay. Then maybe just a vague sense of how things are supposed to happen."

I had a limited interest in this conversation. I would much rather have concentrated on the cold against my teeth and the picture I could see outside of the street with the lamps just coming on.

"Why? In a hurry, Tom?" I thought about his stiff cot and the aching back he probably had but wasn't talking about. My own body started to tense up, the same way it would have if I had to sleep on a cot like that.

"I'm not in a hurry, but if you have some idea of what's supposed to happen and you're not willing to tell me about it, then we both stand to be disappointed. That's what I think."

He went to the window in time to see Russell's Range Rover scream past our house, its tires striking a curb as he careened down a sidestreet in a shortcut to Wilshire.

"Bastard. He could've killed those kids on tricycles."

The children looked unconcerned. They pedaled on down the sidewalk, helmets hugging their skulls. Butterflies flickered at the edge of the lawn, too shy, perhaps, to trespass, watching Tom pace back and forth in front of the window. The cloud of timid, flirtatious yellow butterflies took the place of a pretty picket fence, the way they nervously marked the edge of our lawn.

Our own children looked unconcerned. They made more silence than noise these days and if I stumbled into a conversation I considered myself lucky. Just overhearing their talk filled me up. I was so happy to hear Toby's voice and Tom's, I followed the mingled sound all the way down the hall.

"You look like a dweeb, Dad."

Tom dressed for the Zeemie dinner in Toby's room, switching jackets and ties three times before reaching a compromise. He didn't look happy at what he saw in the mirror, just appeased. I knew the effect of a child's deadpan fashion critique. My faint praise rolled like water between two stubborn banks.

"I kind of like that tie with that jacket."

"It looks stupid. Why would anybody wear a tie with elephants on it? Plus your pants are too tight, Dad."

"Pants are fine. Belly's too damn big."

"I think you look great, Tom." I knew he was self-conscious about that middle, but I honestly didn't mind the way it had advanced and retreated over the years. To me, exuberance and appetite were all mixed up together. I couldn't tell the difference between the way he reached for someone's hand, shaking it with genuine gladness, or the way he reached for a second helping. He always wanted more of life, not less, and a bit too much belly just came with the territory.

"Shouldn't we leave?"

Keys, coins, last-minute instructions to Toby and a look around for Granny Settle. She was standing outside, glaring malevolently at the hedge between our house and Russell's. She held her frying pan in one hand.

"And don't come back!" Her eyes didn't leave that thick screen. She swung the pan at the hedge for good measure and dead leaves showered down on the driveway.

"What'd you trap in there, Babe?"

"I'm aiming to teach that cat a lesson. Second time now I caught it begging for food at this address. The thing's worse than those old barn cats."

"I liked those old cats." The barn had been Tom's pet shop. He would kneel in the hay, squinting in the scant light that fell through the chinks in the wood until his eyes adapted to the murky scene, until he could see the batch of kittens to whom light and dark meant nothing, the mewling, shut-eyed newborns that the yellow cat bore every year.

Granny Settle turned to us, still clutching the pan. She scratched the side of her leg and moved forward a few steps.

"Now don't you two do that to me."

Tom glanced at me, then shrugged.

"Time's playing tricks on me lately and it looks like it won't stop until I do.

Seeing the two of you standing there like that . . ." This was no game. She knocked on the top of her head with her knuckles and I could see the bare space at the back of her open mouth, the space she'd never bothered to fill with gold or porcelain teeth, or teeth of any kind. "Have I come back to Oklahoma or am I still in California?"

"You're in Los Angeles, Granny."

"Ah. Why for a minute, I got it all scrambled up."

It was a confusion I understood perfectly.

"Do me one big favor and don't mention this business to your mother."

"I wouldn't dream of it."

She calmed down once Tom kissed her, saying something too soft for me to overhear, something that made her giggle like a young girl.

Dark wooden floors and brass dominated the hotel lobby and a big ceiling fan fed a current of air that churned over our heads. A bamboo barrier sealed a closed world of discretion and comfort. I felt like we were completely surrounded by sea, in a place detached from any mainland, floating free. I could imagine great waves breaking beyond these trustworthy walls. Latitude, the restaurant tucked away upstairs, felt as distant as a tiny point on an antique map. I must have looked alarmed, thinking of Zeemie personnel fanning out over the island.

"You don't like it?"

"Very much. I'm just a little surprised."

"These guys have more than earned it. Ready?"

I swallowed hard and adjusted the strap on my dress. I checked my makeup in a mirror and nodded. I thought about the salesmen, hoping I could remember their names. There were no crowds in this lobby, no sense of time passing at all. A couple sat plunged in one corner of a down sofa. They were talking so intimately, embracing in a way that was just part of a continuous conversation. Kisses punctuated, but did not stop a lover's dialogue that had no beginning or end. I could have watched them forever, but Tom took my hand and led me to an elevator.

"Will that little guy with the red beard be here?"

"Quit a few months ago. Everyone else is the same except Mathers. He's bigger than me. Must've put on about twenty pounds. Oh, and Joe. He stopped drinking and all he talks about is recovery. And his new girlfriend."

"Is this a briefing?"

We took the elevator to the fifth floor and there the air thinned. It wasn't raucous, Latitude couldn't possibly jostle. But we'd risen to the top of the hotel and the atmosphere demanded more. An escritoire stood in the hall, next to an Indian painting of elephants, kneeling and elegant in that bow to a slim-legged rajah. I tugged on Tom's tie and a woman in a long satin dress smiled and asked us to sign in.

The room was large enough for a group like Zeemie, but all the body-builders made it seem like a snug fit. I pasted on my smile and followed Tom through the crowd to a table. Getting there was as rigorous as any contact sport. There were brief, free zones with a light bump here or there, until Tom lunged ahead into one bear hug, then another. They did love him; these thick, roaring men with shaved heads and shaved loins loved my husband for his products, for his attention, for the seriousness he brought to their peculiar passion. Tom listened to them, that was his secret, he listened much more than he talked and probably any product he sold would have endeared him to the men who knocked back power shakes and power bars and who knew what else since I'd been part of this frenzy. I was introduced or reintroduced, I smiled until my face hurt. Then it seemed we could sit down, should sit down at a table full of hands waving. I thought of those greeting cards in my bedroom. I should have paid closer attention to the signatures. Did you thank people for sympathy cards?

"Why, look!"

I knew all the faces there, but I suddenly forgot the names that went with them. They were so expectant. So shiny and expectant.

"Polly Harrison!"

"Polly!"

"Welcome back!"

I returned to the dream I'd dreamed, not knowing whether I was a hero or just a celebrated guest. What was the source of all the excitement? I stared at Tom. Just what had he told them?

"Tell."

I recognized her. Tom called her the Vital Force. I called her the Loud-mouth. She sold Vital Victuals, newest in a long line of Zeemie meals, and she was unstoppable. She'd gotten married, I saw. Good thing she had access to frozen trays of high-energy food. It took a lot of strength to lift the diamond she had on her left hand.

"How did the two of you get back together? Reconciliation is *so* nineties. We are all *dying* to know your secret."

A glass of champagne was in my hand before she finished the sentence. Tom took charge of the conversation, steering me away from her investigation by spotting someone he had to talk to on the other side of the room. Mathers, pudgy beacon of light, beamed at both of us.

"Tom! Polly! You two look . . . much better than me!"

Poor fat Mathers had three young kids his wife was probably baby-sitting right now and Joe Deacon had a very new girlfriend. She sat next to him holding one of his hands inside both of her own; Joe looked sheepish and proud all at once.

"Polly, this is Melissa."

"Very pleased to meet you."

I rushed into a seat beside her and Tom took the empty seat next to Mathers.

"Oh, we'll scoot down. That way you can sit next to your husband."

It didn't seem that she knew anything about us. Perhaps she hadn't been briefed. Maybe I would get through this evening in one piece after all.

"That's just fine, Melissa." We were sailing through a brand-new latitude after all: I would make sure this boat was really seaworthy. "An old married couple like us sees enough of each other as it is."

Ignorance was bliss. We smiled, fast friends now. She even let go of Joe's hand, patting the top of my cast carefully. "How long till you're out of this?"

I didn't have a chance to answer because Melissa was a real talker. Blessings showered down on me. She was the best kind of nonstop talker there was, only needing the vaguest nod, the slightest affirmation that she was being heard at all. I relaxed and began to enjoy the evening. It would be a night of tribute and ceremony, a fool's parade of blown-up bodies and helium hair, inflated to match oversized body parts. I was served a pretty little salad, filled with bits of curly lettuce and an edible narcissus poised on the edge of the plate. As I sipped on champagne, it began to look like one of Kate's old barrettes.

"Don't you think so?"

"I know so."

I should have listened, but the way her eyes traveled the tables, it didn't much seem to matter. I was caught up in my old cathartic horror of this business, the business of the body beautiful. I loved me more after these events. My own flaws felt gracious and good.

Steamed fish was served with a requisite low-fat sauce on the side. A meticulous spiral of baby vegetables spun in the center of my plate. I tucked into my food and waved happily at Tom. I was in the middle of something that went way beyond vegetables. I could see and spy, record at my own pace. I nodded at Melissa, hearing nothing, and turned to the couple on the other side. The woman had something to do with accounting, I thought. Joe turned all the way around in his chair to face the podium, where a speech was about to be given. I could tell by the drop in the noise volume. Anticipation was hopping from table to table, quieting the room in a wide circle. Melissa hadn't quite caught on.

"And don't tell your husband, Polly, because Joe wants to tell him himself. But we're going to get married! I thought I'd never get him to propose."

Joe was a dedicated bachelor, a dedication that had taken years to develop. Not like Russell, who was still living a version of that life. Russell was young enough to be ignorant of what lay ahead, what was beyond the light bumps and jolts he felt now. But older, seasoned Joe Deacon was a pro and Melissa had brought him down. I listened to her now with real interest.

"I mean he doesn't have a thing to worry about. It's my clock that's important. Guys don't even have clocks."

"You're right about that."

"He worries about the dumbest things, though."

"Like?"

"Oh," she lowered her voice, but not because of the speaker who was moving to the limelight now. The speaker I knew so well. Olympia McMichael, queen of the beasts, truly dressed to kill. Her body, crisscrossed with black cord and covered, when it was covered, with red spandex, made me think of a javelin aimed at our table. She gave Tom a long look and began shuffling through index cards. "Like when he worries that when we have kids, we'll stop having . . . you know."

"Having energy?" I thought of Joe, exhausted, and wolfing down Wafers. "No one sleeps. That's just part of the deal."

"Oh, he doesn't care about that. He just doesn't want to give up sex for kids."

"Ladies and gentlemen, it pleases me to be here this evening." I put my finger to my lips and gave Melissa a reassuring pat on the knee. Tom saw me do this and I thought of a time much further away, right after Kate began to take her first wobbly steps around the apartment. Tom solemnly decided to wear pajamas to bed and the first time he slept like that, in generic gray cotton belonging to fathers over the world, the stab at modesty backfired. We made love frantically, in a rush of fear and sudden strangeness. We were careless and noisy, in a way we'd never been since Kate had been born. When it was over, we didn't ask what it meant. Instead we both lay still with our hands on each other's chests, waiting for our hearts to die down to the same beat.

"Your husband wants to sit by you. Polly, we have got to get together for lunch."

"Wonderful plan. Let's do."

"Holding up all right?" He smoothed the back of my hair and took the glass out of my hand for a drink of water. "I'm beat."

We sat back to listen to Olympia. A former contest addict, she'd sworn off now with a recovery plan as detailed as any twelve-step program. She held herself down to one bodybuilding contest a year, but this meant taming that urge to sign up, to compete, to train exhaustively. And, as Olympia breathlessly described to the Zeemie people, that was something you did one day at a time.

"We all came to this . . ." Her arm opened out in a balletic indication of the room and the world it held safely inside. ". . . with the same impulses. Beginning builders and professionals attack this regimen for the same reasons. We started training because we didn't like how we looked. And we took a solemn vow to change our bodies and our selves."

She allowed for a moment of pure reflection. The sober moment lengthened and threatened to turn to something truly dark and morbid, as everyone considered not who they were presently, but who they had once been. We were saved, though, by none other than Quadzilla. He rose from a table in the middle of the room, glass of mineral water in hand, and toasted Olympia. Quadzilla's quads were legendary and so was his fidelity to Zeemie. He had gotten on the bandwagon early, well before The Wafer took off, combining a love for whey protein with a vendetta against steroids. When the applause leveled off, I poked Tom gently.

"Need I say more?"

"About what?"

"This bodybuilding craze is nothing but vanity. This has nothing to do with strength or health. It's all about being beautiful. Or what these people consider beautiful." I came up for air. I was glad I'd finally put my finger on what I found so absurd.

Olympia was crowing about Zeemie Powder and its high-energy-producing carbohydrates. Something was terribly exciting, it seemed, about medium-chain triglycerides, branch-chain amino acids and valuable electrolytes. My eyes grew heavy the longer she talked. To keep awake, I pictured Olympia on an elephant, an elephant that knelt to a flinty rajah or just any old elephant. The ones on Tom's tie would do. I motioned to a waiter for another glass of champagne and created more animals still for the queen of the beasts to mount. Zebras, giraffes, lions . . . they all turned docile in my imagination as they waited for Olympia to climb on board.

"She needs to hire a speechwriter."

Tom stared straight ahead and his profile seemed stony and cold. He didn't look around as he spoke. "Sorry you're bored, Polly."

"Oh, I didn't mean . . ." But I did mean. I didn't like these dinners and I thought I was on to something about the vanity issue. I sipped at my champagne, but it tasted flat.

"Zeemie didn't just create The Wafer. Zeemie created a miracle product. We've discovered what it means to supplement the natural way. We've felt our endurance increased, our recovery time speeded up with a simple protein snack no one has been able to duplicate. No one."

Olympia fixed bright eyes on Tom. There was nothing accidental in the gesture, in the widening of the eyes, the pursed lips, the slide of the hand to the upper arm and back down again as if just thinking of Tom led to shivers of emotion.

"Is she transparent or what." I said it out the side of my mouth, not letting my face move too much.

Tom turned his head to me, but this time I was the one who kept looking straight ahead.

"The Wafer was the brainchild of Tom Harrison, as most of you know. It started with reverie, I'm told. A dose of dreaming."

Olympia had gotten to the good part. What had happened once was bound to happen again, this time with Zeemie Powder. The Wafer sent Tom to the top of his company, to take charge of legions of Zeemie hustlers. He rose to head of sales on the strength of a memo to the guys in product development. The Wafer. Slipped under the tongue, sacred as the bread of communion, it provided a quick burst of energy for serious musclemen. Olympia's features slid into a feline expression of pleasure. Her eyes narrowed to newborn kitten slits and I imagined someone's hand sliding up and down her rump, eliciting a satisfied purr. Whose hand lay there?

"I don't want this." I handed my glass to Tom. The champagne was no good.

"Then don't finish it, Polly." He whispered hard, as if he were mad about something. What did *he* have to be mad about?

The company president had joined Olympia at the podium. Now there was a match made in heaven. I tried to keep my face still, my attention nailed to the two of them, but I couldn't. I wasn't thinking about Olympia McMichael at all. I was thinking of the Sovereign Hotel, about a conversation that could have taken place in bed. Lovers talked, didn't they? I had failed at that, flown from the scene as fast as I could, but others lingered, I supposed. And in those magic moments anything came to mind and mouth. Maybe Tom was lying in bed, talking about how seriously people (his clients, thank God) took weight lifting, about how gyms were the new church, when bammo! The notion metastasized into The Wafer. There was nothing holy about that. It was cancerous, a killing spree hidden under the skin. People were clapping now. Thunderous applause rang for Tom, for Zeemie, for the glory of the body. Tom bought the Corvette around that time and our life began to change in subtle ways from that point on. I hadn't known why until now. I was finally piecing it all together.

I couldn't see because of tears. They all fell at once in an unpretty cascade, but at least I could get up out of the chair. Tom looked alarmed and Melissa looked beatific, Joe's hand now caught again in hers.

"Oh, you two are so wonderful." She winked at me. "Polly's so proud of you, Tom. Behind every good man there's a good woman and I've sure bumped into one tonight."

I kept crying and smiling, nodding at Melissa. She really was my friend. Tom put his hand on my back.

"I have to go up there."

"I'll meet you in the car."

Getting out of the room wasn't hard, since most of the attention focused on Tom. Just as I was pushing through those doors, I heard him begin his thanks.

The engine rumbled and burst open. Tom gunned the motor.

"The Vital Force said to apologize for her outburst."

"I don't know what you're talking about."

"The crack about reconciliation."

The boss's wife. I'd forgotten all about that weird reality. I actually was the boss's wife, though I seemed to have lost my touch. She was probably afraid Tom would reassign her to a shitty territory.

"Well, I don't apologize for mine."

There was a lot in the car with us as we drove away from Latitude. Questions, memories, new understanding that seemed to mean less trust, not more.

"Which outburst, Polly?"

"I didn't have more than one. I'm talking about bursting into tears."

He pushed in the cigarette lighter and pulled it out to look at the throbbing red glow when we came to a stop. He missed cigarettes. He missed patting the pocket in his shirt and having that cigarette as a little island of time in a long, streaming day. I missed them, too. We hadn't done Schick or nicotine circles or any of that. We started jogging. Every time I thought of a cigarette during the day, I made myself step into running shoes and think of how they didn't match cigarettes. I didn't want my sweat to smell like nicotine ever again.

"Funny. I heard several. You managed to let everyone at the table know how much scorn you have for this business."

"No one heard."

"Maybe, maybe not. But I did."

"So what?"

We were at a red light and he yanked on the emergency brake and turned to me.

"Does it ever occur to you that maybe I'm proud of what I do? That there's an outside chance the way I spend most of my waking hours doesn't shame me, doesn't strike me as stupid or ironic or boring? At least, not the way it does you. You seem embarrassed by what I do, Polly. What is it? Sales or what I sell?"

"I'm just pointing out something."

"Well, it's my turn. You managed to zero in on the fact that this is all vanity. I've seen a picture of Olympia before she became Olympia. She was the kind of girl you'd never look at in high school, the kind that always left something sticking out of her locker, a sweater sleeve or something. She was scrawny and nondescript."

"She sure isn't now."

"But that's the point! Why are you so hard on these people? She changed her looks and her whole life. I'm part of that and it doesn't make me feel like a jerk. It makes me feel good." He blew out a long, furious breath. "You don't have to train to look good. You don't need to do anything, Polly. You were a beautiful kid and now you're a beautiful woman. But how about if you ease up on the rest of us?"

"Thank you. Sort of." He released the brake and we started driving again. I was glad to be sitting in the dark.

"You get along fine without fancy clothes and fancy hair. People still turn their heads to look at you."

He and Beth were ganging up on me. This wasn't so different from conversations I'd had with her. On the other hand, it was completely different.

"What if I belittled what you did?"

"The kids take care of that."

"Answer my question, Polly."

"All right. I'd feel angry and miserable. I'd probably find somebody who loved country music in general and mine in particular."

It was quiet for miles, the kind of quiet you would never forget as long as you lived. And in that silence words grew, amplified, echoed with new meaning. I thought of words I'd said I could never take back. Words I'd overheard that I would never stop hearing. And all of them, every single syllable, seemed carved into my bone. My bone, on which the flesh lay trembling, was scarred now, tattered and tattooed with words.

We were home. Tom parked on the street even though he hated to. Granny Settle's truck took up most of the driveway and he couldn't get her to remember to pull it any closer to the back of my Pacer. I heard a nightingale singing somewhere inside the liquidambar tree.

"All right. That takes care of most of what I had to say. Tell me why you were crying back there."

A SOLD sign stood in Russell's yard. It had been there for about two weeks. I'd always known the house would be sold, so that wasn't a surprise. I wondered if he'd gotten the price he wanted.

"Can we talk about that later?"

I thought I should rest my thoughts for a while. I wanted to sleep. I wanted nothing more than a sound sleep without fears of Barney or anyone else invading the hours before dawn. Anyway, The Wafer kept generating new waves of meaning and I wanted to hold still and quiet so I wouldn't miss them. I watched as Tom opened the door to the cat, Russell's cat, who still cried to be fed, no matter who came after him with a frying pan.

"Why doesn't he break down and feed him? Come here." He held the scruffy cat in his lap as the animal banged his head against Tom, against the steering wheel and against my heart.

"Feel this, Polly."

He took my hand and ran it over the cat's rib cage. Each rib felt sharp and chiseled. I was ashamed to have let things go this long.

"What do you say we take him in, Pol?"

I didn't say anything. He leaned over and kissed me. The cat was pressed between the two of us, but we barely noticed. That cat didn't move a muscle.

Thirty

We rolled down the windows of the Corvette and just breathed the sweet night air. I must have fallen asleep once or twice as we talked. He did, too. I opened my eyes to find him slumped against the window. He still snored; I don't know why it surprised me to find that out. Someone was pulling up behind us and the headlights burned into the inside of the Corvette, shining bright as a police floodlight on a suspect. Gone was Russell's Range Rover. A long, black limo had taken its place. A couple of young girls in strapless gowns poked through the top of the moonroof. They looked like a pair of identical saplings, about to be set into a patch of ground someplace. I stared through the window as the girls got out of the car and glided toward Russell's front door. I looked at the side of Russell's house and wondered how my name would look up there. Then I pictured the headlines in the *National Enquirer.* "Moms Who Tag . . . Mischief or Madness."

"Tom. Tom, wake up."

I slipped out of the car and walked blearily up the path. I wanted to get into bed fast before I was fully awake. The house was warm and muffled, wrapped in a deep sleep. He leaned against the door frame and didn't go anywhere.

"Thanks for coming tonight with me, Polly. It must've been hard."

His arms were folded over his chest. I tried to see myself inside those arms, the kind of picture that would make. But I just couldn't think myself there, no matter how much I concentrated. I really was tired.

"Well. Guess I'm off to the pantry." One movement, very slight, the widening of his bright eyes, made this a question, not a statement. I looked down the dark hall and back at him.

"Toby wants you to drive him to basketball tomorrow, so don't forget to set your alarm. He should be in great shape for camp."

He gave me a wry smile and I took off my shoes so I wouldn't wake anyone. It was hard to turn my back on him, but I did it.

I listened to that nightingale sing until the first bit of light intruded upon the darkness. By the time I smelled coffee and beef fat, heard water start to run through an ancient pipe that ran over my head, everything was clear. You couldn't *think* your way into someone's arms. You had to *fight* your way in. Tom was right about asking for a plan. I finally had one.

"You gotta be kidding."

Both children looked disgusted. I sat on the old wooden bench in the garden. Wisteria was beginning its glistening green creep up the sides of the trellis. I slipped my hand over Toby's and he jerked it away.

"What about that stupid cat?" Toby tossed a clod of dirt over the fence. "Tell *him* to feed it."

"Toby. Shame on you."

"No, Mom. Shame on *you.*"

"Maybe you guys should get another mother. I mean it. Everything I say lately is awful and stupid."

"Nobody even wanted a cat in the first place, ever think about that? And now you're telling us that we have to feed it and clean up its crappy litter box while you and Dad go to a hotel for the night."

"Granny Settle thinks so, too." Kate nibbled a spinach leaf and chewed on it for a long minute. "She thinks it was a really bad idea to start feeding that cat. The other thing, Mom?"

It was a slight change, very slight. But the henna rinse had been gone for several days and nothing had taken its place. No hair shaved on the bias lurking under a length of longer hair. Kate's untreated head shone under the sun.

"Even if you've got this big plan, which you don't seem to have since you keep changing back and forth, it would be really nice if you'd pretend to care about what Toby and I thought. I mean, I'm not stupid. I don't trick myself into believing that my opinion is actually going to change anything. But it would make things seem—"

"—less mean." Toby frowned at the rows of corn. "You're just like Granny Settle. You go around and *do* stuff. Then you're all surprised when nobody's happy."

Toby stood up and moved next to his sister. In another year he'd be nearly her height. They hadn't fought since Tom had been back in the house. I hadn't heard one vengeful word. No bitter, complaining notes had been slipped under my door late at night.

"If you want to know the truth, Mom—"

"I do, Kate. It may not seem like it sometimes, but I do."

"—It was better before Dad moved back. We didn't have to pretend it was normal having our father sleep in the kitchen. We didn't have to pretend to like animals. Just because you and Dad like cats doesn't mean we do. And it's going to be even weirder when she leaves."

"What? You've been on my back since the day Granny Settle arrived."

"Yeah, but it's different now. I'm used to her."

It would have been a ripe moment for a statistic. On dog feces, on the extended family. Come to think of it, Toby hadn't coughed up any facts or figures for at least a week or two.

"Well, you guys. I don't know what to tell you."

"I don't see why you're going to a hotel anyway. Can't you guys just do it at home?"

The elevator at the Sovereign smelled like lamb and cloying perfume. I'd forgotten many of the rooms had kitchens and quite a few foreign visitors lived there for months at a time. I was glad nothing had changed. Everything seemed at least as shabby as it had before. I hoped the Sovereign would suggest the enormity of the job ahead of us. I didn't think our new life should be based on trying to stomp out memories that wouldn't die. I thought it had to reach out and surround every single thing that stood between us. I chose this old haunt hoping I wouldn't have to actually come out and say that. But Tom was a literal man. A good, flat-footed, literal man. The elevator door ground open painfully and we stepped out onto the sloping third floor of the hotel.

"I thought this place would be perfect for an armistice."

"Oh." His voice brightened and he smiled for the first time that day. He bent over the door and frowned as he worked the key into the lock.

"Put some muscle into it. The keys always stick in these doors."

He looked over his shoulder at me. His hair curled gently over the collar of his shirt.

"Oh yeah? How would you know?"

"These old hotels are all the same."

I was wearing good perfume. Usually I was in such a hurry, I squirted fragrance any old place, but tonight I had perfume on my skin, not my shirt. I kept thinking excitement would kick in any moment, probably the second Tom got that stubborn door open. Instead of excitement all I felt was a light wave of sickness that rose from my stomach to my mouth. Probably I was just nervous. Probably things would be easy and natural, a true reconciliation. This creaky hotel was probably full of buried hatchets. Tom rammed his shoulder into the door, just as I had imagined Russell doing to get into Kate's room, and it banged open. I sighed, looking up and down the empty hall. It was too late to run.

"There. Got it."

The room smelled stale. It could have been closed for decades. Tom went straight for the windows and threw them open. We were facing the ocean and it didn't take long for salty air to sweep over both of us.

"Better, huh?"

He began pulling out drawers and turning on faucets, prowling through the room. I hadn't counted on him being nervous. My version of things had never gone like this. Tom put our suitcase on a luggage rack in the closet. Then he turned on the television and stretched out on the bed.

"Hand me that extra pillow will you, Pol?"

I tossed him a gold velour pillow with a fat button sewn in the middle and he caught it with one hand.

"I think I'll take a hot shower."

Zap, zap, zap. Those television channels never stood a chance. Tom pressed the remote control frantically. "Man oh man. The reception really stinks. Hope the shower works better than this. Man oh man."

We both knew it didn't. We both knew the shower actually hurt with its single painful setting you couldn't adjust. I stepped into the bathroom and leaned on the door to get it shut, but it was better once I got inside. I remembered the cold that came through that coverless vent in the bathroom wall and how hard it was to get everything lined up inside the tiny medicine cabinet. My bottles and tubes barely fit and I knew the hotel shower cap wouldn't cover my head completely. My bottle of Secret even fell into the toilet, just like it had when I'd stayed here nine months ago. So much familiarity helped slow my pulse. Maybe if I'd chosen a different hotel, one where nothing had happened to either of us, a hotel featuring printed instructions in the bathroom about voltage and covered drinking glasses with those white paper hats, I would have fainted from fear by now. But that didn't happen. By the time the hot water stung the back of my neck, I was feeling very pleasant. I knew my evening at the Sovereign wouldn't be anything like I'd imagined, but that was beginning to be all right with me.

The curtains were drawn when I stepped out of the bathroom. With the windows still open behind them, they swelled up like velvet bellows and deflated, releasing fat little blasts of air. The sound was off and Fred Astaire was whirling Ginger around with a foolish smile on his face. The reception looked perfect to me. I was naked, but in a friendly way. Tom was naked, too. Fred's and Ginger's shadows danced all around us and the glow from the television set lit our bodies kindly. I pretended we were as much in sync as the two of them.

Tom patted on the empty spot beside him.

"Gee, you look beautiful."

"I do?"

He nodded. He put his fingers on my cast and drummed lightly. Then he leaned down and kissed the top of my arm.

"This hurt?"

"No."

"I bet it did that night."

"I wouldn't know. I passed out."

True, my wrist didn't hurt me a bit. But it looked as if it was killing Tom.

"It should have been me straddling that guy. He wouldn't have come at all if I'd been living at the house." He leaned down and gave my arm another kiss.

"How about we bypass the past tonight?"

"You could make that into a country song."

It was probably six o'clock. Elsewhere children were being driven from kitchens because dinner would soon be ready. I didn't feel hungry myself, but the light released by the billowing curtains suggested that ravenous hour. I slipped my hand into Tom's. We were both sitting up straight with the covers pulled over our laps.

"How come you don't volunteer for stuff anymore, Polly?"

"Oh, I stopped doing that ages ago."

"That's too bad. You were dynamite."

"I was?"

"The best. You're a born public speaker. You light up the whole room. Know what I used to think of when I'd be sitting there in the audience?"

"I don't know. A nation full of terrible schools. No pencils for millions of schoolchildren."

"I used to think of what you would look like up there without any clothes on. Or maybe just a boa wrapped around your neck."

"Tom!"

I could have sat like that until the earth spun off its axis. His hand was pleasant and warm and the way the light hit his face in sections kept catching me off guard. I didn't want one more thing in the world right then. Not one more thing. Here we were having such delicious, meandering post-coital talk without the coital. And that was just fine.

Tom began to talk about centering. Centering was something all his sales-people had to learn to do, even the Vital Force. He offered to teach me to do it. They'd been to a one-day seminar and it wasn't tough once you learned a few basic principles.

"Hey, what's up?"

If I had known about centering, I would have done it then. Gotten off the tangent my thoughts had taken. I wondered if The Wafer had been born in the same way, in lazy talk that went skimming over the top of absolutely every-thing. I must have sat up straighter, thinking about that.

"Come on, Polly. Isn't the point of coming here to really talk?"

"All right. There's something I want to know."

"Anything." His hand slipped away from my arm.

"I just had this flash of you and her sitting around talking. No clothes on, like us."

"Oh, God." He rubbed his hands over his face. "I wish none of this had ever happened."

"But it did, Tom. You're the one who asked me if I thought details would help."

He slid down and turned on his side, with his hand propping up his head. I wished he could hold mine up, too. My head felt heavy and graceless as an oversized bloom on a skinny stalk.

"What do you want to know?"

"What you talked about."

"Oh, that. Business."

"God damn you! I knew that. I just knew it. Sitting around, all sexed out, you two came up with the idea of The Wafer."

He was smiling without smiling and he held down my broken wrist, as if he thought I might knock him out with my cast.

"I don't know about the sexed-out thing, Polly. But part of what came from one conversation did turn into that product. So what?"

"So what? Quit playing dumb." The only trouble was, it wasn't an act. He truly didn't see why this would drive me crazy. He was struggling, his forehead was struggling, creasing and crawling with lines that tried to intersect, but didn't.

"But why would *that* make you mad? That was exactly the thing that drove her crazy. That was all we had to talk about afterward. We didn't have kids to discuss or Granite or anything besides her sales figures and mine. At the end, she always wanted to get me to talk about the two of us, the way it was when we were kids. It was weird. Like she wanted what we'd had."

"She had it! She had you!"

"But that's the point. She didn't have me at all and she knew it."

It was damp in that old hotel. I shivered and pulled the blanket up over me. Johnny Day's cold times had entered here and I felt them as he must have. *I've seen pictures of all of you.* I wanted to see those pictures, too.

"So, all right. You talked about business and didn't talk about me. You showed her a picture, though. She told me that."

"Just the one I carry in my wallet."

The picture showed a knobby-kneed girl blowing a kiss to the camera. Beyond her stood the giant Ferris wheel. That garish wheel that had been our city skyline, our big night on the town.

Tom seemed to be catching cold, too. He rubbed the top of his arm briskly.

"She got a look at the picture. The story I kept to myself."

"What story?"

"The way I gave the guy all those quarters to keep us in the air longer."

I remembered that long ride, the way the air felt on my legs. Tom's kisses as the wheel turned and turned. I had always thought it was our good luck and good love that kept us going around when everyone else's ride was so much shorter.

"You mean, you rigged that up?"

"Of course. How did you think that ride lasted so long?"

I thought about having that much love for someone else. That much love and desire that you would map out strategy beforehand, paying somebody to keep feeding that wheel, to keep it turning all night long.

I felt my chest tighten. Oh, God, not now. Not again. The bathroom downstairs, the silent audience that stood on while I coughed and choked and gasped for air. Don't let me have an attack now.

"Polly, honey. You all right? Hey, here."

He pulled my body down over his and just held on. He held on tight this time, and didn't let me go. I breathed along with him, as if he were swimming me to safety. One, two, three breaths just like his, I was using his rhythm, not mine, not the raggedy gasps that were catching at me, threatening to drag me under the water. Air came closer and closer, it was less difficult to trap in my lungs.

"Better? Polly, don't scare me like that."

"Why didn't you do this that night? Why didn't you come and hold me? Why did you choose her and not me?"

"I didn't choose anyone, Polly. I didn't know what to do."

"So you didn't do anything."

"I went home. I hid out with the kids." He took a deep breath and my chest moved with his as he did. "You're right, I didn't do anything. Just like those rabbits in Babe's garden. I was just as stupid as all those rabbits."

They would freeze, hide inside a row of corn or next to a blackberry bush until they were out of danger. As a child, I thought about what a lousy mother nature was, arming her children with the wrong instincts. As an adult, I had a different idea. Maybe by holding stock-still, some of those jackrabbits survived their predators.

Gradually, holding on to Tom, I could breathe in the old regular way. We had successfully climbed inside a new moment, one that wasn't good or bad and I didn't want to tamper with what we had right then. We were talking. We were naked. We were beginning to get hungry. I could hear Tom's stomach complain and Fred and Ginger had long ago danced off the television screen.

"Let's go get some food."

"Great idea."

I tugged on the blanket. It was drafty as ever in the old hotel.

Thirty-one

*T*he next morning the city looked rested and well, even if we didn't.

"What time did you tell the kids we'd be home?"

"I didn't."

Can't you guys just do it at home? I remembered Toby's outburst and stifled a yawn. We'd talked all night long. Talked. I figured both kids would study our tired faces and assume much more had taken place last night than conversation. I promised myself to worry about Kate's casual attitudes later, when I had some energy.

We drove slowly down Ocean Boulevard, trolling for interesting sights. It was too early for anything jarring. The long stretch of green that stood guard over the Pacific Coast Highway was coming to life, stretching its sore limbs just like we were. Seniors were out in force, power walking or simply walking, their fanny packs proudly bumping with every step. The young who jogged past them were mildly tolerated or flatly ignored. Several golden retrievers galloped past on leashes, their tongues lolling out of the sides of their mouths. Golden retrievers seemed to be the dog of the moment. In Los Angeles there really were such things as dogs of the moment.

"Some scenery. This is our Great Divide. Kind of pathetic when you think about it."

"You sound like you miss it, Polly. You've never even seen the Great Divide."

"But so what? I miss lots of things I've never laid eyes on."

A Mercedes cut sharply in front of us and Tom tailgaited him as punishment. I didn't like the tinted windows in that car and could only relax when they turned down a side street.

"What else do you long for?"

"Oh, you know. Wide-open spaces. A pack horse and freeze-dried food, that kind of stuff."

He smirked and drummed lightly on the steering wheel.

"Wide-open spaces belong in your lyrics, not your life. Polly, you'd last about two minutes in the wilderness. Now that I think of it, you did last about two minutes in the wilderness! Grand Lake, camping . . . ring a bell for you?"

"That was not the wilderness."

"You got a bug bite and made me drive you home."

He was having a very good time. It was the same big grin he wore back then. Somehow my defection from the campsite had become his victory.

"Forget the lake for a moment. Wouldn't you rather look at a human than a rock? Describe one tree you remember from Granite and then describe one person."

"I remember lots of—"

"—That's why people take vacations. To go breathe good air and gawk at vistas for two weeks and then *head home*. You look at pine cones long enough and you become one. I don't know why you keep glamorizing what you were so anxious to leave in the first place. Man, I'd kill for a greasy hamburger."

"It's nine o'clock in the morning."

"So? Hey look, that guy's open."

He swung into a little parking lot and I stayed in the car. I watched as he swaggered back bearing a cardboard carton of food. I hoped the second cup I saw was full of coffee.

"You can't beat this. I defy you to beat this. Want a bite?"

"This from a man who sells vitamins."

"God, this is great." He smacked his lips happily. He handed me a coffee and watched me doctor it with sugar and cream. "Russell's sure disappeared from the scene. How come?"

The fog was lifting slightly, sly as a skirt over slim ankles. Sun was beginning to touch the top of our heads.

"Now that I think of it, he hasn't called since the last time I spoke to him on the phone. Seems like he'd at least come over to see how you were doing."

My stomach jumped. He'd ordered onions on that burger and it was much too early to smell onions.

"Have you spoken with him?"

"Once. He was on his way out, though. I thanked him for everything." I *did* thank him and the way he roared off in his car told me what I could do with all my heartfelt appreciation.

"You didn't go out with him did you, Pol?"

"Here." I found a Wash 'n Dri in my purse. "What do you mean by that?"

"I don't think it's a real complicated question."

I wasn't looking at Tom. It was easier to look at his car and think about car accessories. If any of us had a notion, we could have outfitted Tom with a whole array of Corvette-related gift items, but he didn't even have a Corvette keychain. A misshapen piece of leather dangled from the ignition instead.

"I guess we did go to In Cahoots that one time. He knows I write song lyrics. Oh, and I bumped into him one evening by accident."

"So . . . you haven't really been out there. I mean, in the literal sense."

He had flecks of hamburger bun on his chin, but I let them sit there. My coffee was stale and the nondairy creamer didn't even faintly resemble cream.

"In the literal sense, you have a lot of nerve even bringing this up."

He looked out the window for the longest time. "Do you still love me, Polly?"

Love. It really was a kind of sickness, a different sort of sickness than the kind Frankie Doray had diagnosed. Love was a supernatural germ that invaded on its own terms, a parasite that entered the host body, living on and on, resisting conventional cures.

"I tried not to. I gave it my best shot." The words were surprisingly easy to say.

Tom looked at me and cocked his head.

"How did you do that?"

I didn't think details would help us now. I thought we'd better bury our dead in large and small ways, even though I knew the dead had a clever way of coming back for more.

"Oh, there are lots of things you can try. In the end nothing worked. I was a big flop. I couldn't make myself stop loving you."

I wiped his chin as gently as I could because I meant it. I hadn't been able to cure myself of this sickness, this chronic condition of heart and mind. I was in love with my husband. I wanted to rub the palms of my hands together and have the friction this produced smell exactly like the two of us. I drank down the rest of the bad coffee and fastened my seatbelt.

"I don't feel like going home yet. Let's just drive by the water. Let's stay gone for a while."

Bobby Denario's Bentley was parked exactly eighteen inches from the curb. He was a fanatic about things like that. My mother spotted us from the window and jumped out of an armchair to greet us. She didn't smile as she ran down the path in her red mules. She opened the door to the Corvette and squeezed in beside me.

"Mother! We weren't expecting you until day after tomorrow."

"Bobby and I thought we'd get a head start on things. You don't mind, do you? I love this car, Tom. Take me for a quick spin, won't you?" She gave me a kiss on the cheek and it hurt. She struck my cheekbone like a woodpecker.

Tom put the car back into first gear and I squirmed in the seat. We had been driving for a couple of hours.

"*Can* you forgive me, Polly?" She'd softened her hair color since the last time I'd seen her, added some gold to warm it up. Movie star blond was a thing of the past, although my mother was still infected with Hollywood.

"For what?"

"For not flying to your bedside when this awful thing happened. Bobby and I were trapped in a health spa. No phones, no faxes." Her breasts rose and fell dramatically. "I'll tell you all about what it's like to be trapped with Bobby when we get a moment alone."

I thought I was in luck. We had swiftly left my condition for her own. I was wrong.

"Just look at this." She cradled my cast and rocked it gently back and forth. Hard to do in such a small space.

"Actually, Mother—"

"—You need relief now more than ever. That's why we've come early."

"I don't think Granny Settle wants to move. She's happy here with us."

"Don't talk nonsense. You don't have the space or the circumstances to care for your grandmother. You two have enough on your hands. This is a daughter's job."

If my mother minded being squeezed into such a small space with me, she didn't say so. She opened the window a crack and took a deep breath.

"Bobby and I signed her up for that Friendship Circle. The historical society has also expressed interest in featuring her at a film festival they sponsor. The trick is to keep her busy all day long with one thing and the next."

"Gee, Carla, do you think that's wise? I mean, she keeps herself busy enough here. She's managed to make her own friends, come and go when she pleases, maintain a little dignity." Tom's big hands squeezed the steering wheel.

"Why, Tom Harrison!" When she became nervous, she grew even more affected. "Shame on you. She's going to feel all the *dignity* in the world. We're going to make her a dignitary, a spokeswoman from times gone by! My mother-in-law will be there and a couple of women from the Friendship Circle have absolutely decided they'll be bosom friends. Once she sees her beautiful new room, she'll feel just dandy." She pulled down the visor and checked her face in the mirror. "I think Bobby and I have handled this whole thing *brilliantly*. Of course, if things do heat up, I've got a purseful of medication."

"She's not sick, Mother."

"No, but she's cantankerous as hell."

"That's not the same thing."

"I thought for sure you'd be on my side. I thought you'd be grateful for a little privacy." She took off her sunglasses as Tom pulled away from the stop sign. She bit down gently on the tortoiseshell stem of the glasses. "You two look wonderful, by the way. Tired, but wonderful. You ought to get away more often." She gave me a significant wink. "Mother. Mother. Saying that is like rolling a rock around in your mouth. When was it exactly that you stopped calling me Mama?"

Kate, Toby and Bobby Denario all stood at a kind of attention by the front door.

"Lorraine Middleton called four times, Mom. It must be a *really* good job this time. She even left her home number."

"Mom, a letter came from school."

"I got your grades."

"It's not about grades. It's from Mr. Cloaker. It's got one of those red wax seals he puts on everything like he's the king."

"Can I get in the house, please? Hi, Bobby. Nice to see you."

"Nice to see you, Polly. How ya been, Tom? Put your bag down. Make yourself at home, ha! Hey! I've been poking around a little bit out back. Now, if it was me . . ."

Granny Settle was right. He did favor turquoise. This time it had turned up around his belly. Blobs of shapeless turquoise were set into a wide leather belt. Tom followed him outside gratefully and I let Kate and Toby interrupt each other until they both got fed up and walked away to make phone calls. I leaned against the wall for a minute recovering, then bent over and slipped my shoes off as my mother watched.

"Once we get that Ryder packed tomorrow, once we get all the beds back where they *belong,* you can get a cleaning girl in here."

The dining room doors were shut. I could hear faint voices on the other side of the door. My mother put her hand on my back and guided me toward my bedroom.

"Polly, I need to have a little talk with you. Now, don't get all stiff. There are just a couple of things I need to get off my chest."

She squeezed the door closed to indicate what kind of a talk it would be. Mother-daughter. Adult to adult. Reasonable.

"What in God's name is going on in your house?"

I sat in the one chair I have in my bedroom. It could have stood a slipcover, but it was the one unquestionably comfortable piece of furniture I owned. It didn't have the lumps and bumps of my bed, nor the aged rigidity of my sofa. I relaxed and watched my mother pace.

"I walk into your dining room and I find your grandmother sprawled on a bed. I walk into your kitchen and find a bed in your pantry. Kate casually mentions that her father sleeps there. This is *not* what I expected, Polly."

"So?" I coughed loudly.

"This is where Tom belongs, darling. You know how to get him here as well as I do." She patted the bed, imagining I didn't get it. A little piece of hair fell over her eyes and she shook it out of the way. There was not one gesture in my mother's repertoire that was not self-conscious. Everything she did was steeped in an awareness of her own sexuality.

I stood up. I wasn't comfortable in the chair anymore. "Here's the deal.

Something happened about nine months ago and Tom and I split up. We're getting back together, but it takes time."

"It doesn't take a rocket scientist to figure out what happened."

She paced the room in her stocking feet. Her feet padded softly over the carpet, wheeled, turned and padded again. She looked like a lawyer, banging out arguments before a packed courtroom.

"I saw this coming long ago. I started dropping hints a long time ago and you didn't hear me."

"Oh, I heard you, Mother. I heard you loud and clear."

"Then why didn't you *do* anything? Why didn't you do more with your appearance? Why didn't you flirt? You never used the gifts God gave you. You just slumped around in those clothes of yours! I told you and told you and told you."

"So it's my fault."

"Now, sweetie. That's not what I mean. Men just *need* so much. They need much more than we do, but they're not very good about asking for what they want even if they know what they want in the first place. Now, Tommy's getting older."

I wished she hadn't done that, slipped insidiously back into her apron, the frilly one with pockets covering her breasts. *Tommy is the sweetest boy ever. Tommy, come help me move this old box. Tommy, taste this for me, darling. Good? Good.*

"Don't look at me like that. We all are. And if he needs a little fussing over, a little something extra as the years pass, where's the harm in that? Now, take that Fanfest."

"What does that have to do with it?"

"Take what happened there. Just shows what can happen when a woman exerts herself in the right way."

"Nothing happened at Fanfest, Mother."

"That's not what I hear. Johnny thought you were simply marvelous."

"He thinks you're simply marvelous. I've heard nothing from him, absolutely nothing. But even if I did, even if something happened today or next year or in ten years, it wouldn't be because of what you're talking about. I didn't play pinup girl. I didn't entice him. Want to know why?"

"Well, yes, after all this time. Yes, I do."

She was still lovely. Even though her coquetry was foolish and transparent, my mother was still the prettiest woman Granite, Oklahoma, had ever produced. If she could return to those days, so could I.

"Maybe because I don't like having men howl like hounds and I don't want the whole town to gossip and talk about me behind my back. I don't want to be blackballed from women's clubs or sing in church choirs so I won't feel guilty for being a rotten wife. That's your game, not mine."

Everything was so obvious and true and simple. And I hadn't figured it out until this minute. My songs knew, though. My songs were much smarter than me. *Used to be I could see love on your face. Nowadays I see gel rouge. That makeover took away something I miss. Did Maybelline do that to you?* But my creed of natural allure had begun to feel like arrogance. I wanted to rewrite that song or, at least, enrich it with a different kind of nuance. All the color drained from my mother's cheeks. She sat down on the bed, bereft for the moment of histrionic gestures.

"That town. To keep from dying I may have gone a little overboard." She straightened her shoulders. "Style is always misunderstood in small towns. Minah Overstreet and I both—"

"—ran around with your skirts over your heads until she moved to Las Vegas and that is *not* style, Mother."

The slap stung. It had been years since my mother had struck me and I'd forgotten how to dodge her open hand.

"Watch your mouth, Polly Ann. Minah Overstreet is my best friend."

"And I'm your daughter. You know what? I think our little talk is over."

I heard her voice in the living room. I heard her say she'd love a cocktail. Would the men join her? I didn't fall asleep, I made myself go to sleep, as if it were a safe latitude I could visit for a while. When I woke up the light was on outside and the men were playing basketball on the lopsided old hoop we'd rigged up on the garage. I watched as a white paper slid under the door.

Polly,

I am trying to make amends here. That is why I'm moving your grand-mother to Palm Springs, to relieve both of us. I will say one thing. I loved you the wrong way, but who knew those things back then. It's true. I loved me first and you second and with kids that's bound to backfire. I'm sorry about that slap but all my life people have said horrible things about Minah and me. All we ever wanted was to squeeze a little fun out of life and, believe me, that wasn't easy in Granite.

P.S. (It might be easier on the whole family if we both pretended that silly slap never happened. Oh don't fuss with breakfast tomorrow. Bobby and I will just eat at the hotel.)

Carla

Thirty-two

I was reading the paper the next morning when my grandmother called to me. I thought I was the first one up.

"Polly Ann, I need you. Come quick."

Her hair hung down her back, color-stripped to a metal gray and thinner on one side than the other. She must have pulled that bun too taut on one side.

"It's started. A little ahead of time, but it's started now. Sit yourself down here."

She was on the edge of the bed in the dining room, but there wasn't any space near her. I brought a chair around in front of her knees.

"It won't be slowed down now, so there's nothing to say or do."

"What won't slow down, Granny?"

She lifted her gown up off the floor and I gasped. Her feet were blue.

"Take my feet in your hand, child."

I faced my own flesh and blood and every bit of me was shrinking before every bit of her. I didn't want to see or touch or feel her. My granny was so old. How could I save the woman who saved me for years and years, if I couldn't even bear to touch her flesh?

"Go on. Take my feet in your hands, gal."

They were heavy. I lifted one, then the other. They were icy cold. Dull, dead weights I lay upon my knees. Without her asking, I began to rub them with slow, regular circles I hoped would bring them back to life.

"Polly Ann, where does the cold stop?"

I ran my hand up her ankle and it was like crossing the tundra in search of a kinder clime. "Here. Right here. I'm going to call Dr. Edwards. Your circulation's—"

"You'll do no such thing. You'll rub them until they hold me up and then you'll go about your own business like I plan to go about mine. Just to there?"

Maybe I should have lied, kept my hand on her foot instead of showing her exactly where cold turned tepid, then warm. She was computing her remaining hours and days and my hand was the gauge. I watched her lips move and her eyelids flutter in some daydreaming REM. She reached out for something on her bed, a plump package bound with twine, and put it inside her nightgown.

"That something you want me to take care of?"

"You sound just like her. Rub harder."

I thought about how it felt to be surrounded by the enemy. It was true. I had slipped briefly into my mother's skin and was taking charge of Granny Settle with that insulting chirpiness you use when you kneel to tie a young child's shoe. I pressed so hard on her foot that the skin on my hand was hot from the friction. I let one foot down on the ground and then the other. She tested them gently and finally stood up. I stayed where I was sitting and looked up at her.

"Don't do me that way, Polly Ann."

"All right, I won't."

I wondered if she felt up to a bath. I didn't ask as she moved to the front window to shoo Feldman away.

"That tricky old vulture. Just look at him. I'm dying and he can't wait to set upon my flesh. Go turn the hose on him, Polly Ann."

I picked up a pair of my scissors from the floor by her bed. She dropped them any old way after she was through with them and they could have cut a person's foot straight off. I went for the dust on the table after that. I would busy myself until her thoughts changed direction.

"Go and hose that man off our front sidewalk before I do it myself. Jewel taught me that, bless her heart. Your dear Grandmother Jewel taught me to get rid of anything I didn't want around with a good garden hose."

It wasn't the weight of those icy feet in my hands that made me sure of what she already knew. It was that, calling Jewel "dear." My granny was truly dying. She was forgiving her trespassers, calling off the dogs for the end of time. My grandmother was leaving me. Every single thing, every monstrous ordeal, every minutely ragged hem in my life would take place out of her view, out of her range of comment. I had those scissors in my hand and I was squeezing them tight.

"Well? What is it, Polly Ann? Don't just sit there with your mouth open."

She grabbed one edge of the curtain and shook it with exasperation. She held on to that curtain made from old skirts, stories and the dirt she carried all the way from Granite. Life flew out of those curtains into me. Her life. This must have been part of the gift she brought. The gift she'd driven all the way out here to give me and Kate and Toby. Feldman saw her angry face in the window and moved on. I didn't have to hose him down.

She held on to the package that was still inside her nightgown, though it looked like she might lose her grip on it any minute. I was afraid of sounding like my mother, so I didn't talk. I didn't say anything at all. I made myself coffee and heard the thunk that meant water was running somewhere else. I pictured her lowering down into the tub, hands clinging to the side, setting one foot, then the next down, down, down into swirling waters.

She was leaving my home the way she entered it months before . . . matter-of-factly, with her pure, unblinking view of the world pulled down over her eyes like the brim of a familiar hat. She stuck her forearm in front of her face to block my kiss.

"I *told* you, Polly. I can't abide gush. Now, I've come and gone and that's the end of it. Here, this is for you."

She handed me that box she'd hidden under her nightgown, now wrapped in paper salvaged from a grocery bag.

"Go on. Open it up."

Granny Settle slipped her hand inside one pocket of her overalls and looked at my mother, who sat waiting in the Bentley. Bobby Denario lay on the horn and waved at us happily from the cab of the Ryder. She turned back to face me and shifted her weight heavily. Inside the package was a fine belt filled with geometric designs. I ran my fingers over the diamond pattern, pausing when I got to the buckle. It was a badge of some sort, but the engraving was worn so smooth I couldn't read it.

"That belonged to an old friend of mine. Former Texas Ranger I used to know."

"A Texas Ranger? You never told me that story, Granny Settle."

"That's a story that belongs to me, Polly Ann. I never shared it with anyone." Something crossed her face, some pleasure in awakening a memory closed to the public. While my grandfather was tending to his precious cow ponies, could a Texas Ranger have been tending to his wife?

I tried to envision Russell armed with a six-shooter and a badge, but it didn't work.

"Just what is so funny, Polly Ann?"

"Nothing. And this? What's this made of?" I slipped the belt tentatively inside the loops of my jeans.

"I finally figured out a use for that old horse at the end. I must've made fifty of those blamed belts from his tail. Had a Cherokee fella do the dye and the fancy weaving. Damn animal dropped dead just as they were catching on. Call the children over here. It's time."

I motioned to both of them and they pretended not to see me. They didn't want to be anywhere near us, that was clear. I made a few menacing sounds and Kate finally crossed the front lawn. Toby stood slouched by the side of the Bentley, then pulled himself reluctantly off the car.

"All right. All of you listen now."

Kate was livid, as orphaned now as she'd ever been in her life. She slid the welcome mat around a few times with her foot, scowled and waited for her grandmother to speak. The last to fall for Granny Settle, she would probably feel her absence more than anyone else. Toby stared at his father's back, not about to participate in any more goodbyes.

"I see both you children are angry and I'm wondering why that is." She peered at Toby until he had to look at her. Kate slumped against the front door and rolled her eyes. "I think it's because I came in here and monkeyed with your lives for a time and now you're left with nothing to show for it. Am I right? Answer me, Toby."

He went at a hangnail fiercely, pulling the loose skin until it bled.

"I dunno. Leaving is weird. Anytime someone leaves it's weird. Jeez, it's no big deal."

"Kate?"

"Everything is just as messed up as usual, that's all."

"Say it straight out, children."

"Say *what?*"

"Mom!" Toby pleaded with me, sucking on his finger as he whined. I shrugged. I didn't know what she was after any better than they did.

"Say what's on your minds." She paused and stroked the side of her face. "Unless you're scared to, that is."

Kate stuck her chin out.

"I'm not scared. I'm tired of being pushed around. You came barging into our house without asking us how we felt about it. You tore the curtains off our windows and put dirty old skirts up instead. You planted all this stuff you decided we'd have to take care of!"

She paused and took a deep breath. "And then we started to get used to everything. We started getting used to our dad being gone and you being here. I knew I'd smell meat every morning and I knew I'd see you every night in the yard with a garden hose or watering can. I knew you'd look through my windows while you watered, too, and listen to my phone conversations."

Toby piped up, then. He rammed his shoe into the cement, making it squeak as he talked. "I got used to watching you shave your face every morning like a guy." He hesitated for a second. "I sort of got used to it."

Kate's arm brushed mine. I realized it was the first time she'd dared to touch the cast.

"You made us *know* you. You never stop talking about the times when you died and the time coming up when you'll be gone for good. When you decide to really die, it won't be just an old lady Mom talks about sometimes. It'll be somebody who lived in our house and made us know her. It'll be you!" Kate didn't shout, she whispered. My granny didn't retreat, she advanced.

"That is what you're fussing about? Death?"

She brayed with laughter as my mother rolled down the window on the Bentley. Her voice was icy as she called out to us.

"Polly, this is an awfully long goodbye. The freeway is going to be a nightmare if we don't hurry up."

"Coming. Give us another minute or so."

"Both of you children hear me now. If you two want a church talk then go to church. I've already done my dying and those church people don't have a single thing to say to me." She scratched her head thoughtfully. "Don't stand there looking so sorry. I know how I got to be this old and how many years it took for my face to look the way it does and for my bones to feel like they do. Time didn't just pass. I took every minute that was given to me . . ."

She paused, looking at the belt I now wore. ". . . and some that weren't. Some I snatched like a thief. I know what happened to me and what didn't. I know the story of my own life, just like you'll know yours one day if you don't turn your heads away from the truth. That's all that's important, children. Don't pay a bit of attention to the rest."

The car door snapped shut. My mother wore Keds in honor of moving day and a Minah-inspired baseball hat. She was striding up the lawn, planting her feet soundly in the deep tracks left by my granny's tires.

"Children, I know you're sad about Granny Settle leaving, but trust me. I'm moving her to higher ground."

Granny Settle's eyes dimmed slightly as my mother slipped her arm around her waist.

"Let's all kiss goodbye and get the show on the road, why don't we?"

She took off her baseball cap and stuck it in a back pocket. She ran her hand through her hair with splayed fingers. I'd seen my father do it a million times and I wondered if he would have been happy to know the same gesture clung to my mother.

"Polly, if that truck is still in the driveway Friday, call the number I left tacked on your bulletin board."

"You sold it?"

"For scrap. That way Mama can deposit the check in her account."

"You thought of everything, didn't you?"

The air between us crackled. Our night hadn't ended. I could hear her slap and others like it. The sound of one hand clapping. It was exactly like that sound. Granny Settle had assumed the glazed look that meant she was somewhere else.

"You bet I did, Polly."

She returned to the curb with great care, this time sidestepping the tracks in the front yard. One day she would be as old as my grandmother. But on that day she would remember not a wild, one-eyed beast named Star or the sound of a cowboy's song at midnight. She would remember the cool water that flowed under a bridge and a pack of men howling like hounds. She would remember a kid hellbent on braids and spoiling every distraction she invented in a deadbeat town.

"Granny, I have to tell you something. She's got your whole life planned out once you get there. She's got friends made for you and days organized. She's going to call every shot."

"I may be old, but I'm not an old fool."

"You mean you know?"

"Of course I do. They think I'm senile and that's fine by me. They even use hand signals when they don't want me to know what they're talking about."

"Why are you playing dumb?"

"I'm not playing anything. Palm Springs. Granite. Those are only words and I'm not listening to words anymore. I'm listening to more important things now. By the way, Polly Ann . . ." She tried unsuccessfully to stifle a burp. "Your grandfather paid me a visit this morning and he was a sight for sore eyes. 'Course who wouldn't be after three weeks on the trail? You might need to use a little Borax in there now that they've gone."

"They?"

"Brought that damned cow pony of his right on in with him. Used to be he had some respect for a woman's house, but I guess all that's gone now."

I took her hand and we walked to the back of the yellow Ryder to peer inside. Her belongings barely littered the floor of the deep metal cavern. She owned so little, really. A few suitcases and a scattering of large boxes taped shut, taped silent. They held all the secrets that were left after eighty-two years. I turned to face her, just as Tom joined us.

"Sure is a lot of fuss for these few things. Why the hell'd he rent this truck?"

"Tom, you're asking me? I'm the last person they consult."

"These boxes really don't take up much space."

"Nope."

Tom put his arm over my shoulders and pulled me closer to him.

"Even in the house your boxes didn't feel like much, Babe. This house is much bigger than it looks."

She stopped burrowing for candy or dirt and looked at me hard. Tom was putting a big question to my granny and to me. Her eyes glistened. They looked bright as the hope stones in Johnny Day's velvet skies.

"Wait here for a minute, Granny."

I thought of Shel Elliot and Johnny Day as I headed toward my mother in the Bentley. I'd cut my teeth on those meetings. This would be my most difficult pitch ever. She watched me approach in the rearview mirror. I opened the door and slid in beside her.

"Love your car."

"No you don't. What are you up to, Polly?"

"I don't want her to leave."

The air inside the Bentley was chilly. No air blew at my knees, but I was as cold as could be.

"I wonder, Polly, if you appreciate what I've tried to do here. The effort I've made. Or is this all about your childhood? Are you still mad about the unhappy childhood you imagine you had? Because that's so fashionable right now, isn't it, to suddenly recall how awful your parents were."

I knew she wouldn't take a swing at me. Public brawls weren't her thing since she'd married Bobby. He smiled down at us, parked up above in the cab of that Ryder. I waved at him, sure my mother wouldn't try to poke me with her beloved looking on.

"Well, I've got news, honeybun. You weren't so unhappy. You rode horses and played in the sun until you were brown as a nut. You hummed. You had Tom."

I may have hummed then, but now I sang. Off-key, with an untrained voice that embarrassed everyone who listened but me. My mother and I would always distrust each other. A little tightness went out of my shoulders when I realized this. It wasn't easy having Granny Settle in my house. In fact, it was crazy. But it was better than consigning her to my mother and a phony Friendship Circle.

"She's dying, Mother. Let her die here."

My mother tapped the steering wheel three times and spoke. "You two are just thick as thieves, aren't you? I don't remember a time when you weren't." Her eyes bore into mine. They were like a cartoon version of eyes, emitting harsh beams of light. "I redecorated for her."

"Perfect for guests. Better yet, you can rent that room during the Classic to a cute little golf pro."

"Edith Denario's heart will break."

I laughed out loud. "You can do better than that, Mother."

She was testing my resolve and when I didn't budge, she struck the steering wheel one last time. "All right then, she can stay. But *I* bury her in Palm Springs."

"Perfect."

And it was. I remembered Tom's formula for successful negotiation. Seal the deal and get out. I slipped out of my mother's sleek Bentley fast and went inside to wait for whatever happened next.

. . .

Granny Settle omitted something in her inventory. I sat in the dining room until it had a name. Alfalfa. What I smelled first in that barren room was alfalfa, the kind my grandfather let me make rooms of as a kid. Those rooms had been a fortress, protecting me from the deadly monotony of Granite. I was allowed to stack as many bales as I could assemble until four walls stretched around me, sealing me in and the world out. I never brought along books or dolls. I sat fierce and alone until I invited Tom inside. Later that summer my grandfather removed one fragrant block, then another as he needed them, until there was no bastion left. Just swallows and scrawny barn cats and the sound of the horses nickering softly for oats inside the airy stalls.

"Mom?"

I smelled a horse and the lather that foamed under its belly as it labored along at a slow trot. I smelled dry hills waiting for rain and a length of worn rope. The stale odor of a man's exhaustion hung heavy in the room.

"Mom?"

I turned my head toward Kate's voice, which rubbed irritably against all the other voices I was beginning to hear in the room.

"You all right?"

"Yeah, fine."

"So, she's back, right?"

"She's back."

She sighed and frowned at me. "Is Dad really back, too?"

I nodded and opened my arms for her, not knowing if this was too much, too soon. It wasn't. I folded my arms around a beautiful daughter and held on for as long as she would let me.

"She's *such* a pain in the ass."

"I know."

"But it's better she's here. I mean, your mother's plan stinks. God. This room stinks, too. You oughta open some windows in here."

I did, but even as I struggled with the last window, forcing it open with a wadded-up dishtowel, the acrid smell of an animal's hide and an old man's dusty skin had begun, by slow degrees, to fade away.

Thirty-three

"*H*e's taking us to Disneyland. Stewart's dad said not to bring my own money."

"Here. Always have some money of your own."

Pocket money was such a guy point of honor. I watched as Tom opened his wallet lovingly.

"That ought to cover a pair of mouse ears."

"Right, Dad. Thanks!"

He grabbed a jacket from the coat hanger and raced out the door, remembering goodbye as he hit the front yard. He waved at us and threw a bargain shopper into Russell's driveway.

Kate shuffled into the room, looking like a brightly colored parachute. With her baggy purple pants and an enormous T-shirt, she looked lost inside all that triumphant cotton. She glowered at the closed door.

"Why was he born? He comes in my room, takes my stuff without asking and ruins it." She held up a pair of jeans to illustrate her point. A white rose bloomed in the middle of one leg.

"He probably spilled something and then tried to bleach them."

"I'm going to make him buy me another pair. I'll be back tomorrow morning, Mom. I'm sleeping at Dinah's."

"Hold on."

She would have preferred to rush out the door on that last beat. Tom lay his newspaper in his lap.

"Dinah? You two are friends again?"

"We were always friends. We just didn't do stuff together. I'll be back tomorrow morning."

"Where are you going now?"

I looked at her backpack, slung over one shoulder.

"Can I have some privacy in this house?"

"When it's appropriate. Tell me where you're going."

The newspaper rustled and fell to the floor. Kate turned her attention to the light switch, flicking it on and off a few times.

"The movies."

"Alone?"

"Not exactly."

Tom stood up and she rolled her eyes.

"I am going to the movies. After that, I am going to Dinah's house and if you don't believe me, call her mother." She opened the door and then slammed it shut, turning to face us. "I don't have a date, all right? But I'm meeting this guy at the movies and we're going to get something to eat afterward and then he's going to take me to Dinah's house."

"A date. That's wonderful. What's his name?"

"See? I knew it would be like this. His name is Evan Nolin and what is the big deal?"

"You're making it a big deal by keeping everything so secret. Now, how long has he had his license?"

She was ready for this. "A year and three months and he's only had two parking violations. No speeding tickets or wrecks. Can I just go now?"

She looked at Tom and then examined a spot on the floor. "Okay. One speeding ticket, but it wasn't his fault."

"I need his phone number."

"It's on the kitchen table."

"Be careful, Kate."

"Be good."

"You can always call us if something doesn't feel right."

She backed out the door, waved at both of us and walked toward the sidewalk. I forgot to ask her something and it felt ridiculously important to get the answer. I ran outside, ignoring the way she just kept walking.

"Hey. Does he skate?"

"He plays golf." She didn't turn around, but she lifted her voice and her hand in a wave. "We're both freaks."

I turned back to the house, grateful Tom was inside. But he looked more frantic than I felt. His left hand, jiggling change in his pocket, was a reproach aimed at somebody and I didn't know who he was mad at, Kate or me.

"I should enter this day in a scrapbook or something."

"This isn't a date, you heard what she said, Polly."

"Look who's in denial."

Tom patted his empty pocket nervously. The cigarettes were long gone.

"You know, that handyman was right. We do have a dry-rot problem. Damn window frames in the back are practically turning to dust."

He brushed his way past me, nearly squashing the cat, who had eased into the hallway looking for company.

"We should give this cat a name. That way he'd have a real home."

"Why bother? He knows where he lives."

A true nomad, he looked perfectly at home. Just as at home as he had at Russell's. How many times had I seen him there? Once, twice? Those times were receding, getting more difficult to pinpoint with every new day I added to the calendar. Time was different now. Days were an accomplishment. One week followed by another seemed my crown and glory.

"You like that, don't you?"

The cat's big eyes watered as I tickled his belly. He was delirious with pleasure and claws snagged the edge of my sleeve. I pressed the pads of his paws to get free. I heard light footsteps behind me.

"You're going to spoil the animal the way you carry on."

"Look at you!"

Granny Settle looked like a beautiful old girl in her straw hat and white gloves. Her hair tickled her back in a thin braid and there was even a red hibiscus blossom wound into the plait.

"It was the girl's idea. She did this."

She stared solemnly at the door, then checked her watch. There was such a soft knock, I thought I imagined it. The caller tapped again, avoiding the doorbell, even though it worked this week. I pulled it open to find Feldman. He looked dapper in a dark suit and tie. He leaned heavily on the metal head of a golf club, which now served as a cane.

"Ah, Babe. You look—"

"—like a damn fool. Goodbye, Polly. Tom is calling you."

I watched as Feldman tried to help her into his car. She batted him away and slowly waved at me before I closed the door. I could hear Tom hollering outside.

Tom was gesturing out by the garage. Big sweeps of his arm, as if he were hosting a great party where guests flowed into the house with covered casseroles and simple flowers, their freshly cut stems wrapped in yesterday's newspaper.

"Poor Mr. Feldman. She's either trying to hose him down or go square dancing with him. She'll drive him out of his mind."

"Come and see what else Babe's been doing."

I'd been watching what she did all along. It lolled about me in a wonderland of bright rustic colors. Only the hardiest fruit and flower, bred to endure tough conditions, was represented in back. Granny Settle's horticultural sense had been formed in the hollows of the hills she'd fought her whole life. From a distance, the red clay had suggested fields of wild poppies that made heads of passing drivers snap right and left. Cameras were brought from the trunk of the car to the side of the road as innocent tourists snapped away, filling frame after frame with shots of dirt so deceiving and red, they even imagined a heady perfume floating in the air around them. What's that flower? they asked and never discovered. Who would have dreamed there'd be so many flowers in a place called Granite?

"Tom?"

"Over here. She brought this out from home."

A table was set in back of the garage, covered with the one linen cloth she reserved for Christmas and Thanksgiving. In the center stood a silver loving cup I'd never seen before. A translucent pink plate was laden with cookies. Oatmeal raisin, my personal favorite. A dark glass wine bottle was corked and covered with a piece of silver foil. I opened up an envelope with my name on it. The writing leaned backward, but was exquisitely neat. She must have used her magnifying glass.

Dear Polly,

I have made you and Tom a little picnic by way of thanks. I know I am old and underfoot, but I'd much rather be those things here than any-place else I can think of.

These cookies are not for the children. They are for you and Tom.

"This is so sweet. Here, read this."

"In a second. Look at this, Polly. Date's on the trophy along with her name."

"I bet this is the last trophy she won. Oh, God. It is. This was the last year she did trick riding."

"And this must be moonshine." He lifted the foil off gently and twisted at the cork that bulged over the top of the bottle. "God bless Babe. She brought the still out."

"Oh, Tom! Do you think it's her plum wine?"

I sat down on the bench and watched as Tom worked the cork out of the bottle, breathed in the smell.

"We just got lucky."

I rolled up my sleeves for a walk on the wild side. No sunscreen, no salve stood between my skin and the sun. Maybe I would burn. Or maybe I wouldn't. Maybe my skin would take to the broken skies over a mutilated planet. I thought of the skies in Palm Springs. Maybe my granny would have flourished in the desert. Maybe kissing bugs and brutal temperatures rising over a mean-eyed gila monster would have challenged her to live on for years and years. Maybe lots of things . . .

"Cheers."

He let some of the wine splash into the loving cup, then swirled it around with his hands on both handles. Tom sniffed once or twice approvingly, then rubbed over the silver edge with a napkin, offering me a sip of whatever was in that loving cup. He looked like a hippie priest in his old khaki pants and scruffy shirt. I thought of The Wafer briefly, but the thought was as thin and ephemeral as the protein cookie itself.

"Cheers."

We drank deeply. It was as if she had filtered a rich burgundy wine through thick layers of figs and peaches. Plums, too, I thought. The faint taste of metal made me remember something. I pulled a tattered grocery list from my pocket. EGGS, ORANGES/GRAPES, P. SUGAR and some lines scrib-bled on the other side of the page. I read them and handed the paper to Tom.

He saw her smile and didn't regret
All the money he'd have to spend
He'd pay for a ride straight into the sky
A ride that would never end
A Ferris wheel of days and years
They would travel as lovers and friends.

He was a kid who knew all about love
He knew it all back then
Love wasn't a ticket you paid for
Love wasn't a prize you could win
Nobody taught him and nobody told him
And nobody said it would end.

He fed a wheel of desire
He felt it turn round and round
He hoped they would get stuck at the top
And never return to the ground.

He still thinks of that night at the fairground
Now they have kids of their own
He wonders just what he has paid for
Just what kind of ride he's been on
He misses that young girl beside him
He's never felt this alone.

He fed a wheel of desire
He felt it turn round and round
He hoped they would get stuck at the top
And never return to the ground.

"Was this how it was, Tom?"
"Sometimes. It's not that way anymore."
Tom pulled me onto his lap. If my weight was a strain he didn't let it show.
"You're the perfect weight."
"Oh, yeah?"
"Light enough so you don't put my legs to sleep."

"And? Finish."

"Well, heavy enough I'm never scared I'll break you in two."

We watched the bullies, the moochers that were out in force. Two jays appeared, hopping first from the branch of the jacaranda to the fence post. They became more brazen still, landing on the gravel under a line of salvia. They didn't break up Granny Settle's rainbow, but hopped cautiously from one line of color to another. They halted at purple, cocking their heads at us and screeching for cookies. Tom tossed the fattest one a raisin. A squirrel turned irate, crawling down the trunk of the tree head first. Its tail twitched as Tom tossed more crumbs to the birds.

"Give him something, too."

The animal kingdom moved closer and closer. They seemed charmed, as charmed as we felt. There was plenty for everyone and the semicircle drew in tighter, eager for more.

"Drinking in the sun . . ."

"Yeah. Makes your head spin a little. These cookies are just like I remember."

"I used to badger her for these cookies all the time. She didn't forget."

Tom looked up just as Russell appeared on the balcony next door. He was still in his bathrobe and quickly stepped back inside. He rarely came out to that little lookout of his. He left his windows open more often. Jazzy music now played constantly in Russell's house and a car I'd never seen before parked at the curb night and day. The owner was careless. Parking violations sometimes turned up under one of the windshield wipers.

"These cookies are something. How many have I . . . ?"

"Eaten? I don't know. I've probably had four by now. Funny, I don't feel full. I could probably finish all of them."

"Let's do. Let's be gluttons and eat them all. I'm in the mood."

"Okay."

"Here, Pol."

The clean blue world, spotted with purple underbellies of fat clouds speeding west, spread over our heads. It was the finest day we'd had in weeks, a day that peeled back a second city shining fitfully through its drab, toxic shell. We watched and listened, bright-eyed as the crow peering at us from a post on Russell's property. I felt the edge of my grandmother's note.

"I think I'm doing very well considering."

"Considering what?"

"The news about that Texas Ranger. It gives her a whole dimension she didn't have before."

"A good dimension or a bad one?"

"Neither. It makes her make more sense. The things she says and does."

"How come her dimensions aren't good or bad and mine are?"

"Because she's my grandmother and you, dear love, are my husband."

"Oh."

I actually loved that "oh." I loved the blank and I loved filling it in when I could. I slipped my hand through his hair and pulled on it to tease him. He slipped another bite of cookie in my mouth and whistled "The Wichita Lineman" as I chewed.

"Glen Campbell. We must have played that record a thousand times. It finally wore out."

"You sat on it, Polly."

Tom stood up and waved his arms at the crow. The bird ducked its head into its chest and contracted, then flared its wings wide open and flew off the pole.

"Now why'd you do that?"

"Feeling a little ornery. Feeling a little . . ." He sat back down quickly and swiped at his forehead with his sleeve. "Man. Is it getting hotter out here or is it my imagination?"

Fingers had begun tickling the back of my neck and throat. The rim of the garden seemed to draw closer, the flowers throbbing and pulsing with color. I stretched one leg unsteadily, then the other.

"I don't know about hot. It feels like I'm riding inside a kaleidoscope, though. You, too?"

"Colliding, yeah. They're definitely colliding." He glanced at the hose and shook his head no. "And hotter. Guess we shouldn't drink in the sun." He stood up and wove toward the table, the loving cup still in his hand. His tongue flickered over his lips. "I think I may go inside for a little while. I think I just might have a nap and let this wear off."

"A nap. Good. Perfect."

We pushed through the dense air together. Every step was harder to take than the last one. I hoped we could make it inside. I wanted nothing more than to close my eyes against the light that had grown glaring and painful. The fingers weren't tickling anymore. They were kneading the back of my neck, weakening it and weakening me.

We staggered through the house using the walls as guides and tried to squeeze through the doorway of my bedroom at the same time. Tom stood limply to one side as I stumbled into the room.

"Polly, I don't think I can make it back to the pantry."

"I don't think I can make it to the bed."

It seemed to float in the middle of the room and meet me. I sensed the edge of Tom's body as he collapsed next to me, but I couldn't reach out to touch it. I closed my eyes and as I did a dim, silent world drew me inside.

Thirty-four

*I*n the dream, I passed through the fence with caution, stepping on the wound wire strands between the metal barbs with my foot, holding another set of wires with one hand so that I squeezed through the space without being snapped up inside. I eased through slowly, with bent knees.

Careful.

Hands off.

Don't you go in that lot alone.

Not now. Now I walked toward them, my knees still bent and shaking slightly. I didn't use my voice. This wasn't a place for words.

Their long necks extended over the water, taut lines bound to trap fish. But there weren't any fish in the dead pools. The horses sucked lightly at the top of the water. Delicate, they swallowed dark water and hung their tired heads together over a tree stump. Their eyes streamed and closed shut, blocking out the sight of a creeping girl, another silly kid, when they'd had them scrambling up and down their poor backs all day.

I want to pet them.

Find yourself something else to pet.

I was close enough to see the whiskers on a muzzle and hear a low snort erupt in a whinny. I was close enough to see a dark shape sidle out of shadows by the barn. Not a sound as it sliced closer, but dirt was recast, banking slowly on two sides. A path was being marked across the barnyard, a path you could almost step on, almost follow as it wound its way past the pile of logs and debris to the center where the stump was. Movement wasn't all at once. Movement was a shivering flank and one flickering ear. An eye snapping open, then another. It hopped from the back of one creature to another, catching on. Catching hold.

I was drawn up in it. I watched that snake in the dirt. I felt grit grinding against my own belly. There were no words to stop that edging, glinting line that would split the clot of horses into a moving stream. I cleared the stump, was inside the circles of mares and old geldings. They were not Star. They had no wicked history, no beginning, no end beyond the Settle Ring. I crawled behind their eyes and inside their ears, hearing and seeing what they did; when the milling started and the stomping, I wasn't afraid. I was part of the heavy barrel chests and gray, splitting unshod hooves that rose up to beat the air, first one, then another. I was under their bellies as they reared and I saw their leathery parts exposed and taut, as they took a step back and leaped forward again. Rage and fear freed them from no history and long, baffling days going round and round in a dead, dull circle. They became animals again, suddenly alive as the silent venomous line slipped toward them. Hooves pummeled the snake into a bloody, ragged patch of skin. Again. Again. They struck the carcass again and again, finally flinging it over their backs, landing it broken and still. They wouldn't be subdued, but snorted and pranced along the line of barbed wire, their necks arched and glistening, well after the snake lay stiffening in the yellow brush outside the corral.

I emerged from the dream and felt Tom's warm mouth at my neck. Still reluctant to leave that place, I kept my eyes closed. I didn't want words, not yet. I didn't want to leave a world of pure being. I didn't want reason; I wanted the oblivion of beasts. I wanted to slash the air with my hooves, to take a serpent between my teeth and heave it over my hide.

Tom and I left wherever we'd been carefully, offering each other touch first. My hand left his warm face and began its journey. I wasn't frightened or furious, like those horses. Instead I was perfectly still inside, though my arms and my legs were beginning to move. Tom, too. His fingers kneaded the back of my neck, easing the stiffness there. He touched my throat tenderly, as if it were the most breakable strand in the world. Then he began to kiss me and we slowly wound our arms and legs about each other until they were as tangled as old vines.

325

. . .

"Where are you going?"

"I'm turning."

"Don't." I didn't want to lose this again. I lay drenched in sweat, a miraculous sweat that ran down the center of my chest. I ran my finger over the film, not wanting it to leave the surface of my skin.

"I missed you, Polly. I missed you so much."

"I missed this."

I slid my head up his chest. It was slick and hot. I could still hear his heart pounding under a shell of skin and bone.

"Sometimes in the kitchen during one of those wild times with all of us milling around, you'd look at me over their heads. You let me know that later after the house was quiet, everything would switch back again. We'd lie there like this." He tucked a piece of hair behind my ears and kissed the tip of my nose.

But I'd skipped over the time he was talking about and the time we were in. I was out beyond the moment we had, fighting hard to get back. Frankie had been jealous of our talk, moments like this. But was she equally jealous of others? Where had I been in that push and grind of two bodies and where had Tom been? Truly with another or, like me, hamstrung by memories and desires that circumvented all others? I wanted to know. I didn't want to know.

"How can we make sure this will never happen again?"

"But we want this to happen. Again, more. Don't we Polly?"

"I'm talking about . . ."

I wanted him to make me a promise right then and there and I waited for him to do it. Then I switched and I wanted him to tell me lies, using language we'd never used before. I wanted to hear the guttural sound of love, down in the dark places where it could be found. Rough sounds of me. Rough sounds of it and her and how she had never, ever been me. New needs, new desires, scary pleasures of a changing order. There would be time for it all because time belonged to us. It always had. We stuck out the silence, letting each other stray and return.

He lifted his head and stroked the top of my stomach with one finger.

"I'll never be like Olympia McMichael."

"Thank God."

"Hey, did you dream while you slept?"

"Yeah. Any more of that wine left? That Babe. Your grandmother slipped us a Mickey."

I slid my arms around Tom and lay back down again. This time it was effortless. I didn't think or speak again until it was already over. This second sweat slipped up out of nowhere to consume us both.

Sweet Remedy

We lay awake one midnight
Dawn would soon break through
We mixed a light elixir
That started nice and cool
It turned out sweet remedy
Was disconcerting brew.

We got a wild notion
To just skip the cozy part
We'd turn into strangers
Coming closer in the dark.

As soft lights danced around us
Then flickered on and off
We said those old words of love
And shared those tender thoughts
Then heard a brand new version
Of all those pretty plots.

We got a wild notion
To just skip the cozy part
We'd turn into strangers
Coming closer in the dark.

Hold me in the dark.

Touch me in the dark.

(Repeat)

We've somehow come to the middle of our lives. Which means that every morning Tom and I rise from our bed and slug it out in the workshop. Despite the occasional day filled with nothing but splinters and smashed thumbs and a concrete floor littered with a chaos of wooden shavings, we are making something. It can only be produced in our halting, handmade fashion. Nobody can really tell us how it's done or do it for us. We work in a mobile unit. It can be the kitchen or the garage or the garden. But we're hammering things out together in any small space of the moment.

Kate's scream was pretty halfhearted. She held a corncob in her hand, waving it in her brother's direction. "Take it! Yuck, here."

"Okay, sure. Cool." He peeled the green silk from the corn with his legs spread apart, as if he faced an opponent twice his size. "Check this worm, Mom. Should we toss it out?"

We had our corn. Granny Settle kept her promise. Hard labor got us here and she left little notes everywhere, reminding us of what should or shouldn't be done. Tom found a message under the windshield wiper of his car. It gave the absolute deadline on picking the corn. Any later, Granny Settle warned, and the corn would lose its flavor. No sweet milk would run from yellow kernels packed as tight as teeth.

"Keep it. We'll cut out the bad part and eat the rest."

Toby peeled the corn and watched as the worm inched over his finger, then held it out so Kate would cringe. Once in a while he rattles off a preposterous fact or figure, but mostly the transfer of power has gone smoothly. When he erupts now it's for the sake of taking a stand. He's got his dad back and, though things are far from perfect, he seems to know a good deal when he sees it.

"Who's going to get that phone?"

"It's always for Kate."

Tom stood up, rubbing the small of his back. "Will one of you two go and get that goddamned telephone?"

Kate groaned and flipped her ponytail. She looked like she belonged at a sock hop, which I didn't mention because I loved that look and didn't want to see it disappear. The baggy pants are slimming slowly. I can vaguely make out a shape, a very attractive feminine shape, under all the inflated clothing. The caller was going to give up the way she was walking.

"Kate, move it!"

She finally scrambled up the steps and I took the long pause to mean Evan or another.

"Guess what? It's for you, Mom."

"If it's Beth, I'll call her back."

"It's not Beth. It's some accent named Johnny."

Tom slid his sunglasses up on top of his head and stared at me.

"The only person I can think of is Johnny Day and why would he call me? Probably a salesman."

"Yeah, probably some jerky salesman." Toby tossed a corncob at his dad, a big grin on his face. "Tell him we don't want any."

Granny Settle called out to me from the spot where she sat in the shade. "Look out for him, Polly Ann. That's a man who is generally up to no good. I don't care what he sings."

I had a funny feeling as I crossed the sidewalk. The funny feeling that accompanied wonderful news, the best in the world. The same funny feeling that could also mean a violent flu was on its way from Asia.

"Hello?"

"Hang on. Gotta put you on hold."

His voice crooned over the phone and I had to smile. Johnny Day's hold music was his music. *I'm back from beyond now, baby. Does that mean anything to you? I know all the faces and places. 'Cause I've been there a time or two.*

"Polly, is that you?"

"Yes."

"Lemme ask you this, Polly Harrison. You in the mood for a little good news?"

I cleared my throat and tried to say something sensible. "What do you mean, Mr. Day?"

"Mr. Day, is it? Well, fine. Hell, anything's fine. The wife's back, Polly. Interested in knowing why Lola came back?"

I had to keep my mind on his voice. Nothing else could intervene and that was hard because there were flares and fireworks going off in my head, sending me running in every direction.

"I drove over to her place. Of course that took every bit of courage I had. I went over there, not caring who saw me or who heard me and, Polly, I dropped down on my knees in a serenade. Care to guess what I sang?"

"A love song."

He blew his nose loudly and I looked at the receiver. Then I looked at Russell's house. Long-gone Russell's house.

"Is that the best you can do? I sang 'Guided Tour,' that's what I sang. Gave it a melody and you know what, Polly Harrison? The goddamned thing worked. She was bawlin' her eyes out! She still hums it around the house. Anyhow, about that time a buncha youngbloods started courtin' me. Started acting like I couldn't do anything wrong all of a sudden. Keith Hart, ever hear of him?"

"Of course. He's huge."

"He's not huge. I'm bigger than him, but you know the fella I mean. He wants to tour with me. See, he's a college boy. Smart. Thinks literary, too much so sometimes, for the good of his songs. But anyway, I know just how to play these boys, so I say, 'Fine, Keith. But how about if we do a Guided Tour.' Guided Tour, Polly. You with me?"

"I . . . could you explain—"

"—Do I have to spell this thing out for you? I want to sing your song on tour. Here's what we need to do on this thing."

He went on to mention a few changes to my song.

"Rome, Mexico, France. Now my fans are Americans, Polly. When they travel, they pack up the whole family to see the U.S.A. and they're going to want Johnny Day to do the same thing. I know what I'm talking about, honey. The trickiest newsletter Carla ever wrote was the one explaining why Mama loved England."

I listened as he eased me out of my own song. He stepped in to fill the vacuum.

"So, I say we write a new song, based on your idea naturally, and we take it to a few old, familiar places your guided tour didn't include."

I listened as he rolled along. It was like being carried off by a current strong enough to gouge out riverbanks and capsize small craft. Tom hovered by the door.

". . . and I'm gonna kick off the tour in Branson. We're thinking October on this thing. Tell me something, Polly?"

I looked at a jar of pickles Kate left out on the counter. I felt just like one of those spears trapped in vinegar.

"Yes sir?"

"Oh, now it's sir. Tell me this, Polly. Did I make someone happy tonight?"

"You certainly did."

I reconstructed our conversation after the line went dead and hung up the phone carefully. Although I cringed at the thought of such a corny serenade, my song had worked wonders on his estranged wife and now Johnny Day was going to include it in an upcoming tour. So if the tour was to be recorded, my song would naturally be included. Wouldn't it? I didn't know exactly what this news meant, but I'd find out.

"Good phone call?"

"You tell me."

He did as he came straight at me with a crazy mix of daisies and cosmos, assorted spinach leaves and ferns, a little of everything the garden had to offer. Tom defined this as a lucky break even when I didn't. I wanted a tour to Nashville, not Branson. I wanted full authorship, not coauthorship. But Tom was there, drenching me with reality, not dreams, though maybe I'd have a little of both before the day was over. One thing was sure, though. Fresh, healthy things were muscling their way into my kitchen. I had to figure out canning right away, if I wanted to hold on to the riches of the season.

EPILOGUE

*M*y mother buried Granny Settle as she was instructed to do, not daring to defy a piece of paper taped to the wall of my dining room. The notice specified "A Plain Pine Box With No Foolishness On It" and Granny Settle had pressed down so hard on the word "No," the pencil lead punctured the paper with a fierce hole. Unfortunately, the note hadn't set the tone for the funeral and my mother had gone all-out. It had been an afternoon of cowboy eulogies and windy messages about the West from Palm Springs luminaries, resulting in a death that significantly outdid the deaths, past or future, of any members of the Friendship Circle. I knew, because I eavesdropped on a few of them in the back of the crowded funeral parlor. They whispered about her meanness, which had become legendary. What kind of woman wouldn't come to her daughter's lovely home to die? Especially when the daughter had decorated with such care. Worse still, my granny would never RSVP. *I never did get a single reply from the woman. All that postage and never one word.* I stood behind Mildred Adams, former secretary of the Friendship Circle, at the service and didn't dare ask whether it was my granny's behavior that made her tender a letter of resignation.

"Tom and I had quite a picnic that day. Just what did you put in those cookies? Or was it the wine?"

We stared down into the austere coffin, half expecting her to rise up and tell us. I tried not to think about how they'd made my grandmother's face so beautiful, what chemicals they'd injected to plump up her desiccated skin, what cosmetic wizardry had produced such a tended, tender face. She'd never bothered about such things in life. What would she have said about this attention to every feminine detail? I noticed my grandmother's eyelashes for the first time. Had she just been granted the eyelashes I saw now, carefully combed and darkened to flip up teasingly from a lifeless face? And the clothing, what would she say to that? She was in full Western regalia, a turn-of-the-century cowgirl costume, hers or someone else's. She wore the gold belt, the belt she had rightfully won. The tips of brand-new boots peeked out from the edge of the long skirt. Those shiny soles had never once cut across a dusty corral.

"I'm out of that cast, Granny. No one would ever guess what happened."

I looked over my shoulder, thinking I heard someone enter the cool, empty room. Everyone had taken a turn paying respects, ogling her getup and imagining the life she once led. The same life she rudely withheld from friendship circles, my mother's circles, circles of any kind. She wouldn't have them at the end, the intimacy, the telling, for it was her end and hers alone and these weren't her people. I saw that in the dignified, disillusioned way my mother shook hands and firmly pressed on before all the assembled mourners.

"She looks like a parade float." Rory held my shoulders down as he said this, probably to prevent me from jumping out of my skin. He winked at Tom.

"Rory!"

"Seriously. If we propped her up for the Rose Bowl and made a bunch of paper flowers to go underneath the casket, nobody would know the difference."

He opened his hand and put it on my hair, not going any further in any direction. I could hear voices outside in the hall and I was glad Tom and Rory were standing next to me. I'd almost forgotten what I'd come into the room to do.

"Help us with this, Rory. Tom, here's yours." I opened my purse and handed them one plastic bag each, both of them filled with red Granite dirt. They turned up in my lingerie drawer the night before she died, right next to a bag of sachet filled with potpourri so old it had lost all its scent.

"She tell you to do this?"

"No. She just stuck them next to my underpants. She must have figured I'd know what to do."

"Cool." He opened the bag suddenly and stuck it over his mouth and nose like a feed bag. His eyes closed as he took a few deep breaths.

I went first, crumbling the dirt between my fingers and then sprinkling it over her body as if I were seasoning a fine broth. I dug my hand into the bag and grabbed a whole fistful, scattering it about her shoulders and carefully combed hair.

"I hear the kids. They've probably got Mother with them. Faster."

We did what we could with our hands and then turned the bags inside-out over her body, not wanting to lose a bit of what she had so carefully guarded.

Rory had gotten older since I'd seen him last. And it wasn't something that registered in more gray hair or an extra wrinkle or two. His body had a new tilt, a new bit of hard-won information and I wondered suddenly if he'd sold his Harley.

Tom touched the back of my arm softly.

"I think she means it this time, Polly."

Steadied by Tom's hand, I took one last look down at her body, marred and sanctified by a few handfuls of red dirt.

"Then I'd better kiss her goodbye."

I leaned down and that's just what I did.

ABOUT THE AUTHOR

*L*inda Phillips Ashour is the author of *Joy Baby* and *Speaking in Tongues.* She teaches writing at UCLA, has received a Beck Fellowhip at Denison University, and has been a fellow at Yaddo. Her reviews have appeared in *The New York Times Book Review,* and her short stories have appeared in *The Paris Review* and *The North American Review*. She lives in Los Angeles.